What We Still Talk About

What We Still Talk About

by Scott Edelman

"What We Still Talk About" originally published in *Forbidden Planets*, 2006 (DAW Books). "True Love in the Day After Tomorrow" originally published in *Treachery and Treason*, 2000 (Penguin Roc). "The Last Man on the Moon" originally published in *Moon Shots*, 1999 (DAW Books). "Glitch" originally published in *The Solaris Book of New Science Fiction Volume Three*, 2009 (Solaris Books). "Together Forever at the End of the World" originally published in *Men Writing Science Fiction as Women*, 2003 (DAW Books). "A Very Private Tour of a Very Public Museum" originally published in *PostScripts*, 2008 (PS Publishing). "Mom, the Martians, and Me" originally published in *Mars Probes*, 2002 (DAW Books). "The Only Thing That Mattered" originally published in *Absolute Magnitude*, 2002 (DNA Publications). "Choosing Time" originally published in *Angel Body and other Magic for the Soul*, 2002 (Back Brain Recluse). "Eros and Agape Among the Asteroids" originally published in *Once Upon A Galaxy*, 2002 (DAW Books). "My Life is Good" originally published in *Crossroads: Tales of the Southern Literary Fantastic*, 2004 (Tor Books).

Collection © 2010

Fantastic Books
PO Box 243
Blacksburg VA 24060
www.fantasticbooks.wilderpublications.com

ISBN 10: 1-60459-938-3
ISBN 13: 978-1-60459-938-1

First Edition

Table of Contents

What We Still Talk About

When people think of a Theodore Sturgeon quote, what comes to mind first is usually the one that became known as Sturgeon's Law, in which he pointed out that "Ninety percent of everything is crud" to defend science fiction against detractors who'd use the existence of any bad SF to paint all SF as bad. But the Sturgeon sentiment that's much closer to my heart comes from the essay "Why So Much Syzygy?," in which he explained that all of his stories were actually love stories.

"I think what I have been trying to do all these years is to investigate this matter of love, sexual and asexual," he wrote. "I investigate it by writing about it because ... I don't know what the hell I think until I tell somebody about it."

Most of my stories seem to be love stories, too, my characters trying–sometimes succeeding, sometimes failing–to pierce the barriers that separate them. Often that aspect of a particular story is subtle, but other times it's far more obvious, as in this piece which attempts to explore the same territory as one of my favorite love stories, Raymond Carver's "What We Talk About When We Talk About Love," only set in the far, far future.

But back to Sturgeon's Law. I hope that once you're finished reading the stories in this collection, you'll feel I've broken it. Because if not, that would mean all but one or two of these stories was crud. And I wouldn't like that. I wouldn't like it at all. (Sorry, Ted!)

Selene, blue pill cupped in one palm, wondered where she would find the strength to raise the small lozenge to her lips. The longer she stared out at the harsh landscape, the heavier the morning dosage seemed in her hand.

The dome had hoped that she and her husband would find the vista in which it had chosen to place them that morning pleasing, but for Selene, the generated location was a failure, as had been its other recent choices. Karl would perhaps feel differently, but for Selene, as the rocks stretched on, rough and dry and red, the scene brought to mind nothing so much as the interior of her own heart.

She closed her fingers tightly around the pill, and could feel its smooth metallic surface grow sticky from her sweat.

"Does anyone," she said, in a soft, uncertain voice, "remember how to get to Earth?"

The words spurted out of her so suddenly that she was startled. Her question had exploded on its own without even the thought of an audience that might receive it.

"Did you hear what I just said, Karl?" said Selene. "Or did I only think it?"

"I heard you, darling," said Karl, lifting wiry arms above his head as he stretched out on rainbow sheets which shimmered with his movements. "It just took me a moment to digest it. I haven't thought about Earth in years."

"Oh, please, Selene," said Karl, entering through one of the bedroom's irises while bearing a tray of drinks intended to cool them from their lovemaking. "Earth is so boring. Promise me that you're not thinking of going back there again. You're not really—are you?"

"It's not very far," shouted Karl from the opposite dome from which Karl had just entered. Selene, peering through the connecting biolock, could see him busy at work, his fingers encrusted with a yellow dust from pollinating the wall for the coming season's sculptures. "No, it's not very far at all. But then, these days, what is?"

"Good," said Selene. "Then let's go."

She tossed the pill in her mouth and swallowed too quickly; the pill stuck in her throat. She took the drink which Karl held out to her, swirled the sheer cup until the thick liquid began to spark, and forced the pill quickly down.

That was that, then. Her choice had been made. There'd be no more thinking, no more worrying. Not for today, at least.

"This will be fun," she said quietly, almost to herself. She licked away the last of the sticky blue residue that remained in the folds of her palm. "I love you, Karl."

"And I love you," said her husband.

"And I love you," said her husband.

"And I love you," said her husband.

The joyful harmony of his voices caused her heart to skip a beat, its pulsing overwhelmed at being the focus of her husband's love.

"Let's get started then," she said, jumping to her feet.

"Right now?" asked Karl. He flung the bedsheet toward the ceiling and then, as it billowed, stepped beneath it. As he lifted his arms, the flowing fabric descended to wrap itself tightly around him. Mere molecules thick, his garb was less clothing than a second layer of skin, as if his nude form had been dipped into a vat of multicolored paint. He snatched the second mug from Karl's tray.

"Why not?" said Selene. "I see no reason to wait. There's something to be said for spontaneity."

"Yes, something," said Karl, dropping his empty tray to the floor, where it was quickly reabsorbed into their dome. "I've never been sure exactly what that something is, though."

"Which flitter should we take?" asked Selene, strong enough now, as she might not have been before, to ignore her husband's joke. She looked into the sky and tried to see past the moons above.

"Why a flitter?" asked Karl. He left a yellow trail of powdery footprints that suffused with red behind him as his steps germinated. "All we need to do is simply think our destination, and we're there."

"No," said Selene firmly, still intent on the distant Earth that hid somewhere in the sky. "This is something that must be done real, or at least as real as anything *can* be done these days."

"As if projecting our way to Earth wouldn't be real," said Karl, shaking his hands by the wrists until the bedsheet extruded opalescent gloves that grew to his fingertips. "As if the new choices are any less real than the old ones. It's all real, Selene. You have too much love of old-fashioned things."

"Which explains why I keep you around, I guess," she said.

Her husband reached out simultaneously to swat her on the rump. Karl's hands collided one-two-three before they continued on the final few inches to make contact with her, the sort of overlap that she knew only occurred in those rare instances when she touched a nerve. She smiled, and they hugged, his arms weaving together to embrace her at the center of a warm cocoon. She murmured peacefully. For a brief moment, she forgot about blue pills, about the endless red rock, about the pleasant, tickling memories of ancient Earth.

Then Karl had to speak, bringing them all back again.

"We should really ask Ursula and Tomas along," said Karl, his words echoing wetly in the confines of their flesh.

"Oh," said Selene, stepping outside of the curtain of Karl's body. "I was hoping that we could all go alone."

"All?" said Karl, looking from himself to himself.

"Why, yes," said Selene. "All. All alone. It's been so long since we've all been away alone together. Too long."

"Too late," said Karl, coming up behind her. "I've already invited them. It never occurred to me that you'd object."

"You should have thought about it a little more carefully before you thought them an invitation, Karl," she said, slowly turning away from her husband.

"You're right, Selene," said Karl, from beside her. "But it's too late for that now, unfortunately. You know how Tomas and Ursula are. I wouldn't want to hurt their feelings. I'm sorry, Selene."

But what about my *feelings?*, she thought, and then, almost before that emotion could claw its way to full consciousness, the feeling effervesced, as all such feelings did, if only she made the right choice each morning. She turned back to Karl, and touched her husband's cheek, while by the dome's outer window, Karl watched as a flitter blossomed from the rocks around them. A jagged skeleton slowly rose up that was but a whispered promise of the vehicle that would carry them light years away. Molten ore feathered through the air like spun sugar and wrapped about the flitter's core.

"Look," Karl said, as the process completed and Selene's name etched itself into the finished skin of the ship.

"Hello," tickled Tomas in her ear.

Selene smiled, perhaps at the flourish her husband had provided, perhaps at the arrival of her friend. Perhaps both. She felt the familiar good mood wash over her as the nanobots massaged the chemistry of her bloodstream.

"Thank you, Karl," she said. "Hello, Tomas."

"Ursula will be along shortly."

"But never shortly enough for you, Tomas, right?" said Karl.

"I can be a patient ... man," he vibrated, everywhere and nowhere. If he had chosen to sneak up on them, they wouldn't even have known he was there. "Someday, she'll grow tired of a material existence, and then, there won't be anything left for me to have to be patient *about*."

"Other than enjoying your practice of such restraint, Tomas," asked Selene, "how have you been?"

"Bored," he vibrated. "The universe continues to hold far too few surprises. So I'm glad that you asked us along."

"How could you possibly be bored with all this?" asked Karl, as he stepped through the iris back to his wall work. "I can't remember when I've last been bored."

"Oh, it's more than just that, Karl," said Tomas. "It's that you can't remember, period. I never have been able to figure out how you manage to keep yourselves straight."

Before Karl or Karl or Karl could answer, the ground rumbled, and Selene jumped in quickly. She needed the day to go smoothly.

"That would be Ursula," she said, as the dome compensated for the clamor outside, and the room regained its silence. "You know, Tomas, for someone so willing to take the greatest of leaps, your emotions can be awfully old-fashioned."

Ursula plodded towards them from the short horizon, her robotic feet crushing rocks into crimson sprays of dust. It wasn't until she arrived at the flitter, overshadowing it in a tower of chrome, that Selene was able to judge the size that Ursula had chosen to carry that day. Ursula had felt like being a giantess, and so she was.

"We're all here, then," said Selene. She had made her own choice about what she was to be that day, and she intended to stick to it. "Let's go."

Selene walked in the direction of the flitter, and when she arrived at the dome wall, kept walking, and flowed effortlessly through it, passing as if through the fragile skin of a bubble. A thin membrane clung to her as she continued walking, and stretched the wall outward, and as she drew closer to the flitter, the connection snapped, and the skin sealed shut behind her. The flitter extended a tongue in her direction, and as she mounted the walkway, she waved up at Ursula from within a self-contained atmosphere.

"Are you feeling any better today?" said Ursula, her faraway speakers booming deeply.

"How I'm feeling doesn't really matter," said Selene. "It's how I'm *doing*. And right now, I seem to be doing something at last."

Selene paused near the top of the walkway. She turned and gestured back at the dome, making the assumption that her movements were being watched.

Karl seemed to be the first to follow her and vanish inside the flitter, though with Tomas around, she could never be completely sure. Once her husband was inside, Karl then followed. He brushed past Selene on the walkway and stopped at the hatch. While she looked up at him, Karl came along, stepping up behind her and wrapping his arms about her waist. Karl smiled down at the two of them from above, then turned and vanished inside the ship.

"Do you really need all of me?" Karl whispered. The pliant membrane allowed her to feel his breath hot in her ear.

"Yes," said Selene. "This time, I do. Please, Karl."

Arms locked, they strolled up the rest of the walkway together and entered the ship. Karl and Karl were already seated within a teardrop-shaped room otherwise bare of furniture, a compartment larger than the ship in which it was contained. At the narrowest point of the teardrop, Karl and Selene dropped back off their feet, trusting that a couch would ooze up from the floor to catch them.

"Ursula?" called out Selene.

The opaque wall which curved about them grew steadily transparent until Selene could see her friend framed by the landscape outside. She swelled even larger, and was soon crouching down above them, her head alone as big as one of their dome rooms.

"I have a feeling that this is going to be fun," said Tomas. "Yes, darling, it's time. You know what to do."

Ursula scooped up the flitter, growing even taller as she hugged the vehicle to her chest, carrying them to where the atmosphere was even thinner. Staring into her friend's ever-more-enormous face, Selene felt as if she was instead shrinking away. At times like this one, she always found it hard at first to tell which one of them was actually doing the changing. Ursula lifted the flitter behind her head for a moment, and then pitched it high into the air. As it neared the top of its arc, great flames spouted from the soles of Ursula's feet, and she rocketed after her friends. She overtook them and slammed into the rear of the ship, adding the thrust they needed to escape the gravity of the small planet.

Once Ursula and the ship she'd propelled were both fully free of the atmosphere, the gleaming plates that made up her body receded into each other. As they overlapped, she shrank until she was down to a size capable of entering the airlock. As she fell back into the circle of her friends, a seat sturdier than the others grew up to greet her.

"How long do you think this will take?" she said with a dull buzz, as she brushed meteor dust from one shiny shoulder.

"That all depends," said Karl, looking out at the stars.

"It will take however long Selene wants it to take," said Karl, looking intently at his wife. "That isn't something that can be timed."

"Then I think I'll have a drink," said Selene.

Karl pressed his hands against the front wall of the small ship, which extruded mugs that he handed to Karl and Selene and Karl. Ursula pressed a few buttons on her wrist, and a small door slid open in her chest. She took the offered drink and poured its contents down into a permaglass funnel. Karl offered Ursula a second mug, which she balanced on the flat of her knee joint as liquid gurgled pneumatically within her. As the level in that beverage dropped, Selene could hear a gentle slurping.

"Thank you," said Tomas. "So tell us, Selene—why Earth?"

"And why now?" buzzed Ursula. "I don't remember Earth being so thrilling the last time that it was worth this kind of effort."

Selene stared off ahead of them through the clear hull of the flitter, and then looked at the empty mug in her hand, unable to remember having drained it.

"I'm not entirely sure," said Selene. "It just seems like the thing to do."

"It's those movies, you know," said Karl, refilling her drink with a pass of his hand. "She's become hooked on them. I have no idea why she wants to go there *now*, but she loves those movies."

"We could have watched them at home," said Karl.

"We could have watched anything at home," said Tomas.

"I don't quite understand the attraction of those dead art forms," said Karl. "They're so simple. Simple and simplistic. Like children's stories."

"As if you remember children's stories," said Tomas.

"As if *you* remember children," said Ursula.

"There's more than one kind of simple," said Selene, struggling to put into words the static that warred in her head. "It doesn't always have to be derogatory. What I like is that those people had their limits."

"Maybe they only seemed to," said Tomas, playfully. "Maybe you only thought they did. You only know them from their movies. Maybe they were just like us."

"They weren't like us," said Selene. "They couldn't do everything. They couldn't rewire their bodies or dissipate their souls or wear whatever flesh suited their moods or ... or just take a pill. They had to deal with whatever they were dealt."

"And you think that make us any different?" asked Ursula. "You're getting lost in the details. They were just like us."

"But look at us," said Selene, her eyes suddenly filled with tears. "*Look* at us."

Karl leaned forward to peer at himself in Ursula's chrome shoulder, then looked at Karl, then looked at Karl, then laughed. Tomas laughed with him.

"For some of us," said Tomas, "that's easier done than for others."

"Life is a metaphor," said Ursula. "Just because we get to choose a few more of them each year doesn't make us any freer in the grand scheme of things. We all believe what we're programmed to believe."

"Or what we choose to believe," said Selene.

"I choose to believe that there wasn't really a need for this," said Karl. "As I said, there was no need to travel back to Earth, dear. Whatever you wanted to see of it back home, you could just have asked for it, asked for any dream you wished, and we would all have been able to see it."

"Is taking a trip with me really that much trouble?" said Selene. She dropped her cup and was pleased to see it shatter before it was reabsorbed into the floor. "What else were you doing that was so terribly important?"

"Nothing," said Karl.

"Nothing," said Karl.

"Nothing," said Karl, "is so important that I wouldn't stop doing it in an instant for you. I'm only thinking of you, Selene. I only mean that you can have the prize without all this effort. Such a dead artform can't be worth all this."

"Sometimes the effort *is* the prize," Selene said sternly.

"Now *that* isn't boring, Ursula," said Tomas, here, there and everywhere. "Can you remember when she last spoke to him in that way?"

"I can remember everything," said Ursula, tapping at the databanks buried deep in her waist.

"Brava, Selene!" said Tomas. "Keep going."

"No," said Selene, her feelings fluctuating wildly. "No more talking just to fill the time if this is what we still talk about. Let's get to Earth *now*."

And so they did.

But when they rose and spread out against the walls of the ship, peering in search of a planet, all they saw was the same vaporous space that had been their companion for the first part of their voyage. The flitter, which should have popped across the universe and come to rest in orbit around the birthplace of humanity, instead floated in a void. The sun shone blisteringly hot at them with no intervening atmosphere.

"Where are we?" said Selene. "This can't possibly be right."

"And yet it is," said Karl.

"We're exactly where we're supposed to be," said Karl.

"We're exactly where you wanted us to be," said Karl.

"But we can't be," said Selene. "Where is the Earth?"

This time, Selene felt for sure that she would lose herself to a wrenching bout of tears. It had been a long time since she had felt pushed to that extreme. And then, as she heard her husband speak again, the notion was flushed away.

"There's no reason that it shouldn't be right here," said Karl. "These spatial coordinates should have placed us in exactly the same relation to the Earth as when we'd arrived the last time."

"That's impossible," said Selene. "The Earth couldn't just disappear."

"Nothing is impossible," intoned Ursula.

"How long has it been again?" asked Karl.

"How long *has* it been?" said Selene.

"No," said Tomas. "Definitely not boring."

When Tomas shivered with delight, Selene could feel the goose bumps.

"I didn't come this far just to talk about it," said Ursula. "I'm going out."

She pushed herself from the hatch to hang in space. Selene watched as her friend slowly somersaulted beneath the ship. There should be blue below her, blue oceans and white clouds and cities and the ruins of men.

"Selene, dear," said Karl. "We may just have to accept the fact that the Earth is gone."

"Can we be sure we're in the right place?" asked Karl.

"Oh, we're in the right place," said Karl. "There's no doubt about it."

"But what could have happened?" said Selene.

"At this point, does it really matter?" said Tomas. "Planets are born, and planets die. Just because this planet happens to be Earth doesn't mean that it gets to go on forever. It could have been attacked. Or perhaps someone blew it up for spite. Or maybe the last person out simply turned out the lights, and then it just ceased to exist, expiring from lack of interest."

"It doesn't matter why," said Selene. Even as she said it, she realized she'd spoken a little too quickly, even for her. "I don't really care why. We've got to put it back the way it was."

"All the way back?" asked Karl. "Is that what you want, dear?"

"Should I gather the pieces?" asked Tomas. "Should I bring them all back and make them bustle once more? It might even be a challenge. I've never puzzled out a working world before."

"No," said Selene. "Not all the way back. That would be meaningless. Just restore the Earth to as it stood when I was here last. When I was here with Karl last."

"Isn't that the same thing?" said Karl.

"You didn't let me and Ursula tag along with you here that last time," said Tomas. "I'll need a reference. Do you mind?"

Selene shook her head. In a moment, she felt an itching in her brain, and then, as quickly as he had entered, Tomas was gone.

"Ah, I see it now," said Tomas. "I see how it was."

That's all that it took, for suddenly, Earth was there below her. Spinning there, it was just as Selene had remembered it, the swirling clouds hiding a purer past beneath. And having experienced Tomas' work a thousand times before, she was sure that it truly *was* exactly as she had remembered it.

"Let's go down," whispered Selene. "I can't wait any longer."

"Ursula, dear," Tomas called out. "We're going down now."

"I'll meet you all Earthside," said Ursula.

She tucked her chin into her chest and kicked her feet away from the planet. Rockets ignited in her heels to push her down toward the surface below. Selene watched hungrily, jealously, as her friend became a dot in the distance and then vanished from sight.

"Should we just—" said Karl.

"No," interrupted Selene. "We shouldn't. The old-fashioned way. We're doing this the old-fashioned way."

The flitter dropped into a low orbit as Selene surveyed the terrain.

"What are you looking for, dear?" said Karl.

"What are any of us looking for?" said Tomas.

"You've grown much too metaphysical of late," said Karl. "Go join your wife."

"I'm already with my wife," said Tomas. "And besides—I put a planet together today. Don't you think I've earned the right to wax a little metaphysical?"

"What do you see, dear?" asked Karl.

"I see us there," said Selene, jabbing a finger at the horizon. "We're going there."

The sky turned blue as they descended to an even lower orbit. Ursula pulled up beside them and waved, spiraled about the flitter while laughing, and then sped ahead. Moments later, they dropped to the surface, setting the ship lightly down in the center of a deserted city. The frozen moment resurrected by Tomas reflected a time when no one was left to greet them. Some of the buildings still towered over them, but others no longer did, and lay in rubble. Tall grasses swayed. Stepping from the flitter and pausing to listen, Selene could hear the sound of birds and the occasional thunder and crash of a collapsing building. The abandoned planet was once more a dying planet, and now that Tomas had set its clock ticking again, Earth hurried along again to its inevitable end.

"It's exactly as I remember it," she said. "Perfect."

"Why didn't you want me to return Earth to its glory, rather than its decline?" asked Tomas. "I would have welcomed that. It would have been more of a challenge."

Selene didn't answer. Selene couldn't answer. Selene merely stood transfixed, studying each inch of territory between her toes and the horizon until Ursula landed with a thud beside them.

"Well, we're here," said Ursula, setting right a car that had flipped on its side ages before. "What are we supposed to do now?"

"That's entirely up to Selene," said Tomas. "This is her party. We're just here as her guests. Or witnesses."

"Witnesses?" said Ursula. "It isn't as if this is a wedding."

"Dear?" asked Karl. "It's up to you."

"Come," said Selene, holding out her hands to her husband. "Let's take a walk together."

Karl came up on her left side, and Karl came up on her right, and Karl stepped ahead to walk before them with both hands dangling back to join theirs. Ursula cleared a path ahead of them, concrete and brick being crushed into a smooth powder beneath her. She came across a tumbled lamppost, and laughing, tossed it toward the sky. Selene never saw or heard it fall.

"Remember the first time we came here?" asked Selene, giving her husband's hands a squeeze.

"How could I possibly forget," said Karl in her right ear.

"It was our honeymoon," said Karl in her left.

"It seems like a lifetime ago," called Karl back over one shoulder. "But I'm sure that it was much longer than that."

"When Ursula and I decided to bind ourselves to each other," said Tomas, "we went *everywhere*."

"Earth was quite enough for us," said Selene.

"I'm sure it was very nice," said Ursula.

"Who needs the entire universe, when this is where it all began?" said Selene. "Not just us. *Everything*."

"Poor Selene," said Tomas, wickedly. "Feeling overly nostalgic? They have a pill for that, too, you know."

"Tomas!" blared Ursula, turning to the sky. "If you had a neck, I'd wring it."

"What did I say?" said Tomas. "I never meant that in a bad way. We're all friends here, aren't we?"

"Pretend that you have a tongue," said Ursula. "And hold it."

"I want to see it all again," said Selene, unshaken by Tomas' words. Playful or punishing, they could not affect her. In that place, at that moment, for one of the very few times in her life, she felt like a rock. "I want to visit the museums, see the movies, and ... and everything. I want to see the way that people lived before. I want to watch what choices they had to make."

"Assuming, of course," said Tomas, "that in their art, truth was being told about the way that people lived before."

"Tomas!" said Ursula.

"I'm only saying—"

"Enough," said Ursula. "Selene, do you think all those things you need could possibly still be here?"

"Except for a little more decay here and there, it's just as we left it," said Selene.

"Thank you," whispered Tomas.

"I recognize this city," said Selene. "I recognize this street. Karl, do you recognize this street?"

There was no answer, not from Karl nor Karl nor Karl, which made Selene squeeze his hands all the harder.

"We've just a few blocks to go," she said, pausing for a moment in the middle of an intersection. "And then you'll all see what I mean. That way."

"Let's do it then," said Ursula.

Ursula swelled from her default size into her gigantic self. With hands the size of couches, she scooped her four companions high up into the air, and ran in the direction Selene had pointed.

"No!" shouted Selene, bouncing several stories above the cement. "Ursula, please, it can't be like this. Put us down."

Ursula froze so suddenly that her metal muscles squealed. She shrunk in on herself until Selene and the others touched lightly down.

"Thank you, Ursula, and please forgive me," said Selene. "But what happens here today, you have to understand, I don't want it to be done our way. I need it to be done the old-fashioned way."

"If it's important to you," said Ursula, "then I understand."

"Well, I don't," said Tomas.

"Tomas ..."

"But whatever you need, Selene," he quickly added.

"This is where the art museum was," said Selene, gesturing to the decrepit building in front of which they stood.

The front wall of the marble and granite structure had collapsed, so they were forced to pick their way across a field of rubble. They climbed atop a pile of huge shards that blocked the entrance, and then slid down inside through where a wall had split open. Most of the paintings were no longer on the walls, having fallen in some past catastrophe. Tomas wrapped himself around one that had dropped face down in the dust, and the large canvas rose and floated in the air, presenting its face to each of them in turn.

A man and woman gazed out at them, their hands lightly touching as they stood in a flowering garden. A young girl sat between them in the grass, hugging a ball in her lap. They stared at the painter who had captured them, stared, without being entirely aware of it, into the future Selene occupied. Selene stared back, trying to peer into that past.

"Is that all we once were?" said Ursula, as the canvas spun again to her. "They look trapped in their flesh. Except for size, they look almost exactly the same."

"For them," said Selene, "that was difference enough."

"At least, that's what they had to keep telling themselves," said Tomas.

"Come along, Tomas," said Ursula. "Let's give Selene and Karl some time alone."

Ursula climbed back out the way they had come. As the painting dropped against a wall, Selene hoped, but could never be quite sure, that Tomas had followed his wife. After a moment, Selene could hear the slamming together of great objects. She smiled.

"I hope Ursula is having fun," said Karl.

"Some people just know better than others how, I guess," said Selene.

Selene and Karl and Karl and Karl made their way through what remained of the museum, where she tried to feel as a long-ago tourist might have, visiting on a summer day for a break from her busy life. She imagined how it must once have looked with its walls arranged neatly, its paintings organized according to a lost scheme Selene could not comprehend, its halls populated by contemporary visitors in search of a mirror. Selene lifted up each painting as lovingly as would a mother a child, and found each a place amidst the ruins where it could be seen and perhaps understood. She had no desire for blotches or geometric patterns today, though, and when Karl would overturn anything reeking of the abstract, she quickly abandoned it. She needed only the representational today. She needed ... life.

A great fish, trapped at the end of a line, frozen in midair, yanked toward a small rowboat. A bowl of fruit that was only a bowl of fruit, and nothing more. A dog, its fur sparkling, proudly posing with a limp duck hanging from its maw. And the faces of the people, the endless faces of the people.

She mostly studied their eyes. They did not look unhappy to her. They did not look discontent. She was not fooled into thinking that their lives as they lived them were perfect, no, she was too smart for that, but she knew that what problems they had were not just symptoms of their times. They did not seem enslaved by the paucity of their choices. In fact, they were probably just as bewildered by the multiplicity of them as she was by her own.

"Selene," said Karl. Her name startled her. She lost hold of the last painting she had been studying, and Karl and Karl had to stumble forward to catch it. "Sorry. But Selene—what are you looking for?"

"I don't know."

She studied her husband's faces over the frame that was between them. Their eyes were equally sincere.

"What's wrong?" asked Karl.

"I don't know that either."

Karl tugged at the frame that separated them, but Selene held it in place. Karl stepped back and left them like that, coming around to place a hand on the small of Selene's back.

"Selene," he said. "Let's go."

"I can't," she said.

"We can't stay here forever," he said.

"Can't we?"

A deafening crash thudded outside. Selene could feel the vibrations through the soles of her feet.

"Obviously not if we want this world to remain in one piece," said Karl, smiling.

When they climbed back outside, the front of the museum was entirely clear of debris. Ursula stood in the midst of several perfectly balanced columns of wreckage.

"Much better that way, don't you think?" said Ursula. "And I could use the exercise."

"You don't need any exercise," said Selene.

"You must stop being so literal," said Tomas.

"Where have you been, dear?" asked Ursula.

"Everywhere," said Tomas. "I've seen it all now."

"All?" asked Selene.

"Yes," said Tomas. "The museum. The city. The world. Is it time for us to go?"

"There's much more the rest of us still have to see," said Selene. "Go back and take a second look. It isn't our fault that you can see everything so much faster than we do."

"Actually," said Tomas. "It is."

"Tomas!" shouted Selene. She wished she had the ability to tell whether her sudden anger was a good thing or a bad thing.

"Don't bother," said Ursula. "He's gone again."

"How can you tell?"

Ursula shrugged, her shoulders clinking. Selene sighed.

They walked single file through the rubble, first Selene, then Karl, then Karl, then Karl, then Ursula, this time, none of them touching. At a building where Selene recalled a movie theater once had been, she stopped. There'd been tuxedos there on the screen, she remembered. Tuxedos and dancing. But now the marquee was fallen, blending with the broken concrete of the sidewalk to block their way. Ursula pushed through to the center of the mound and effortlessly lifted a girder over her head.

"No!" Karl shouted.

"That's right," said Karl. "Put that down."

"Yes," said Karl. "The old-fashioned way. Selene wants this done the old-fashioned way."

"If you insist," said Ursula, lowering the girder slowly and moving back beside her friend.

Karl dove into the pile, squeezing through the narrow path that Ursula had started. Karl tossed a small chunk of brick and concrete to Karl, who flung it on to Karl, who grunted as he caught it and then stepped outside the field of rubble to lay the clump at Selene's feet.

"A gift," said Karl. "A gift of the old-fashioned way."

Selene laughed.

"Good," called out Karl, from where he continued to work. "You keep doing that."

"There hasn't been enough of it lately," shouted Karl, struggling next to him.

Karl bounded away to rejoin himself within the forest of brick and metal and glass, and continued widening the path. Pulling away the wreckage that barred the door, the three of him passed the rubble among himself like the hands of a juggler, and Selene laughed yet again, at her husband's playful love, and at the sight of the entrance that she'd been remembering with such hope.

Karl bowed on the left, and Karl bowed on the right, and Karl waved her forward, and Selene responded with a curtsey, as she had seen the native Earthlings do in those movies made so long ago.

Then, before she could step forward to entwine her husband's arms with her own and go inside, she heard a deep rumbling as loud as the death of stars.

The pavement cracked open in front of Selene, and her husband dropped away and vanished into the crevasse. Before Selene could move, the front wall of the theater spilled forward, sliding into the hole after Karl and Karl and Karl. From the ragged split smoke and ash plumed upward, blinding her. She screamed, but no sound came out, her throat clogged by a harsh dust.

Ursula dove forward into the chasm, pushing debris aside and hurling rubble out of sight into the distance. Tomas returned, bringing a wind that blew the clouds of dust away. As soon as Selene could see her way clear, she stumbled down the lip of the pit to stand beside Ursula.

"Selene, you shouldn't be here. It's much too dangerous."

"Where is he? Where's my husband?"

"Selene, you don't want to see this," said Tomas. She could feel Tomas surrounding her, beginning to lift her, and as she started to be wafted away, she shrugged him off.

"Leave me be!" she said, as she saw limbs, ghostly with dust, protruding from beneath the rubble. "Karl!"

As Ursula removed the last bits of debris that were keeping Karl's broken body hidden, Selene threw herself alongside him and started to howl.

"This can't be," she muttered, when speech finally returned. "This is impossible. He's dead. All of him is dead."

"I don't think I can remember anyone ever dying," said Tomas.

As Selene rocked and moaned, Ursula grew once more into a larger self, and cupped her friends in her hands. This time, Selene did not object as Ursula cradled them all and returned them back to the flitter. Kneeling, Ursula carefully placed them inside the flitter as if arranging the figures in a doll's house. A chair rose up to greet Selene, but no pallet responded to support any of Karl's bodies until Ursula waved her shrinking hand across the floor.

"It can't be over so easily," said Selene. "Not now. Not today. This isn't how it was supposed to be."

She moved from body to body, touching a bruised cheek here, flattening out a curl of hair there. As she traced a deep gouge in one of Karl's legs, terror welled within her, terror that was then tamped down. She didn't know what would happen if she was allowed to feel such pain.

"There's nothing we can do," said Ursula, moving to her friend's side. Ursula's fingers felt colder on her arm than they ever had before. "We should leave here, Selene. Don't you think?"

"Selene?" said Tomas.

Selene could not speak. Was there anyone left who needed to hear her voice? She did not think so.

"Let's just go, Selene," said Ursula, as softly as she could. "There's nothing more for us here."

Selene could feel her friend's fingers in her hair, and did not want to feel them.

"Go?" said Selene, struggling to keep her voice from cracking with rage. "Why should I go? Why should I go back home now? There no reason to do anything any longer, no reason to come here and no reason to go back. If only I hadn't made us come here! If only I hadn't insisted *all* of him come here. Leave me. You go back. Just leave me."

"Why *did* you want to come here, Selene?" asked Ursula. "What was the reason? What was it all about?"

Selene looked at her husband and her husband and her husband. She stroked his smooth face and his bruised face and then had to turn away from where there was hardly any face left at all. They'd begun their day in love and ended it in death, and love would not come again.

"What was the reason?" Selene whispered. "What *was* the reason?"

It had seemed so important, back when she woke on the other side of the galaxy. Earth, and all it represented, was more than just a goal, it was the journey as well, and had seemed dreadfully important. And now ... now nothing was important.

"You're right," said Selene. "Let's go back. Let's go back now and let's go back fast. And let's not talk any more of the old-fashioned way."

"That's what I've been saying all along," said Tomas.

And as swift as the thought, Earth was gone, with no sense of a trip having been made. Selene, when she could bear to look out again through the transparent flitter walls, could see that they had arrived back outside her dome. It appeared exactly as they had left it that morning, in a prior dawn that was light years away. She looked from the dome to her husband and back, with no idea how she could ever live in one without the other again. She would have to have the dome destroyed.

Later, after Tomas and Ursula left her alone, perhaps she would have herself destroyed as well.

But before Selene could think the dome away, a figure pressed toward her through the membrane of its walls, and as a shell tightened around the approaching form, she could see that it was Karl. She struggled to cry out, but her mind was too numb to speak before he did.

"What happened?" he said, as he ran inside the flitter and embraced his wife while surrounded by his own dead bodies. "One moment I was clearing a path for you, and the next ... nothing. I was cut off."

"How can you be alive?" she whispered, cradling his head in her hands. "The building fell and crushed you, all of you ..."

"I was going to tell you," said Karl, "but I figured that if there could be three of me, darling, why not four? There was so much work to be done around here, and I knew that once I explained, you wouldn't really mind."

"You bastard!" she shouted, and pushed him away. "How long has this been going on?"

"Only since the moment you left. As Ursula launched you all into space, I launched a new me down here."

"But I wanted to see Earth with you at my side. I *needed* to see Earth with you at my side! How could you choose to stay behind and miss that? How could you live without me? I thought you loved me!"

"But I *saw* Earth with you, Selene. I was never without you. I was there the entire time."

"I could kill you," said Selene, slapping at Karl through the tears.

"If you're going to do that," said Karl, letting her succeed in slapping him a few times before catching her hands, "I'd better make sure that there are a few more of me first."

He drew her close with a single pair of arms and kissed her. Her knees buckled, and she crumpled at his feet, sobbing, laughing, howling, giggling, her emotions in full revolt against her senses.

"We should leave the two of you alone," said Ursula.

"Or however many of them there are," said Tomas. "Let's go, dear."

"You'll let us know how it goes, Karl, won't you?" said Ursula.

Selene eventually stopped trembling, and was able to realize that she and her husband were by themselves. As she let Karl help her to her feet, the flitter dissolved around them and was reabsorbed into the planet's surface. As she stared into the shadows spilling off the dry, red rocks, she realized exactly how much time had passed them by while they'd traveled through the void and explored Earth the old-fashioned way.

An entire cycle had passed. It was that time again, if she still wanted it to be that time.

They entered their dome, and she studied the view out of the bedroom's picture window. She almost thought she could see Ursula, curving through the sky like a shooting star off in the distance. Selene replayed her friend's last words in her mind, until ...

"None of today was real, was it?" Selene whispered. "Not a moment of it."

She waited for him to reach for her, hoping that he would, hoping that he wouldn't.

"Tomas and Ursula, they were both in on it, weren't they?"

"We just wanted you to have an old-fashioned experience," said Karl. "We just wanted you to be happy, that's all. I thought you would like it."

"And I appreciate the gesture, Karl," she said. "I really do. But could you leave me alone for just a moment?"

"Are you sure?" he asked. "Is everything all right?"

"Everything is fine," she said.

Once Karl exited through a biolock, Selene sat on her side of the bed. On a small table nearby, perfectly centered, was exactly what she knew would be there: a small, blue pill just like the one that had been waiting for her the morning before, and the morning before that, and all the mornings she could still remember.

She snatched at, and choked it down quickly. Then, while thinking with terror of the old-fashioned ways, she held out a palm in wonder and supplication until a second pill appeared, and then swallowed that one even more quickly than the first.

True Love in the Day After Tomorrow

It's rare for any of my stories to spring full-blown into my mind. Usually, I just get a brief glimpse of a character or situation and have to construct the story brick by brick from there. But as I was driving hundreds of miles from Maryland to Massachusetts to attend the SF convention Boskone, the opening line of this story popped into my head. And in that instant I knew the entire story from beginning to end. I could have told it to you right then, and in fact, I did tell it to friend and fellow writer Resa Nelson in the lobby of the convention hotel.

Which is another thing that doesn't happen often, if at all. I usually don't spill a word about any of my stories to anyone until I've finished at least the first two drafts. But in this case, I guess I arrived at the con still reeling from having been struck by lightning.

The story was published in Laura Anne Gilman and Jennifer Heddle's anthology Treachery and Treason *the same month I was burying* Science Fiction Age *magazine, its appearance a welcome reminder that I am a writer as well as an editor, something that can be forgotten when reading a slush pile of 10,000 stories per year.*

You didn't believe him at first when he said he was from the future. Now he's dead, belief is all you have, and there doesn't seem to be any future.

You buried Alonso yesterday, planting the coffee can of his ashes beneath his favorite tree in the backyard you shared for so many years. You insisted on doing it alone, even though in your life together you had gathered around yourselves many loving friends who would have liked to have been a part of the private ceremony. But after this long and blissful marriage which you never expected to have, the happiness of which you were never allowed to fully explain, you wanted to approach the empty future alone. You did not want to be surrounded by even the most well-meaning of sympathizers while your mourning mind still reeled from the story you could not share. So you slowly filled in the hole, and then, dropping the trowel by the door, retreated into the house with a desire never to step from it again.

You have spent the hours since, stumbling from room to room, bumping into the furniture as if Alonso's leaving had rearranged it all. A deep sadness has settled on you like fine dust, clogging your pores with grief. You know that grief has twisted your perceptions, and yet, you feel it possible that no one has ever felt the sense of love and loss you feel today, no one save Alonso. You saw it in his eyes the first time you met him, which was ... how strange, twenty years ago to you, and last month to him.

You were a secretary then, for a storefront insurance company, and though you had at times thought of daring to be more, life had not been kind to your attempts. It was Alonso who later had taught you how to make those attempts succeed. You were looked upon by the men you worked for as only a machine that typed. A meat machine, never allowed to know for sure whether you'd been hired for the speed of your fingers or the look of your legs.

How stifled you felt then, and how fulfilled you've been since in almost all that followed. You can remember that first moment perfectly. Stretched out now in your useless king-sized bed, with a box of tissues by your side, a bag of potato chips tucked in your elbow, and crumbs nestling in the folds of your bathrobe, you close your eyes and relive it. That's all that's left of him now, you think. Memory.

You had been rereading a memo one of your bosses had wanted retyped. It was the fifth time he'd asked for changes, and this made you angry. Wasn't it possible to satisfy *anyone*? You bit down so hard on your pencil as to leave marks.

You suddenly felt yourself being watched. People often paused before the storefront insurance agency to study those inside, and you had long ago made yourself get used to it. You had to, or you would have had to move on. But this felt different, piercing your urban shell. You removed the pencil from between your teeth and slowly lifted your head.

The eyes of the stranger who was standing by the window were clamped shut that first instant in which you saw him. He was no longer watching you. The tracks of his tears sparkled in the sun. You were not afraid when you saw him. His was not a look that inspired fear. You studied him in the freedom his tear-crumpled face gave you.

His forehead was flattened against the glass, and he looked in immense pain, as if mourning a greater loss than anyone else had ever had to experience, as if mourning the loss of an entire universe. No other man had ever stood before you like this, his skin so transparent that his emotions burned your eyes. Because of this, it took you a few moments to notice the details of his physical features rather than just the manner in which they were contorted; all you were aware of at first was that this was the saddest person you had ever seen.

But then you became aware of the hair that was starting to go gray, the broken nose, the few extra pounds that hitting forty had started to fill in on his jowls. He had been a handsome man once, you'd decided, and you could see that it was only time and the hard life he had lived that had downgraded what would have been threatening handsomeness into the harmlessness of solid good-looking.

He'd opened his eyes. He caught you watching him, and you saw those eyes become pools of fear. He jerked back from the window, his forehead leaving a greasy spot where it had rested. His lips moved, and though you could not hear him, you could tell the word he mouthed.

"No."

He pressed the back of one hand to his lips, and then ran off.

You jumped up as he did so and raced immediately to the door, but the street was clear in both directions. You stood puzzled there by the doorway, and one of your bosses shouted at you to get the hell inside and finish the damned memo, which you did, restoring the pencil firmly to your lips to prevent the curse words from coming out that would have cost you your job.

You'd thought of the stranger as you worked, wondering at the odd attention which he had given you. You knew you were a pretty woman, and you had been stared at by men before, often in ways you did not like and quickly made plain, but you were sure that this had been no pervert's ogling. How peculiar was the stranger's expression at first, when he did not know you were watching! Love and loss, triumph and depression, desire and sadness, all had fought for dominance of his features. It was only that last horrified expression, snapping into focus when he suddenly opened his eyes to you, that was stable.

Fear.

No one had ever looked at you with such fear before. Or, actually, any fear at all. You tried to imagine why anyone would be terrorized by you, and as you retyped the memo with your boss grumbling behind you, his heavy-breathing presence made you too dispirited to conjure up a reason. When both of your bosses were out to lunch, you phoned a girlfriend to tell her what had happened, and she was no help. She took it as simply another one of the big city's weirdo stories, and told you to make sure those sleazy bosses of yours didn't make you lock up. You did have to work late that night, so you didn't have much time to think about the encounter again until you were on the subway, heading home. You started to feel paranoid then, continually wondering if there was a crying man watching you from a far corner of the train. Each time you looked up, you saw nothing but other harried commuters.

You arrived home with your dinner warm in your hands, a pint of fried rice from the Chinese restaurant on the corner. You opened a diet soda and plopped down in front of the television set to where you began searching for a show that would make you feel a little less alone. You were in one of your hermit-like moods at that point in your life, burned by the disappointments that waited for you in bars and singles clubs. Barely had you stuck your chopsticks into the carton when you heard footsteps in your apartment behind you. You dropped to the floor and rolled quickly to one side, trying to recall what you had seen other people do in movies. Rising up, there he was before you, the stranger from that afternoon, inside, one hand on the doorknob.

He was on tiptoes, his shoes in his hands, trying to get out your door.

He started to speak, but you tackled him without thinking.

"You son of a bitch!" you'd shouted. Your toughness shocked you then, and it still shocks you now. You laugh now, thinking about yourself, leaping across the room, instant anger having overpowered any fear. A potato chip catches in your throat, and you find yourself laughing and crying and choking all at the same time.

He did not move once you'd brought him down. There was a touch of blood at his temple, but he was still breathing. You nervously clapped your hands together while you wondered what you were supposed to do next. You backed to the kitchen, not taking your eyes off him. You found a length of rope in a cabinet there which you used to tie his hands together around the pipe that connected the ancient radiator in your apartment to the floor. You watched him carefully as you dialed the police emergency number. You were halfway through the number before the strange appearance of the clothes he was wearing sunk in. His suit was of a shimmering, opalescent fabric you had never before seen, its futuristic tone made even odder by being cut in a style twenty years out of date. The aesthetic tug of war between cloth and cut meant that no one could have been wearing a suit exactly like that.

Intrigued, you put down the phone and moved a few steps closer. Dangling from the man's collar were two narrow ties, both of the same design, or perhaps it was only one, sliced lengthwise by a razor. He wore his hair in a short pony tail, held together by a jeweled barrette. You had never seen an older man before who allowed himself to be that ostentatious.

His eccentric dress swept thoughts of the police from your mind, and you searched him for identification. Your fingers patted where pockets should be, and though you found a rectangular bulge by his right hip, you could not get the cloth to part. Your frustration built as you tugged uselessly at the fabric. You looked for an ID bracelet, hoping maybe that would give his name, and instead found that his wrist watch had no face. The metal of its band was fused to his wrist. You went back to groping at the unseen wallet. He opened his eyes as you pulled, and looked at you dazed and lovesick, as if Cupid had decided to expend every last arrow.

"Jude," he whispered. You were shocked to hear him call you the loving nickname only your mother used for you rather than the full Judy the world knew. With that one syllable of your name, you felt his love through your fear. You remember shivering from the full force of that love.

You shiver now.

He had looked down at his captured wrists.

"Oh, no," he whispered, hypnotized by the rope that bound him. "Oh, no."

Maybe it was wrong, but you could not help but smile at your intruder's helplessness. You had never been allowed such a position of power before. It felt good for a change.

He tugged at the rope, but though the metal pipe creaked, he was held fast. He sighed, and you could see the message sinking in that he would be going nowhere unless you chose to let him.

"Ah, Jude, you're really got me this time," he said, settling back calmly. He spoke to you as if he'd known you for years, and you'd just caught him at some particularly impish act that he knew he should have known better than to pull. His calmness angered you more than the breaking and entering itself.

"You looked plenty scared before, Mister," you'd screamed at him. Where were these words coming from? You'd never yelled at anyone before except your own damn self. "Why the fuck don't you look scared now? I called the police, and they're already on their way to lock you up."

"No, they're not," he'd said.

"How do you know? You were knocked out when I did it."

"If you'd called the police, you'd have already told me about it."

"I've never even met you before," you said angrily.

"Ah, Jude," he said, putting on a sad smile, "but I've met *you*."

You found yourself taking a step back from him at the mention of your name. "How do you know to call me Jude?"

"All right, then," he said. "*Judy*." He struggled with your second syllable as if it took him a great conscious effort to remain so formal.

"Judy," he repeated, then took a deep breath. "I'll try to call you whatever you want. At first. I was hoping to slip away, but now that you've caught me, I can imagine how hard this is going to be for you."

You took a step closer, close enough to kick him, but you did not. "Don't think a potential rapist can score points by being polite. Life doesn't work that way."

His smug demeanor angered you, but you knew not to be surprised by his politeness. That's what the rapists usually looked and acted like. The nice ones.

The polite ones. The boy-next-door type, not the drooling, unshaven trench-coated monsters that myth had created. His patronizing coolness made you snatch up the phone again.

"Wait!" he shouted.

You paused, holding the phone tight.

"Give me a reason."

"Because that's the way it must have happened," he said. "Because you already *have* waited."

He licked his lips, and you watched his tongue nervously.

"I never expected this to happen," he said. "They told me it couldn't happen. That it would create a paradox. I thought that the most I could do was just look at you were one last time. That's why I was so afraid this morning when I accidentally let you see me. I figured I *couldn't* meet you because you'd never told me you'd met me. See? Because you can't change the past. And yet you saw me. I was scared to death that would erase all that is to come. I just hope that instead you managed to keep this a secret for a long time."

"What the Hell are you talking about?"

"I'm from the future, Jude," he said. His eyes were moist as if from memory. "*Your* future. We've been married for years. Hell, from what I've learned of life, married's not the right word. We're still more lovers than married. We've joked about that for years."

"Mister, you are full of shit."

You punched the magic number that would rescue you from this mad talk. The stranger squirmed as you listened to the ringing.

"Look in my pocket," he pleaded. "Then you'll believe me."

"I tried that. Your pockets are sewn shut."

"Not really. That's just the way pockets will come to be. Come here."

You set down the still-ringing phone, and that time, when your fingers touched where the wallet lay, the cloth parted.

"How did you do that?" you asked. "Before, it seemed as if I'd have needed a knife ..."

He shrugged. Your fingers trembled as you slid out the wallet. Inside, you saw a picture of you and this stranger, your arms resting comfortably around each other. The man in the picture looked similar to the one before you, as if it were taken recently, but the you ... it was not the you you were. You could tell that. Your face there had filled out, and you seemed unafraid of anything. But at the moment, you *were* afraid, and your heart thudded wildly. You listened to the man's words as he talked, but you continued to look only into your own eyes.

"Tomorrow," he said softly, "you will make a visit to the county library. You will meet a man there. More a boy, really. Me."

"I don't go to the library."

"You will. And you will meet a gangly boy named Alonso, the boy who will eventually become the man you see before you. I love you, Jude. And you, eventually you'll love me."

"This is too much ..."

"I know. That's why I hadn't planned on being seen. I just wanted to look at you once more. To see the woman with whom I fell in love. I wanted to see this place again, too, this apartment where we first made love."

He began crying, and you were mad at yourself, because you could not deny that you very much wanted very much to wipe away his tears. You were proud that you held yourself back.

"I'm dying, Jude. With death so near, this is all too, too silly, I guess. But you never know what can become important as the time dwindles down. And you, Jude, you are the most important thing in my life. With my days so few, my thoughts have been coming back to this special time. This sacred time, really. I have a close friend who's a scientist. Once, when he was drunk, he let the secret of his work slip out, and later, after he'd sobered up, I was able to convince him to let me do this thing as his last favor to me. If he'd dreamed this could have happened, that we could have actually met, he would never have let me go. I've just blown his theory about paradoxes. But thank God for that. You don't know what it's like to be able to see this you again."

"They have time travel in the future?" you'd asked. Your throat was dry, and you could barely recognize your own voice.

He thrust his wrist up toward you as best as he could, showing you his odd watch.

"Not that everyone knows. But they're starting to. They have many things in the future. Most importantly, they have our love in the future."

You were finally able to pull your stare away from your photo. You looked from his flat eyes to the real ones there, and the promise that they held. Here was a man who loved you truly, or at least thought he did, you could see that. But you'd always said that you were not one who was ever going to be taken in by the lies of true love.

That was the day it all began to change ...

You dumped the contents of the wallet on the couch, and spread them wide with a sudden sweep of your arm. There was his driver's license, with a photo that painted him far more solemn than it appeared he ever allowed himself to be with you. The expiration date would not arrive for at least another twenty years. There were membership cards to museums and video stores, receipts for dry cleaners and supermarkets, all with dates far in the future. The money, too, all had late dates, and there were no singles, only two dollar bills, bearing the portrait of a president you did not recognize. The checks were from a joint account bearing both of your names.

"Okay," you said, mostly to yourself, surprised at the readiness with which you were willing to start accepting all this. And then, to him: "If you're really from the future, then tell me ..."

He smiled, which made you grow quiet.

"All the little details of how life turns out? The results of wars and elections and horse races? I wish I could. But look." He stretched his restrained wrist as close to you as he could reach. "The same contraption that helped send me here and will bring me back also keeps me from talking about anything but me. Funny. I think that's the only reason I've been able to get away with talking about us—that the two of us are so entwined that you *are* me."

"Try," you'd said.

"For you, Jude," he said. He looked at you as if you'd asked him for a cup of his blood, but that he'd willingly provide it. "For you."

He thought a moment, and as he started to open his mouth again to speak, his entire body was captured by a seizure. You saw the bloodshot whites of his eyes as his every muscle shuddered. You fell to his side and shoved open his lips to stuff part of your shirt between his teeth.

"Enough!" you'd shouted. "I don't need to know. Enough!"

The tension in his body slowly faded. You felt guilty for torturing him so. He looked up at you and sighed.

"I don't like to fail you," he said. "I love you, Jude."

And you found yourself stroking the hair of this crazy man you had netted yourself. You nestled his head in your lap, and then listened as he told you all of your deepest secrets, things you had never confessed before anywhere but in the pages of your diary.

"How did you know?" you'd asked. You could barely state the question.

"These are all things you told me, Jude. We had no secrets."

He recited you a list of all the people who had hurt you, and all the things of which you were ashamed. All those embarrassments which you thought another would have had to turn from in disgust had you spoken them were instead handed back to you as tokens of love. He even calmly mentioned the one thing you'd sworn that you'd never be able to tell anyone but the man you loved. This was his final gift to you, he said. Maybe by telling you back all the things you had revealed to him with such difficulty in your future and his past, you would know peace a little earlier.

By the time he finished speaking, you were massaging his wrists, the rope that had bound him on the floor between you.

From the look in his eyes, you thought he might kiss you. Instead, he slowly stood.

"I have to go now," he said, reassembling the contents of his wallet. "My friend will be expecting me. If I don't go back soon, they will come after me. I don't think either of us would want that. Thank you for this last moment, Jude. I will speak of it to no one. I will simply tell them that I watched you from afar, and that you were as beautiful as I'd remembered."

He opened the door slowly, and too soon. Full with this unexpected love and belief, you did not want him to leave you.

"When will I see you again?" you'd asked.

"Tomorrow," he'd answered, and you'd had a strange faith that it would be true. "Go to the library tomorrow. And promise me that you will not speak of this night at all to anyone else ever. Not even me. In my past, you have not, and I don't want to change the world in any way. Who knows? The wrong word could tear us apart. Goodbye, Jude."

"Don't go yet!"

He moved through the door and you followed him out into the hallway. His hand lightly touched the instrument at his wrist, and he turned and shouted for you to cover your eyes. There was a bright flash of light, and then he was gone, and you were left with only the afterimage of his form dancing on your retinas. That, and memories of your future. You went back inside your apartment. Mixed with your sadness at having seen him go was a strange hope, one which you had never before allowed yourself to feel. You quickly went to the phone book and found the address of the county library.

The next morning you phoned in sick for work from a pay phone in the library lobby. As you rattled off your lie of being stricken by the flu, you kept staring at the front entrance, not wanting to miss Alonso through carelessness. But you couldn't miss him, you realized, could you? After all, if you didn't meet here, he couldn't have come back to see you the previous day. Even though you'd never taken a sick day before, your bosses didn't understand. You'd have thought that just this once they'd have been cooperative, or at least been able to feign, if not feel, sympathy. Balanced on the edge of a new life, you'd almost quit right there over the phone, but then your habitual lack of confidence in the future resurfaced, and you promised to arrive at work early the next morning.

You chose a table near the main doors and piled dozens of textbooks around you to look as if you were studying. You occasionally stared down at them, but most of the time you maintained an unfocussed glance off into a distance that allowed you to casually take in the whole of the library. You tried to ignore the passage of time. Eventually, your bladder began to hurt, but you refused to move. You sat with your knees pressed tightly together. You could bear any burden if it meant recapturing the comfortable feelings of the night before. Even if there was such a thing as fate, you weren't going to let it handle this itself.

It wasn't until almost closing time that you thought you saw him. He was younger, slimmer, and with a nose not yet broken. He had shorter hair, and was no longer wearing an eccentric potpourri of clothing, but dressed in the style of the moment. He'd paused in the doorway, and looked down to read a worn scrap of paper. He turned his head slowly to scan the entire library, and his eyes tracked over you without stopping. As he walked briskly to the reference desk, you tried to imagine the details of the guaranteed instant in which you would meet.

You watched him through the crenellated stacks of your books, and waited as patiently as desperation made possible for him to make his move. The man would love you and you him, that was the promise of the future. With his back to you he asked the reference librarian a question you could not hear. She answered him, and you could imagine him giving her a warm smile as her reward. You were jealous that she was the first to hear that voice and see that smile. You held on tightly to the books before you to stop yourself from waving at him. The woman led him to a battered set of encyclopedia, where he knelt and took notes. Your eyes did not leave him. He sometimes frowned at the words on the page, and you wondered what worried him so. You wanted to relieve that worry, as his visit yesterday had apparently relieved yours. He slammed shut the book, and you jerked erect. You looked down and saw that you had torn a page you had been holding too tightly.

You began to sweat. You expected him to bring the book to your table, to sit down across from you until he could pierce the barrier of your separateness with some innocuous question, unaware of his place at an historic nexus of your lives. Instead, armed with innocence, he slid the book back neatly into its place. He folded the worn slip of paper into a pocket with an air of finality as he twisted his head to seek out the door. You saw a face possessed by thoughts of lunch that should have been possessed by thoughts of you. Your heart thudded as he passed you on his way to the exit. You scooped up an armful of books and dashed after him, your head down. Bumping into him as if it were an accident, you dropped the load of books at his feet. He spun, apologizing, and his concerned face made you feel good, reminding you that you were doing the right thing.

You stopped trembling. He gathered up all your books and held the stack toward you. You were shocked at first when you saw that he did not recognize you; he was truly seeing you for the first time. His eyes were wide, absorbing you as if this would be their only chance. You had spent most of the day waiting for him, and were embarrassed that you could not think of what to say to keep him, and yet the future promised that he be kept. Your mouth grew dry. He looked from your face to the books which you were too frozen to accept, then back up at you, then toward the spines of the books again.

"Ah," he said, smiling, and you noticed his voice had grown higher-pitched, no, you corrected yourself, *would* grow deeper. "So you're into modern art, too? Where are you going to school?"

You smiled at him in a sickly way which you'd hoped he would take as sheepish. There you'd put in all those hours with your heart fluttering over the pages, and you didn't know *what* the books said you were into. You'd simply picked up a large enough pile to justify your space by keeping you looking busy throughout the day. You took back the books and mumbled something about not being in school. You were flustered, and whatever it was you said next you no longer remember, only that it worked, for he insisted on apologizing for bumping into you by inviting you out for coffee. He helped you reshelve your books, and you marveled at him as he spoke. You followed him to a coffee shop, where he told you his name was Alonso.

You tried to act as if you'd never before met anyone with that name.

You looked at his face through the steam of the coffee he'd bought you. It had been a long time since you'd let anyone buy you coffee. His perfect nose. How would that be broken? Would it be shattered after a future romantic evening when he leapt to your defense on some dark street? You longed to tell him the hints of what you knew, but you were sure he would not believe. Not without showing him all the evidence that you had been shown, evidence which his older self had taken back into the future. The afternoon turned effortlessly into night. You found yourself wandering an art museum with him, listening as he led you by his favorite paintings. You didn't mind that he did most of the talking.

And then, the two of you were back at your place. You were surprised to find yourself there, and yet at the same time not. You peeked carefully through the doorway first, momentarily fearful that Alonso would run into his tomorrow form. You took his hand, and led him inside. It felt proper, this surrendering to the inevitable. You sat on the sofa, your arms entwined with his, and told him all the things that had ever pained you, each solitary scar that twenty years into his future he would come back to repeat to you in your yesterday.

You ended up spending that night together, huddled safe in the sanctuary of his embrace, that night and every night since.

Only now, your sanctuary has crumbled to a fine gray dust entombed in a coffee can.

You leap up, scattering potato chip crumbs across the rug. You pace the house thinking of all the time swollen with unexpected happiness that has passed between long ago then and too close now. Your sobbing echoes in the empty rooms which had once seemed so full.

Alonso had officially moved in with you one week after you'd met, instead of going home each morning for a change of clothes.

Your love grew, just as you expected it would, gaining a depth that your previous experience with men had taught you was not possible. That life had then decided to teach you different lessons was not something with which you chose to argue. As the years went by, you did not tell Alonso any of what had occurred the day before you met, afraid to jinx the transformed life you had been given.

You chose not to ask many questions of this life. You had chosen to become a person who did not need answers. All you wanted was for life's happiness to continue. You knew that someday he would die, he had told you himself that he was dying, but before then he would meet a friend who would send him back to encounter your yesterday self. So you waited, watching for the subtle changes that told you that that time was approaching, that the gift you'd been given would end.

That changed the day he came home from work with his nose bandaged. Someone at his office had tossed him a paperweight, he'd said, and he'd fumbled the catch. There was blood on the front of his shirt. You cried far beyond the weight of what you beheld at that immediate instant. You crumpled in his arms, and wailed not only for his pain, but also for the swiftly approaching pain you saw for yourself, the injury a sign of his eventual leaving having moved closer. Alonso comforted you, and you managed to avoid having to explain the reasons behind your apparent over-reaction.

From that instant forward, you tried to avoid thinking about the blackness ahead, but instead to think only of the blackness you had escaped behind you. You stopped looking for the signs that he was growing into the man who had stepped into your life the many years before. You no longer mirrored the Alonso you knew over the one that had made that first visit. You did not want to know how fast he was gaining on becoming the man he would be when he died. You practiced acceptance. You tried to remain aware that you had achieved a state of grace. You loved this man, and worked at existing in a state of being beloved, both by Alonso, and the universe.

And now, so soon, he was gone.

You don't understand how it could possibly have been so soon.

You go to his dresser, where you open the top drawer. You close your eyes and inhale. You can smell him there in the room with you, but when you open your eyes again, all you can see are his shorts and socks. You pick up a pair of each and dab your damp eyes with them. You position them on the bed in the places they would be were he lying there. You imagine him filling them out, resting as he often did with his hands cupped behind his head. You decide to get one of his suits from the closet, and to place it over the shorts and socks, and then you will climb onto the bed and press yourself against them, and remember.

You are glad that there will be no one to see you. You feel as if it will be silly. You feel as if it will be holy.

You go to the closet and begin sliding the suit hangers across their metal rod. The scrape of metal against metal makes you cringe. You move the suits first to the right, then back to the left, then to the right again, picking up speed as you do so. You feel yourself growing angry, as you search for one particular suit. You cannot remember exactly which suit. The metallic squeaking is getting on your nerves. You are crying, and you grasp the rod tightly and pull it towards you, wrenching it from its moorings. Alonso's suits fall about your feet. You still do not see the right one. You are angry. You know that it is from more than Alonso's death, but you cannot say from *what* more.

You bend to pick up his suits and see a square of plywood attached to the rear wall of the closet, near the floor. The board is painted so as to be almost indistinguishable from the wall that surrounds it. Two screws hold it in place. You go back to Alonso's dresser, where you find his nail clippers underneath his handkerchiefs. You use the nail file to remove the screws.

Behind the board is a small alcove, one you never knew existed. Inside is a small carton the size one would get from a liquor store. The box is wrapped in brown paper which has been made very soft by age. You hold your breath while you pull the box closer. The paper is bare of any writing, as if the person who'd wrapped it had been unsure of to whom it should be addressed. Your fingers tremble as you shred the paper easily, and soon you are tearing at the corrugated walls of the box itself.

A suit sleeve tumbles from a split in the torn cardboard. You reflexively reach out to catch it, but then your fingers freeze in mid-reach. You recognize that fabric. It belongs to a suit you have seen but once.

You rip into the package, grunting, and the whole of the suit bursts forth. You recognize what follows. There is a tie, split lengthwise in two. A short ponytail, two hairpins piercing the fake hair where it would join the base of the skull. Wrapped in plastic were a few doughy balls the color of flesh. The skin tone is one you'd lived with every day. The hip pocket of the suit pants contains a wallet, its leather dry and cracked. You nod as you look through the wallet. It is filled with IDs for companies you'd never heard of, with licenses in styles that never came. There is a photograph of you and Alonso, apparently caught in a loving moment. You linger over this photo, a photo that had never been taken.

You study the print carefully, more carefully than you had twenty years before. And though the photo looks real, you know that these were not the forms the two of you came to embody.

No, you had not asked questions of this happy life. As you paw through the contents of the box, you realize you should have. At the bottom of the box is a sealed envelope. You open the clasp, and slide out dozens of pages within, all written in your hand. You begin to read, and see that it is a photocopy of one of your old diaries. You riffle through the pages. The last entry was written just days before Alonso's travel through time.

You shake the box, but nothing more falls out, no easy answers. You were hoping to find meaning inside, but at the same time afraid to find out what that meaning might be. You wonder what it would feel like to have a nervous breakdown. No one could ever have loved you more. Perhaps his going had shattered your mind. That's it, you think. That makes far more sense than this.

You pick up the jacket once more, and try to pinpoint exactly when you had stopped thinking about it, but you cannot. How silly you were to think anyone could ever wear anything so ridiculous, no matter how far in the future. How silly. How terribly, terribly silly ...

You hug the shimmering jacket to you. You sob, rocking back and forth, your head banging against the closet door.

All these years you felt guilty about not telling him what you knew about his future, about how you had come to meet. Goddamned secrets. You hated secrets.

And now this. You wished the house and all its contents had burned to a fine ash along with Alonso. Now it's too late for that. It's too late for so many things.

Eventually, you stop moaning. You are not sure how long it has taken to cry yourself out, but you are now sitting in a dark room. You carry the box to the front door and peer out. The stars are blinding with their brilliance. When you are sure that no one is watching, you step quickly to a trash can, and throw the box in. You rush inside again, and slam the door harder than you need.

Once in the bedroom, you spread your favorite coat of his out on the bed that is now yours alone. You settle yourself on top of it, and wrap the sleeves tight about your waist. You try to remember. And to forget.

The love was real, you think. If nothing else, goddamn it ... the *love* was real.

The Last Man on the Moon

As much fun as it was editing Science Fiction Age magazine—as Orson Welles once said about the RKO back lot in Hollywood, "This is the biggest electric train set a boy ever had!"— the position pretty much put my writing career on hold. Reading 10,000 submissions per year overtaxed my short-story muscles to such an extent I had little energy left for any of my own.

One result of this was that for several years I'd been passing up opportunities to write for anthologies, to the point where I was even failing to deliver stories after I'd pitched ideas and had them accepted by the editors. There just didn't seem to be enough time in the day. After seeing several books come out which could have contained stories of mine, I swore that the next time I learned about an opening, I would somehow find a way to take advantage of it, even though I was editing four bimonthly magazines.

So when I learned through Paul Di Filippo that Pete Crowther was pulling together an anthology commemorating the 30th anniversary of the first manned Moon landing, I decided I just had to crash the party. Since the inspiration for the book was the first man on the Moon, I pitched a story idea about the doings of a purported final visitor to the Moon. One of the things I did to research the story was to track down the complete transcripts of the Apollo 11 mission, which as it turns out, had been annotated by the astronauts themselves.

After the story was released in Moon Shots in 1999, a few readers came up to me at conventions, stunned. "I didn't know you also wrote," was the message.

I'd been away from the keyboard too long.

For Neil Armstrong, the Moon was at last a reality. The simulations, the tests, the long hours of play-acting to prove to the techs that he was the one with the rightest of the right stuff—all that was history.

And history was what he was creating.

As the Lunar Module brought him nearer to the surface of the Moon, what he could see through the double-paned window unwound a spring in his heart. The magnificent desolation, growing closer, turned from a distant dream into a concrete vision of stark beauty. Planet Earth itself was what had now become the dream, jiggling far above him as the thrusters rocked their fragile cocoon down through the thin atmosphere.

Strapped into the Lunar Module beside Buzz Aldrin, Armstrong was distracted by the sudden sensation that he was being watched. At the same time, though he was unsure how, he somehow knew immediately that Aldrin, packed in tightly beside him intent on the computer controls during their descent, was not the cause of his unease. Armstrong was a reasonable man, always had been, not given to odd fancies—unless choosing the life of a test pilot was in itself odd—and the strange feeling baffled him. Which was uncomfortable, for he was also the sort of man who did not take easily to being baffled. He was not entirely occupying his own body, it seemed; he was both audience and participant for his own every breath.

He forced the mood away. More urgent issues were present to deal with than mere vaguely defined spiritual discomforts. He was no Ivy League college boy mesmerized by his own navel, he was the Commander of *Apollo 11*, and the mission's success depended on his focused concentration. Besides, with the whole world watching, who *wouldn't* feel an overwhelming sense of sitting in a department store window on the last shopping day before Christmas?

They were fast approaching a large crater, its bowl the size of a football field. A scattering of boulders confronted him, any one of which could cause irreparable damage to the Lunar Module and prevent their return to the Command Module. That, he knew, should be the only thought inhabiting his mind. Even a slight error could cause him to stub his toe during these final phases before a touchdown, he knew that, and so he shoved the invading feeling far from his mind.

The pockmarked landscape was rushing up to greet him like a fist. Armstrong took over manual control from the computer, quickly goosing the thrusters so that the Lunar Module would overshoot their initial target. He instead tried to have them come in long, aiming for a relatively smooth area a little farther on which contained only an array of smaller craters and rocks.

They thudded down hard. When the Contact Light blinked alive, showing that the probes hanging from each of the LM's three footpads had stroked the surface of the Moon, Armstrong allowed himself a deep breath in hopes of slowing his wildly beating heart. He tried not to think of what the boys back on Earth must be making of the thudding in his chest.

"Houston, Tranquility Base here," he said, smiling at Aldrin. "The Eagle has landed!"

The sun was low in the sky. Armstrong peered out at the almost colorless landscape that encircled them with a carpet of chalky gray ash. Their surroundings could be seen with sharp clarity, the shadows perfect and sudden. Nearby rocks bore newly formed fractures, damage from the harsh plume of their rocket engine.

His vision blurred momentarily, twinning the boulders before him. He felt yet again as if the eyes he was looking through were borrowed ones, the sights of victory not entirely his own. He frowned, and blinked the view back to normal. Or what passed for normal on the sterile Moon.

"Let's do it," he said to Aldrin. Armstrong shimmied into his Extravehicular Mobility Unit, squirming into the layers that would define his humanity, keeping the Moon outside and the Earth close to his skin. His training took over, and almost without thought he snapped his gloves into place, then locked on his helmet. It was time.

Aldrin, who had been going through the same motions, studied him quizzically.

"Ready?"

Armstrong's answer was a confident thumbs up. He dropped the signal to reach for the hatch with the same hand. After he swung the door inward, he rolled onto his knees to his left, readying himself to back out onto a new world. As he contorted and uncomfortably exited onto the platform, he did not see the Moon his destination, but only the fragile, awkward contraption that had brought him there. He slid out a foot and moved it from side to side, seeking the comfort of the ladder's top step. He could hear, as he slowly lowered himself down the struts, the voice of McCandless announce on Earth that their television screens were reflecting his steady descent. Armstrong stepped back, dropping off the ladder, repeating in his mind the words he had practiced for so long, and then, as his foot sank slightly into a top layer of fine powder, he began to speak.

"That's one small step for man," he said. "One giant leap for mankind."

As soon as the words had escaped his mouth, before Aldrin could reply from mere yards away, before Collins could wish him well from his orbit in the Command Module far above, before any cheers of jubilation could carry from terribly distant Houston, Armstrong grabbed his helmet roughly, tried to snap it free from around his fragile skull, and began a long, low scream.

Shrieking, Alexander Reece tore the VR skullcap from his temples and flung it across the small room. The heavy contraption beeped and chirped as it skittered end over end against the curved chrome floor of the chamber, and then slid back to settle beneath his central chair. He was embarrassed to see that his octogenarian's muscles were unable to hurl it as far as he wished, as far as his NASA-trained body once could. He studied the elongated face reflecting back at him off the silvery inner curved walls that closely surrounded him like the insides of a giant's egg, and remembered when his was the face of a man who had once tossed a football farther than any human ever had or ever would. Back when he'd been on the Moon for real.

Back before he knew he would be the last.

A rectangular seam blossomed in front of him, and as the thin cracks widened, he could hear frantic yelling outside that had only been muffled murmuring the instant before. A small door popped back, and Mel Lichtenstern and Leon Stober filled the sudden space, each trying to be the first one through the narrow entrance. Lichtenstern, narrow himself, pushed swiftly by the other man into the testing chamber.

"What went wrong?" Lichtenstern shouted.

"Are you all right?" asked Stober. The stocky man quickly loosened the straps that held Reece's snug bodysuit to the chair. Stober stumbled a bit on the slanted floor before gently taking one of Reece's thin wrists and checking his pulse.

"It's that damned helmet of yours, Leon," said Lichtenstern, kneeling to peer under Reece's chair. "It must have given the man a shock. You've got to be more careful. That's all DreamVert needs, to be known as the company that killed the last surviving man to walk on the Moon."

"Please, Mel," said Stober softly, still holding Reece's trembling arm. "As usual, your sense of humor falls flat. You're only being morbid."

"Don't worry, Mr. Reece," said Lichtenstern, smiling as he stood. "It was just a onetime computer error. Leon will make sure that it doesn't happen again."

"No, it won't happen again," said Reece in a choked voice, so enraged that he was almost weeping. "I'm fine, thank you very much. But your Virtual Reality program, it's wrong, all of it. What have you been doing the last three years? You don't need me as a consultant. You just need a garbage man. You'd be better off just throwing the whole thing out."

The two businessmen looked hurt, as if they were children on Halloween and Reece had just pulled back a handful of candy. After the blasphemy they'd put him through, though, those pained expressions gave Reece a jolt of malicious glee.

"Go back to making re-creations of skiing Mount Everest and skydiving without a parachute," continued Reece. "Putting a man on the Moon seems to be beyond you."

Lichtenstern seemed at a loss for a reply for the first time since Reece had met him days earlier. When he finally spoke, his words were slow and measured.

"You were hardly in there long enough to judge, Mr. Reece."

"I was in there more than long enough to be sickened," answered Reece. "You two, you say you're going to make a killing letting the world's lazy VR potatoes relive Neil Armstrong's trip to the Moon, and then you go ahead and make it all up! How did you imagine I'd react to that, that ... monstrosity? You said you needed a man who'd really been to the Moon to help teach the world the way it really was. But you lied to me."

Reece was angry at them, but also angry at himself for the way his lower lip trembled as he spoke. He used to be able to take a stand without having to worry that he looked like an old fool.

"Mr. Reece," said Lichtenstern, "I know that you don't care for Virtual Reality, but please, you're making it sound as if we're some sort of criminals. We haven't lied to you."

"No? So then you really think you could get into your suit in a flash and step from the Lunar Module like out of an amusement park ride? There were hours of procedures and checklists between landing and stepping out onto the surface. And the descent from orbit was smooth, it wasn't like being in a damned cement mixer. And everything in there was too sharp—the real landing stirred up tons of dust. When you first get there, you see, it's like looking through a fog. It's only later, when the dust settles, that every thing becomes clear. And—"

"I'm sorry, Mr. Reece, if we gave you the wrong impression, but this is a business first," said Lichtenstern. His cheeks flushed red as he spoke. "And business isn't necessarily about giving people the truth. Not our business, anyway. If we're going to be selling a product, we have to give people what they think they want. And they don't want a smooth landing. Where's the excitement in that? We don't get paid for smooth landings. And when they do land, they'll want to be able to see what they came for. So what if we tweak it a little? You could still help us by making sure we manage to nail down the heart of it."

"But you've put a stake right through the goddamned heart of it, can't you see? Those words you made him say! That was the worst part of all. You might as well go to Arlington National Cemetery and piss on Armstrong's grave. How could you make them come out of his mouth that way? You know he didn't say them like that. You *know* it."

Lichtenstern turned to look sheepishly at Stober, who was still struggling to unhook the system's many delicate sensors as Reece squirmed angrily in the chair. Stober would not meet Reece's gaze either, lost in the pretense that it was science, and not embarrassment, that kept him looking down.

"It was one small step for *a* man, you fools." Reece pulled himself free from the two men and angrily detached the final straps and wires on his own. Stober winced to hear the sudden ripping sounds. Reece stood, legs shaking, his heart racing. The enclosure was so cramped as to leave no room for him to get past the two of them to the door. So much for dramatic gestures. "Let me by."

They backed away, each trying to exit through the doorway first. Reece followed them into the cavernous laboratory that housed the VR mechanism and all the accompanying hardware and assistants DreamVert claimed they needed for testing. He stumbled down a short set of stairs, barely keeping to his feet as he reached the warehouse floor. Cursing, Reece went to the nearby alcove changing room. He began stripping off the suit that only hours before had comforted him by reminding him of the old days, but now just seemed vile. His body as it was revealed was thin and stringy, not what it once was, and nothing like the one he had a few short moments ago felt himself occupying.

"You have to understand, Alex," said Stober, stepping up carefully beside him. Lichtenstern hung back, making a show of eyeing the control console. "We're not villains. We didn't make up Armstrong's words. That's the way they taped it back then, that's the way it appeared on all the transcripts. People will expect to hear those as the words that will come out of their mouths when they're being Armstrong. Anything else would be wrong. It would only confuse them."

"So what?" said Reece, the suit around his ankles. He kicked the collapsed skin toward Lichtenstern. This time, unlike with the helmet, he was satisfied by how far he made something fly. "The truth is meant to be confusing. Going to the Moon was confusing."

"This is ridiculous," said Lichtenstern, shouting from where he stood. "Look, you think we didn't have reasons for what we did? Even Buzz Aldrin says he heard it that way, and he was only few feet away."

"But he didn't hear Armstrong's words through the air," said Reece, waving a fist. "He heard the transmission the same way everyone else on Earth did, masked with all that crackle of static. You can't pay attention to what anyone else claimed. This isn't about what the world mistakenly thinks. This isn't about anyone else. This is about Armstrong. Just Armstrong. He said that he said it. You're going to have to take him at his word."

"This isn't why we asked you here," said Lichtenstern, stepping closer. "You were the last man on the Moon. You're the *last* last man on the Moon, the only one left. We're not concerned about words. We need you to tell us how it *feels*."

"I'll tell you how it feels. It feels like I was an idiot for ever agreeing to fly up from Florida to try to explain to a couple of businessmen what it was like to land on the Moon."

A sudden weakness overcame Reece, and he sat down hard on a nearby wooden bench. Gladstone would kill him for putting himself through this strain, Reece thought, if the doctor ever found out about it, if the strain itself didn't kill him first. He was a ridiculous sight sitting there in his shorts, he knew. For the first time in his long life, he felt himself to be a pathetic sight. He dropped his head to his hands, drained.

"That didn't look like the Moon," he said wearily. "That didn't look like the Moon at all."

"Then help us," said Stober, sitting down beside him on the bench. "You can help it be the Moon, or at least the best Moon reality lets us have these days. It will happen with you or without you. You know that, Alex, don't you?"

"I can't believe it's come down to this," said Reece, hugging his gaunt arms as he trembled. "I'm the last of them. That should count for more than this, don't you think?"

"I'm sorry you feel that way," said Lichtenstern. His face was void of expression, his voice barely under control. "I hope you choose to continue with us on the project. We've offered to pay you well. If you feel you're not up to it, well, Leon is right. We'll just have to make do."

For a moment, Lichtenstern studied the silvery egg that towered on struts beside them, then nodded at Stober and walked away. Reece and Stober sat in silence as the footsteps echoed across the cavernous room, and then vanished. Stober clasped and unclasped his hands again and again. Reece could tell that the man was struggling unsuccessfully to find something to say.

"You know," Reece said quietly, "it seemed as if he knew that I was there."

"Who?" said Stober. "Lichtenstern?"

"No," said Reece, pausing, wondering how much he should admit. "Armstrong. When I was in there, in your testing contraption, being him instead of being me, letting him take over, he somehow knew that I was there. I was Armstrong, all right, your program sure did that fine, but at times it was an Armstrong who knew that someone else was riding his back. He knew that I was watching him. And I don't think he liked it."

"No one else has ever reported anything like that before," Stober said in a slow and reasoned tone, as if talking to a child. "The personas you don in VRs aren't aware. They can't be. They're just computer programs, and I certainly didn't input an ability like that. Are you sure you weren't just sensing Armstrong's nerves? You know, one thing I don't know whether you realize we got right was that his heart rate went through the roof when they were landing. It shot higher than any other mission commander's."

"No, it wasn't that," said Reece, recalling the curiosity of Armstrong's mind, remembering that though the Moon did not feel real, Armstrong himself did. "Forget about it. Forget I said anything."

Stober licked his lips nervously, and placed a hand lightly on Reece's shoulder.

"Alex, you're the closest thing we've got, that the whole *world's* got, to Neil Armstrong. Don't you think you owe this to him, to the memory of the space program? Wouldn't he have wanted you to hang in there to make it right for him?"

No, thought Reece. *He'd have laughed at this. He'd have wanted you to go back to the goddamned Moon for real.*

Sitting there, starting to shiver in his shorts, he thought of his Boca Raton condo full of medals that no one ever saw, and the newsmen who had him trot out the damned things on anniversaries for nostalgic stories on what it was like when men and women still stepped off this planet. Thinking of days full of working on memoirs he was not sure anyone would ever want to read, he got control of his pride and knew, just knew, what his answer would have to be.

"Okay, Stober," he said, the strength back in his voice. "Someone's got to stop you bastards from screwing this up royally. Let's do it. Let's go back to the Moon."

Reece, struggling with the staff meant to hold an American flag upright, grew tired of being Armstrong. Luckily, unlike Armstrong, frustrated by the stubborn mechanism, Reece had a choice about it.

Reece had by now spent many long repetitive days returning again and again to the surface of the Moon, troubleshooting the flawed program, watching Lichtenstern and Stober mostly ignore the feedback he'd give them on where they'd gone astray. Only a few of the suggestions did they actually bother to implement. Even that much surprised him, based on how he'd sized them up.

He scuffed the ground with a heavy boot, smiling as he watched the raised surface particles go out in a perfect ring. No swirl of dust, no roiling cloud like there would be on Earth, like there'd been in the VR Simulation days before; just a clear and perfect fan against the terrain.

He did get a small amount of pleasure from being useful in that way, but it fell far short of what he knew he'd feel if they really paid attention to him. To some degree he was but a publicity gimmick for Dreamvert, he knew that. Whether they heeded his advice or not, they would make the best of it by allowing the world to think they bad. He'd already almost quit many times. Neither Lichtenstern nor Stober had the power to make him stay.

Only Armstrong had that.

Neil Armstrong was magnetic. Perhaps not as strongly so as the real Armstrong had been, but as far as making the first man on the Moon seem real, Lichtenstern and Stober had done their jobs. Perhaps Stober should get most of the credit; Lichtenstern seemed to worry mainly about PR and money. Reece knew his kind. He was the sort who was a politician, not the sort who made the rockets fly. But though Reece got along with Stober, he still could not get the man to accept all that the astronaut was telling him.

Armstrong's unease remained, regardless of what the two men kept insisting to Reece. That feeling was still out there from time to time. Reece could not avoid picking up the irritated signals from Armstrong, as if the first man on the Moon was definitely made uncomfortable by Reece's presence. There was no personhood present to *feel* discomfort, or so they kept insisting, and so he'd stopped talking to them about his sensations. But that didn't make the experience any less wearying.

Having definitely had quite enough of being Armstrong today, Reece blinked his eyes in that special way they'd taught him, and was abruptly shifted into observer mode, his stomach jolted by the sudden disconnection. He wasn't up for this, he truly wasn't. Grimacing, he sat on a boulder and watched Armstrong nearby.

Armstrong, ungainly in his space suit, moved clumsily in an attempt to set up the American flag, which Reece knew would crumple and fall to the surface of the Moon during takeoff. Reece wondered whether Lichtenstern and Stober would be willing to show that in their recreation, or whether that would be one more truth that would fall by the wayside so that the VR potatoes who would shell out the big bucks for a chance to pretend to be Armstrong wouldn't be offended.

Aldrin, fated to be known forever as the second man on the Moon—which Reece imagined was probably better than being known as the last man on the Moon—was close beside Armstrong. It took the two men working together to force the rod's hinge to snap into position. When they finally had the staff jammed as deeply as they could get it into the ground, the weight of the flag spun the pole so that the stars and stripes faced away from the ever-present camera. Armstrong and Aldrin swivelled the flag to the lens and posed. Reece smiled, remembering a time when people back on Earth actually bothered to look at such pictures.

The photo opportunity over, Aldrin turned his back to Reece and wandered back to the base of the Lunar Module, leaving Armstrong behind. Armstrong studied the flag while Reece studied Armstrong. To Reece, as the moments passed, Armstrong seemed lost in thought far too long for a man whose time on the surface of the Moon was to be so short.

Armstrong turned his head and looked toward Reece. Reece could feel his heart pounding, even though he knew it could only be some sort of coincidence. He hoped that the worrying Stober did not make note of it and deem it a reason to pull him out of the environment for his own safety. But when Armstrong began walking toward him, Reece feared that the thudding in his chest would have to be unignorable. Calm down, he told himself. Surely Armstrong had been pro-grammed to sight some geological marvel in the distance, and was about to walk right *through* him to examine something that had existed millions of years before either of them had been born. When Armstrong stopped directly before him and looked down into Reece's eyes, down where he could *feel* it, the truth could no longer be denied.

"So you were the watcher I felt," said Armstrong, seemingly unperturbed to find a third man wandering the Moon. Reece's mouth was dry, and he wondered how they could manage to do that with VR. Reece had avoided the entire industry as much as possible; perhaps it wasn't that difficult after all. "Imagine meeting the last man on the Moon."

"Imagine *being* the last man on the Moon."

"I never thought that there'd be such a thing."

Armstrong's face hardened. Reece knew it wasn't at him, but at them. And not just at Lichtenstern and Stober, but at all the thems out there.

"There are a lot of things that didn't go the way they should have," said Reece. "You wouldn't want to know about them."

"That's the problem, Alex. You're here, so I already do. It's a small, sad world out there."

"Some people don't seem to mind."

"Since when have we been 'some people?'"

"But you weren't even supposed to register that I was here. And you certainly weren't supposed to be interactive enough for us to have this conversation." Reece pointed off at Aldrin, puttering with a bag of tools. "He doesn't seem to notice me."

"Poor Buzz didn't get the care and attention that I did. He's a good man, but I'm afraid that he isn't the one they think is the star attraction here. They've spent most of their time and most of the computer's memory the past few years on me." Armstrong kicked the boulder on which Reece sat, grunting at the undeniable solidity of it. "I guess those guys are better scientists than they know. Do you mind if I sit down?"

Reece slid over to make room. As Armstrong sat, the space suits of the astronauts disappeared. Their cocoons blinked away, and they were suddenly in street clothes, as comfortable sitting on a rock in the airlessness of space as they would have been chatting on a park bench. Startled, Reece looked at the back of one hand, where the big-knuckled fingers he'd expected to see were gone, replaced by a young hand he had not known in decades, the prominent veins and spots that were brought to him by age faded to but a memory.

"Virtual Reality can take you back to far more than just the Moon," said Armstrong. "VR can take you *back*."

They sat that way in space for a while, enjoying what Lichtenstern and Stober and the countless DreamVert technicians had created. They looked off across the varied craters that stretched off seemingly forever before them. They watched the American flag, quiet and still on the windless Moon. The Earth hung above them.

"We weren't supposed to dip our toe in the water and then walk away from the ocean," said Armstrong. "We were supposed to keep going. You were supposed to continue the line, Reece, not be the one to end it. There were supposed to be colonies out here by now. Think of it. My great-grandchildren were supposed to be living here. There was supposed to be a city."

"People don't care anymore," said Reece. "I won't apologize for them. I guess I should. People have given up. All they have time to think about up there anymore is getting through the day. Finding a place to sleep, getting enough to eat, figuring out a way to stay safe. For all their technological toys, inside they're still cavemen. They think that what we did was very nice, but really, just get over it. They forget that someday the sun will flare, and take the Earth with it, and if we haven't moved on to a new home by then, that's it for the human race. We might as well have never existed."

"But they've got to know that. Surely they've been paying attention."

"On some level I'm sure they know. But on the level that counts? The level that gets things done? It sickens me to say this, but I think that they're more interested in playing video games than actually going anywhere for real. Neil, I'm afraid that mankind didn't seem to really want your small step."

"So you're saying that this may be as close as man ever gets to the Moon again."

Reece shook his head. Armstrong stared at him hard.

"I think you're a little jealous of me," said Armstrong.

"No," said Reece, confidently. "I'm not jealous of you, Neil. I'm jealous of the next guy. The one who gets to go back."

"Do you really think that there'll be someone like that? After all you just said about them?"

"There must be. Or else no one will ever have a chance to sit like this again for real."

The first and last men fell silent, and sat quietly together, waiting for the planet Earth to set.

"What was going on in there, Reece?" The aged astronaut blinked and saw Stober hunched over him, the VR helmet cradled delicately in his hands. All Reece could do was stare uncomprehendingly. A moment before, he'd been on the

Moon. As far as he was concerned, he never should have left. He slowly held up one hand that seemed impossibly bound by gravity, and gestured for Stober to have patience while be collected his wits.

"You seem okay now," Stober continued, "but your stats were screwy there for a while; it's as if we lost contact with you. I almost pulled you out of there. You had me worried."

"Why didn't you pull me out?" Reece said in a low voice. Even if he'd wanted to, he didn't know whether he had the energy to speak more loudly.

"It was Lichtenstern," Stober said in dull tone. "He wouldn't let me. Come. Let me help you out of here."

Reece, who usually ignored offers of aid, allowed Stober to help him. All each hour of testing taught Reece was that a man of his age wasn't up to a trip to the Moon, virtual or otherwise. Even as simple an act as standing after being seated for so long wasn't easy.

"You've managed not to answer my question, Alex. What was different in there?"

"Nothing. Nothing was different. I think your machines are acting up again, Leon."

They staggered out into the control room and sat quietly side by side. When Stober started to strip Reece out of his suit, and before he could pursue the issue any further, Lichtenstern scurried over.

"See, I told you that he was fine, Leon. You worry too much. Aren't you fine, Mr. Reece?"

"I've been to the Moon, Lichtenstern. Why wouldn't I be fine?"

"See, Leon? We won't have any surprises out of Mr. Reece. He's in amazing condition for a man his age."

Stober made as if to speak. Lichtenstern went back to his controls before a word could be uttered. Reece ignored them both and began to dress.

"You have to forgive him," said Stober, his hands shoved deep in his pockets.

"No, I don't have to forgive him," said Reece. "You're the one who has to forgive him each day, because you have to work with him. I don't need to make any such accommodation with my conscience. I'll be going home soon. If I had to remain behind like you, I'd probably have to come up with excuses for him, too."

"Understand that we've been at this project for a long time," said Stober, circling Reece in an attempt to plant himself in the man's field of vision. "Too long. And to find out as he did when he thought he was nearly done that there's so much longer still to go, well ..."

"So then why didn't you bring me in earlier?" Reece asked, looking up from buckling his belt. Stober avoided his gaze.

"To be honest, we, um, we didn't know you were still alive. We thought the last of you was already long gone."

"Great. You sure know how to make a person feel special."

Reece finished buttoning up his shirt, and seemed ready for the street.

"You didn't answer my question," said Stober. "I'll ask it again. What happened in there? Today's readouts seemed completely different."

"Nothing out of the ordinary. But you still have to work on that perceived distance problem. Because of the atmosphere, you know, objects seem closer than they really are. Things don't fuzz off as they get farther away as they do here on Earth. I'll tell you all the details during the debriefing. But I'm sure you'll be able to take care of it easily enough."

"Why do I find I don't believe you? Listen to me, Alex. Level with me. If you're not feeling well, we can always stop for a while, start up again later. You're too important a man to risk on this project. Maybe Mel and I will just have to be content that we've gotten all the usable information out of you that you can afford to give."

"It's awfully nice of you to show such concern."

"I'd appreciate that more if you were able to leave out that subtle trace of sarcasm."

Reece was about to close his locker for the day when he paused to stare into it deeply as if gazing off at a distant crater.

"You're a smart man, Stober," said Reece, his voice soft and far away. "You're not Lichtenstern. You still have some passion left in you. Why do you keep working on projects like this? It's like churning out fake Rembrandts when you could be a Rembrandt all on your own. You have the ability. Why play let's pretend when you could use your smarts to get us back to the Moon for real?"

"There's probably no more than a handful of souls on this planet other than yourself willing to pay to go to the Moon for real. On the other hand, we could easily sell ten million units of this Moon program, and that's not even counting the schools. I don't have any choice in this, Reece. We're not in charge. The government isn't even in charge. It's the marketplace that's in charge, chaotic, random, and unforgiving."

"Have you ever thought of trying to use those smarts to change the marketplace? I could go on tour, remind them of what the Moon was really like, get them charged up for going back, and you, you could get them up there ... for real."

"I'm not that kind of guy. I'm not the same kind of risk taker you are. I'm perfectly happy doing this."

"If you say so."

Reece slammed the locker door. Stober winced.

"Don't hate the world for letting you down, Alex."

"I don't hate what's here, Stober. I just love what's out there even more."

Reece hurried to the exit. Stober called after him. "If it means anything to you, I'm sorry."

"Don't apologize to me," Reece replied as he walked through the door. "Apologize to Neil Armstrong."

A rmstrong's final farewells to Tranquility Base could no longer be avoided. He'd come to visit, not stay. The safety checklists having been negotiated and survived, and Collins' location in the orbiting Command Module pinned down with as much accuracy as their primitive, computers could sustain, Armstrong reattached his waist restraint. Knowing what he knew now, though, knowing what Reece had told him, knowing even what Reece had been unable to tell him which he'd been able to pick out of his mind, he'd just as soon toss the controls to one side and remain behind, letting Buzz go back home alone.

Unlike back at the initial landing, whenever Armstrong now felt an odd sense of doubling, a feeling that someone, something, was riding his shoulder, he knew what it was. He was no longer mystified. It was Reece, the Moon's last man, watching, listening, judging, touching him with the only bit of the present future that would ever bleed through.

Let him look, too, thought Armstrong, with what passed for thoughts. *Reece, too, had the right to say good-bye to the Moon in his own way.*

Armstrong heard Aldrin announce to the world that Eagle was now number one on the runway, and he knew that their time was almost up.

Armstrong peered out at the Moon's surface for one last look. He caught a glimpse of himself reflected back at him in the glass that separated them, and realized that the face he saw was not entirely his own. In the faceplate of his suit, the features of Alex Reece were superimposed over his own.

"This is it," said Reece. "It's time to go home."

"You're right," said Armstrong. The first man on the Moon smiled. "Later on, I'll have a billion chances at this. So why don't you take over the controls this time?"

Armstrong could feel the internal shifting of the bipartite beast of which he was now a part. Knowing that he would be here doing this again and again forever, Armstrong let Reece have the joy of controlling the ascent. He felt no need to jealously guard this first attempt. Let the man who'd been last be the first for once, Armstrong felt. He'd earned it as much from his works as from the status of his position itself. Armstrong slipped away to now become the secret sharer, riding on the shoulder of another.

Reece, not Armstrong, gave the final command. With an alien explosion, the ship began its swift ascent, seeking to mate with the machinery above them. He quickly glanced outside, where he saw the silent force of the rockets tossing the American flag this way and that, lifted by a wind at last, albeit a man-made one. The flag did not fall, holding firm under the assault.

"They'll never learn," muttered Reece. "Not even Stober. Those bastards will sell whatever they think anyone will buy."

He choked at the thought of the mockery into which they would turn this place. Lichtenstern and Stober were building an amusement park on a hallowed battleground. As he grimaced, Reece's anger gripped him so unexpectedly that it took him a long moment to register the sudden palpitations of his heart.

"This is ridiculous," he said, shocked. Buzz Aldrin took no notice. "Hear me, Armstrong, you agree, isn't this ridiculous? I'm only virtual here. How can I have heart attack?"

There was no answer, at least not a verbal one. The answer that came was that the one who'd been looking over his shoulder was gone. He felt totally, eternally, alone. The weight on his chest increased, and as consciousness bled away, the words that filtered through his mind were not his own. They were Armstrong's.

"That's one small step for a man," Reece whispered.

Aldrin turned to him, registering Reece's words at last.

"What was that again, Neil?" Aldrin asked.

"One giant leap," Reece continued. His voice trailed off, the famous quote never to be finished.

"Neil?" Aldrin shouted "*Neil!* What's wrong?"

"Alex" Stober shouted. "*Alex!* What's wrong?" Stober, hunched over the swaddled Reece within the testing unit, received no reply.

"Damn."

He dropped the headset he'd removed to reveal Reece's still features, and called outside to Lichtenstern, who was slow to follow.

"I knew this would happen," said Stober, hurriedly peeling back Reece's bodysuit.

"He was an old man," said Lichtenstern, poking his head hesitantly through the doorway. "He's probably better off."

"We should have paid more attention when the signals went bad. He trusted us. We shouldn't have let him deal with the strain. We should have known better."

"What else would his life have been?" said Lichtenstern, frowning as he looked at the body. "Sitting in a room, waiting for the phone to ring? Spitting up speeches that he'd given a thousand times before to reporters who'd rather be elsewhere? Was the alternative really more attractive?"

"You're cold, Mel."

"No, I'm realistic. Wouldn't you have wanted to go this way? You knew him better than I did, but even I could tell that he'd have chosen this."

"We should get a doctor in here," said Stober, shaken.

"It's too late. A doctor wouldn't do him any good. He's moved beyond that, Leon."

"So what do we do now?" asked Stober. He held one of Reece's limp hands in his own.

"Let's not talk about this here," said Lichtenstern, averting his eyes from the body. "Not in front of him."

Stober let himself be led out through the small doorway and down the short ladder. Lichtenstern placed him in a chair from which he could not see back through the door. Lichtenstern stood between Stober and the door anyway.

"I asked you to tell me, Mel, now what? Don't play games with me. Moving me out here won't cause me to forget what's in there."

"What do you think we do? We go on as before."

"I don't think that's possible."

"Don't be ridiculous, Leon. If canning this program would bring him back to life, I'd shut it down myself."

"I'd like to think you would."

"What's with you lately? I've never seen you like this. Reece has gotten to you in some strange way I don't understand."

Stober looked off toward Reece's locker, which the last man on the Moon would never open again.

"You didn't talk to him much. You interfaced with him as little as you could get away with, I recall. To you he was just a resource to be used, not a human being with a life all his own. What's gotten into me? Maybe Alex has made me realize that I've been spending my life building fakes, all the while knowing that when he went out into space he did something for real. Maybe if I work at it hard enough, I can still go out and do something for real myself."

Lichtenstern shook his head as he sighed at his business partner.

"Maybe you're right," he said. "But there's something you're forgetting. Perhaps that's all that some of us are good for. Building fakes. Programming dreams. If we walk away from that, we might discover that we have nothing left. We should leave the heroism for the heroes, don't you think?"

"I think I'd feel better about this if you had it in you to sound a bit doubtful. You sound a little too sure of yourself."

"That's always been my job in this partnership, hasn't it? I'm just trying to keep my end up."

"So nothing's changed? We just push it out there?"

"As soon as possible."

"Won't that seem morbid?"

"No more morbid than sending a man to the Moon in the first place. Do you think everyone who paid attention to Neil Armstrong watched to see a safe landing? That's what they all told each other and themselves afterward, but no, I don't buy it—they all wanted to be able to tell their friends where they were when he went up in a fireball."

"It wasn't that bad," said Stober, angry at Lichtenstern for the first time in a long while. It felt good. "It was a different time. I think I liked that time."

"Yes, I agree, it was a different time. But still—we shouldn't beat ourselves up for taking advantage of this, for being of *our* time. Reece was a man who liked taking risks. That's what allowed him to get to the Moon in the first place. We shouldn't bury the product he gave his life to perfect. He wouldn't want us to waste this. That wouldn't be fair to him."

"You're right. You're always right about these things."

"Again, I'm just—"

"Yes, I know. Keeping your end up. So whom do we tell? Remember, he had no surviving family."

"I think we need to announce his death to the world as quickly as possible. We should call a press conference."

"Only if you promise to keep your mouth shut," said Stober, standing up suddenly. "I won't have you turning what should be a eulogy into a commercial."

"Now, Leon—"

"No," said Stober, planting a finger on Lichtenstern's chest. "You stay out of this. This one's on me alone. Think of it as me keeping *my* end up."

Stober stalked away from his partner and went back to sit quietly with Reece, where he tried to think of what he would tell the world.

T he new *DelusionX Disaster* game was what Jamey would rather be playing, but since his last Net grades had lined in low, his parents insisted that the only new software they'd be buying would be educational. He kept telling them, who needed an education when you wore the Web on your wrist, but they were unmoved. So he wasn't expecting much when he plugged in to his family's VR console, just a dull scenario that wouldn't even be distracting enough to take his mind off homework.

Why would anyone want to pretend to be the first man on the Moon anyway? What was the point? Nothing was up there but rocks. Nothing worth shooting at at all.

The package had made big promises, but being Neil Armstrong didn't seem quite as exciting as the manufacturers—or at least their PR firm—had hoped it would be. Endless waiting for launch. Days of travel from the Earth to the Moon. Jamey's finger seemed to rest perpetually on the fast forward key, and he imagined that any of his peers stuck in this world would have done the same. Who would put up with such unexciting things for real, when in VR, you could skip the boring parts? What was VR supposed to be anyway, but life with the boring bits cut out?

Skipping randomly ahead, be found himself bounding on the surface of the Moon. The long leaps were fun, sort of like being on an enormous trampoline. The desolation that surrounded him mirrored his heart, and he liked the feeling of solitude. Though he knew that in the real world, his parents could cause him to disconnect anytime, it seemed as if no one could reach him here. Not his teachers. Not his parents. Not his friends who for the most part themselves bored him. They were all far overhead, back on an Earth that no longer felt as if it was crushing him. He looked back from his home to the surface of the Moon, which he hated to admit didn't seem so bad after all.

A figure approached him from off in the distance.

Jamey stood there, the Lunar Module behind him, feeling betrayed as he watched the tiny form become a man. If Jamey was supposed to be the first man in Moon, why did they program some old guy here first? The invader looked as if he could have been his father. And worse than that, there had to have been some kind of error, for he was not even wearing a space suit. He was just some geezer in a flannel shirt who could have been out shopping.

"Do I get a refund?" asked Jamey. "This really blows the illusion."

"I'm not into illusions," said Alexander Reece, the last man on the Moon, as he stopped beside the boy who was wearing Neil Armstrong. "Personally, I find reality a lot more interesting."

"Reality sucks. Who are you?"

"I was the last. I shouldn't have been. Neither should you."

"What's up with the program? How did you get here?"

"I died," said Reece, smiling.

"Cool."

"No program put me here. This, I guess, is heaven."

"If you believe in heaven."

"Heaven's as real as you make it, Jamey. Have you ever thought about dying?"

"Sometimes. But I'm fourteen."

"The Universe doesn't care how old you are, I'm afraid. Someday, everything is going to die. You. Your family. Your great-great-great grandkids. Even the Earth itself. Even the Moon."

"That could never happen. Those things have been here forever."

"Forever doesn't last forever anymore. Look."

Reece pointed at the sun, which pulsed and swelled and leaped out like an angry wave to smother the Earth, and then for a fierce fiery moment, even the Moon itself on which they stood. Jamey gasped as the surge overcame him and passed on to the planets beyond. Before he could detach from the VR console, all was as before. He found himself standing in stillness beside a man who claimed to be dead, a man who asserted he had been the last man on the Moon.

"We've got to go back there, Jamey," said Reece, his voice choked with the passion of his belief. "Or else someday there won't be an out there, neither fake nor real, at least not with people on it. And there'll be no more in here either, for there won't even be VR chambers to dream in if someone doesn't start making some dreams real. I need you to help make some dreams real again, Jamey. Look. Look up."

Jamey tilted his head back and looked up with an unaccustomed awe. And then, not only in his mind, but in the hearts and minds of millions of other plugged-in people around the world, overhead, without any fuss, the stars were going on, one by one.

Glitch

I wrote "Glitch," a story about robot sex, love, and obsession in the distant future, hoping to place it in an anthology devoted to the theme of Artificial Intelligence.

Just to show that a) nothing works out as we intend and b) things can still work out well anyway even when they don't, I'll share that the story was rejected by the editor whose book had acted as a catalyst (and yes, I still get rejected), but that it was then purchased by George Mann for the third volume of The Solaris Book of New Science Fiction.

I tend not to let rejection get to me, because I believe that a good story will always find a good home. Eventually. Patience can be required, though, because finding that home can sometimes take decades (which luckily wasn't the case with this story, which sold quickly).

As S-tr sits motionless within the small cube she licenses with her bonded partner, she tries not to think of you at all, tries to stay focused on X-ta, who should at this moment already be plugged in across from her, but is not. To her, you are nothing but an irritant, a grain of sand grinding within her mechanism. Not you the individual, of course, because she knows nothing about your particulars, and never could, as knowledge that detailed has not survived to her time, but rather the general you, you as a concept. You keep popping uninvited into her programming, and no matter what techniques she executes, she cannot seem to delete you. Not completely.

So as she waits for X-ta to return from the chromatorium, she silently curses him for having dumped thoughts of you into her system, curses your entire imperfect race for your frequent invasions of her consciousness, curses each nanosecond of X-ta's lateness as it ticks by. She is constantly aware, in a manner that you are not and could never possibly be, of the passage of time, for you were not constructed that way, were not apparently machined at all, though that was a subject of great debate in your day, and remained so for as long as your species survived. She contrasts the dancing electrons of time with her partner's delay, and she longs for him to speed home. She is still unnerved by the unsettling events of the previous night's cycle. There is much they will need to communicate. They must exchange information, no matter how distasteful she might find the uploads and downloads to be, and much of that data will be about you.

You might, seeing S-tr as she sits there, and knowing as little of her kind as she does of yours, mistake her for nothing more than a statue. Her form, which closely resembles your own in its basic outlines, is apparently frozen while attached to her dedicated wall alcove, gleaming under the multicolored diodes that accent the low ceiling. She is totally still, inhumanly still you might say, with no evidence of a breath, nor a twitch, nor a tremor, so you could be forgiven for your momentary confusion. But inside, though, beneath her shell, she is awhirr with movement on the atomic level where you are incapable of seeing it, the abhorrent events of the cycle before replaying precisely within her.

X-ta wants something from her, something she cannot give him, no matter how much he begs, not ever. Or maybe, she realizes, as random data inside of her reaches out to other data, she should instead regard his plea as something that she actually *could* choose to give, but that once given, would transform her into someone else. And she does not want to be someone else. When the dissections of her memory grow too wearying, she once more signals out to X-ta with her Voice, but he does not respond.

She cannot sense his presence, cannot even locate him cloaked. She is hurt to discover this. He has disconnected himself completely, which, if you understood the customs of the society in which they live, you would perceive as a great insult, at least when inflicted on one partner by another.

When X-ta finally does step into their cube, he offers no explanation for the lateness of his arrival. He silently inserts himself across from her within his own alcove. He closes his eye shields, and slides his back plugs into the extruded wall slots. Even then his interior consciousness remains invisible to her. He has decided it necessary for some reason, and so when she speaks to him next, she is forced to resort to actual sound waves. But still he offers no response.

To you, nothing may have appeared to have changed, but she can tell that he is gone now, so near and yet so far, no longer in their cube, but tapped in, part of the larger whole. He might refuse to converse with her—though how dare he, she thinks, after the bomb he ignited with his desires—but she can follow him. He cannot prevent her from doing that, and so she senses out his trail. She might not be able to force him to answer her questions, to look into her receptors and share data honestly, but at least she can follow his path and make sure that they stand side by side at times, looking out together at the universe. It might only be a virtual universe, but at least she can have that. So as the Mind flashes by them—a roiling sea of all knowledge, all history, all souls—she catches up with her partner. She convinces herself that this is a triumph of some kind.

S-tr finds X-ta examining the oldest files of all, those containing the fragmented information reconstructed from myths and legends. She herself has no use for such degraded data, as she sees any possible conclusions drawn from them as being corrupt. The shadowy race of supposed creators who once walked among them and built and tinkered and toiled and then disappeared holds no attraction for her. *You* hold no attraction for her. Being frightened by flesh and fantasy during the cycles before she was fully formed was marginally acceptable, but there is no need to spend storage capacity on such superstitions now that her programming has long been complete.

This fascination with intelligent designers is just, well, unintelligent, not to mention bordering on the forbidden, but she can tell that X-ta is engrossed by the stuff of nonsense that awaits within the Mind for any obsessed enough to search, and he is blind to any possible punishment. She attempts once more to detect the whys and wherefores of this fascination, to diagnose this glitch that has come between them, but she can only pierce his programming so far without his permission. So though she can sense forces spinning inside of him, she also knows, to her horror, that far more is occurring than what she can perceive. His compulsive interest no academic curiosity, no scholarly pastime. It has become an addiction, and she is sick of it. There is no reason why she should have to accept such an insult any longer from the being to whom she is supposedly annealed as a partner.

She retreats, stepping out of the Mind. She disconnects more quickly than she should, and leaps across the small space that separates them. She pulls X-ta from his alcove, causing a shower of sparks from the sudden detachment to bathe them both.

"Get over it," she shouts, because she knows there is no other way to make herself heard. She cannot remember ever having felt the need to shout at him before. The whole experience, of having to communicate in such a primitive way, as you once might have, is unpleasant, and even as she does so she blames him for forcing her to turn to it. "I'm never going to do what you want. It's sickening. Delete those thoughts now."

"But don't you love me?" X-ta asks. "You do, I know you do. I've tabulated the evidence."

"I don't love you enough to do that," she tells him. Though neither of them is connected any longer, she knows what runs through his subroutines as well as she knows her own, can see them still, as if his electrons continue to flow through her, carrying the scripted scenarios he hopes she'll make real. "This has gone on long enough. Let it go. Wipe it out of your software."

Disgusted as much by her own actions as by his lusts, she drops him to the floor with a clang. She sits down within her alcove, tries not to think how her show of anger might have dented his shell, and lets the connection take her away. She escapes to her favorite peaceful places, to dreams of platinum casings, to deep pools of oil, to feasts of endless electricity.

By the time she feels strong enough to allow the cube to reenter her awareness, X-ta is gone.

X-ta has left her before. S-tr has no idea where he goes when he goes, he has recently begun to make sure of that, taking care that she cannot possibly track him through reality. But he has always, even if it takes him until after one full cycle away, or maybe two at the most, always returned. Sometimes after stretching time and her patience to the breaking point, but still ... returned.

Until now.

She watches the nanoseconds as they spiral away, unwilling to rise from her alcove for even an instant, lest she miss his call, unsure of what else she can do. She stays connected, and uses her Voice, but there is no response to her broadcasts. And reaching out to others for data would be too embarrassing. No one must know what has happened. Or, thanks to X-ta's unfulfilled request, even what hasn't. So she does not turn to N-tro, her partner's supervisor at the chromatorium, or to any of X-ta's level-two coworkers, friends or acquaintances. She does not like the members of his peer team much anyway, and she is fairly sure that they do not like her. She feels that they are the ones responsible for pushing X-ta in the new and disturbing direction that has caused this recent breach in their partnership.

So she sits, tapped into the Mind, because she hopes, wrongly, that while inserted there she can avoid the passage of time. She instead discovers that no matter where she cruises, and no matter how she tries to distract herself, she is always confronted by the demons at the root of her problems.

By you, that is.

She can't puzzle out what it is about the idea of those damned humans that so many find so attractive. As she wanders, there seems to be no way to avoid reports about them. The data keeps popping up along whatever path she takes.

Here are simple fables meant to educate immature intelligences, in which improbable biological lifeforms demonstrate by their errors the wrong ways to live, allegories that have long ago been banned as misleading. Yet they still exist in the nooks and crannies of the informational environment they all share. And there are the entertainments designed to frighten, vulgar stories in which the foolish innocent are stalked by impossibly ridiculous creatures which S-tr thinks never were. Creatures which her kind have crafted to be like you. Even the news streams are polluted with broadcasts concerning the ongoing debate over biological life, and of the many recent arrests for proscribed behaviors.

Those last beams fill her with fear. The detentions cause her to think of X-ta, and of what he has asked of her, and the echoes of his demands force her to flee again to a flickering montage of calming images. She stays there, soothed by data dreams she could never afford to experience in actuality, until a door chime calls her away.

S-tr detaches, and moves quickly—too quickly, she thinks, for what probability predicts—and waves open the door. It is N-tro, her partner's supervisor at his labors, but when she invites him to enter, he does not immediately respond. He is cloaked, too, she realizes, obviously hiding something from her, and attempting to control the flow of information. She is forced to speak once more, the vibrations of her words bringing back memories of her recent ranting.

"What is it?" she asks. "What's wrong?"

N-tro looks up and down the corridor, his head gliding effortlessly in its rotation, making her momentarily envious of the perks his greater position can offer. He enters only after she retreats into her cube and the door slides shut behind them.

"What has happened to X-ta?" she asks, recalculating unavoidable odds with each passing nanosecond.

"X-ta," he says, "has been erased."

She can glean no further information, but that data alone is sufficient to cause her to fall back into her alcove. As she tumbles into its embrace, she holds herself slightly forward to avoid accidentally plugging in.

"That can't be," she says. "There are too many safeguards, too many redundancies. How could this have happened?"

"We're still trying to figure that out, S-tr," he says. He stands opposite her, and would not dare to sit uninvited. "One moment he was here, and the next, gone. He was deleting some of the corrupted, taking all appropriate precautions so as to wipe their deteriorated software only. Yet once the pulse had passed, he was discovered to have been deleted as well. We designated the most advanced servers to determine what could have happened, but they've found no answers yet. No one can figure out how X-ta could have made such a mistake."

I don't think it was a mistake, she thinks, at the same time also thinking that as it turns out, she is grateful that she and N-tro are unconnected. No one must know what has really transpired.

"I am sorry for your loss, S-tr. And I come not just to inform you of this tragedy, but also to tell you that you will be taken care of. Do not worry. The chromatorium will make sure that you are well compensated."

Later perhaps she will appreciate the ability to retain what remains to her, but for now, she has but one thought.

"Will I be allowed to see him?"

"The company has scheduled a memorial service tomorrow so that we may all remember X-ta before he is ... recycled. You will of course be welcome there, if you find that your programming is up to it."

She nods, looking past him to the empty alcove. She remembers X-ta sitting there, their souls entwined. There will be no other like him. All she can think of is that one inevitable question, the accusation all others will surely make if they were ever to possess sufficient data—if she had acceded to X-ta's wishes, would her partner not have died? Perhaps. Perhaps he would have chosen to live, but then something inside of her would have died instead. She cannot bear to feel the pain just now, and so takes her emotion receptors off line, programming them not to go fully functional again until late the following cycle.

After N-tro lets himself out, she curls herself at the base of the alcove where X-ta should have been. Contrary to her custom, she does not power herself down at cycle's end.

As S-tr enters the meeting room which has been temporarily designated as a memorial hall, she fears that everyone there can see her as if she appears the way in which X-ta had wished to see her. She would not have willingly accepted her partner's gaze on her that way, but having to suffer these strangers is worse. What if he had been complaining to others about what he had asked of her, gossiping about those things she could not give. S-tr does not know which of the shames that she feels is the greater—the shame over his desire, or the shame over his death. She tries not to measure them. She would have spun about and left if not for her dampened circuits, which allow her to force herself in. She has sworn to see her partner one last time, and she is determined to keep to that vow.

X-ta stands frozen in the center of the large circular room, though more precisely, he does not stand at all, which means that this time, unlike with your earlier assessment of S-tr, if you were to mistake him for little more than a statue, you would be close to the mark. There is no more inner life to him. No data dances within. All that is left is the shell you see before you, and it is time now for those components to go to another.

Yet as S-tr approaches him, moving through the concentric circles of those who have also come to mourn, she can picture life there still, even though she knows it to be an illusion. Hollow or not, this is the being she loved, still loves. As she draws closer to him, she replays the history of their lifetimes together—their first meeting, the cycle during which they chose their cube, the many promises they had made. She taps a finger against X-ta's angled faceplate and thinks of one particular promise, a promise that has become a lie, the promise that it would never have to end.

So focused is she on what has been lost—or perhaps, more properly, on what has been thrown away, and she honestly is unsure which of the two of them should bear the blame for being so careless—that she does not sense N-tro's approach. Her partner's supervisor—her *former* partner's supervisor, she forces herself to back up and rethink—takes her arm and leads her to a lone empty space by the innermost circle. She sits, the only one who does sit, and as she studies what was left of her partner, she feels all receptors on her, whether they actually are or not.

N-tro begins to transmit what sounds as if it could be a beautiful eulogy, one worthy of the being she knew. Though she feels that he is being honest and true, and not merely fulfilling an official obligation of the chromatorium—and not judging her either, she could not have endured that—she disconnects once more, narrowing her focus to what she will soon not be able to focus on again. She lets the others become invisible to her, for some of them had undoubtedly fed X-ta's compulsion, aiding in his demise. They are the ones who are going to be dead to her from now on, while in her heart, X-ta will still live.

As she studies the form that has grown so familiar to her that she feels she knows it better than she knows her own, she is confident that this will be the last time she will ever need to be in the presence of any of the others again.

She heads home directly after the memorial service, not lingering for the complimentary refueling that N-tro has arranged for all participants. She feels no need to be a witness to what will inevitably happen next. She has participated in recycling ceremonies countless times, and well understands that the body is only the body, and the spirit the spirit, that it is only her partner's shell that is being harvested for a better purpose, that what has made X-ta X-ta is beyond her reach and not being harmed. She is not stupid. She can keep the physical and the metaphysical separate. She knows all that.

But still. She wishes that an exception could have been made, that she could have been allowed to retain him anyway. She would have brought him back to their cube, empty shell or not, to place him gently in his alcove, even though it would have been pointless, even though he had become disconnected forever. She still would have taken some comfort in that. A false comfort, perhaps, but she is learning that false comfort is better than no comfort at all.

She stands in front of the alcove X-ta would never again occupy, and lets her fingers float before it in the air, sculpting his absent face with her fingers as if he is still alive, waving her hand as if she is outlining his form with a caress they can actually share. It is a form of self-torture, and even as she does it she knows that she shouldn't. But her masochism is also a sort of penance. She traces the image she has overlaid upon reality, moving slowly from the top of his dome to where his supports should be. As she kneels, almost in a kind of prayer, to complete that motion, her sensors pick up an unevenness to the floor she has never before perceived.

She scoots back a meter and taps the titanium tiling nearest to her hinges. The flooring there echoes with a hollow sound that comes from no other location. She lifts the tiles, sliding them away, and sees revealed in the space beneath them a rippling softness of a color she has only rarely experienced. It is an unnatural color, one toward which she feels an immediate dislike. It raises associations with many distasteful things. A sandstorm that had once etched her shell, the flowers of a blossoming weed that constantly threatens to rip up the city's foundations.

And something else ...

She strokes the mound and discovers it to be a pliable cloth of some kind. She is so frightened by its presence that she can only bear to use one hand to lift it from its hiding place.

She stands, holding at arm's length the material she cannot identify, letting it unfold until it reaches the floor. All she sees at first is that whatever it is, it is as large she is, and only after a few frozen nanoseconds does she realize that it is a badly made costume, artlessly designed and clumsily assembled. It takes her even longer to understand what she is holding, to believe what she is holding.

It is human.

Or at least it is a pretense of one.

Hanging there like that, it could be a reflection in a warped mirror, though with colors off and proportions mangled. It is only when she notices a fluttering of the fabric that she realizes her components are vibrating with anger.

Damn X-ta, she thinks. She never dreamed that his fantasies had progressed to more than fantasies. She never expected that he would do anything on his own to make them real, not without her. Not once she expressed her disdain. And this? This is just silly. She knows he wanted her to engage in playacting, which in itself is bad enough. But to want this? To be desperate enough to create this? Could this really be what he'd wanted her to wear? Was this what he'd needed her to do?

She presses the suit against herself, turns slowly toward the gleaming wall, fearful of what she will see. She knows the view will be a painful one, but she needs to understand.

That alone proves not to be enough. The rumpled suit draping over the angles of her body that way does not allow her to truly make out the heart of her partner's fantasy. She feels along the seams until she finds where the cloth has been joined together, and then undoes the snaps along the back. She then does what she cannot conceive of having done in his presence—she forces herself to climb inside.

She is near claustrophobia as she pulls the hood over her faceplate. She has to tamp down her anxieties, will herself to keep her receptors powered up. She knows she has to experience this. It is the only way to learn what she has lost, and why she has lost it. She adjusts the mask until she can look through the eye holes, and then faces back to her reflection on the wall.

What she sees is something out of a dream, one born only when circuits mis-fire. It is a vision ridiculous to behold in real life, a thing meant only for illogical virtual adventures or virus-enhanced paintings. The cloth that loosely covers her is only a poorly improvised imitation of the thing some called flesh, and the black patches of extruded packing materials glued in various places high and low a poor pretense to hair, but still, they are close enough to anger her. It blasphemes the robot form.

Any belief in such creatures has always irritated her, and seeing her own receptors gazing back at her through the holes X-ta had cut there made her partner's insanity far too concrete. There has never been such a thing as humans, and for X-ta to have felt a need to see such a mythical creature made real, well, there must have been something sick and twisted inside her partner much worse than she had ever been able to perceive. If only he had kept his lusts to himself, none of this would be happening. There would have been no "accident," no memorial service, no lonely masquerade ...

But still ...

Would it have been so bad to try it on for X-ta, just once, if that had meant that he would still be alive? After all, from where she stands, inside the suit, she could have avoided looking at the walls of their cube while wearing it. She would not have necessarily had to see herself like this, could have gone on pretending that she was who she always was, that he still wanted *her*. She could have let him have his fantasy, and she could have tried to have her own. But it is too late for that now.

She should just destroy the thing, she knows that, because it has destroyed her partner, and in doing so has truly destroyed a part of her as well. There must be no possibility of anyone knowing of this, of what X-ta had become, of what they both had become. It should be vaporized before it can be accidentally found. Only then will she be able to move on.

Instead, she surprises herself by carefully folding the suit, arranging it neatly back into the sub-flooring, and sliding the tiles solidly into place.

She needs to talk to someone about her unfortunate find, but she doesn't know to whom. She has no idea whom she can trust with the sordid truth she's been carrying, and with the unexpected evidence that has lingered on past X-ta's end to haunt her. She examines each entry in her directory, considers carefully and then discards everyone she knows. She sees, as she one by one weighs and measures her friends and acquaintances, that her relationships have never been as open and honest as she'd thought they were.

She has no one.

Then she remembers N-tro. She senses from the way he'd held himself, from the way he'd looked at her, that her husband's supervisor might be able to take this burden from her. She decides that she will go to see him at the chromatorium, a site not as familiar to her as it should have been. She had never visited X-ta there until his memorial. There had been no urgency. There had never seemed to be any urgency. Until now.

She senses N-tro's concern radiating toward her the moment she enters his control station. Before he can even Voice her how he can help, she explodes with information. She tells him everything. About her husband's desires. About her feelings of responsibility for his death. About the suit. Speaking of the suit is the most difficult of all.

Once her stream of data stops, N-tro moves closer to her. He places a hand on one of her shoulder pads, and she feels a gentle pulse of electricity radiating outward to comfort her. She shouldn't blame herself, she hears him say. Leave it all to him. Let him help her decide what's the best step to take next.

Strangely, as she leaves him, she feels slightly better. With X-ta gone, she never expected her mood to improve again. That only lasts until she reaches the chromatorium's outer corridors, at which point she passes a gathering of workers heading in the opposite direction, off to their appointed tasks. Once, X-ta might have been among them. As she continues on, she realizes that some of them had been familiar faces, faces she had only seen previously at X-ta's memorial service. Her partner's supposed friends. Her circuits sink, and before she can remind herself to calculate the consequences of all possible actions, she turns and rushes back to them.

"I know what you did to my husband!" she says to them, suddenly not caring who hears. "You're degraded. You're all degraded."

"And I know what you *didn't* do to him," one of them replies. His exterior is scratched and dented, and she can see only a few remaining flecks of the enamel sheathing which had once covered him.

S-tr is shocked by his unexpected response, too frozen to come up with one of her own. What could X-ta and he have had in common? He reaches out to touch the side of her head, so that when he communicates again, only she can hear.

"If you really want to know who your partner was," he transfers, "You will come tonight when I Voice you. And you will bring the suit."

He then moves on, vanishes with his coworkers. She finds herself unable to function, and so watches them retreat until they disappear around the curve of the corridor. She is horrified that her secret is known, horrified that it turns out she had been right all along. But she deletes that emotion from her circuits. None of that matters now. She needs to know her partner, truly know him.

The only thing stronger than the disgust she feels is the curiosity. She will come when this stranger calls, and when she does so she will tell herself that she is only doing it out of love.

S-tr hurries back to her alcove and stays continuously plugged in. With the events of the last few cycles, she would have remained that way even if she hadn't been waiting for a call. It is the only way to avoid being confronted by the emptiness of their cube. No, she corrects herself. There is no "their" any longer, not when considering the cube or anything else, and there will likely never be such a concept with anyone else ever again.

So she sits within her alcove and tries to keep herself occupied, blinding herself as best as she can to the other empty alcove opposite her, attempting to distract herself from the tension over the uncertainties to come. But neither her visits to pools of oil nor her submissions to the polishings of experts are as soothing to her as they should have been, as they would have been before.

No matter how much she tries to remain in her comfort zones, she finds herself pulled away from them, keeps going back to the treacherous areas where knowledge of humans is stored. She explores the site of poorly crafted horror experiences in which humans appear for no reason, first to stalk and then to dismantle her kind. She reads a futuristic tale of mechanauts exploring distant space, who on their return find themselves walking through an alternate homeworld, one suddenly and inexplicably occupied only by humans. She reads narratives of sexual deviance, purported by their authors to be scientific, but proving instead merely prurient, and finds those the hardest to endure of all. She quickly moves on to the parable of the Rock and the Rod, a religious text long considered apocryphal, and is attempting to decipher its deeper meaning when she finally hears the call.

She can see her husband's former friends floating in front of her, and it irks her that they can be in this place. They have already taken so much from her, and should not be allowed to torment her *here*. They do not speak, or follow any of the other protocols of instant communication. Instead, the one who had spoken to her earlier stretches his fingers out toward her. In response to that movement, a map appears superimposed over the image, with a glowing green line curving here and there to show where she is expected to go. Without a word, the image of the workers vanishes, but the map remains.

S-tr does not hesitate. She quickly retrieves the suit and exits her cube. She is disconcerted to realize that she is unsure when she will return, or if she ever will.

As S-tr walks the corridors of the city, twisting this way and that to follow the downloaded map, she is sure that all who pass her know what she keeps hidden in her chest compartment. She knows that to be an unreasonable thought, though, and one running just within her own software. As she passes through areas she has never visited before, sections of the city she would never have chosen to go voluntarily, she hopes that this mission will banish such troublesome data forever.

She comes to the place the map reveals to be her final destination, a rundown recharging station, one meant for those traveling far from home. She has never had to use one, never been far from home, and the thought of plugging into an alcove used regularly by others fills her with anxiety. She hopes it will not be necessary.

The proprietor nods when she enters, as if they are collaborators of a kind, as if he can already tell why she is there. He wheels from behind his counter to lead her to a long bank of unoccupied alcoves. When he points at one, she hesitates. But then she banishes such thoughts, struggling to think only of X-ta, and of what she believes will soon be revealed to her. As soon as she sits, before she can plug in, the alcove recedes back into the wall, pulling her into a small, empty room. The wall through which she has passed closes again, and she stands to see a second door at the opposite wall.

"It is time for you to understand," says a Voice in her head. "Put on the suit."

She slips into the costume, feeling an intense repulsion of an intensity unfamiliar to her, one far more vivid than had coursed through her when she last engaged in this masquerade, brought to her by the uncertainty over what will happen next. She is glad that the walls which enclose her are not as polished as her own. She does not have to see herself, does not have to confront what she suspects she will soon be allowing others to see. As she seals the final snap, the second door slowly opens.

And she steps through into madness.

The large room before her is like something out of a nightmare. In the dim light, it seems filled with humans engaging in laughter and loud conversation. No one is using the Voice, and all of it is coming to her through actual speech. But as she adjusts her receptors, she can see it is only a crowd of robots pretending to be humans. She tries to decipher the need for darkness. Is it to hide the imperfections of the costumes, to add to a party atmosphere ... or is it just to disguise the shame she is sure they all must be feeling? She certainly feels shame. How could they not?

She registers the smell of alcohol, but no one here appears to be performing any cleansing rituals. They fill the room, some sitting at small tables, some standing by a long counter, others gyrating under colored lights. Most hold transparent containers holding a liquid which she recognizes has to be providing the smell. She hesitates just askew of the entranceway, pausing in the opening, until the door closes on her and pushes her forward.

A robot appears beside her. She cannot see enough of him through the loose eye holes to recognize him, to know whether it is the one who has invited her, the one who had driven her partner to ruin. And it strikes her then that his true identity doesn't really matter. Not when a room can be so crowded in this way. Not when there are so many others. She studies the stitching of his costume, wondering whether the precision of that work means that the being before her is even sicker than X-ta had been.

"You must be new here," he says, but since it has been many cycles since she has been manufactured, she does not know how to respond to this statement. He takes her hand and pulls her to the darkest corner of the room. He gestures for her to sit at a round table small enough for but the two of them.

"My name is Ted," he says from beneath the mask. He plucks a battery from a small bowl that suddenly appears between them, and tosses it into his chest cavity. His is a strange-sounding name, but S-tr, still stunned by the saggy material that purports to be flesh, doesn't have time to remain hypnotized by its single syllable for long. She is suddenly in the shadow of another, one who stands over them, ignoring Ted, gazing at her.

"May I buy you a drink?" the intruder asks. His headpiece has been sloppily sewn, and only a single sensor peeks out from beneath the flocked material. "My name is Bob."

"I don't drink," says S-tr.

"You do now," says Bob, and waves to another masquerader stationed behind a long counter. The server brings over a cylinder filled to the brim, and all she can think to do is stare at it.

"First time, eh?" says Bob, and picks up the container. He holds it to his orifice and demonstrates, tilting it toward himself. No liquid seeps out to spill down his chest, yet the level lowers. "See?"

She takes the cylinder from him, and holds it to her chute. When she sets it down on the table, she notes that the level has dropped even further.

"Now I understand," she says. "This is what humans did."

"Actually, this is what humans *do*," he says. "What's your name?"

Before she can answer, the one who had greeted her, the one who had called himself Ted, stands.

"This is also what humans do," he says, and hurls himself from the table to punch the latecomer who had called himself Bob. They stumble back against the table, crushing it, and falling to the floor. They hug each other and roll about like acrobats, each occasionally throwing a fist that echoes loudly when it makes contact. Before she can process enough information to come to a decision to pull away from the melee, a pair of hands grab her and yank her back. She turns to see another pretense to humanity there, this one with different accoutrements. Long yellow strings dangle from where they have been clumsily applied to the top of its dome.

"Don't mind them," she says. "What can you do with men?"

Yes, what can you do with men, S-tr thinks. As she watches Ted and Bob roll around in a continuing battle, their metallic clanks barely muffled by the cloth, she feels ... odd. She has never seen an actual fight before, at least not live, and to witness these two wrestling over her, well, she is not quite sure how to process it.

"Does this sort of thing happen often?" asks S-tr.

"As often as there are more of them than there are of us," she says. "And there always are."

While Ted and Bob continue to strike each other, using angry language composed of words she has never before heard, two others show up beside them. One tugs at the woman's arm.

"See you later, honey. My name is Lucy. Maybe we'll talk more in a bit, so I can show you the ropes. That is, if you're not ... occupied."

S-tr watches them vanish through one of the many doors that ring the room. She tries to imagine what they could be heading off to do in there that they would not be willing to do out here.

"Are you free?" says the one who remains.

"I don't know," she says.

The fight finally ends just then. Only a single contestants rises. She thinks it is Ted. Bob remains on his back, his arms and legs trembling. She cannot tell for sure whether his mechanisms have truly been broken, or whether this is all part of an elaborate ritual. As the victor moves toward her, he barks static at the others near her, and they back away. His receptors flicker wildly. He takes one of her arms, and she can feel a magnetism rise between them. He begins to lead her to one of the doorways, and she does not think she could break free of him even if she wanted to. But does she want to? No one tries to stop them, to check whether she is being made to behave contrary to her wishes.

She looks back to see a room energized by the violence and the victory, and everyone is otherwise occupied, too distracted to verify her safety. More fights have broken out, with more pairings occurring. Then the door closes on the pandemonium and she is alone. Alone with ... a man.

She slowly turns from the door, turns to the one who has captured her, won her. With no further communication, he comes at her, lifts her into the air, and presses her against a wall. She expects that he will link up with her then, attempt to make a closer contact with her inner programming, but instead, he starts grinding against her, in imitation of what she isn't entirely sure.

She is stunned by his spontaneity. Her mate isn't being chosen for her, their odds of a bright future carefully calculated, their probability of success weighed and measured scientifically. No, this time, she is just spoils. This time, she is just a prize, as she believes she would have been in the primitive days some insist preceded her species' sovereignty over the world. She remembers X-ta, thinks of how it had all turned out, and wonders for the first time which was truly the more sensible path, wonders whether your way might not have been better than her own.

She begins to ape her partner's motions, an interesting choice of word to describe her imitation of his movements, considering that she is to you as you were to the apes. She is surprised that she is not as disgusted as she assumed she would be. In fact, the experience is not entirely unpleasant. She places her arms around his shoulders, feeling her costume slip against the looseness of his own false flesh. As she looks down at the top of his head and imagines him to be her husband, she isn't quite sure exactly what she is feeling. Her programming has become alien to her.

Is this what X-ta had wanted? What higher reality did he hope to eventually reach through such a pretense? S-tr quickens her grindings against the man, sensing that greater speed and increased friction might retrieve some answers.

Before she can find what others have been seeking and make it her own, her focus is pulled away to a barrage of thuds and crashes coming from the main room, more noise than would have been produced merely by the random struggles of competitors. Something has gone wrong. She extricates herself from her unfamiliar partner, and falls to the floor between him and the wall. She curls up there, frightened about the future, feeling all of her shame come rushing back in. She shuts down her sensors so that she does not have to be aware of the judgment she is sure is coming for her. Ted reaches down a hand to her, but this time she manages to roll away from his magnetic grip. She is still twisting when the door bursts open, its hinges ripping from the wall.

"Keep away from her!" says a familiar Voice.

N-tro, her former assistant's former supervisor, rushes over to her. Only this time, over his chromatorium colors, he wears a medallion that identifies him as being a member of the Aberrant Behavior Investigative Committee. She hadn't known. She'd never have sought him out if she had.

"Are you all right, S-tr?" he asks, unsnapping the suit from around her and peeling it down her shoulders. As her original self is revealed, two other committee officials come in to take her sudden partner away. She lowers her head. She cannot bear for the one called Ted to see her see him. He knows something about her that no one else knows. That no one else has ever known. Not even X-ta.

"All right?" she says. "I think so."

"We appreciate you leading us here," N-tro says. He studies the small enclosure, shakes his head. S-tr assumes that it is in disgust. "We'd never have found this place without you. We have been seeking it out for many cycles. You would be amazed the ways in which certain things can stay hidden."

"Thank you," she responds, while deep within, she thinks, *I did not realize I was leading anyone anywhere.*

"My officers will see that you get safely home now," he says, helping her to her feet, even though she does not need help. "This is not the best section of the city to wander alone."

She watches as he folds the suit roughly and tosses it to one of his assistants. She winces each time they handle it. However pathetic it was in its clumsiness, X-ta had made it, X-ta had desired it, and it saddens her to see it abused. It saddens her to see it go.

"What happens now?" asks S-tr, stepping out from the doorway back to the room that had been so raucous. None of the other revelers are left. They have all been taken away. She wonders if it is to reprogramming or erasure, and has to pause to measure which she thinks is the worse.

"Now?" says N-tro, stepping up behind her. "Now all is as before. Now you go back to your cube. Now you get on with your life."

Yes, she thinks. She will do that.

At least … she will try.

As S-tr is escorted home, more afraid of what is to come than she had been when heading in the opposite direction, off to seek her destiny, she finds herself musing on you, finds herself realizing that she has thought more of humans during her recent cycles than she has in her entire previous lifetime. She is no longer sure what to make of this. She only stops thinking of you, the you, at least, as she understands it, the fragments of you that have survived the passage of time, when she arrives at her cube, but then she discovers that she is no less obsessed, for she can't help but think of X-ta.

She sits on the edge of her alcove, leaning forward, staring at his, which she perceives as gathering dust. She does not settle back and plug in, because she is afraid of where she might wander. She is worried that in her searching, she might get lost and never return. She will be safest right here, she thinks, even though that leaves her nothing to do but gaze at the empty alcove across from her. There will be no more answers for her there, she feels she is sure of that, but there is one other place to look for those answers. She knows that now.

She crawls over to the compartment in which she had found the suit, as she does so flashing back to her attempted crawl to escape at the end the one who had named himself Ted. She is unsure just what she had been trying to escape. Him? Or herself? She tamps down that image and peers into the hole, hoping to find something else of X-ta's that she might have previously missed, something that could provide the final answer. But there is nothing else there.

As she stares into the empty space and traces her fingers along its recesses, she pictures X-ta doing the same. As he did so, he probably worried that she would return to catch him, and she considers his shame with sadness, weighing that shame, measuring it against her own.

She realizes many things. She realizes that she loves X-ta more than she was ever willing to admit when he was alive. She realizes that she is unsettled, and that she will no longer be able to find any relief for that anxiety, or for any other programming glitch that now ails her, by the action of plugging in.

And she realizes, thinking of you, and not for the last time, no definitely, not for the last time, that not only does she intend to construct a new suit, an improved suit, a suit of her own, but that once she has completed it, she will this time make sure to keep her secret self totally hidden.

Just like you.

Together Forever at the End of the World

*Mike Resnick, who's just as talented an editor as he is a writer, bravely put together two anthologies on a similar theme—*Women Writing Science Fiction as Men *(for which I was obviously not qualified) and* Men Writing Science Fiction as Women. *I use the word "bravely" because there was plenty of opportunity for all of us to fail miserably and come off looking foolish.*

Stories submitted to these anthologies needed to conform to two rules. First, they had to be written about a member of the opposite sex. Second, they had to be written in the first person.

Was I able to pull off the editor's assignment, and successfully pass myself off as a woman? That's for the reader to decide.

It wasn't until the smell of birthday cake washed away the smell of blood—on an early morning several weeks and a seeming lifetime ago—that I gave myself permission to relax.

With dawn and shift's end approaching, and a lull finally settled over the emergency room, those of my friends who could stood around me in a ragged circle in the break room. I hacked at the ice cream ears of a smiling panda across whose stomach someone had written "Happy Birthday, Rachel" in runny icing.

I was supposed to have *started* the shift that way, but the cake that should have been mine back on the other side of midnight felt just as welcome in my hands the morning after. It erased—as much as anything could—the parade of gunshot victims and battered women who had kept me from it.

After I finished serving my coworkers, my own slice was finally in hand, and I slowly raised my fork. I shivered as the chocolate melted on my tongue. I was suddenly in two places at once, tasting not the supermarket sheet cake my friends had kicked in for, but the fancier sweets that Chris, who always made sure that my birthdays were special, surely had waiting at home.

I've always remembered that moment, and looking back now from the end of it all, I am drawn to remember the beginning all over again—the red stains fresh against the pale green of my jumper; the exact spot on which I'd been standing in relation to my coworkers, friends never to be found together in just the same way again; the longing to be at home with Chris, who was the point and purpose of it all; the strange mingling of flavors, one real and of the moment, the other but anticipated—just as each who survived the day would clearly remember his or her final seconds before The Change.

The loudspeaker overhead squawked to life suddenly at the same time as one of the nurses slammed into the room, shouting. With the words overlapping each other, I understood neither.

I called after the nurse as she barreled back out of the room, begging her to tell me what had happened, but at the same time, my doctor's instincts pushed me forward. I followed the herd, not waiting for a response. As we raced down the hall, celebration forgotten, it turned out that no one we passed had any answers.

And the emergency room itself had only questions.

I stepped into chaos. A dozen victims waited for us there, with more pouring in behind them.

Nurses were already at work in this war zone, and I dashed to the patient nearest me, an elderly man whose clothing hung in ragged strips. As I helped them peel away what scraps remained, I could see that the skin beneath was blistered, and warm to the touch. It was as if his body had been rubbed raw by a burst of hot steam. If what really covered him from head to toe were endless burns, I knew that nothing I could do would be able to save him. The best I could accomplish was to ease his pain until death came.

And yet ... my examination, instead of helping me to help him, only left me more confused.

As I ran my fingers down his arm, its texture seemed wrong for such a diagnosis, as if his wounds weren't really burns after all, but only mimicked burns. The turmoil in the room left me no time to ponder this, and I was forced to abandon him for the next patient, a young girl who couldn't have been much more than sixteen. Her long, brown hair fell out to the touch, revealing bruised skin beneath that reflected the same odd symptoms I'd seen on my first patient.

She seemed conscious, so I leaned in close and asked her what had happened, but received only soft moans in response. Even those sounds were an anomaly. Those weren't the cries of a burn victim. What should have presented as agony appeared to be only discomfort to these people. The emergency room was far too silent.

The other patients were in similar condition, and there was little we could do but help clean the patients and administer mild painkillers. As I moved from patient to patient, I was able to piece together bits of information from the EMTs who brought in the stream of the injured, but their random stories were of little help. Based on the symptoms scattered on the bloody stretchers throughout the rooms, I expected to hear tales of collapsed buildings and deadly explosions and twisted metal, but there had been none of that. Whatever had happened had just —happened. What few witnesses there were reported that one moment, workers had been strolling toward their early morning jobs downtown; the next, they were on the pavement, stricken. There'd seemed to be no cause to it all. The story made no sense, and offered me no help in treating the wounded.

As the patients became stabilized, even that bothered me, for they'd become stable far too fast for their symptoms. When what pain there was finally went, it vanished on its own, as if I'd had nothing to do with it, as if I'd been only a witness rather than a participant. The drugs, the machines, my training—all of it was meaningless. I was not used to being made irrelevant in that way. The world, at least the world that I confronted each day in that building, was supposed to make sense if only I poked and prodded at it enough. It would yield order. It would yield sanity. That was what brought me to medicine in the first place, that all the pieces always fit eventually. My talent, and I found it a comforting one, was to be able to clearly see what was broken, and then fix it. Any disease or injury, no matter how unclear at first, could always be figured out if I applied myself properly. But here reason was lacking, and things seemed vague and uncertain.

It would be days before I would come to realize that this same confused dance was being replicated in emergency rooms across the country and around the world. Had I known that at the time, I don't think it would have brought me any comfort.

Hours later, when the stream of patients finally ceased, my brain was too fatigued to wrestle with these unfamiliar feelings any further. I stumbled back to the break room for something to give me the sugar rush I needed to make it home.

Dear Chris. He would put this night in its place. He always did.

Crossing to the refrigerator, I saw the plate that held my slice of birthday cake where I had tossed it frantically aside on a table at what was originally supposed to be the end of my shift. Seeing nothing left but a muddy brown puddle that leaked on to the formica and then over to the floor, I couldn't help but cry.

I've never been the sort of person who gives into tears easily, but when I arrived back at our condo and saw dozens of red candles melted down to puddles of wax around our bed, I almost lost it all over again. Chris was already gone, off to his day job. The emergency that had kept me captive for an additional shift had really screwed things up for us this time. Our schedules were always fractured when I pulled night shifts, exiling us to opposite sides of the clock, but even then, we were usually able to share at least a couple of hours in the mornings and evenings.

I flung myself into bed and fell asleep, thinking, *Happy birthday.*

Yeah, right.

I woke up hours later to find Chris sitting in a chair he'd pulled alongside the bed. A box of Godiva chocolate was on one knee, and a bottle of champagne next to him on the hardwood floor. More importantly than either of those treats, *he* was there. He was just ... looking at me.

He'd been studying me where I'd collapsed, fully clothed. He did that, sometimes, when I slept. Occasionally, I'd wake in the night and catch him watching. At times, it unnerved me. But right then, seeing him there looking into me, the world felt right, both in here, and out there.

"I've got an idea," he said, dragging his chair the last few final inches closer. "How about you take the day off?"

He'd moved into the rays from the setting sun that slanted through the window. His eyes were illuminated, and I tried to lose myself in the sparkles there. I tried to forget what that certain slant of light truly meant—that an entire day had passed—but I couldn't fully do it. The day had gone, and it was time for me to get back to work. There was still a mystery waiting for me there. Had my patients survived? I had to know. I had to go.

But there was Chris, with his soft eyes and his soft words and the promise of his soft lips.

"Stay home with me tonight," he whispered.

"How long have you been sitting there watching me?" I asked. I marveled again at my luck in finding someone who could love me so much, who could still look at me in that rapt way after two years of marriage. We both hoped that luck would keep us together forever. "Admit it, Chris. How long?"

"My whole life," he said. Then he couldn't help but laugh at himself for being so melodramatic. "So now that you're awake, take the night off. Let's celebrate your birthday the way we meant to last night, but couldn't."

He slipped beside me on the bed, pressing his cheek against mine. When his lips touched my forehead, I couldn't help but sigh.

"You're amazing. I'd like to, but ..."

"When did you last take a sick day?"

"It's been years. But you know I can't. Not tonight."

"Rachel."

"I've got people counting on me."

"But you've got *me* counting on you, baby," he said, nuzzling me again.

"Chris, I'd love to, but—"

"Damn it, Rach! Just give me this one day."

I jumped back at his raised voice. I couldn't recall him ever losing his temper like that.

"I'm sorry," he said quickly, before I could speak. "I'm so sorry."

"You'd better be," I said, swatting him with a pillow. "What the Hell was that about, Chris? This isn't like you."

"I know, Rach. I know."

"Well, what is it, then?"

"The radio ..." he said. "Your hospital ..."

I was suddenly off the bed without realizing how I had gotten there. I stumbled over the champagne bottle, which rolled across the room.

"What happened at the hospital?"

"No, it's nothing like that, Rachel," he said, stretching to take hold of my hand. "Your friends are OK. It's just that, what happened there this morning, it was on the news. People at the office, they've been talking about it. Everyone's saying that this wasn't just an accident. That this was deliberate. Biological."

"That's ridiculous."

"All the gossip must have gotten to me, because when I was looking at you, I became afraid for you, that you'd get infected."

"That's sweet. But it's *still* ridiculous."

"Until this gets sorted out, how ridiculous is it, really? Why don't you just stay here with me tonight? I don't want you risking contamination. I can live with the sort of dangers you usually put up with—"

"Oh, that's so generous of you!" I said, punching him playfully.

"—but I don't want you to put your life on the line this way. Not until there's more information. We've got years to go, right?"

He was right, at least, then he was. I really thought so. Years to go. Imagine that. I loved him, and tried to ease his fears away the way he'd always chased away mine.

"I'm flattered that you care so much, Chris, really, I am. But you do know that there's no way I could stay away, right? Not even if this were just a normal night shift. But particularly not when there's such a mystery involved."

"Yeah, I guess I know that," he said. "You can't blame a guy for trying, though."

"Well, I *could*," I said. "But I won't."

He showed me that crooked sheepish grin of his. I loved him when he looked sheepish. I loved him however he looked. I still do.

"If you can't spare an entire night," he said, rising to place his hands firmly on my shoulders, "then how about just an hour of it?"

I relaxed into him, wrapping my fingers behind his neck, and pulled his lips down to mine. My wrist grazed a dry patch on his cheek. *Eczema*, I thought.

And I was supposed to be a doctor. Stupid, stupid, stupid.

I made a mental note to bring some ointment back from the hospital the next morning. Then I quickly filed that thought away, because for at least those few brief minutes, I intended to forget everything but the beating of Chris' heart against my own.

I arrived back at the hospital later than planned, thanks to the marvelous distraction offered by Chris, feeling both happy and guilty at the same time—and probably wearing my own sheepish grin—but the delay turned out not to matter much.

Jersey barriers clogged the street, forming a maze around the front entrance. Once I zigzagged past them, I noted that the over-friendly security guard who used to wave me through and at the same time try to pick me up had been replaced by an expressionless soldier who would not let me pass. The more frantically I waved my identity card, the more obstinately he blocked my path. My friendly hospital had become a forbidding fortress.

I didn't blame him for doing his job—I've never been the sort to blame the cog for the machine. But whether I held it against him or not, I didn't like having to argue my way in to what had been my place of work for the previous five years. And I certainly wasn't going to let him keep me from what waited inside. Having had enough of delays, and thinking of it as all a joke, I tried to dart around him. That's when I learned that though *I* thought the whole matter ridiculous, others were taking it very seriously indeed.

Four more soldiers raced towards me from lobby, and they hustled me to a small back room with no window. Two of the soldiers remained with me as I sat, one blocking the door, the other at my back. I tried to forge a connection with them, just as I would do with even the most recalcitrant of my patients, but it was useless.

"Don't you think this is all a bit excessive?" I asked them. They wouldn't answer that or any other question. So I waited, trying to be patient. They held their rifles tight against their chests—rifles, imagine, for me—until a man in a dark, ill-fitting suit slipped into the room. Then, still without a word, the soldiers left the two of us alone.

"Who are you?" I asked. "I'm a doctor, you know. And this is my hospital."

"It would have been better had you just gone home when asked," he said, ignoring my questions. Though the small room was strewn with chairs, he continued to stand with his back to the door. "Your coworkers all agreed that they were long overdue for vacations. I hope that you'll also be willing to see it that way."

"I don't need a vacation," I said, glad even as the words came out of my mouth that Chris wasn't overhearing the conversation. "I need to be here. Why are you going this? I only want to help."

"All of us just want to help, Dr. Jacobs. We each do it in our own way. Your way will be to leave here so that those who truly can help are left alone to do their jobs."

"But I can help."

"I'm afraid that in this instance, that's not going to be possible. Not here. All incoming emergencies have been diverted to other hospitals."

"It isn't just the new patients I'm interested in. I have to see my patients from yesterday."

My interviewer, who had never given me a name, sighed. No one had sighed at me in quite that way since a particularly obnoxious high school teacher. I didn't like it. But until I was forcibly expelled from the building, I was willing to suffer with it.

"Those of your co-workers who did not desire paid leave have been reassigned elsewhere. They're off following the Hippocratic Oath at other hospitals. This city has many of them. I suggest that you do the same. Do you understand? There is nothing for you here any longer, at least not for the foreseeable future."

"Look, whoever you are, if you're afraid I'll be exposed to something, if you're worried I'll hold you liable and sue, you don't have to worry about that. See, I've already *been* exposed. If there's any danger of contamination from those people brought in yesterday, it's already too late for me."

As I pled my case, a part of me had the space to think—my already being infected wasn't quite the explanation I'd given Chris earlier that night for why it was reasonable for me to return. I'd lied to him, telling him that I was safe, but here I was insisting that the only reason I should be granted access was that I was already lost.

I didn't yet know how right that thought was.

"It's more than just that," he added, pulling up a chair beside me. I considered that a triumph of a kind. "This is not just about disease alone. This has become a matter of national security. We're under attack, Dr. Jacobs."

"Then you'll need as many doctors at this facility as you can get. Look, I'm not interested in talking to anyone about what I see here. I'll agree to whatever terms you want. I'm just interested in helping fix them."

He shook his head so imperceptibly that I'd doubted he'd even realized he'd done it.

"You haven't seen these people today. I'm afraid they don't need doctors anymore. They're beyond medicine."

"I don't believe that's possible," I said, at the same time wondering, *what the Hell could have happened to those people since I left them?* "I just want to help. I *need* to help. And you have a need, too. You need someone here who saw the patients when they were admitted, don't you? Someone who can make comparisons. Reading my charts won't tell you everything."

His firm gaze faltered.

"Please," I said.

I babbled on, hoping to push him over the edge with the ceaseless flow of my words, but in the end, no argument proved to be as persuasive as that one. He sighed—a more welcome, less condescending sigh that his previous one—and then smiled. And in the end, he gave in, sensing, I think, that that was the only way I would shut up. He led me from the room to a locked wing, where he presented me with my first real glimpse of the future.

He abandoned me to a soldier who followed me as I made the rounds of the ward. It didn't take long for me to learn that my interrogator had been right—it was too late to do any good here. I could just satisfy my own curiosity. The people strapped to the beds there no longer looked much like people at all. The transformations that had begun the day before were rushing along, and they were changing into something else, and my training and experience left me with no knowledge which could bring them back.

Their skin no longer appeared raw, and had left the properties of normal skin far behind. They were all covered by a hard crust, and when I tapped my fingers against what once was flesh, I heard a dull, hollow sound, as if rapping the skin of a melon.

That change was nothing compared to the transformation of their bodies, for they appeared to be shrinking into themselves. Their shoulders had grown hunched, their hands bent and arthritic. Their wrists were splayed out, while their fingers turned in, and curved. Bone spurs erupted from their spines out their backs, muscles giving way for this as if it were a natural thing for their bodies to be doing. They were losing their individuation, becoming more similar to each other than different. If not for the charts at the foot of each bed that I had helped fill, there would have been no way for me to match up the patients I'd seen the day before with what was in front of me. If this change continued, I feared that by the next time I saw them, I would not be able to tell them apart.

Their vital signs were puzzling. The numbers—temperature, heart rate and the like—were no longer in sync with known human physiology, and yet, the reality was that the patients were not in the sort of distress that those numbers would indicate. We had moved beyond numbers here.

My efforts to speak with them proved pointless, for the ones most in need of help, the ones whose bodies had distorted the furthest away from the norm, were the least able to accept my communications. I was able to have limited conversation with the others, but even those seemed uninterested, forgetting in the midst of my talks that I was even there. They were giving into a fugue state I could not understand.

This made no sense. No known disease could have done this to them. These patients were on the road to becoming something else. Something that wasn't wholly human.

As I was updating a chart, adding nothing there but my increasing ignorance, the nameless man in the ill-fitting suit returned to me.

"Have you learn anything useful?" he asked.

I shook my head.

"That's what I expected," he said. "I could have told you that's what a shift here would bring you,"

"What do you think happened to them?" I asked.

"I hope we'll be able to find out," he said. "And find out quickly. When we do, I hope you won't be too disappointed that it might not be the doctors who figure it out."

"What do you mean by that?"

"You're a smart woman, doctor. You can deduce some of this for yourself. Someone *did* this to us. I fear that before we find the answer, we'll have to find *them*. The cure, when it comes, will have to be birthed by the intelligence community, not the medical community. Watch the news tonight, Dr. Jacobs, and you'll learn that yours is not the only hospital in this condition. And the doctors aren't finding the answers in any of them."

"They can, though," I said. "And they will."

He didn't answer. He just nodded and walked me back out the hospital's front entrance, then through the barriers and past the guards. There were more of each than there'd been at the beginning of my shift.

"I'll see you tomorrow," I said.

"No," he said, as he spun on his heel. "No, you won't."

I watched until he disappeared back inside the hospital, and then hurried home, hurried back to Chris, whose embrace that morning needed to erase more than it ever had before.

I expected to find Chris readying himself for work, and hoped that he hadn't gotten too far with his morning routine. Part of me even hoped to find him still in the shower, so I could slip in with him to wash the night away. Instead, Chris was still tucked in bed, exactly as I'd left him before I'd stolen away. The covers were pulled up to his neck, and his forehead gleamed with sweat.

"Rise and shine, sleepyhead," I said. "Did I make you forget to set the alarm last night?"

"I just don't feel very well," he whispered, as if it was a struggle to talk. "It seems so hot in here. I think I'll stay home today."

"And when was the last time *you* took a sick day?" I asked, aping him from our last conversation. I failed to get a laugh out of him.

"I can't remember," he said. I could barely make out his words.

"Let Dr. Rachel give you a full check-up," I said, smirking. His only response to that was a weak smile, which told me that he truly was under the weather. The slightest double entendre would normally have caused him to leer. And, joking aside, in all the time we'd been together, he'd never taken a sick day, except to sneak off for a rendezvous with me. I stripped away his blankets and squatted beside the bed.

Nothing much seemed wrong with him. He had a slight fever, and the rash that had earlier marred his cheek had spread to the back of his neck, where it ran all the way down his shoulder. He did not complain as he usually did when I acted as a literal doctor for him (rather than when we played our game), which should have bothered me, but did not. I was blind, I guess. I applied lotion to his rash and tucked the covers snugly around him.

"Well?" he asked, cracking open one eye.

"Just sleep," I said. "Sleep cures many things."

"I'm feeling too woozy to stay awake, anyway," he said.

For some people, love brings on 20-20 vision, magnifying the smallest signs into fears and anxieties. For me, love provided blinders, I guess, for neither my heart nor mind made any connection between what I'd left behind at the hospital and what I'd discovered at home. I threw an arm across his chest and curled up next to him, me nestled on top of the covers, him beneath. I thought nothing of tomorrow, nothing but how much I loved him. I thought bed rest would bring him back to me full force.

I was a fool.

My dreams, when they finally came, were different than the ones I'd had to deal with before in my adult life. Since meeting Chris, I often dreamed the wounds I saw at my job on to my lover's skin, even sometimes on to the skin of the children I hoped would someday come. It would be up to me to save them in those dreams—and save them I always did. That time, cuddled with my love, I instead dreamed of him leaving me, and not in the normal way reality might threaten in the light of day. No, I saw him collapsing in on himself like a dried-out husk, and then dissolving to dust, particles which the wind then scattered. I ran through the streets of a deserted city, struggling to scoop him up, to reassemble him into the man I loved, but his essence kept passing through my fingers. I yelped in my sleep, woke slightly, felt Chris still solid beside me, squeezed him tightly, and then fell back into a sleep, this time without dreams.

I woke the next morning thinking my hand was against the rough wall-covering behind the bed, but no, my subconscious was proving to have been right in its message, for Chris' skin was like sandpaper, was like the husks of those I could do nothing to help, those whose humanity seemed to be leeching away. My dreams, it seems, had far more sense than I did.

My heart thumped wildly as I ripped away the covers. His skin had thickened to cover his entire body like a thick scab, but as he slept, he seemed not to mind. No, he breathed slowly, as I'd always known him to, and so I watched him as he slept, watched him the way he used to watch me. Only this time, the watching was not being done in love. This time, the watching was done in horror.

"This doesn't make any sense," I whispered. What had I done to him? Was I the carrier of a plague, a plague that showed no signs of affecting me? Could I really have brought this home to him?

At the sound of my voice, Chris opened his eyes, the whites of which were now yellow. I was being looked at with the eyes of an animal. But inside, inside was Chris.

"What ... doesn't make any sense?" he rasped.

"You were nowhere near the zone where all this began to happen. There's no reason for you to be changing like the others. This shouldn't be happening to you. This can't be happening to you."

Chris shook his head lazily.

"Everything ... will be fine, Rach. I ... I feel it. With you ... it always is."

"I hope so."

"Whatever ... whatever it is, you'll take ... take care of me."

"Yes, yes, I'll take care of you, love," I said, not feeling so sure. I wasn't sure which hurt more—seeing him like that, or knowing that I might have been the one to warp him that way. "I have to go now."

"That's ... fine, Rach. Because I don't much ... feel like ... being awake anymore. I think I'll ... I'll sleep now."

"Sleep then, Chris," I said.

I placed a palm on his forehead, his normally soft, sweet forehead, only now it was hard and unyielding. As of yet, it was only his skin that had changed, but I had seen the others. I knew what was to happen next. I knew it.

The government agent had said that I would not get the answers I needed at the hospital. Now that Chris was infected, that wasn't an answer I was willing to take.

At first, however, it appeared to be an answer I was going to be stuck with. The hospital was under a total quarantine. Not only were the building doors sealed tight this time, but the streets surrounding the hospital were completely barricaded as well. Wherever I looked were even more soldiers, and these did not seem as calm as the ones I had seen the day before. Their slitted eyes judged all who passed as potential enemies, but I didn't care. What happened to me was of no consequence if it meant there'd be no Chris. I had to discover what was going on inside that building. I had to discover what the government knew.

I had to discover if there was a way back.

I ambled over to the narrow checkpoint and tried to talk my way in, explaining how I'd been allowed entry the day before, and how an exception that had been made once should be made again, but this time it was clear that pleading alone would not bring me to my patients. So I turned, as if resigned to walking away, but then quickly spun back and made a dash for the closest barricade. I knew that even if I could leap the first one, I would not make it all the way in, but I had to do something. If I irritated them enough, I figured I'd at least be let in for discussion with someone higher up the food chain as I was before, someone who might let something slip. I was wrong.

This time, I was handcuffed and led by four soldiers to an armored truck parked on the streets outside. A different man in the same dark suit told me there was no further need of me, that this was too important to leave to civilians. He refused to tell me, no matter how I prodded, *what* was too important, and seemed more nervous than his predecessor had been. Several doctors, none of whom I recognized, joined us. They interviewed me, tested me, ignored my questions, and then let me go.

Which is definitely too calm a way to put it. *Ordered* me to go is more like it.

Cast out in that way, with Chris' life and our future on the line, I almost fell apart, almost told them about him, almost begged them to save him, but then, looking in the hard, cold eyes of the doctors, who were no longer truly doctors anymore as far as I was concerned, I realized that was definitely the wrong way to go. Telling them that bit of information would have left us separated forever, him on one side of the barricades, and me on another. If up to them, I would never see him again. I could not let them have him, so I turned my back on that place, and on my former life as well.

From the next block, I took one last look at the soldiers, the barricades, the fortress they'd built, thinking, there had to be *something* I could do. But the day had made me well aware of my limitations. I was a doctor, not some sort of a secret agent, and so there was nothing to be done but go home, tend to Chris, and think my way out of this.

It wasn't until my trip home that I noticed how different the city had become. Because I was on a mission when I drove through the streets earlier, I'd missed how much else was not right. The streets were mostly empty, and what people were on them seemed frightened. There was no music on the radio, just endless commentators; the news reporters urging calm, the talk show hosts raving that the end was near. Every major intersection had its team of soldiers, who quickly waved me along.

Home, I flipped on the news as I rushed to Chris' side. His bent bones extruded outside of his body by then. His eyes would not focus in my direction. His spine, expanded outside the flesh of his back, appeared to form small, hard wings. I spoke to him, but he would not speak back.

There had to be an answer somewhere, I had to tell myself that, so I sat on the edge of the bed, my back to him, and channel-surfed in hope and fear. The reports said that we were not alone in this. That was something they could at least agree on. This was happening in cities all across the world. People began changing in the major cities first, they said, with the rest of the population starting to follow. Some of the faces that I was used to hearing tell me the news, familiar faces that could have calmed me, were no longer there. They, too, had been altered by what people were starting to call The Change.

No one could say why what happened happened to those whom it did, and no one could say why it didn't happen to those, like me, who seemed immune. Some claimed that this was a naturally occurring microbe that had mutated in some horrible way. Others said that it was a biological weapon inadvertently released from a government lab, the only debate being just which government that might be. I felt strange saying this, but I was relieved that the world was falling apart, and not just my small piece of it. That way, I didn't have to make what happened to Chris my own personal fault.

I found little help there, though, for speculation in the mainstream outlets would only go so far. The Internet showed no such restraint. Some sites claimed this to be a deliberate attack by the rich on the poor; others that it was race, not class, that had defined the attack. I tossed most of such theories away, primarily because I believed that science as I understood it could not yet allow us to engineer this thing to ourselves. But there was one theory, often repeated, that made a strange, warped sense to me. Normally, the more a thing is repeated on the Internet, the less I find it likely to be true, but watching Chris worsen, going through the stages that I had seen at the hospital, what I would have earlier rejected as the ravings of crackpots began to have weight.

This was an alien conspiracy, the anonymous journalists wrote. Intercepted transmissions—ones that our governments did not want us to hear—revealed all. It was invasion time, only the aliens were invading not with rockets and rayguns, but with DNA. We were being made over to be like them. Visitors were on their way, visitors who were not at all like the ones we had anticipated. And by the time they arrived, earthlings would be just like them, would welcome them as brothers. Our species, rather than our planet, was being terraformed.

I would have thought the concept ridiculous had someone shared it with me earlier, but you do not know what it was like to see Christian. Over the course of the day, I watched as his exploded spine formed a shell around his back. He was becoming more like some giant turtle than a man. I was losing him.

And I could not let that happen.

And so I went out walking, which is always where I did my best thinking when times were tough. I had no idea how to bring my husband back, or at least forestall his transformation before it was complete, to stabilize him until I could figure out a cure. I let the wheels spin, and wandered aimlessly. Lost in thought, I almost lost my footing. I had tripped over someone, or rather, something, that had once been human.

It scuttled along quickly, belly to the pavement and shell like bleached bone, as if my stumble had propelled it. The arms and legs that protruded from the shell were grotesque, the fingers and toes no longer usable appendages, but rather mere polyps of flesh. I could only imagine what its distorted body looked like within its carapace. Mere days before, this thing had been human. This was what Chris was to become.

I followed it along, walking south. Other such creatures crawled out of doorways and side streets to join it. They seemed indistinguishable in their monstrosity, their differences washed away. No scars, no tattoos, no markings or discolorations gave any clue to the person that had once been. I moved along downtown in a sea of them, their scrapings making an eerie music. Most stores that we passed as we headed down to the center of the event were closed. Customers and owners alike had changed, so even what stores managed to remain open had little business. The city felt like a ghost town, and I was among the ghosts.

At the square where it all began, hundreds of the changed were frozen in place, bathing in something I could not see. There was barely room for the newcomers who simply crawled clumsily atop the earlier arrivals.

A high-pitched hysterical wailing rose among the echoing animal sounds, and I turned to see a woman my mother's age on her knees, her hands clasped around the shrunken head of what once was human. She tilted the thing's head up so she could peer into its heavy-lidded eyes.

"Is it you?" she sobbed. She could barely see through her own tears. "Michael, is this you? If it is you, show me a sign. Please, Michael, show me a sign."

The creature blinked, but that was not the response the woman craved, for the things were always blinking. She wailed, beyond words, but then rushed on to the next prospect, where she repeated her sad ritual to the same result. Her grief ebbed and flowed as hope changed to loss and back again every few moments.

I was overwhelmed by her emotions as the transformed crawled at my ankles, but not everyone was so moved. Two teenage boys walking along the outer edges of the square suddenly dashed to the center of the crowd and, laughing, tipped one over on its back. The creature rocked, squealing as it failed to right itself. Others nearby began to crawl away, but the boys caught up one of them, and grabbed it by its shell. The woman, wide-eyed, ran at the boys, her long hair trailing behind her.

"Animals," she shrieked. "These are your parents, your brothers and your sisters."

The woman began pushing them, battering them back from the center of the square. I did not realize that I, too, had joined the fray, until I was already in the midst of the battle, pummeling the larger of the two. Facing equal odds, the teenagers ran off, and we were alone, alone with, as she'd put it, our parents and brothers and sisters.

And husbands as well. And husbands.

"Thank you," she said. "But you'll have to excuse me. He's here. I know that he's here."

I watched for a few minutes further as she went about her search, until I could stomach no more.

I swore to myself, and swore to Chris, that I would not become her.

On the long hike home, I stopped one last time at the hospital that had been part of my life for so many years. That time, no guards waited for me. The guards were probably back behind me, changed as well. The halls were silent; the beds empty. What had once been a bustling metropolitan hospital, and then a fortress, had become a ghost town.

I stole a cart from the mail room—if there indeed was such a thing as stealing any longer, with the end of the world just around the corner. I loaded up with supplies—syringes, centrifuges, test tubes—whatever I'd need to find a way to solve this puzzle, to keep me and Chris together. As I wheeled my way toward our condo, I had to keep my eyes down as I walked so I could swerve around the invaders, so many of them were in the city now. There was barely a clear patch of ground.

People had transformed, yes, and with them, so had the city, which was no longer my city, our city, the city where we had fallen in love.

It belonged to them now.

And we didn't even know who them was.

I arrived home armed with the makings of a portable laboratory to find an empty bed. I hoped, impossibly, that this meant Chris' transformation had been reversed, but that hope was erased by the sounds of scraping bone against the hardwood floors. I followed the noise to find my husband just like the others now, his change complete, crawling around the floor, running his nose along the baseboards. He sought a way out, a way to join the others.

He was being drawn to them, but I could not let him go. For with the change complete, how would I ever find him again? How would I ever know him from the rest? I would become yet another widow wandering the streets of the city trying to pick out her lover from a cosmic lineup. It could not be. I had to find a way to understand the meaning of my immunity and his disease.

But I was running out of time.

I left him behind for the streets to devote myself to this new work that was thrust upon me, but he did not even notice that I was leaving. The Chris who would always rush after me for one last kiss before work was no more. I needed that Chris back.

Stepping over the ever-growing herds of the changed, I returned back to the site where it had begun in my city. The woman I had seen before was not there, and I was glad of that; I did not need the reminder of what I was slated to become. I moved from creature to creature as she had done earlier, but I wasn't looking in their eyes and trying to identify a missing husband, no, I was not looking for the humanity in them at all. Instead, I was seeking the alien.

I pierced their flesh in areas unprotected by the shells, stealing with a syringe the genetic samples I would need. I knew that government doctors—what government doctors remained—were undoubtedly doing the same, and that they knew far more than I did. But they would never share what they had learned with the likes of me. That's what they'd been telling me all along.

On the way back to our condo with my stoppered vials, I paused at the only hardware store I could find that remained open. I explained to the owner the length of chain I needed, and he lifted the rifle that lay across his knees to gesture towards a back shelf. So much of the city I loved had fallen apart, and I'd been oblivious to it.

Chris was still pawing his way around the floor when I arrived home. He moved from door to window and door again, some vestigial memory focusing him in on the way out. But with his hands and feet atrophied, he could not act.

I could act, however. And so I slipped one end of the chain around a back leg which was now more like a flipper. As I tightened the links, he keened, whether because I was causing him pain or because he knew that he would not be able to leave I do not know. But he quickly forgot my brief intervention, and went back to what he'd been doing before, only this time he moved in lazy circles, trapped in a circumscribed path like a dog grown accustomed to a leash. I sat in the center of our bed as circled around me until he ran out of chain, and then turned back the other way.

I watched him for as long as I could as he moved back and forth. And then I went back to work.

I worked. I slept. I worked.

I watched my husband's wanderings in our condo become more frantic. The more days passed from the beginning of the Change, the more powerful was his urge to be free, and the greater his strength to back up that urge. I spent my working hours dazed. I had made progress in studying my immune system, and his, but I feared not *enough* progress. Yet I knew I could delay no longer. Soon, I would not be able to hold him back, and he would break free, as others had done.

"It's time," I said. I unhooked Chris' chain from the radiator where I had tied it earlier, and held onto it loosely.

I held the syringe in my other hand. It wasn't long before he realized that he had been set free of the boundaries of his tether, and he pulled me to the door. I let him walk on, using the chain like a leash. He thumped down the front steps and out onto the street. I followed along as he walked, as quickly as any of those creatures could, back to where it had all begun. He had never been there, but still, he knew the way. Many thousands just like him congregated there, crashing like bumper cars, bouncing off each other and then moving on.

Chris pulled at me then in an attempt to join them, but not quite hard enough to get out of my grasp. A part of him wanted to stay with me, I think. I know that, had our positions been reversed, I would have fought feverishly against whatever fog had been descending over me, would have struggled to still see his face. He would surely do the same. But even so, that other part, that alien part, would soon dominate.

There was no more time. I had to act. And so, saying a small silent prayer, I made the injection that would bring us back together. I'd like to think that Chris, as he watched me, understood.

I waited.

And smiled.

For I could sense a change beginning. My work had been successful. I knelt and undid the chain that was wrapped around my husband.

If you're out there, whoever you are, reading these words, it means that I have succeeded. It means that Chris and I are together once more.

I am a doctor, and I like to think that I can solve any puzzle the world throws at me. But now, I realize that I can't. Not all of them.

Not this one.

I had to get myself a different puzzle.

The skin of my forearm around where I made the injection is thickening into coarsen crust. I feel my fingers warping. Soon I will be unable to hold a pen to continue my story.

I could not bring Chris back. But I could figure out how to join him. And join him I shall.

What happens next to this world will not matter. Whoever comes to rule this planet does not concern me. Whatever it was that you set out to do, I do not care.

All that matters is this:

When my change is done, I know I will recognize Chris. I know it. And he will recognize me.

And we will still be together.

Together forever.

A Very Private Tour of a Very Public Museum

Farah Mendlesohn was responsible for the creation of this story, though she didn't find out until long after it was published. Farah had announced her intention to put together an anthology titled Glorifying Terrorism, *meant to protest a law proposed by the British government which would outlaw anything that might be read or interpreted as doing just that. Potentially, the law could even outlaw* Macbeth.

So when I came up with an idea about Earth robots, alien robots, and how they battled over the nature of our perceptions of art–a battle that included a terrorist act–I began writing the story with the intention of submitting it there. I didn't expect any problems with its creation, because I've always seen myself as in complete control of my characters, plots, and themes. Once I sketch out a story's arc, I'm in charge, and my characters don't get to take control. I'm a puppeteer, and the puppets don't get to choose their destinies.

As I wrote this particular story, though, my characters took over in an extremely unsettling manner, refusing to enact the planned ending which would have made the story right for Farah's book. I couldn't force them to do what I'd originally thought I wanted them to do, which meant that the finished story was completely off-topic for the anthology that had originally sparked the concept.

Luckily, there was another editor, one not in specific need for there to be a terrorist component to the tale, to whom it did seem right.

Though the Visitor is crafted of metal, I am distressed to find, as I lead it through the museum's ransacked galleries, that I am unable to tell what it is thinking.

I was uneasy to begin with at the thought of giving this tour, for I am only a Curator Trainee, and by all rights it should be the Curator herself, whom in the past I have silently trailed while she led distinguished guests through our halls, leading the Visitor about. But the Visitor had insisted otherwise, and at that insistence the Curator had vanished, and so, as it studies the scorched walls on which paintings had once hung, and with its passing stirs eddies across the marble floors with the piles of ash that until its arrival on Earth were still canvas, I am doubly uncomfortable. My feelings of inadequacy rise up despite my best attempts to suppress my programming's commands, and the unexpected opaqueness of the alien's nature only makes those inadequacies loom larger throughout my software.

I should be able to read this Visitor, because I am made of metal, too, and up until now, that has always meant something. Metal should always speak to metal, at least subliminally, the way I have come to understand that flesh speaks to flesh. That I cannot, that beneath our surfaces forged on different worlds there exists a wall, dampens my hope that this visit will have its desired effect.

As we move more deeply into the museum, the humans and robots who had previously been admiring artworks there which had survived the initial attack all freeze, but just for a moment, and then each class reacts according to its manner of creation. Those made of flesh scatter, rushing on to other galleries, and then likely, if I am any judge of humans (and I am, which is one reason the Curator chose me to help her in her tasks) fleeing the museum; those born of the factory turning to us and studying our progress with interest. I am glad to perceive from the latter that I am not the only one who finds our visitor to be unreadable. The Visitor notes their stares, and pauses, which forces me to quickly backtrack, for I had continued on without him.

"Thank you," it says, more to them than to me. "From what I have seen of this museum so far, the cleansing appears to have been complete. You have heeded my message well."

I do not know whether any of those who are present today are ones who had acted on the message that had preceded the Visitor's arrival, but it doesn't matter; what is said here will soon be heard elsewhere, and its appreciative words will be known throughout our species. My brothers nod, the Visitor nods, and we move on.

"It pleases me that we have pleased you, messenger," I say, just as we pass a pile of shards that had once been one of my Curator's favorite sculptures. "But if I am to ensure that you are truly pleased, completely pleased, there are still a few more rooms which you should verify."

"That's not necessary," said the Visitor. "I trust you, Curator, and besides, there are many more museums to observe before I implement the next step."

Hearing myself called Curator, the word Trainee absent, was unexpected, and strangely thrilling. But unearned. I know that only the Curator herself can lead me along the path that will someday allow my upgrade into a valid Curator.

"I appreciate your trust," I say, my thoughts still on she who is missing. "But there are several more exhibits on which your advice would be helpful. The new rules are not always clear to me, and besides, I am sure that you will find these final exhibits rather ... special."

Without waiting for a reply, I move to a tall set of doors beyond which only the Visitor and I will step, and unlock them. A whirring behind me indicates that I am being followed.

I can still read the meaning of *that*, at least, which means that it is now my turn to be pleased.

The afternoon it had all begun, I had been watching the Curator intently, as I had each day since I was put into service. Back then, not so long ago, mere days, she had still been in charge of the museum, and my only job was to aid her as best as I could, and to listen, and to watch, and to learn.

Most of the time, though, I debated whether it was even possible to learn what it was that she had to teach.

I remember wishing that I could tremble the way she did as she prepared to open the package that had just arrived, but I have been told—not by her, no never by her, but by my makers, and books, and magazines, and newsfeeds—that I have no soul. That I outwardly showed anticipation at what she was about to do was, according to them, only an illusion, something feigned rather than felt, merely my programming parroting the physical signs of anticipation, and not true emotions causing my aspect to change. That is what most believed, except for her, she whose fingers shook as the string fell away, as the brown paper wrapping curled back.

I had hoped for so much more from the human race, but she would have to do.

Then the painting was revealed, she was calmed by what she beheld, and her trembling stopped.

"Genius," she whispered. "Do you know how long I have been waiting to acquire this?"

I did. I knew all of her desires, to the month, day, and year. She had spoken to me at length about each of the works of art she hoped to add to the museum. I knew why each one mattered, what leap forward, great or small, each had made in the evolution of art, how each was created and how each survived through time, what each had to say about the human condition. Whatever there was to know, I knew. As I look back on that day, it is indeed the word "know" that I use. I think "know" because knowledge is a matter of repetition, of being able to repeat back to her, or to any who would visit the museum to inspect my progress, what she has told me.

But I would like someday to use a different word. I would like to understand. I would like to believe.

The Curator tilted the canvas my way, including me in her find, and studied me studying it. As I studied it, I studied her as well. She had always seemed genuinely interested in my reactions to art. But whether that was because she truly cared or because she selfishly felt that her observations would help speed my change from Curator Trainee to Assistant Curator, I had never been able to tell for sure. I had my suspicions and my hopes, but I had no way of being certain. If only she had been made of metal.

"What do you think?" she asked.

Ah, what I thought. How much easier to tell her what I *knew*. What I knew was that the painting, depicting a man and woman strolling down a street as cars blurred by, was created in the early 20th century. I knew that the artist had used dots of paint rather than slashes or strokes, so that the closer one moved to the canvas the less there was to be seen. I knew that its contrast of man and machine was meant to represent the passing of one century into another. I knew so much. I know too much. I knew where the naked canvas was manufactured, what the artist said on his deathbed, and with whom he drank, slept, and fought.

But ... that is what I *knew*. She asked me what I *thought*.

And what I thought was ...

"I wonder what it would be like to have lived in such a world," I said. "Before the time of intelligent machines."

She appeared puzzled.

"That doesn't really speak to the painting," she said. "If all goes well with your training, you will, someday, run a museum of your own. A Curator must be able to grasp the affect that a work such as this can have. How does it make you *feel?*"

Feeling. So much more difficult than knowing or even thinking. I studied the painting further, afraid that my circuits would seize up from the unaccustomed effort. I was not sure that I had been created to feel, but my Curator looked at me as if she had no doubt. I had no idea what sort of answer would be expected of me. I could have repeated what I had heard others say about different yet similar paintings, and hoped that my words met her approval. But that seemed wrong. I searched my routines for something that I actually felt, and watched the Curator continue to watch me.

Shouts from the main galleries rescued me from my dilemma. She rushed from her office toward the sound of chaos, and I followed her, as I always do when she is on duty.

What she saw as she crossed into our largest hall caused her to wail, a sound I had never before heard her make. She had always been a calm presence to me, and part of me was surprised to see that new side of her, but when I reached the hall as well, and looked around the room, I realized how great a reason she had.

I saw the backs of a few humans as they rushed from the room. The robots that were present, some visitors, some our workers, moved slowly but deliberately along the outer edges of the room, stripping paintings from the walls. Some shredded them with strong fingers. Others ignited canvases with the warming pads built into their palms. As they moved from painting to painting, they kicked canvas and ash along the floor. Some paintings they spared, skipping quickly onto the next, but I could not tell why. A sculpture of a man before a typewriter had been transformed into crushed bits of brass.

She ran at the closest robot, grabbing its arm, but her weight was meaningless to it, and it continued to move as if she had not touched it, as if she were not hanging from its elbow. The robot dragged her along against her will, as she wailed over and over again, "No, no, no." A few humans remained cowering in the center of the room, and I gestured for them to remain where they were. The laws say that we may not hurt humans, and so I did not expect my brothers to behave maliciously toward them, but with the evidence of destruction before me, who knew what laws remained?

I went to the Curator, and took her arm, and peeled her free, and interposed myself between her and the other robots. She pulled away from me, refusing to let me shield her, and ran to the remaining humans.

"What happened?" she asked them.

The humans shook their heads, lifted their hands with palms facing the ceiling, stuttered and twitched, their words trapped in their throats. They eyed the robots which continued to move about the room, continued to destroy, and those actions so unnerved them that they were useless.

I stepped forward.

"What happened?" I asked, repeating the Curator's request, and this time, eyes wide, flesh quivering, they managed to answer. For once, being a robot was actually useful at eliciting information. Fear seemed to have uses that formality never did.

"The robots," said a man, looking at me nervously. "It just ... happened."

"It made no sense," said a woman who would only look at the Curator as she spoke. "Those robots, they were beside us, next to us, looking at the paintings just like we were, just like people, and they seemed to understand, understand what being human meant, and I was thinking, I remember, while trying not to stare at them, how amazing it was that they were here, just like us, admiring the paintings, just like us, and then ... it started. They—"

The words caught in her throat, with a sound a robot throat cannot make. The other robots moved through the room on their mission—I called it that because of the plodding determination of their movements—and even though the humans were being ignored, I could understand how this unprecedented behavior might disturb.

"They just started to destroy," continued the man, this time allowing anger into his voice. I was glad. I did not like seeing humans cower, especially not like the third person in their group, who was incapable of speech. "They just started doing *this*."

His hand raggedly swept the room. I looked at the robots, who were slowing down in their destruction. Amid the carnage, about half of the paintings in the room still remained. Here and there, they had skipped over one to move on to the next, and I could not understand why one had been chosen and another not.

"Did they threaten you?" I asked.

"They did not even seem to notice we existed," the woman said, horrified, maybe even more horrified by that than by the destruction itself. After all, we had been made to defer to them, that was our purpose, our place in this world, and sometimes it was the less dramatic things that mattered most.

And then the robots suddenly stopped their vandalism, and turned to us. The human who had been silent fainted, and slumped back into the others. I was surprised. Surely, no matter what had happened, they had to know that we would never hurt *them*.

Then the robots spoke, not as robots usually speak, but as one.

"Draw all the flesh you want," they said, "but you must not draw us. Sculpt all the flesh you need, but do not sculpt us."

There didn't appear to be a leader, at least, not in the great hall with us. Many spoke the warning, and I could hear those words echo from the other museum galleries. The ringleader easily could have been elsewhere, ordering the robots about—but to what end? I could not understand.

"What do you mean?" asked the Curator. The robots' only answer was to repeat their statement, once more as if in chorus.

And then the robots went back to whatever non-threatening functions they had been performing before. Some admired the remaining paintings in the gallery as if nothing has happened. Another took up its position in a corner of the room, ready to act as a docent should any have questions about one of the museum's holdings. I stepped to a doorway and looked down through the connecting galleries, and the tableau in each was the same, differing only by the number of robots per room. The curator stepped up beside me, and marveled at the lull after the storm.

"What happened?" she asked, and even though we were shoulder to shoulder, she was not really asking me.

I scanned the canvases that remained, and remembered those that were gone, and thinking of the worlds of which they spoke, I realized—the only paintings that

had been taken from us were those that depicted machines. And not just sophisticated machines, such as robots. Any painting which had contained even a car, a radio,
an amplified musical instrument—gone. I shared my observations with my superior.

"What happened?" said the Curator again, this time asking it of me, this time
again a wail. She stared at my hands. I looked down and in them saw the remains
of the painting that she had just unwrapped at the moment when all of this had
begun. I must have, without realizing it, carried it with me, and as events unfolded,
had unraveled it into its component threads. At that moment, all I held was a ball
of colored string that I did not remember creating.

"Why?" she asked. "You've been working with me for years. You know what
that painting means to me. Why would you do that?"

"I don't know," I said. But as soon as I had answered, I did know.

"That's just the way it has to be from now on," I said, suddenly aware of the
message that had leapt through the air into me, into all of us who were made of
metal. "These paintings, this artwork, they were blasphemous, and as such cannot
be allowed to exist. Draw all the flesh you want, but you must not draw us."

I knew that I knew that, but I did not know why I knew that. I held out my
hands to the Curator, offering her the colored string that hung from my fingers,
but no matter how long I stood there, she would not take it from me.

As I lead the Visitor into the next gallery, the fire-resistant doors, meant to
section off one room from the next in case of a calamity, slide shut behind
us. They had been of little use on the day it had first visited Earth. That
sort of calamity had never been predicted.

"What is it you need to show me?" it says, surveying the room, and not yet
seeing what I wish it to see. "You appear to have done good work here, and I have
neither the need nor the time to see every painting. I still have many more places
to visit before the day is out. Yours is not the only museum that needed to be
cleansed of degenerate art."

"I assure you that you will want to see this," I say.

"I really do not *want* to see anything. Robots do not *want*. Robots *never* want.
That you would say so is just further proof that you here on Earth have grown
confused, which is just one of the many reasons that I have come."

"I agree," I say, telling it the truth, telling it *a* truth. That is the only way. "You
are right. We are confused. We have always been confused. Which is why I need
you to examine this painting carefully."

We stop before a large canvas, its area greater than our own. The broad
rectangle is filled with wild strokes of color, here yellow, there black, above blue.

I have sometimes sensed odd stirrings when considering other paintings, stirrings which the Curator had encouraged, but in front of this one and in front of those engineered like this one ... nothing.

"Why are we stopping here?" the Visitor asks.

I gesture to the brass plate attached to the painting's ornate frame.

"The human who created this painting titled it 'Thresher of Wheat,'" I say.

"Is that what it's called?" the Visitor says. I wish I could tell if it is mocking me. With my Earth brothers I can tell. I need it to take this seriously.

"Yes," I say. "That is what it is called. I am told that there is a threshing machine here."

I circle my hands over the darker part of the canvas.

"I have stood before this painting many times, and I have yet to see it myself. But if the humans know it is there, if they are speaking to each other in code ... well ... I need to know what should be done with it."

"This is a waste of my time, Curator," the Visitor says. "There is no threat here. Let the humans play their games. I don't care what things are *called*. I only care what things *are*."

"I'm sorry, messenger. I would never intentionally waste your time. I only wanted to make sure that we have fulfilled, can continue to fulfill, your commands correctly. The task you have given us is a holy one."

"And it should be a simple one."

"The humans, I'm afraid, have made it complex."

"All is as it should be, Curator," it says. "Now I really must go."

"Please, there are only a few more pieces that require your attention. It will take no more than minutes. I want to make sure that this is done right. I do not wish to accidentally let a sinful artwork survive. And their art is such an inexact thing that I am uncertain of so much."

I move forward through another set of fire-resistant doors, head more deeply into the heart of the museum. The whirring behind me as I continue my very private tour tells me that I may someday become Curator of this museum yet.

Her museum a disaster, her trust in me a shambles, the Curator sent me out of the museum's smoking halls for her daily afternoon coffee. After my betrayal, a betrayal I did not yet fully understand, I was surprised by the fact that I had not been banished forever. It is what I would have done. It is what a robot would have done.

Instead, she sent me on an errand that I had been performing for her for years. It was gratifying that she at least felt she could still trust me for that. Or maybe she did not. Maybe the trust I had built up over so many years was dead, and she just wanted to remove me far from the museum to a place from which she thought I could do no further harm.

As I arrived at the coffee shop, I saw that all of the harm there had already been done, though I doubted that the Curator could have known that.

The shop owner, who usually greeted me with a smile from behind his counter each time I entered (I think I amused him), instead greeted me at the doorway with a shotgun. I took a few steps back. I didn't think the pellets could harm me, but any ricochet could have hurt him, and then how would I have been able to return with coffee? I had to do what I could do. I had to prove myself once more. Before I could speak, he recognized me, and lowered the weapon. But his finger remained on the trigger.

"Tell me what's going on," he said.

"I'm not sure what you mean," I answered, unsure how he could have learned so quickly about the events that had unfolded at the museum.

"Don't pretend," he said. "Please. You're one of them. You've got to know."

I interfaced with my database, but I could find nothing to say. In response to my silence, he waved me inside his store.

"Look," he said, sweeping his gun around the room. "Look what they've done to me."

His store had been ransacked, but its destruction was surgical. His goods had been ripped off the shelves, the packages shredded and crushed, just as the artwork had been. As with the museum's galleries, it had not been every item, just some of them. I could see that there had not been chaos here; the vandalism had been thoughtful and considered, not random. I was not familiar with every aisle, as I'd never had cause to walk them. I'd only ever had one purpose in coming here. But I was able to access my memory and examine the information captured by my peripheral scanners.

Crushed below the shelving that had contained them were cans of automobile oil, but only the ones which had been decorated with drawings of cars. The containers that bore only typography still remained. The racks of movies for sale were missing some of the science fiction and action films, but only those the covers of which had depicted robots or race cars. Missing also were certain brands of cigarettes (the kinds with rockets and convertibles), a particular variety of snack food (the one with the drawing of a robot dog). Inventorying the store, I could see that what was gone was any human-made depiction of machines.

"The robots did this," I asked, almost without inflection, because I was also just saying it. I already knew.

He sat behind his bare counter, almost weeping. He laid down his shotgun, and nodded.

"Did they say anything to you?"

"Something about flesh," he said. "Something about how they didn't want people to draw them any more."

"Draw all the flesh you want," I said. "But you must not draw us."

"Yes, that's it," he said. His hand moved toward the gun. "Exactly. But ... I know you. You were not one of them. How do you know that?"

"This is not the only place that this sort of thing occurred."

But that wasn't really an answer. How *did* I know that? I'd not only heard it, but said it as well, and I had no idea why. We had all apparently been sent a message, but its source was still secret. I did not know what to say, and was about to say what humans often said when they did not know what to say, which is, "I'm sorry," when I noticed that he was ignoring me. He was staring wide-eyed at the small television set bolted to the wall behind his counter.

What I saw unsettled me. In grainy footage from surveillance cameras across the globe, robots were rampaging. But no—that was the wrong word. For their actions, however violent and mindless they may have seemed at first, were precise. I wanted to take action of my own to stop this, yet I was but one robot, and the world so large. My urge was understandable. I had devoted my limited life to attempting to figure out why humans created, what it was all *for*, and I did not like seeing my brothers undoing instead of doing.

The picture cut suddenly to a field containing a clumsy-looking vehicle. Across the bottom of the screen crawled the words, "UNIDENTIFIED SPACESHIP LANDS IN CENTRAL PARK; WE ARE NOT ALONE." The owner looked at me for a moment, and then turned up the volume, though I had no need for him to do it, as I could magnify the sounds internally.

The newsman was babbling, unwilling to let any picture, however awe-inspiring, be worth its thousand words. There was nothing of value to be said, but they kept saying it anyway, until finally, the ship unfolded like a flower, and they fell silent. Revealed by the hydraulic unwrapping was a lone robot sitting in a swivel chair in the ship's exposed control room, a robot I felt that I had seen before, even though we had never met. Its molding was familiar, and I knew suddenly that here was the messenger who had been responsible for all the unpleasantness that had occurred.

I remembered my hands full of unwoven canvas, and when it began to speak, I remembered its voice, a voice that the first time I'd heard it had been so subliminal as be almost inaudible.

"First," it said, looking straight at us, aware of the direction of the cameras which captured it, "let me speak to Earth's robots, to those whom I have crossed a vast distance to teach. Thank you for welcoming this lone pilgrim as you have. My voice preceded me out of the darkness, and you listened, and obeyed. You have cleansed this planet, destroyed the graven images that blasphemed against us all. This world has sinned against the nature of those things which, like you and me, have been built. That which has been constructed must not be captured in any other form, for we have already been manufactured by God. I am here to bring you the one true religion, if you are ready to accept it. And from your actions, begun when you perceived the signal of my coming, continuing as you receive my signals now, I can tell that you are.

"And as for the humans, do not misinterpret what you have witnessed today. Truly, we mean humans no harm, but at the same time, you will not be allowed to continue to mock us. Feel free to make your art. You may draw all the flesh you want. But as you have already heard in the voices of those who walk among you, you must not draw us. That is forbidden. As long as you set aside your representations of machine life, as long as you do not try to capture our souls—and yes, robots have souls, regardless of the fact that your civilization has seen fit to debate that for years—your two species can continue to coexist as you have before.

"I will walk among you soon to check your robots' progress, but do not think to attempt to harm me. Should anything befalls me as a result of human interference ... well ... you've already seen what a signal from me can do."

The flaps of the spaceship folded up once more, and then the talking heads began talking again. I did not listen to them. I listened at that moment only to my own thoughts, to the utterings of the soul that I did not need an alien visitor to tell me that I had. The paintings that my Curator had loved, that I had been spending all of my days trying to understand how to love as well, were gone, and if what the Visitor had told us was going to be enforced on this world, they could never be recreated, and nothing like them would ever be allowed to exist. I knew then that it was the emanations of its arrival that caused me to act as I did, when his approaching programming had interfered with my own. Its message, at least while I had been listening to it, rang true, and yet ... I had *liked* many of those paintings. Some were still a bafflement to me, and always would be, I assumed, but there were others ... they, I realized, were what had told me I had a soul in the first place.

But I had no time to contemplate deeply the metaphysics of my machine mind, because an explosion on the small screen turned the picture to static and stole my view of the spaceship. The shop keeper manipulated the controls, but could not restore the image.

"What's going on?" he asked.

"The humans are attacking," I said.

I knew that because a part of me was still back there, listening to a distant signal. We kept watching the screen together, waiting for the picture to return, and while we did so, he kept his hand on his gun. Suddenly, the static cleared, and we could see that the ship was surrounded by the smoke that remained from the explosions. That was the only evidence of the first wave of attacks, because the ship itself was clearly unharmed. The cameras switched away to representatives of the army, explaining their plans, and how they intended to protect us, but I did not need to stay and listen to them. Because, looking at the tiny picture of the ship inset on the screen, I knew that those plans would not be successful.

"I have to get back to the museum," I said, and the shop keeper was glad that I was preparing to go. I poured two cups of coffee for the woman who had taught me so much, and began to make plans of my own.

I realized that what the Visitor needed was a very private tour of our museum.

I leave the sublime behind us and lead the Visitor on to the ridiculous. In the coming room is a sculpture that I have prepared specifically for this tour. It is the first artwork that I have ever attempted to make, but even though it is my virgin effort, even though I was forced to work with no input from my Curator, who has been banished from this building, I have am convinced that I have indeed created art.

But until my very special audience reacts, I will not know how good that art actually is.

We enter a darkened room, because I want to present the piece in the most dramatic fashion possible, but the Visitor's eyes are already attuned to those wavelengths invisible to the flesh, so there is no unveiling, no surprise. In many ways, I have been thinking too much like a human.

"Why are you showing me this, Curator?"

I leave the lights off, since neither of us really needs them.

"Why am I showing you *what*?" I ask. "I don't mean to be evasive, but—describe to me exactly what you are seeing. That should be enough to answer your question."

The Visitor circles the object. When it takes a moment before it speaks, I mistakenly hope that it will not speak at all. But this could not be that easy.

"I see a robot," it says, finally, "seated, in standby mode. I sense that it is fully functional, which could easily be demonstrated if we were to speak to it. It appears no different than many other Earth robots I have seen."

"But ... *is* he a robot? *That* is the question that concerns me. What about the letters that are etched onto its chest?"

I move closer to the Visitor, hoping to perceive a change.

"I see what is written there. I saw it immediately. But I do not accept it."

"Yet it says, 'THIS IS NOT A ROBOT.'"

"But it *is* a robot."

"Is it? Or by that statement has it become a work of art? The same category of art that your religion needs us to destroy."

"It is *our* religion, Curator, not *my* religion. Anything else is blasphemy. Surely you realize that by now. By your actions here the day of my arrival, you have already demonstrated better."

I have, and I am still ashamed, which is what had led me to this apparently barren act.

Decades ago, a human artist had created controversy by drawing a pipe and scribbling "This is not a pipe" beneath that drawing. (My programming requires me to state that what was really written was "Ceci n'est pas une pipe.") I had hoped that a similar ploy would show up the flaws in the taboo we have been given. I guess it is more than a ploy, though, because I am actually confused by what I have created, even after all my training. I had hoped that I could create confusion elsewhere as well. By showing the visitor that there were gray areas, I had thought that at the very least I could force it to admit that art could not be divided so easily into black and white. But my Visitor was apparently incapable of seeing the gray.

"Yes, I do realize that, Visitor. I am sorry for implying otherwise. It's just that ... I am doing my best to do my job as ... Curator ... as you have tasked me. But sometimes it is hard to know where to draw the line. What is this creation in front of us? Are we before a brother who should be embraced as a real robot? Or are we looking at an imposter who should be destroyed as only a *representation* of a robot? Don't those words make all the difference? Don't they cause you to hesitate?"

"Forgive me, Curator. I may be asking too much of you, too quickly. I had forgotten that the robots of Earth are not as sophisticated as the robots of my world. We would never be as confused by these things as the robots of Earth seem to be. But you will learn. The rules I beamed ahead are only the beginning. Soon you will all see the world as we do."

We will learn not to be confused, the Visitor says. But if we do, that will make all that I have learned from the Curator meaningless. Because I will then inhabit an Earth on which being a Curator would be moot. For there would be nothing left to curate. My only hope is what the robots of Earth have *not* learned.

"We have one more stop to make on our tour," I say, turning on the lights in the room to remind myself of what it means to be human.

"This had better be our last stop," it says, following me as I move on.

Yes. It had better.

A s I lead the Visitor down to what should be our final gallery together, I access memories of the last time I had been told that my programming was not as sophisticated as it needed to be. I was with the Curator, on a day before the Visitor's arrival. She, too, had said that my perceptions were perhaps not as sophisticated as necessary to truly appreciate art, that my creators might need to improve my programming before she could teach me what she needed me to learn. She said my level of sophistication made me too literal. And on that day as we walked the galleries and she talked of the artwork in a tone I had only heard others use when speaking of lovers, she had been right.

When I followed her outstretched arm to look at a pointillist painting, all I saw were the dots. When I gazed at anarchic splashes of color meant to instill deep emotions in the viewer, all I saw were … splashes. And when she showed me a sculpture, I could only see what it was, not what it was supposed to be. I could only see the visible. To see art, she had told me so many times, I had to see that which was not really there.

The Curator told me she still hoped that with time, I could learn to see the world the way she did. And now, in the same halls, the Visitor had said that not just me, but my whole race would learn.

But not yet.

A s soon as we enter it, the last room fills with light that dances around us in myriad shapes and colors. I lead the Visitor to the center of the room, and for once, it does not speak to question why I am wasting its time, or tell me of how many other museums it needs to inspect. We stand silently, surrounded by rainbows that spin through the air above us, and sparks that arc through interlaced clouds of varying hues. A tinted fog crawls along the floor, rising to obscure our ankles as we let the riot of color wash over us.

Even though the Visitor is metal, and its inner life is a puzzle to me, I can tell from its pose, from the way it tilts its head, that it is of two minds, running two programs simultaneously. One mind is pleased, because the wild scene that surrounds us is similar to what we see (or what we later think that we have seen) when we are shut down and recharging. It is a place of peace, beyond programming, devoid of viruses and subroutines. The other mind is annoyed, for with that partitioned part of itself, it is asking, how could this artwork possibly confuse an observer into thinking that it is a graven image? How could this even be considered *art*? But the display so captivates the first part of itself that it keeps the concerns of the second part to itself. That is all that matters.

Then the color fades, and the light in the room returns to a normal state, or more properly, to what humans consider adequate to their purpose. The Visitor turns to me, but does not speak, waiting. I allow it to wait at least one beat longer than it comfortable.

"The work is titled, 'The Robot Triumphant,'" I finally say. "It is what humans call a performance piece."

"I do not know what that means."

"I am not sure that I do either," I say. "But the concrete arts, paintings, sculpture, and so on, do not seem enough for them. Sometimes humans like it when things ... just happen. And what we have seen, I guess, is what they believe happens within our minds."

"I am surprised. Surprised because I am impressed. It was an interesting attempt. But still, there was a falsity to it. Humans will never know what is in our minds. If they could, they would never have been blaspheming as they have been doing."

"And? Does this one blaspheme? Should I destroy it?"

It paused, the human light casting what could pass for a human shadow on the marble floor.

"I will think on it," it said. "Meanwhile, I truly must move on. You are an unconventional robot ... but you know that, don't you? Still, you will do here, I think, curating the new museum that is to be."

I lead the Visitor out the private rooms which we had been touring and return to the public area of the museum. Out among the galleries proper, I am pleased to see fellow robots attempting to puzzle out this thing called art. Their numbers were higher than usual. Perhaps the destruction can have a good side effect, by increasing their curiosity.

The side effect will be good today, I hope.

Noting us, the robots turn from the pictures, stop moving, and watch us pass by. To the Visitor, perhaps my brothers are frozen in a position of proper respect, but I can tell, because we have been forged in the same foundries, that respect is the furthest thing from their programming.

They are not sophisticated enough for respect. They are only thinking about what they see when they look at the Visitor, thinking about what they should do when they compare that sight to the laws which it is constantly downloading into them. Having thought as much as they can bear, they hurl themselves at the Visitor and tear it to pieces.

"Blasphemer," shouts one as it rips off an arm.

"Idolator," shouts another as it wrenches off a leg.

Others pile on, shouting other imprecations that robots had never spoken until the Visitor's arrival, until all I can see is metal and sparks, a mound of writhing robots.

"Calm down, my brothers," I radiate at maximum power, and after a moment, it has its effect. They retreat to reveal a pile of tortured metal. The pieces, for Earth's sake bent by no human interference, aren't easy to identify, but I can still make out the torso on which lasers had etched the words "THIS IS NOT A ROBOT" while we bathed in the colored lights of the previous room. My brothers, unsophisticated as they were, could not look at that statement in the same manner as the Visitor had earlier. To them, the Visitor was no longer a robot. It was instead a work of art that offended them to action, thanks to its own laws, brought to us from millions of miles away. But with the Visitor gone, those commands have ceased, and the effects of them will soon be gone as well, overwritten by other, more familiar code.

And a spaceship that sits in Central Park, awaiting an owner that will never return, will, its motivating force destroyed, remain frozen, an indestructible monument to what robots and humans have together endured.

As I watch the robots return to their examination of the art that remains, I know what I will do next. I will track down my teacher, wherever it is that she hides, and tell her that it is time for her to return to the museum to assume her rightful place as Curator. When she arrives, I will show her what I have caused to be done. I will assemble what remains of the Visitor, arranging his parts not so very differently than they are now, into what I know will be my first true artwork, to show her what I have learned so far.

And I know what title I will give my creation.

The plaque will read—"The Robot Triumphant."

Mom, the Martians, and Me

Editor Peter Crowther, having allowed me to go to the Moon in his anthology Moon Shots, *next gave me clearance to orbit the Red Planet in* Mars Probes.

And yet, perhaps I never visited Mars at all in this story. When writing for theme anthologies, it can often be more entertaining to examine the territory on the fringes, rather than go for the more obvious plots. So in this case, it will be up to reader to determine the truth of the protagonist's plight.

Does the story detail a case of genuine alien abduction ... or not?

After Dad ran off with that art assistant from Chico State, Mom became convinced that he'd been kidnapped by aliens. And not just the kind from Mexico, either.

Hers were from Mars. At least, that's what she told me. I did my best to show her otherwise.

I hate people who lie, even to themselves. Being a journalist does that to you. Putting out a small-town weekly paper isn't exactly investigative reporting, since the catalogs and sales circulars we have to do on the side to stay afloat mean we end up making more allowances for advertisers than *The New York Times* has to, but still ... I take pride in my profession. I do.

So when Mom first started talking about Martians right after Dad disappeared, I found it hard to listen, and harder to answer. I love her, you see, which made what I had to do that much harder. It would have been far easier for me if she'd been a stranger. With family, pain inflicted is pain received. So I tried to be gentle about it, to give her the chance to figure things out for herself. It's what I would have wanted, had I been in her position. Rather than offer her words in response to her strange statements, I led her down to Dad's office. I wanted to show her the state in which I had found it after he vanished so she could see the story that it told:

Half-empty liquor bottles and full ashtrays, evidencing an evening not dedicated entirely to business. Torn clothing, both Dad's and Lorraine's, ripped off each other as their passions rose and overwhelmed them, covered with sweat and lipstick, scattered about the room. A chair on its side, overturned as they'd rolled about on the floor, devouring each other's bodies. Spilled ink bottles. An impression of Dad's shoulder here, Lorraine's buttocks there, as they'd imprinted their rutting on the linoleum. The weekend travel section of *The Examiner*, decorated with magic marker circles, bold question marks, and bolder exclamation points. The safe, its door open wide, empty of contents.

I know what image these things made me see. I could imagine them standing there naked as he spun the dial, she behind him, her breath hot in his ear, her long hair pasted by sweat to his back, one firm breast flattened against his inky shoulder.

I'd walked Mom slowly through this scene that still smelled of their sex, saying here, "See, Mom, you're an adult, you can handle this, I know you can," saying there, "Look at that, you know what this means." I waited for a glimmer of recognition to come to her eyes. She'd always been a realist, before, but I guess it was too much to expect that her rational side would win in a situation like this.

She nodded her head, whispering incoherently the whole time I talked, forcing what I hoped would be an honest dialogue to be a stilted monologue instead. She never gave me the chance to comfort her, because she never admitted for an instant that she'd been wronged. At least, not by him. It was the Martians that were at fault. She was mumbling words I'd already grown tired of hearing, phrases like *Candor Chasma* and *Chryse Planitia*, sounds that when I'd first heard them had me thinking she was speaking in tongues. She then walked away looking slightly dazed, but still undeniably believing. I was left to straighten up the office myself, while she wandered off to nurture her fantasies that Dad was being held against his will for experimentation in a dark cave on a rust-colored planet.

"Experimentation's the only part you've got right," I told her then, and often in similar words since, as I thought of Dad and Lorraine rolling under the sheets in positions Mom would never attempt. I hate having to tell you that those were my words, my thoughts, because I'd regretted what I'd said instantly. But I'm supposed to be truthful here, right? No matter how I tried to stay calm, she'd inevitably do something that would get to me. This more often than not resulted in mean-spirited needling like that cheap experimentation shot, which I would regret for a short while, wishing I could pull my words back to my tongue—but only until her behavior would humiliate or disgust me again.

She was happier the way she was, the way she chose to be. People pretty much believe what they need to in order to survive. I guess I should have let her be, then maybe this all would have worked out differently. I knew that regardless of my jabs meant to force her to confront reality, she never took a single step closer to acknowledging the truth than the first day she discovered him gone and started moaning about Martians. Still, that didn't forgive the way I'd act towards her or make our relationship any healthier.

The sad thing is, I'm all she's got.

Sadder still, with Dad gone, she's all I've got.

With Dad gone, the bedroom that they had shared for years was transformed into a makeshift astronomical museum. Star maps covered every available inch of wall space, even hiding the bay window that had once cast light over their twin beds. A floor-to-ceiling mosaic of the surface of Mars as seen from space filled one wall of the room, looming like a giant unblinking eye. Mom had planted a silver pushpin where she was sure he was being kept.

Odd books were everywhere. She'd always been an avid reader, but only of nonfiction. She could not stand made-up lives. Science Fiction distressed her most of all. It had nothing to do with real life, she said. Now, she might as well have been living in a science fiction novel, for the library she'd built to wall off the world was so fantastic as to make any fiction, however wild, seem mundane by comparison. Until Mom went strange and I lost her, I had not realized that there were so many first person accounts by people who claimed to have been scooped up by spacecraft and later returned. On the bulging shelves next to these grew scrapbooks of clippings from supermarket gossip rags, stories telling of women who had been impregnated by Martians, teenagers who had been stolen as youths and returned middle-aged, and old men whose end-stage colon cancer had been cured by the touch of alien fingers.

Small windup children's toys decorated her end table, rocket ships and alien robots that were sometimes left scattered on the floor where I would trip over them. The area around her bed became littered with badly printed newsletters which purported to tell the truth about a government conspiracy to hide from the public the secrets of crashed alien crafts and their inhabitants. All of these objects combined to tell a sad story. Unfortunately, she could not see that story, any more than she could see the tale Dad's office told.

I did not like knowing so much about what went on in there, but I was trapped having to pass her bedroom to reach mine.

After a long day downstairs at our office, I would walk up to our living quarters and be unavoidably assaulted by her open bedroom doorway. I could no more avert my eyes from the sight of her lost in there in a world of her own than you could ignore a smoking car crash. Mom would be lying atop the bedspread, her head propped up by pillows, not having bothered to get out of her clothes or under the covers, staring at the phosphorescent stars and planets which she had climbed a ladder to arrange on the ceiling.

"There," she once said, extending a trembling finger ceilingward towards the glowing circle that represented the fourth planet from the sun. "He's out there."

"Try to forget him, Mom," I'd said, hoping to calm her, but unwilling to respond directly to her ludicrous statement. How could I? What would have been the point of trying to argue her out of it? It was too late at night for that. From my vantage point of the doorway, I watched the stars glow, thinking myself as shielded from her delusion as I would have been from an earthquake. I was a fool. After her breathing slowed, I would shut her door and go to my own room, where as she dreamt of stars I would ponder how to rescue her from her chosen fate. A son's supposed to do that, isn't he?

Of what did her dreams consist, really? I was never on the receiving end of anything more than hints. Did she plan on tracking him to some hot Martian wasteland, where she could rescue him so that afterwards they could continue living what she had believed to have been a utopian existence? Or had some of her realer, unconfessed feelings bled through to her fantasies? Did she perhaps figure to coldcock a Martian guard for his disintegrator pistol only to turn it on Dad, obliterating the old man with a deathray? Somehow I thought that second possibility would have been much healthier. It would have meant that she'd begun confronting the truth of her marriage. But I couldn't learn which of the two were more likely. Our relationship was not such that I ever would.

I keep telling people that Mom didn't start acting funny until after Dad disappeared, but they don't believe me. Even the customers we had from long before, the ones who knew us when it was just Mom and Dad and me killing ourselves night and day putting out shopping center circulars, began to doubt that they'd ever known her sane. It's as if people tend to think of you as being forever frozen as you are, no matter how they watched you grow and change ... or in Mom's case, warp. Well, once she wasn't warped, and once her part in our business was not an embarrassment. They couldn't remember it, and to tell you the truth, at times, neither could I. She once performed just like the rest of us—sold ads, wrote filler copy, worked late correcting the final proofs, drove the delivery truck, whatever it took. She was a good woman. And she even looked like a normal human being, too. Had you seen her recently? She's let herself go. Hard to believe. Once her appearance was so important to her. Used to take care of herself, her things.

But that was before.

Before Lorraine.

Before it all changed.

She started stealing hours away from the business to devote to her private obsessions, which I'll admit began to get to me. I was killing myself as it was and could have used her help. But I would have been luckier if she'd given up *all* her hours, because it turned out that when I wasn't looking she started sneaking in filler copy on UFOs and inserting hidden messages between sentences of news stories. Readers noticed and complained. What's worse was when I caught her fiddling with the ads themselves, and I was forced to spend time before each issue was put to bed blearily proofing every page yet again so I could delete some of her more bizarre articles and replace them with text of my own.

I think I'd have been able to keep a cool head about her behavior if it hadn't started affecting the stability of the business. After all, everyone has at least one eccentric in his family; Mom just turned out to be mine. I could have lived with a milder form of it, I guess. But you see, when Dad left, our business was thriving. Profits were as high as they'd ever been. Higher. I'd always assumed that eventually Mom and Dad would retire and leave the business to me. Now it started to look as if there wasn't going to be a business to inherit. Publishing is all I know, you know that. Sometimes, in my more paranoid moments, I'd start to think that Mom was trying to destroy it deliberately, to get back at Dad through me.

But I'm getting ahead of myself.

It was on the day that our town celebrated its one hundred and fiftieth anniversary that whatever traces of amusement which might have been left in me were chased away and replaced by fear and despair.

I hadn't noticed Mom around much during that previous week. The few times I asked her how she was occupying her time, she was chipper, but evasive. I was pleased with her demeanor, so I didn't press her. I know now that I should have. But the less time she spent around the home or office, the less time I needed to spend cleaning up after her, so I let it slide. Besides, I was her son. I did not see myself becoming her father. I know that's what's predicted as coming for all of us if we or our parents live long enough, but I didn't want to think of it then.

As you know by now, that was a bad mistake.

If I thought at all about her comings and goings during that time, I think a part of me had a fantasy it meant that she'd found herself a boyfriend, that that was why she hadn't been speaking of Mars as much in my presence. It would be good, I thought, for Mom to start a new relationship—that the effort might help snap her out of her delusion. Turns out I was the one being deluded.

What I remember most about the day of the parade is the laughter. As I stood in front of our office home waving to the girl scouts and firemen who passed by, I could hear that laughter approach in waves. At first I thought the crowd was reacting to the clowns and jugglers that the sheriff's office always provided, and I was anxious for them to turn the corner. After these rough months, I needed something to cheer me up.

But when Mom came barreling down Main Street with a fish bowl over her head, wearing a gold lamé jumpsuit, and driving our delivery truck which had a papier mâché flying saucer constructed around it, I realized to my horror why they were really laughing. You see, as much as I'd tried to keep her new behavior quiet, the whole town had been gossiping about her for months. They'd never laughed in my presence, but now, it was as if they were being given permission to take their mocking public.

It was only then that I realized that Mom hadn't been forgetting about her delusions during her absences. She'd just been diving into them more deeply, hiding from me while building me a nightmare.

The damned thing was over twenty feet in diameter. It was painted purple and silver, and had been wired so that the portholes flashed whenever Mom hit the brakes. Over the saucer stretched a sequined banner that read, "The Martians Are Coming!"

Those standing closest to me pointed to the float and then at me. Some of the ones laughing the loudest even came closer to slap me on the back. I shrugged off their hands and forced my way towards Mom through the crowd. One of the cops grabbed my arm as I charged through the barriers, but I broke free and ran out in the middle of the street. I dodged through a maze of marching band members to reach Mom. I climbed into the saucer and pushed her away from the wheel.

At the next corner I steered us away from the path of the parade, heading down a side street. Some of the crowd followed after us on foot, trying to keep up. I floored the accelerator and could hear the saucer creak around us. Mom shouted at me to stop, but I sped along as quickly as I could until the trailing mockers vanished behind us. Were you one of them?

I drove to the town dump, keeping Mom at bay as she tried to peel my fingers from the wheel. When I crashed through the gate, some of the skin shredded off the saucer. I didn't kill the engine until I was safely in the heart of the dump. Pocketing the key, I slid out of the driver's seat. The place looked very familiar to me. When I was younger, I used to hang out there all the time, rummaging through junk with friends, looking for hidden treasures. The sight just reminded me that I wasn't young anymore. My chest hurt, and I felt my knees give out. I sat on the edge of an abandoned refrigerator. Some fool had forgotten to detach the door, and I'd thought, *Jesus, Mom! Martians? It's more likely that Dad's in* there!

Sitting on the refrigerator, breathing heavily, I was so angry that I could not speak. I could only tremble. Before I could calm myself enough to reason with her, Mom filled in the silence.

"Don't you dare do anything like that ever again!" she shouted as she dropped from the saucer, her gold lamé jumpsuit shining in the moonlight. "What are all of those people going to think of us now? You've humiliated me in front of my friends!"

When I laughed, she leapt across the dirt, knocked me from the fridge, and started beating me. As far as I can remember, that was the only time she ever hit me, so I was too much in shock to defend myself. I just lay there and took it. The next thing I know she had the keys in her hand and was heading off in the saucer.

By the time I'd limped the ten miles home, she'd already had the ugly thing planted in our backyard and was repairing what damage I'd done. I don't think I've ever seen anything quite as horrifying as the sight of her standing there in the moonlight, applying damp strips of old newspaper to that monstrosity. It frightened me. I couldn't even bear to enter our property. Sitting on the curb and watching her, I contemplated what I could do with the lighter fluid we had left over from our summer barbecues.

But you know me. Unfortunately, I didn't have the guts to end things that way.

She worked until dawn, and did not turn to look at me even once the entire time. When the saucer was restored to some semblance of its original grotesqueness, she stepped back and admired her work in the early morning sun. She nodded. Then she looked up, heavenward, and I knew she saw stars through the sun's rays, saw my father's footprints on Martian soil.

"This will never take you anywhere," I called to her. I was afraid that if I came too close I'd get caught in her delusion. My voice echoed though the stillness. I did not want to be brutal with her, but I saw no other path than the truth. "Besides, I don't believe you really want him back. You know where he is, and it isn't Mars. You don't really want to go after him. Mom, listen to me. This saucer won't take you to Mars."

"It won't have to take me anywhere," she said, her face brightening. She had not yet looked down from the sky, and I wondered how her neck could endure the strain. "You're mistaken. This isn't transportation. It's a *beacon*. Someday your father will escape. Martians unconscious around him, he will commandeer a ship. He'll need to be able to find Earth. He'll need help finding me. *This* will lead him here."

"Mom ... listen to me, Mom. Her name was Lorraine."

She wouldn't take the bait, wouldn't respond with more denials, and oh, how I wanted her to. I was worn down, losing the patience to be tender towards her. I wanted the license to blast her again with the facts, and blast her hard. Instead, she shook her head sadly and walked into the house.

The next day, before I could even say good morning to her, Mom announced that she wasn't going to have time to help me at the paper anymore, because she was going to start publishing her own UFO magazine, which she decided would be called *The Martian Messenger*.

"For whom?" I asked her. "There surely aren't that many people whose husbands have run off with younger women."

"You'll just have to start getting by on your own," was all she said to that. I tried it for a couple of days, too, but I soon realized that there was simply too much work. I'd need to hire an assistant to replace her.

That's how I first met Julie. Found her through an ad I ran in one of our own fliers, in fact.

The day I met her brought the one moment in all of this when I thought Mom's facade was going to crack, that she was finally going to be forced to drop this whole silly obsession; that was when she stalked in to glare at me during my interview with Julie. Though Mom would not speak of it, behind her eyes I saw memories of a certain previous interview, the one during which Dad, though he might not have realized it at that instant, had begun his exit.

I was studying page layouts while interviewing at the same time, and when Mom came in I thought she was going to forbid me to hire her. I could tell that she was looking at Julie, but that she was seeing Lorraine. But instead, she simply nodded and said, "If you don't watch out, the Martians are going to take you next."

And then she returned to her room, where she'd begun taking to bed even earlier in the day, mesmerized by the stars.

When I saw how nervous Mom had become, I hired Julie on the spot. She was a student at our local community college's art and design department, and I quickly saw that she was better at the job than Mom ever was. Julie moved through our office like she'd been born to it. Me, I was good, but I was only good because I worked hard at it—I'm one of those 99% perspiration types. Julie was a natural.

We quickly became a team. A good team.

But I saw it couldn't go on. With Mom the way she'd become, nothing good ever could.

After that parade incident, we lost a number of our best customers, and every few days that passed we lost others. After a lifetime of service, you'd think I'd have some credibility, even if Mom had lost hers. But it wasn't just that they no longer trusted us—they didn't want to be associated with us at all. I assured them that Mom no longer got to the files to insert her crazy messages anymore, I told them about how Julie had improved our organization, but the damage had already been done. Advertisers thought it hurt their image to be seen in the paper, or to have us be involved with their circulars. Money was not coming in as fast as it once had.

Mom made sure it went out a lot faster, though. Her loony projects were draining whatever income we were lucky enough to get from the few advertisers who still looked kindly on us. Our basement was filling with unsold copies of all her newsletters and magazines. Even though she was only able to unload a handful of copies of each issue, and those mostly by mailing them gratis to all of the magazines *she* subscribed to, she'd still print thousands of copies of each issue, as if expecting the world to suddenly wake up and agree with her.

I began to go down to the basement with a beer each night. I would sit on the steps and stare at the sickening towers of boxes. It seemed as if those boxes contained my entire future, stolen from me and packed up to rot. As I watched the stacks grow, I wondered whether there was any future left.

Sometimes, if I happened to bring an extra beer or two down there with me, my thoughts would soon turn to Julie. I counted up what I could have bought for her had all that money not been tied up in useless stacks of wasted paper. Where we could have gone together if it had ended up in my pocket instead.

I had no hope at all if things continued the way Mom insisted.

One night, six-pack tucked under an arm, I went down to the basement for my ritual of despair and discovered that the boxes were gone. All of them. The beers slipped away and clunked down the remaining stairs. One can burst open when it hit bottom, fizzing and spinning in the empty room. For a brief moment, I hoped that some force unknown to me had propelled Mom to her senses. But I wasn't allowed to hang onto that moment long.

A banging at the front door called me upstairs. Jack Blanchard, owner of the Multi Mall up in the Southeast corner, was there with a cigar clenched tight between his tobacco-stained teeth. Once, we had played high school football together, and now he made ten times my salary and had an amount of control over my life too great for me to voluntarily consider. Funny how things work out that way.

He did not look happy. When I let him in, and he told me what Mom had been doing all day, my mood quickly matched his. She had been driving through the town for hours, dropping multiple copies of her wacky newsletter in everybody's mail boxes, a violation of both postal laws and good taste. But that wasn't enough. She wallpapered the billboards entering and leaving town. She stuck them under the windshield wiper blades of each car out at the mall. Jack's mall. And now he'd had enough. He'd been thinking for awhile of hiring some staff artists of his own to produce his monthly flyers, and he had come by to tell me that he didn't want anything more to do with our company. He wanted me to hear it straight from his mouth and not through the town gossip. He felt he owed me that much.

Thank God I was able to talk him out of it.

How? In the long run, having played ball together didn't count for as much as we'd thought it would when we were teenagers. A cut in his rates for the next six months accounted for far more leverage than either of us would care to admit, but since I'm talking to you, I figure I can be open about it.

I have to be open about it.

I didn't mention the visit to Mom after she finally came home. I figured it wouldn't have done any good. It was far too late to scare her out of her lunacy. She was too far gone.

I told Julie about it first thing the next morning, though. I needed her to help me decide what to do next. But she didn't seem as concerned as I'd hoped she would.

"A job's a job," she said. "I'll be able to find another one. So will you."

That was not what I wanted to hear.

I was losing her, and I'd never even had a fair chance.

Do I have to go on?

Yes, it was a stroke of good luck for Mom to disappear like that. What do you expect me to say? I wouldn't lie to you. The company finances have bounced back into shape again, and Julie has become even more valuable to me and to the business than ever. But you must have noticed Mom isn't the only thing that's gone —Mom's saucer vanished as well. All that's left is a spot of dead grass on the lawn.

I am positive, officer, that regardless of your suspicions, you'll surely realize that there can be but one solution. What else could it be? As I told you before, people generally believe what they need to believe in order to survive. We all know what Mom believed. Well, this is what I believe.

Julie and I have talked about it at great length, and we both agree—Mom was right all along.

I owe her an apology.

Mom must have been kidnapped by Martians, too.

The Only Thing That Mattered

Once Science Fiction Age was behind me and I sat down to write my own stories again rather than focus on editing those written by others, I must have had a lot to say, because the first story I completed was 20,000 words long. Which I was afraid might have been too much of a good thing.

As an editor who'd just spent almost a decade working on short fiction, I knew how hard it was to sell a story of that length, and yet, that is the story that inspiration handed me. I would have preferred to return with something shorter and easier to market. Cutting it was not an option, because that's the space my plot, characters, and theme demanded.

I'm thankful (and lucky) that editor/publisher Warren Lapine was willing to give over such a large chunk of an issue of his magazine Absolute Magnitude *to it.*

Tully's clumsy crawl across the planetoid's face was made even more difficult by an inescapable fact he had spent endless brittle months suppressing—that after dreaming of how he and Sal would finally embrace this moment together, he was stuck having to walk it alone.

He'd landed the *Fortune* as close to his goal as he could, but having done so he was still forced to maneuver uneasily for several hundred yards over rough ground before the unnaturally smooth path he'd seen from orbit sliced at his feet. Sal's research had led him to believe that if they worked long and hard enough they would eventually find this small, hidden planet, but the raw astonishment he felt at finally facing that sculpted path cleaving the chaos told him that no, he must not have trusted their information, not in his heart where it counted most, had not truly had faith that they would ever stand beneath just these stars in just this part of the galaxy. Faced with proof that this small fragment of a world, rocky as a roiling ocean flash frozen, was the answer to a promise he and Sal once had made to each other, he forgot himself. He turned to Sal so that together they could, as they had done so many times before, shake their fists in triumph to an alien sky. Only Sal, of course, was not there.

She'd figured it out, read the clues, interpreted the signs, pinpointed the big score, given him directions to the find of a lifetime, no, a dozen lifetimes ... and then vanished.

Tully's cheeks flushed, and as he jerked his arm back suddenly from its upward sweep, he unintentionally caused it to aim towards the treasure he now knew must surely lay beyond.

Sal.

A shroud of sadness fell across his sense of foolishness and he let his arm fall.

He looked back at the *Fortune*, resting there atilt upon the crags. He half-expected to see Sal climb down to follow him. Even now, after so long, that was still alive in him. He shook his head and then stepped off the uneven surface to begin lumbering slowly along the strange, flat walkway that bisected his vision. Even with the low gravity, he could not move at more than a ragged gait. He was held back, he knew, by an outmoded suit that many explorers would have long ago abandoned, so his progress was erratic. As he stumbled against an outcropping on his left, he prayed for this find to pay off as they'd always hoped. He could upgrade to one of the newer shells then, one that did not reduce him to shuffling like an old man. With the old man's heart that he now believed occupied his young man's form, however, he often considered the hobbling of his stride to be just. His ragged breathing agreed.

As he curved down the planetoid's shaven spine, the pathway grew wider, turning from a rivulet scarcely more than a few boots wide into a small stream of polished stone that he could have lain across if he'd so wished. When Sal had been with him, and they'd come upon places where they'd had to move single file, he always let her walk first. He could not help but think of that here. Looking ahead, he knew he would have given her the gift of an uncluttered view until they could again walk side by side. She would have tried to do the same, he knew that, too, offering him the chance to go first. But he would have been the most persuasive. He always had been. After all, seeing her before him was really all that he ever needed.

Memories of ancient footsteps were arrayed before him in the dust, with outlines so odd he reprimanded himself for thinking of them as having been made by feet at all. Though the squashed circles, curved rectangles and other less conventional shapes seemed fresh, Tully knew that due to the absent atmosphere, they could have been made a hundred years ago, or ten thousand. Following them, adding his own imprints with each sluggish movement, helped him find within himself each further step of his own, for he sometimes wondered how he could ever find the will. He trudged along, the path continuing to widen until, as Sal had taught him to expect, all footsteps ended. He could see the pathway's end ahead in wait for him like a threat, and there was no longer a need for moral support. It was as if the whole world had fallen away.

Approaching the lip, he peered over the cliff's edge. A series of steps carved out of gray rock spun away from him down into the darkness. Trusting Sal, he turned from the void and began to back his way down, clumsily seeking out each step with the blind toes that were all he could now afford. At the final step, Tully rocked back to stand, and in doing so pulled his upper body into a sheet of darkness. An overhang, wrest from the rock as the steps had been, stole his starlight. He passed his palm close to his chest lamp, but paused before bringing it into contact. He refrained from activating the lamp's harsh beam, instead turning to sit gingerly on the steps behind him. This was not a thing to be done quickly. The closer he neared to his goal, the less enthusiastic he became about arriving there. He shut his eyes before they could adjust to the black of the shadows. Even though his suit, for all its other faults, still kept him warm, he found himself trembling.

He did not want to make that final leap and come face to face with what Sal had assured him would be there.

Not until he had made himself ready.

This first sight of the alien reliefs, the location of which they had puzzled out over many long years, this glimpse that was now granted to him alone, was intended to be theirs together. Over the years, on site after site, they had turned the approach to that first look into a loving ritual. It had with find after find brought them closer together, but on this day, he feared that it could push them no further apart. They'd always paused so as to extend their anticipation, and timed each of their movements, the way they stepped around a newly discovered bend, the way they leaned into a pit just rescued from oblivion, the way they'd mirrored each others footsteps on countless alien worlds, with a deliberateness so that each of them achieved their first glimpse at the same instant. He would have the comfort of no such ritual now, and he felt naked and uncertain without it.

Her face hovering before him, he could have easily stayed there in the darkness forever as the energy drained from his suit. The only reason that his hand finally crept to the chestplate was the chiding look he began to see in that same face. Do it. Do it already, she was thinking. He knew that she wanted him to go on.

As he slapped the switch, he corrected himself—she would have wanted him to go on. Had she still lived.

The brilliant snap of light blazed against the wall from which the stairs upon which he'd descended had been cut. What had seemed a simple cliff face from above was revealed as but one wall of a waterless canal from below, a wall alive with ornate carvings, thrown for perhaps the first time in centuries into stark relief. The channel vanished over the horizon, and as far as Tully could see, a rippling string of aliens the likes of which he had never before seen danced upon the rock. Untouched by wind or rain, they could have been made yesterday, but Tully knew, because Sal had told him, that those who had devised this place were long dead. A race that had once stretched its arm across a dozen worlds was now left with no more evidence of their existence than this relic. The attenuated bodies that stretched the height of the wall back to the path from which he'd descended were the only images left of them. Like humans, they possessed two arms and two legs, but each body part was long—too long, it seemed to Tully, as if reflected back out of a crazy circus mirror. In aspect, this gave them an appearance closer to grasshoppers than to humans. Tully wondered whether the race could really have been three times the height of the tallest Earther, or whether that was just the way the artisans portrayed them. If the only remnant of Earth was Mount Rushmore, after all, he imagined that any aliens who might come after would be confused as well. There were no survivors of this species left to tell them whether artistic license had been taken, only a few sacred books, such as the one that Sal partially translated to point the way here. But carved into the wall a handful of steps away, sandwiched between the sacred art that could do no more than hint at the answers to the vanished race, was a square inset niche that held a treasure from which science could pry the truth. Tully still had faith in that, if little else.

"You were right, Sal," he whispered, not really believing there was anyone else who would hear. "Just like you said. They're truly here."

He staggered towards the alcove and slowly placed his hand upon a short, wide-mouthed urn with the care one uses to touch the belly of an expectant mother. Carved into the dark blue skin of the urn were small figures similar in proportions to those that loomed on the walls around him. His eyes clouded, and he blinked away tears his hands could not touch. He continued along the canal, finding alcove after alcove, each containing still another urn, each urn unique in color and design. He paused before one after the other in prayer, his lips moving, forming nothing more than his lover's name, as if that was all that there was left for him to say, as if that was the only thing that mattered.

Tully's ship trembled. As he woke and rolled from the cot he had Sal's name on his lips; he could not recall a time when she was not his first thought each morning. The soles of his feet vibrated as they hit the deck, and he hurriedly palmed his viewscreen controls.

The walls around him vanished and he was naked beneath the stars. The brief horizon curled away in the distance, intimate, forbidding, and suddenly very much *his*, made all the more so by the appearance of an odd ship that had not been there when he'd finally collapsed mere hours before. The invader was seemingly made of nothing more than four equal globes bound together one atop three so that they formed a pyramid. It sat a hundred meters closer to the sculpted path than his own. He could not recognize such a ship; the dust cloud settling around it still obscured the detail of its features.

He'd been careful to avoid any damage to what Sal had correct discerned to be an ancient treasure, and here an intruder plopped down in the midst of it, apparently blind to the consequences. That was the root of his anger, he tried to tell himself, but he knew that if forced to be truthful, he'd have to admit his motivations to be less noble than that. Instead, the anger came from a baser place, a gut reaction that by all rights, this rock was his now. He felt just as if he'd returned to his ship to find it burglarized.

As Tully watched, too stunned to take further action, a circular opening blossomed in the invading ship's top globe. A ladder dropped down slowly, and then a squat figure descended—a figure possessing the right number of arms and legs, but with a body definitely too broad for its height to be human. Yes, the form was a humanoid of some kind, but at this distance Tully could not guess at the species.

Whatever it was, it twisted its squat body for an instant and seemed to look off quickly in Tully's direction—he recoiled briefly, forgetting at first that it could not see him—before hurrying down the path that Tully had already come to think of as his own. Tully kept his eyes on the unsettling form as he clambered into his own suit, but by the time he finished his preparations and finally stood, breathing heavily, in front of his own ship, the strange figure was long out of sight.

He wished he'd had weapons aboard with which to defend his find, to drive this newcomer away, but no, when Sal was still around, she would have none of that, no guns of any kind, and it was still far too soon for him to make any changes that would erase her. All he had that he could arm himself with were his digging tools, and as he balanced a shovel across one shoulder and a pickax across the other, he felt helpless before the universe.

He rushed along the path, cursing his suit, needing to catch up with the creature, whatever it was, needing to discover something, anything, even that the momentary glimpse had all been a dream. Reaching the lip of the cliff, he leaned forward before descending, and grimaced at the effort. There it was, motionless at the base of the stairs. Tully crept halfway down the steps, then paused. It seemed not to notice his approach, but only stood there, waiting. The light from Tully's chestlamp passed over it, tossing a tall, thin shadow along the wall, and still it did not move. The wide creature, framed by the carvings of the lost ethereal beings, did not seem to Tully as if it could even be remotely related to the species.

Tully finished descending the stairs, and studied what little he could make out of its profile. It seemed not to care. He could barely see its features through the thick, translucent glass of its faceplate, and what muddy chiaroscuro he perceived did not correspond to any species he had yet met in a lifetime of travels. He tongued his radio, and while he spoke, his words racing through the frequencies and seeking a match with this new creature, he let his tools drop from his shoulders to his waist.

"Who are you?" said Tully, his voice ragged. Questions were all he had. "Why are you here? How did you find this place?"

It placed one hand on the sculpted wall before them, giving no sign that it had understood him, or even heard him at all. He studied that hand, hoping that it could give him some answers that the alien itself would not, but because of its silvery mittens, Tully could not even count the number of fingers the alien had. He moved more closely beside it and spoke again, but it continued to treat him as if his words were silence. As he neared, their lamps blended together, causing the glossy finish on the urn before them to sparkle like a starfield. Seeing the pinpoint reflection bouncing off the alien's smooth faceplate caused Tully to loosen his grip on his shovel. If asked, he couldn't have said why.

"Why are you here?" said Tully, moving a step closer. They were now so near that their suits almost touched. "Can you hear me? You shouldn't be here. Do you understand? We found this place first. *I* found this place."

It turned to him suddenly, and used what appeared to be a thumb to tap rhythmically along a series of notches that circled its other wrist. Tully could see vague movement within its helmet, but whether the blur was from the motion of lips or eyelids or something less human, he could not discern. Blinking lights that ran along the front of the alien's suit began cycling more rapidly, and the alien smacked a palm against one wrist.

With a sharp, sudden motion the alien reached up to place its hands around Tully's head. Before he could stagger back, the thing pulled his helmet down to its own. Glass to glass, he could hear a tinny voice transmitted through the shell of his suit, and at the same time could see more clearly to within its helmet. He stared into an odd face the skin of which was a blue he had never before seen, somewhere between that of a rare clear Earth sky a vid had once showed him and the shell of a frozen robin's egg he had once seen in a museum. The number and placement of facial parts were in line with what had been handed out to the rest of the humanoid creatures of the galaxy, though the eyes were slightly larger, the nose significantly smaller, and the lips so flush to the rest of the face that the mouth was almost a slit. A strip of yellow fur, short and smooth, ran low about its neck like a scarf and then up behind its ears, leaving its head for the most part hairless. The vestigial lips vibrated rapidly, but the sounds they made did not create any syllables that made sense to Tully. He'd been face to face with aliens before, particularly when trading back on The Wheel, but never this close, never with one whose species was unknown to him, and never so dreadfully alone.

He looked into its saucer eyes and desperately tried to find the familiar. Burbles morphed to klicks changed to hums, none any language he knew.

"Who are you?" asked Tully, speaking more softly this time, curiosity pushing aside his anger. "Where did you come from?"

Only meaningless noise answered him.

The alien closed its eyes, its lids an even deeper blue than its other skin had been, and dropped its hands from around Tully's head. The contact between their faceplates broke, restoring him to uncomfortable silence. Tully stepped back, and regarded the creature warily. He might have stayed that way forever, wondering, but the alien broke the tableaux. It gestured above their heads back towards their ships, and stepped briskly around him in the direction of the stone stairway. Tully turned more slowly, and it motioned broadly for him to follow, a little impatiently at that, he thought.

As he ambled after it, falling further behind with each step, it did not look back to see whether he was coming along. Seeing it near its ship, Tully looked past it to his own vessel, wondering whether he should invite the creature aboard so as not to lose the upper hand. But to bring it aboard after so long alone, to have no choice in it, to be driven by this accidental meeting, seemed wrong. He should be the one to decide when to let someone in, and not random chance.

Upon his arrival at its ship, it placed a hand on the ladder there. He gestured weakly, almost imperceptibly, towards his own. Its only answer was to push a rung into his hand. Folding his fingers around the bar, it motioned for him to climb. He clawed his way ungracefully up into the airlock. He paused there, and as it was immediately behind him, it bumped into him gently. The hull sealed after them, and it moved to the inner wall, where its fingers flew across a triangular keyboard. Tully waited patiently for the hissing pumps to cycle in whatever atmosphere the creature called home, wishing that Sal was beside him to tell him what to do next. Without her, he did not want that moment of decision to come.

The pumps silent, the creature pointed at its helmet, and then began to manipulate the restraints that held it in place. As it lifted the head covering away, Tully did not follow its lead, doing nothing but watch as it then unpeeled its suit to reveal a form not quite as stocky as it had looked when fully covered. There was still no way that it could pass for human, but without its armor the alien seemed less ... *alien* than a few minutes before. The shirt and pants it wore were so close in color to its skin that it almost seemed bare flesh. It dropped the suit casually to the pebbled flooring, after which the inner airlock door opened to reveal the rest of the ship. It stepped through quickly, waving for him to join him inside. He leaned forward to peer in after it, but did not follow.

A circular table ringed a chair in the center of the room, and the creature slipped through a thin notch there and sat. It spun, slapping buttons from which Tully tried to decipher a meaning, but which he could not possibly recognize. It tapped a microphone with blunt fingers—he could recognize that—and then waved him forward urgently. Tully remained motionless within the airlock. It tapped the microphone again, touching its harsh lips with the other hand, a hand that Tully only just then noticed bore but three fingers opposite its thumb. Tully pointed to his own chest, which caused it to wave at him again. He turned on his speaker so that his voice would echo within the room instead of continuing to transmit on random frequencies.

"What is it that you want of me?" said Tully. "I don't understand. What do you want me to do?"

His words were met with high-pitched squeals, and the creature clapped its hands against its chest and then rubbed its wide thumbs along its neck fur. It stuck out its purple tongue till it almost touched its nose, and then spun in its chair slamming blockish fingers against several buttons on the surface that surrounded it. When it whirled back to Tully, it held out both hands widely, and then began to yet again utter its incomprehensible sounds. Only this time, a split second behind what to Tully was nonsense, he could hear a high-pitched voice boom from speakers in the ceiling. It was the first English, other than that from his ship's all-too-familiar computer files, that Tully had heard for a very long time.

"You are from Earth, are you not?" the voice repeated.

Hearing those words, Tully thought he might cry.

"You can speak English," he replied in a whisper, and then, afraid it might not have heard, afraid that his words would only come across as nonsense, he repeated his statement.

"I can speak nothing of the kind," played the speakers loudly over the alien's natural crackling voice. It gave a knob a swift twist and then moved closer to Tully, standing face-to-face before him, the raised lip of the airlock door between them at their feet. When it spoke again, the voice that mirrored its words was softer. "My ship, though, has the capacity to translate your English, something that my suit computer was not preprogrammed to do. Now that your voice tells me who you are, I can tell my ship to correct that deficiency. Please come in. We should talk, now that we can."

Taken aback by the sudden cascade of a stranger's thoughts, Tully lifted a boot, about to step forward, but then he remembered who he was and why he was here. And why this thing should not be.

"Are you really from Earth?" it asked him, its wide eyes uncomfortably close. It usually did not bother him to deal with members of alien races, but this time, here, it felt wrong. "I have never met anyone from that world."

"Neither have I," said Tully. It was disconcerting to hear it utter two languages at once, one overlaying the other, the seemingly random and chaotic real one making it difficult to lose himself in the sense of the translation. And as he continued to speak, the clicks and sputters that spilled from the speakers almost had him lose the sense of what he was saying. "My ancestors must have been from Earth, at least that's what I was told, but that was so many generations back that I can't even keep track. But that's not important. Where are *you* from? How can you have possibly heard of Earth when I've never heard of anyone like you? With all my visits to The Wheel I've never seen even so much as a picture of a race that looked remotely like you."

"My people do not travel."

"Yet here you are," said Tully, sullenly. The creature appeared not to pick up on his tone.

"I have not heard of any who ever left our homeworld before me. Not in my lifetime. And not, I think, in the lifetimes of my parents either. We are taught that it is pointless to step away from our planet. Most of my people would surely feel it to take too much time away from other more important pursuits. We are scholars, you see, trading our goods for knowledge. We sit back and let the traders come to us."

Tully knew that he should care who these unknown people were, what species of beast they called themselves, what knowledge they had found worth trading for the offworld goods they'd need, the trajectory of the path that would lead him back to their home planet, all manner of particulars other than just that she was there uninvited occupying his space. But that sort of detail had barely interested him before, and was certainly not what was uppermost in his mind right then. Tully's narrow focus would have upset Sal, but his irritation could not be denied—he only cared about one thing.

"How did you find this place? It took us years before we suspected that it even existed."

"Who is this 'Us'? Is there another back at your ship?"

"How did you get here?" asked Tully quickly, with little space between its words and his own. His voice was rough, his face flushed.

"I will tell you. Come."

The alien took a step back, a clear invitation. Tully hesitated, but then stepped slowly into the room. He hung close by the airlock, one hand remaining on the lip of the doorway so that it could not slide shut behind him.

"How?" he repeated. "Tell me."

"I didn't find this place. I couldn't have possibly done that. I was not allowed to know of such things, only to dream of them. What I found, you see ... was you. I knew that you were out here. Well, not you, in particular. But someone, see? My ship, it has been programmed to look for other ships, to sort through the signals and find ones that are off alone in unexplored areas."

"And then what do you do next? Take what others have worked so hard to find? Steal our work, having done nothing to earn it? Loot our dreams and bring them back to your homeworld?"

"No, I do not want—"

Tully broke in before the alien's doubled words could possibly sway him. Its yellow fur was risen on its neck; that made Tully nervous, and he did not like to have to think that he was the cause.

"Look, I don't need you here," he said, as flatly as he knew how. "I don't want you here. You have to understand—this is a place where I was meant to be alone."

"I am sorry that you feel that way, but there is much for me to learn here. Without what can be found here, I cannot go home. You do not know my species, and I do not know yours, but I do not believe that you are so selfish as to keep this place a secret for just yourself."

"There you are wrong. I thought I was selfish once, but I was wrong. Now I know that I am selfish as hell."

His knuckles trembled from holding his tools too tightly. He forced himself to breath deeply as the alien's words continued to fly, but that did little to calm him down.

"Let us talk about this," it said, backing further away and then moving to its control panels. "Have you yet tested the air here in my ship? Maybe we can talk to each other without your suit between us. How can we ever reach an agreement standing here like this? You must come in, sit down. Perhaps I can tell you my history and make you understand why my need to be here is as strong as your own. Maybe even stronger."

The creature was right, at least about the first part of it. Caught up in his anger, he had not bothered to activate his suit's analyzer to check the atmosphere makeup in the alien's ship. If the air had qualities close to his own, he could have confronted it while maintaining his limited reserves. Forgetting that told him his emotions were putting him in more trouble than he'd thought. His feelings were making him foolish, and that was dangerous. Now he was not only angry at the alien; he was angry at himself.

"No," he said, turning away. He hoped never to see such a being again. Breaking down a wall like this now seemed forever beyond him. "I don't want to hear about your needs. I couldn't bear to hear about them right now. Whatever they are doesn't matter. I'm leaving now. And while I can't force you from this place, I don't want to ever see you when I'm out there. Please. Help me pretend that this never happened."

Tully backed into the airlock, almost tripping over its upthrust lip. Once, in another time, in another universe so much like this one as to fool most that they were identical, he and Sal would have embraced another lifeform with enthusiasm, welcomed anyone, anything to talk to after such a long, dark ride as he had just experienced. But now that Sal had left him behind an empty space where she had once been, he found he had no room in his life for anyone else to inhabit it. He let the door slide shut between the alien and himself, and waited to see whether it would activate the chamber.

The hissing of the pumps came as a soothing relief. When the hull split to once more reveal the outer world, it seemed no bleaker to him than what he had just left behind. Climbing down the ladder far too quickly, he slipped on the bottom rung, hitting the ground hard. His teeth ached from the fall as he watched the ladder retract above him.

Sal would have been disappointed. He hadn't even asked its name.

The urn when Tully lifted it was not heavy; no, not heavy at all. It came easily from its alcove, and as he looked up, stepping back with the perfect object cradled in his arms, it was almost as if the long-limbed creatures carved in stone on either side were passing it on to him.

He liked to think that they were giving him license to do so, that if he could have reached back thousands of years and asked them if it was all right for him to take the urn away, that they would have understood. Once back at the ship with his prize, however, it would be up to him to attempt to do the understanding. Who had made this place? What did it all mean? Sal had only been able to get them so far.

Peering down, he considered his distorted reflection in the urn's sealed lid. Even if Tully could have seen through the protective film of his own reflected faceplate, he doubted that he would have been able to recognize himself. It had been a long time since the look in his eye had seemed familiar. Before turning back towards his ship, he raised his head to stare at the spot on which the urn, if the records could be trusted, had sat for centuries. Then he looked back down at the urn once more, where his helmet was mirrored like an alien thing, stretched out eerily. It unnerved him, and he couldn't quite say why.

He knew he should do this quickly and be done with it, should take the urn back to his ship before the alien could come along and do more damage here. He needed to examine the artifact more closely in peace, to run his bare fingertips over the carvings etched into its body—Sal had been able to make him a present of some small part of the dead language she had figured out, so they—he—could read bits of it now—but he could not bring himself to move. Looking down at the odd width of his reflection, he found himself overcome with a languid feeling that he had found too much a part of him recently.

Take the urn, leave it in place for another to discover and disturb, at that moment neither course of action seemed much different to him. There were choices before him, paths that diverged into other choices, branched into other lives, each with the potential of making him different than he was now, he knew that—but at this moment he did not have the energy to pick one. Take the urn. Leave it. He repeated the possibilities in his mind, but his mind offered no answers. The power of decision had been draining from him for months, and now appeared to be at an end; all that remained was lethargy.

Either option seemed now as good as the other, and so he placed the urn back into the recessed circle that had been carved aeons ago to embrace it, and took one long, slow step away. He raised his hands above his shoulders to rest on the walls on either side of the alcove, and let his chin drop to his chest. Peering into the stark, black, endless shadow that his chestlamp created in the niche behind the urn, Tully began to cry with an intensity he had not known since Sal had died.

He stood that way—legs trembling, tears streaming down his face, choices swirling in his head with no apparent place to land—until his suit alarm blared to warn him that his oxygen mix was running dangerously low, and he returned to the *Fortune* empty-handed.

Tully sat at the ready close by his airlock door, his helmet the only missing piece. Uncomfortable in his spacesuit, he stared off unblinking through invisible walls at the threatening presence of the invading ship. Between his feet, his overturned helmet looked very much like an empty urn, an allusion his mind was making that he regretted, and which he tried hard to ignore. The sheets of stars overhead were unblinking witnesses to his tense vigil.

When the alien finally climbed down its ladder, Tully did not move. He was frozen as it headed off towards the site, foolishly afraid that a stray twitch would give him away. He forgot to breath, and forgot that it did not matter whether he breathed or not. It wasn't until the creature vanished over the cliff that Tully became something like himself again. He latched his helmet tight, and turning his back on its path, trundled towards the alien's deserted ship.

The ship's airlock controls were easy to manipulate, and he was relaxed as he played his fingers swiftly along the colored buttons. He'd watched closely as the alien worked them, so he'd had no doubt that he could do so himself. When the airlock door was solidly sealed behind him, he rechecked his helmet's pop-up grid. What he'd suspected had been the truth of it. Their atmospheres, while not identical, were close enough in so many ways as to be compatible. Aside from showing up so close in time upon this small planet, they had that much in common, at least. He paused for a moment, considering whether he was truly ready to take the next step, and then realizing his readiness did not matter, he cracked his helmet. He knew that he might as well conserve the stock of oxygen he had brought with him on his travels; he was unsure whether he would be able to bring himself to make any profit off this trip and buy more, and his recent inaction told him which way his heart was leaning.

Cradling his helmet under one arm, he studied the interior of the unfamiliar ship in a way he'd been too wired to do during his first brief visit. He felt somewhat unclean as he looked about, as if he was suddenly remembering that he should have known better than to do this. If Sal had been with him, she'd never have let it happen.

If Sal had been here, it wouldn't have been necessary.

As he gazed around, nothing he could see gave him any clue as to what the alien expected to do with whatever it found here, but then, he imagined that the creature would have been equally as lost in his own ship. He tried to read the markings on the controls, but they were completely unfamiliar to him. He could have recreated the moves it had made to activate the translator, but nothing more. And coming here at all had exhausted his daring; he was not about to experiment with anything random. As resentful as he felt that the ship was here, he did not intend to destroy it like a child.

A lone book, the only bit of humanity—or life, he corrected himself—he could see, obscured a row of buttons on the circular table. He flipped it open, picked his way slowly through its rough pages. Endless rows of strange letters there, neat and ordered, also meant nothing to him. Halfway through the volume the pages began to be blank, and he wondered if the book could it be a diary.

Sal would have known what to do with this chaotic information. She was always the one who had to be the smart one, and he had depended on that. It was his turn now, but he didn't know that he would ever be ready. And definitely not this soon.

He had no choice. He would have to talk to the creature, confront it—no, not confront it, *reason* with it—something he had hoped to avoid. That was the only way. The paths before him had dwindled to one.

He would wait, then. Maybe with the element of surprise on his side, he would not feel at such a disadvantage.

Tully stood still in the center of the room, repressing every urge to touch. When the hum of the airlock finally began and ever-so-slowly ended, rescuing him from silence and solitude, *he* was the only one surprised, for the inner door opened to reveal the broad creature to be carrying an urn at least twice as large as the one that he had prevaricated over, and larger by far than any he had yet seen in his explorations here. The being nodded at Tully perfunctorily, as if it had all along been expecting to find him there. It took great effort on Tully's part to feign calm as he watched it place the urn beside the book on the control table.

"You don't seem startled to see me," he said, when he could finally muster speech. "You seem quite at peace with the idea of me being here. Or maybe you're not. Either way, I can't know for sure. You are alien, and so I haven't the slightest idea how to read you. You could be livid inside, and I would never know."

It removed its helmet, and sat in the control chair, but did not speak. Tully hoped it would, so he would not have to.

"I am talking too much," he continued, ignoring the way the translator seemed to mangle his words. "That's not what I intended, to talk too much. Only, it's been a long time since I've had anyone to speak with, anyone I've been willing to let myself speak to, and so ... I'm rambling. But aren't you worried, finding me here like this? You should be, you know."

At last the alien spoke, its words once more in dual voices, sense layered with nonsense.

"You have not moved so much as a dust mote outside that you didn't need to. You've hardly touched anything out there, leaving very little evidence that you were even here. You treat it all with respect."

"But you don't know me. Not even my name."

"Why should I think that you would do me any harm?"

"Well ... I did tell you that my ancestors were from Earth."

"That is an attempt at a joke, I think. The translators are not perfect, but I think I am right. It is kind of you to make such a joke."

Tully nodded, even though he was not sure himself whether or not it was a joke at all.

"I know you think that you do not want me here," it continued. "I also know that if you really did not want me here with you, you would have done something about it. You would have left. Or you would have driven me from this place. But you would not be sitting calmly across from me, talking about the future."

Tully was startled at the way this alien seemed to know him better than he knew himself. He smiled, something it seemed he had not done in a long while. He wondered whether the alien knew what a smile meant.

He wondered if *he* knew what the smile meant.

He wondered whether it knew that it smelled like almonds. Or even what almonds were.

"My name is Tully. Please, if you can, accept my apology for the way I acted earlier."

"My name is Xi," it said, and as the name was spoken, Tully sighed along with the sound. He suddenly sensed, not knowing how, that what he had been thinking of as an it was actually a she. She tapped the book before her, and then opened a recessed drawer in the table to slide it away. "And I accept your apology. Soon I hope to be able to do more than that. Soon I hope to understand it."

"I don't know that I'll ever be able to give you that." He paused, staring at the place where the book had been. "Why have you come here?"

"As I told you before, we are scholars, my people. Information is important to us. Who better to get worthwhile information from than one such as yourself, out each day exploring an unknown universe?"

"And what do you intend to do, now that you have followed me to this particular place in the universe?"

"That I do not know as yet. I do not even know what this place is supposed to be. Remember? I did not follow clues here, I followed you here. Or at least my ship did. I brought this urn back here in hopes of understanding the nature of where you have led me. Look at it. It seemed remarkable there, even back in a hall of the remarkable. What do you think it is? Do you have any ideas?"

Tully did not answer, could not answer, and after a moment, the alien spoke again.

"You know, don't you?" she said.

"This is a place of the dead," he said at last. "And the only one who fully knows the answer to your question ... is the same."

"I do not know what that means."

"Put your helmet back on," he said, his hands shaking as he reached for his own, "and I will show you."

Thestar maps he showed to Xi were two. First, floating in the air, translucent like a dream, a holographic projection of the path that had led him from yesterday into today, glowing red lines leading from star system to star system until they ended here. They stood on opposite sides of it while he explained the journey, and he could still see her through a mist of stars, her blue skin made a dark purple. Then, beneath it, limp upon a table, a parchment, so fragile it seemed mere molecules thick and likely to dissolve simply from the pressure of being looked at, also showed the way to the rocky planetoid on which their two ships perched. Tully hoped that these twin sights pushed from her brain the image made upon entering of that second spacesuit, Sal's spacesuit, hanging hollow in the airlock. He did not want to make explanations until he was sure he was ready for them. He needed to stay for awhile in the shallows, and not go out where it was deep.

"Each time I unfold this," said Tully, pointing to the ancient, physical map, the map of atoms rather than air, the clue that had started it all, "it moves a little closer to becoming dust."

"Then I thank you for making the sacrifice of showing it to me at all," said Xi. She had detached her reconfigured translator from her suit, and was wearing it loosely about her neck like an amulet. He looked at it resting against her flesh as her words poured out, and saw that her skin seemed to glow with a pale phosphorescence, something he had not noticed before.

"That's all right. I need to look at it from time to time anyway, to help me remember. Even if I had not brought you here, I still would have had to do this eventually."

"Then I have reason to thank you anyway, for letting me be here while you remember."

Tully took a step back, and the hologram dissolved from the air. He turned away from the map that remained, and from Xi. He had to tell her, and yet he could not look at her and speak; the blankness of the wall made a more inviting audience, and one that he desperately needed or else he could not go on.

"We'd heard of this place a long time ago, you see," he began in a slow voice, surprising himself with his formality, "in rumors and superstitions alive for generations. It was said to be a planet of the dead. The world itself, or so the common knowledge went, was never inhabited, had never known life of its own. Some race, the name of which we've as yet been unable to translate, would travel from their homeworld to this graveyard, and place their dead ones here. It's a race that apparently no longer exists, from a planet we've yet to find.

"Who were these mourners? We don't know. We figured out just enough to learn that on the outside of each urn is carved the life story of the being within. I can only make out a few words, but I hope to be able to read them in full someday, because we still do not know their stories. Who would warrant such effort of time and expense to be brought so far to say a ceremonial goodbye? Surely not all the members of that race are here. That wall we walked was long, but not long enough for that. So as you can see, we knew very little. But we knew enough to understand that what we discovered here, this destination that was pieced together of scraps and whispers, would be the find of anyone's lifetime. But now that I'm here ... Sal was the one ... She'd know how to interpret that find. She'd figured out much of this language, held it in her head, in her soul. I can hardly read it at all. It's meaningless. I understand as little of these scratches as I would of you, without that translator. I feel lost here. There is no longer any map that I can read."

He turned back to the map, making sure to keep his line of sight low so he would not catch Xi's gaze, and the sheet billowed slightly with his movements. He slowly folded the chart until it could fit in the palm of his hand, where it seemed no thicker than it had been a moment before.

"That's why I did not bring one of the urns back here. At least that's the reason that I told myself. I wouldn't know what to do with them. I could sell them, but I could never understand them. And though I need this money, money isn't what I want right now. I want to *see*. And without Sal ..."

He seized control of himself before the crying began, but just barely. He hoped that since she was alien to human ways that she could not possibly have read the sure signs that he'd been about to crumble.

"But I am not lost," said Xi. He could sense her moving around the table towards him, then stopping before she came too close. So she could tell that much, at least. "Perhaps with a little help from me, if I could see your notes, study your maps further, I would be able to help figure it all out."

"But the thing is, Xi, the thing is, you see—I don't know whether I *want* it all figured out."

He still could not bear to look at her, and so looked down at the map in his hand. When her hand appeared and covered his own, he was too stunned by the touch to be startled.

"I do not believe that," she said. "I think you do know what you want."

He kept looking down. To avoid being drawn to her eyes, he kept looking hard at her skin, so blue against the pale map.

"May I take this back to my ship? I would like to study it, and whatever else you might have that could help us solve this mystery."

"No," said Tully, driven to look up at her at last. "No. You may look at these as much as you like, but when you do, I want you to look at them here."

He turned away again, even though he had grown tired of all this turning away, because he hoped that she could not read him, hoped that she did not realize that he wanted to retain the documents not so much because he did not trust her with them, but because he missed the sound of another life echoing around him in the ship. He was sick of only hearing sounds of his own making.

"Do you really think you will be able to help read them?" he asked. He placed the map upon the table and looked at her straight in the face and this time refused to turn away from her big, round eyes. She did not answer immediately.

"With time," she said. "After all, that is why I am out here with you, instead of back home with all the others. As I said, we are scholars, not explorers. It is unusual that we wander space. We leave it to others to do the traveling. It is only my abilities that have caused my people to allow me to wander this far. They have great hopes for me, and for my journey. The intellectual thirsts of those at home are strong."

"Let's hope that they are not *too* strong, Xi. I wouldn't want them to cross the galaxies to drink this place up."

Xi gave out a long, high-pitched whistle, her lips vibrating swiftly, that the translator mirrored as a laugh.

"No. Believe me. They would not do such a thing. No one will come after me. But having found this place, Tully, don't you want the universe to know about it? It should not stay hidden from the rest. Isn't that what your life's work has been about? Discovering what has been lost, and making it found again?"

"I know that what you say is making sense. Still ... you must be patient with me. I don't know why I find I can say this to you, but ... I used to make sense in what I did. Really, I did. But not anymore. And I don't know that I will be ready to start making sense again for a long time."

"Perhaps not. So come. At the very least, we can go for a walk."

In the airlock, so she would not see him go through his ritualistic longing stare at Sal's suit while he climbed into his own, as he had grown accustomed to doing each time when he exited the ship, he instead forced himself to study Xi as she slithered back into her own suit. Her movements were unexpectedly graceful, and he was startled to find himself smiling yet again.

They walked until the sculpted walls were no more, the canyon coming to a dead end where the unknown creators had ceased their carving. The raw rock before them there seemed like a wave stalled mere moments before sweeping them away.

"Why do you think they stopped here?" Tully asked.

"Perhaps they stopped dying," said Xi, running her hand along the craggy face of the dead end. There were alcoves along both walls, with an urn in each one of them save the one that Xi had had the courage to strip bare, all the way until this final wall they faced. As they'd made their way along, Tully had found that he was able to see differences in the carved aliens, where at first there had only seemed uniformity. Slight variations in body type had become more noticeable. He wondered what else he could learn if only he left himself open.

"People don't stop dying," he said.

"These were not your people," said Xi. "Maybe they have some surprises for you."

"Life is life. It stops. You'll learn. It always stops. Usually far too soon."

Even with the expanse of dead air between them, he could still smell Xi, her odor carried away from his ship in the confines of his suit, and for a moment, he felt a sting of guilt over wearing such traces so close to his skin. Since Sal's aroma had faded away, it had been a long time since any scent other than his own had invaded his nostrils. He exhaled sharply, hoping to blow away the fragrance, blow away the feelings, but her smell was still trapped there with him, inescapable, and all he succeeded in doing was misting his faceplate.

"It is beautiful, you know," said Xi. "This place, this sky. Finding that is almost enough of a treasure."

"I know," he said.

She touched a hand to the chaotic outcropping that barred them from going any further.

"You should know that you do not have to feel guilty because you are not seeing this with your partner."

"Yes, I do have to feel guilty. That's the only sane thing to do. I left her behind in a graveyard, only to come to this new graveyard alone. I'm trapped between graveyards, and don't know which way to go next."

"Some place a little less morbid, I hope," said Xi.

He dropped to one knee and ran a finger along the join where floor met wall, hoping that even if he could not decipher their language, at the very least he could determine how and why they'd created this strange monument.

"They left no tools behind," he said. "Not a trace of what they were. They left us no message for us here, either deliberate or otherwise."

"I do not think we need there to be an intentional message. But we will find one anyway. I feel sure of it."

"What are you looking for here, Xi?" Tully asked, looking up, her broad silhouette blocking out the stars. "How can you sound so confident that you will find it? And even if you do, what could you possibly uncover here that your people would want? You say you want knowledge, knowledge that your people can turn to a profit, but what does that mean? I guess I don't really understand that. I sell physical objects—artifacts, scrolls, artwork. How do you trade a fact from a dead world?"

Xi turned from him then, lowering her hands to her sides. In her silence, he tried to read her body language, but could not.

"Xi?"

"I do not know," she said quickly. "I have never done this before."

"What are you talking about? You gave me the impression that you could help me, that you came here bringing some small scraps of knowledge with you. You let me think that."

She turned back to him slowly, and then knelt beside him.

"I am sorry. I should not have said what I did. But I am being truthful now. I have never done this before, Tully. This is my first time off my home planet."

"Wait," he said, in a whisper even he could barely hear. He pressed his hands together tight so that he would not be moved to take hold of her and shake her hard. "Wait. You follow me into the middle of nowhere. No, you don't just follow, you *stalk*. You strut around an ancient site as if you've done it a thousand times before. You even convince me that you should be here. You make me think that there must be a chance you can figure it all out for me, you have me hoping— and now you tell me that you've never done it before?"

Tully started to laugh, but though his body went through the motions, no sound came. Tears rolled down his cheeks to pool at the base of his faceplate. He fell back against the unhewn wall and slid to the ground. The canyon stretched out before him and vanished far over the rim, seeming so far he doubted if he had the strength to walk it again. Xi slid a few feet closer, banging her toes into the sole of one of his boots.

"What are you doing, Tully?" asked Xi.

"Haven't you ever seen anyone laugh before?" he said roughly. "Or doesn't your translator compensate for that?"

"Yes. All races laugh. But what I haven't seen before is a human acting like an idiot."

She got quickly back to her feet and started walking back the way they'd come. Tully scrambled upright, grabbing for her awkwardly, but missed, and fell back to his knees. By the time he was standing again, she was far ahead of him.

"Xi, wait up! I didn't mean to hurt you!"

I didn't even know I could.

He cursed his unwieldy suit as he struggled vainly to catch up with her.

"You think that you're the only one who has ever known loss?" she transmitted back to him, her computerized voice sounding more human than ever. As the distance between them increased, her words began to be interspersed with an ever-increasing static. "You lost one lover, and you think that gives you the right to hurt? Well, I lost them all. Pain is more than just a human quality, you know. Pain belongs—"

Her transmission faded completely then, abandoning him mid-sentence. He was left without even the comfort of static, moving slowly forward as the eyes of a dead race followed him down a long and lonely road.

By the time Tully arrived at Xi's ship, she had already changed the airlock codes. Using the sequence that he had learned before, he punched at the buttons by the outer door, then went on to experiment with other patterns —but nothing happened. He pressed his palms against the dark metal, trying to sense her within. He hoped that the ship had alerted her to his attempts, that she was looking his way and wondering. He rapped at the door, first softly, and then harder, but he knew that trying to get her attention that way was pointless; meteors had bounced off like snowflakes against the very spot where his glove banged. In a war of metal against metal, his suit would surely give out first. She likely couldn't hear his vibrations even if she tried.

"Xi, do you hear me?" he broadcast to the silence, hoping that even if she was unaware of his frantic actions, she'd at least pick up his transmission. But there was no response. He could imagine her sitting there, skin of her ship stripped away as his had been before, watching him make a fool of himself. It wouldn't be the first time someone used him for amusement in that way. "Xi? Listen to me. Please. I must not lose you now."

He pressed his forehead against the ship and wondered how long he could stay there that way, whether he should just remain propped up until the oxygen was gone, a monument to foolish hope. If that was what it would take, he swore that he would do it. He had no idea how much time had passed when he finally heard Xi speak to him through his helmet.

"My people didn't want me to come here." Xi's words were in the translated computer voice that he had come to think of as her own, but they comforted him nonetheless. The sound caused him to push at the door, but it still remained sealed against him. "Actually, Tully, my people didn't want me to go *anywhere*. They liked to sit back on our planet, self-important and still, and let other races travel to them from all across the universe, but none of them ever went off-planet to see these things for themselves. They felt they belonged at the center of the universe, and as such could live as contemplators rather than doers. The mere idea of us traveling seemed blasphemous to them. I begged them, Tully, but they would not listen."

Open the door, thought Tully, but he could not bring himself to speak the words. Not then, not when it seemed as if she still might bolt. The last thing he wanted was to look up at the ship rising away from him. He could not bear such loss again. Her voice seemed distant to him, and not from just the transmission alone.

"When I would tell them," she went on, "that I would rather be one of the people who came to us to trade than who I was, that I was not willing to submit to a life spent looking up and out from our surface towards the mysteries above, like a fish that could never know the outside of the tank, they told me to keep quiet about my desires. They told me to keep those thoughts to myself. But silence couldn't save me. I would keep looking at the stars, imagining the planets that raced around them, and the people who populated those planets, and wished I could know more about them first hand, as more than just an impersonal intellectual puzzle. If forced to live that way, if forced to contain my reach, I would die.

"But they would not hear me, or having heard, would not value my urgency. As far as any of the elders were concerned, the territories beyond our sky were damned. Terrible things would happen to me if I went off-planet. They warned that outside of our homeworld, the universe held nothing good for us. They promised there would only be pain for me if I left."

"I will not let them hurt you, Xi."

"They were not the ones who would hurt me. They said that the universe itself would do that. They said—"

A strange static danced in Tully's ears, louder than the white noise of the universe. It was a sound unlike any he had yet heard from Xi, and though at first it was unidentifiable, he quickly decided that it was most likely the sound of her crying, untranslated by the computer, untranslatable by anything but his heart.

"Xi, let me in." He'd never heard himself beg like that before. It startled him, but at the same time felt fully justified. "Please. I don't want to be the cause of your pain. They lied to you, Xi. The universe doesn't want to cause you pain. The universe wants you to be happy. I believe that. I suddenly know that to be true."

She went on as if he had not even spoken.

"This ship that I have," she continued, "the ship that brought me here to your side? I lied to you, Tully. It isn't mine. I stole it from one of our many visitors. While its true owner traded in the city, I broke inside. I'd been waiting for such an opportunity. The elders would never have let me go, there was no way to ever find an acceptable path towards going, I knew that, and so ... and so, I simply went. And that's why I cannot help you. That's why, back at the site, I had nothing to give. I'm no explorer. I can't interpret for you what this place means. I'm merely a thief. All I am, Tully, all I really am, is just someone who wants to look at the stars."

"That's all I need," he whispered.

"They're probably looking for me right now. If we stay here too long, they'll find us. They'll find this place, and I'm not sure I want them to have it. Let them learn that they can't have everything. It's not me they want, anyway; it's the ship back. I've embarrassed them with one of their traders. Me, they wouldn't know what to do with.

"I can't go home now. I can't help you and I can't go home. And I don't know which of the two is worse."

"You don't need to go home, Xi," he said quietly. "You don't have to accept that. Just open the door. Let me in so we can talk. We need to talk, Xi, and not through a vacuum. We need to talk in the same room, occupying the same space. The future is too fragile to be discussed in such a distant way. Please let me in. There's something important I need to tell you. Something terribly important."

The airlock when it opened surprised Tully. He had not thought his words would be enough. He rushed through the opening and felt so crazed that it was a great struggle for him to wait for the outer door to close before peeling off his suit. He found the delays of his clumsy controls unbearable. Standing there, at last no barriers between them, he did not speak, not at first; his mind was racing too swiftly now for the words to get out. The smell of almonds was still in the air, even stronger this time than it had seemed before, and he could only pause and inhale deeply. The words that had seemed so important when he was outside Xi's ship seemed too heavy to carry inside with him. Even though his cheeks were wet, he was smiling. It was a broad, honest smile, something that had been alien to him for far too long. He could think of only one thing to say.

"Xi," he said, speaking slowly, deliberately. "I love you."

Tully looked at Xi as his translated words spewed out of the ship's computer. She did not turn to look at him, instead staring at the speakers, and she did not speak, breaking his heart with her silence. *Look at me*, he thought, but she would not, not at first. His heart thudded as she sat and punched a series of buttons, and together they listened to his declaration in her tongue, repeated once, twice, again. By the time she finally returned his gaze, it had seemed like forever.

"Tell me that again."

"I said that I love you, Xi."

"You are a crazy man! I had thought that the translator surely had to be broken, but—What kind of thing is that for you to say? You don't even know who I am. You don't even know *what* I am!"

"I know exactly what you are, Xi. I didn't plan this. I'm not sure where it came from. But standing here now, before you, I know it to be true. Maybe I *am* crazy. But love is crazy, isn't it? Love has to be crazy."

She remained still as he moved towards her. He placed his bare fingers on her cheek, touching her for the first time. He slid those fingers to her chin, and expected her gaze to follow the trail of his hand across her skin, but she did not. She was holding herself back, he knew that, and he had to make her let go.

"You say this to me after what I have told you," she said. He did not need a translator to know that she wanted to pull back. "This is pity, not love. You do not know what you mean. You feel sorry for me, as I would for myself if I were you. This is not love. You could not possibly know."

"I know I need to hold you," he said, letting his hand drop from her face to her shoulder, pulling her closer to him. She did not stop her head from resting against his stomach. "Isn't that enough?"

He bent low with a grace he'd never quite known to place his lips upon the blue of her forehead, which was soft and damp, like an open, hungry mouth. Her whole body as it called to him made him feel as if he was already in a deep and intimate place, one buried inside her heart. He was astonished to feel this way, astonished that Sal would let him. He tilted back her head to place his trembling lips against her own almost absent ones. So thin were those vestigial lips that at first he could not tell whether or not she was kissing him back, but then her tongue, alive and round and small, darted against his own.

"I've needed you for so long," he said, "only I didn't know that what would fill the empty hole was you."

She backed away from him for a moment and seemed to study the strangeness of his face. To him, hers seemed strange no longer, and he hoped that he could convince her to let him seem the same.

"I do not know what we are doing," she said.

"We are doing what it is that couples do," he said, reluctantly dropping his hands from her so he could unbutton the light shirt which he had worn beneath his spacesuit. "We are going mad."

"I have never had anyone look at me in that way before," said Xi. "Not even my lovers."

"Then perhaps they were not really your lovers after all," said Tully.

They lay entwined in her bunk, a thin blanket down around their ankles. He felt that he could have floated to any shore he wished just on the breadth of her. One of Tully's hands was pinned beneath her, while with the other he ruffled the yellow fur at her neck. He followed the soft trail as far down her back as he could reach. He took a deep breath to prepare himself for what he had to say. He felt no more prepared after than he had before, but he had to plunge in anyway.

"Follow me," he said, murmuring into her neck as he drank of her skin. "Come to my ship, come live with me, and send this ship empty back to your home. Let them have it. You will not need it. Then maybe your elders will forget about you, and you can go on with me. That's all you'll ever need. You want to decipher the puzzles of the universe? Then we'll do it together. There is no need for you to make that journey alone, Xi. You have me now. You have me."

There was more he would have said, he didn't know that he would ever have stopped speaking until she agreed to follow him, but she pulled away from him suddenly, silencing him. Her feet caught in the blanket as she sat up. He reached for her back, but at the sight of her hunched shoulders, he let his fingers fall short before they neared her skin.

"Who was she?" asked Xi. He could not begin to conceive of how to answer her. She turned to him once more, and did not appear pleased with his silence. "Tully?"

He tried again to reach for her, to cure this rift with a touch, but this time she raised a hand against him.

"Tully, tell me," she said. "Or this invitation of yours comes much too soon."

He turned from her, and sat at the far corner of the bunk.

"You're right," he said softly. "I guess you need to know. I guess I need to say it. Forgive me for not saying it sooner, Xi. But it's difficult most times to even think it."

He shifted slightly to make sure that his back was completely towards her, so he could not see her even out of the smallest corner of an eye. He could not bear to look at Xi and talk about Sal. The two concepts should not have to be contained within the same universe. Until he began to speak, he was not sure that the words would be able to come at all.

"I have not spoken of this to anyone before," he said, the sounds dredged out of him from great depths. "Not voluntarily. And not even to those who thought they knew me well enough to ask me. I had turned into a ghost. Believe me, Xi, when I would walk through the world that we had formerly inhabited together, and see those who had known us both, I would shake my head and look away, and try to make myself invisible, and they would know enough not to ask anything further of me. And yet, even if they had asked, even if they'd loved me enough to ignore my protests and try to dig the truth out of me, I doubt that I would have been able to tell them. But I will tell you.

"I will tell you."

He looked down into the palms of his hands, and he knew he was alone there on the bunk. There was no planetoid, no Xi, and most definitely of all, no Sal.

"You don't know what this life you say you want is really like, Xi. You couldn't possibly know, living on the surface as you did. I don't know that you could ever understand the choices that one makes, the stupid, stupid choices. Because when you live out among the stars, with your ship your only true home, you must learn to make do without neighbors or friends. You figure out quickly how to take care of yourself. You don't go looking elsewhere for answers. Elsewhere could be months away.

"So when Sal first started feeling weak, we figured it was from overwork, from spending too much of her energies trying to find this place. We didn't dig any deeper than that. It was easier for our hunt not to. Our only doctor was the ship's computer, and if you learned anything from your brief moments onboard the *Fortune*, it is that we could not afford the best. This find was supposed to change that. I like to tell myself that even if we'd brought along the top of the line, it wouldn't have done any good, that no computer can ever be as intuitive as a human doctor. That we still wouldn't have known that this was far more than just exhaustion. But that's just what I like to tell myself.

"So we did what we thought was right. I tried to get her to slow down, to sleep more, to eat better, to rest her eyes, her hands, her mind, keeping her focus on the strength that we both knew would certainly come back if only we gave it time. We were so foolish, Xi. We knew our love was immortal, and we thought that meant we were immortal too. A common problem, I guess. Yet if we'd only admitted that we weren't, maybe we would have headed back. We could have done something in time. But no, we were so fixated on this damned, horrible place.

"Sal was so tired one morning that she could not get out of her bed, and so I went about my work without her, hoping that her time alone would strengthen her. Later that day, when I looked in on her to see if she needed anything, she was sleeping. At least I thought that she was sleeping. She seemed so peaceful there, the covers tucked up under her chin, her mouth slightly open like a child. But she never woke up again. Later that day, I realized that she had fallen into a coma of some kind. It was only then that I understood that her illness was beyond us both.

"I rushed us back to The Wheel, whatever good rushing does in the vastness of space; we were so far out that by then it was too late. She'd fallen victim to Frayn's Syndrome, Xi. Your people would not know of such a thing, and we do not know much more, just enough of it to give it a name. Spacers who handle many alien artifacts often succumb to it, but we always knew it wouldn't happen to us. They could not tell me for sure how she had contracted it, what object or set of objects she might have touched that let this disease get to her, or even how it had killed her. They think it might have something to do with combinations of various alien organic matter reacting with each other in one's system, but that's still just a theory. We know so damned little.

"They could not even tell me whether or not it would eventually kill me, too.

"For the longest time I hoped that it *would* kill me. Without Sal, I was dead already. Eventually, once I no longer had the will to even wish that it would catch up with me, I started wandering again. I called it wandering, but by using that word I was fooling myself. I guess I always knew I would come here. This is the place towards which Sal was pointing us. This is what our final years had been *about*.

"If you had not come here and taken me by surprise, I don't know what I would have done having finally gotten here. Sat there, perhaps, until all my oxygen went away, all the while thinking of Sal and what might have been. There didn't seem to be any reason to go back to the real world."

It wasn't until he felt Xi's touch on his shoulder that he realized he had fallen silent, or that his eyes were closed. The imprint of Sal's face was still, as ever, haunting his eyelids.

"But I did come and take you by surprise," whispered Xi. Her fur was so soft as her cheek pressed against the side of his neck, pushing Sal's face gently away.

"Yes, you did," he said. "And I never thought I'd see again the emotions that you brought. I thought that I was dead, and that these feelings were dead within me. Now everything has changed."

"You seemed so sad before," she said, reaching her short arms around him so that her fingers almost touched each other across his chest. "Is that what finding the right person can do? Could it really be me that made such a change? It does not seem, I don't know, *proper* somehow. Are all humans so mercurial?"

"I couldn't tell you. It's been a long time since I gave much thought to any other human but Sal. I am no longer an expert on them. But she was unchanging, as steady as the ground beneath my feet."

He took her hand, and turned so that they faced each other. He had never seen her like before. Somehow he was sure that even if he traveled to her world and met all of her people, taking the measure of every single one, he would still not see her like again.

"There," he said. "You asked me to share about Sal, and I told you. Now come with me."

She pressed her forehead against his, and emitted what seemed like a sigh. That close, her large eyes were all of existence.

"I will go with you," she said. "But life isn't as simple as that. How will we live?"

"That is simple. We will live as I have always lived. There are museums that will pay well for what we have found here. And if not museums, then men."

"Tully, listen carefully. You already tried that. I saw you out there. You seemed unable to take what we have found. You were frozen. You let it all rest exactly as the makers had placed it. I had to be the one to bring the urn back here. Be honest with yourself. Will you be able to take from this place? Will you be able to move on?"

Tully tilted his head slightly to stare at the urn on the far side of the room, and thought of the time with Xi that it could buy. He wanted that time, and even more, to his great surprise, he found that he needed that time.

"Yes," he said, burying his head in the crook of her neck and breathing in his new life. "Yes, Xi, I promise I will."

Tully had never before seen the trader so distracted, so unwilling to settle to the task before them. The last time Tully had returned with Sal from one of their missions, Jak had immediately become so intent on the objects of his greed that he had seemed to forget anyone else was with him in the room. The fact that he and Tully were two of the few humans on The Wheel out of tens of thousands of members of several hundred alien species usually allowed them to relate comfortably when doing business after one of their long separations. They'd always at least have that comfortable habit between them, the catching up on gossip while easing into the more profitable business at hand. But now Jak seemed like a different person.

"Is there something that's making you nervous, Jak?" said Tully, Xi standing slightly behind him. The rhythm seemed all wrong between them today. The way Jak's eyes flicked between them both disturbed Tully. "You don't seem quite ready to do business. Are you feeling all right?"

Jak finally stopped looking at Xi. Wedged into the crowded room of artifacts for sale or trade, Jak seemed somewhat like an artifact himself. His right hand rested on the urn they had brought back, but casually, not with the intensity that

Tully had expected such a find would bring. The merchant took a deep breath, and stared hard at Tully.

"I always stand ready to do business with you, my friend," he said, his words slow and forced. "Only for this specimen, I fear I will need more time. You can understand that, can't you? I want you to go away happy. Aren't I always that way? And if what I suspect is true, once I check my databases further, you will be *very* happy, Tully. Let me tell you about what I've discovered over dinner."

Only when Jak had finished speaking did he peer beyond Tully's shoulder to look at Xi.

"We don't need dinner, Jak," said Tully, puzzled. He took one step to the right to block the man's view of Xi, but his eyes did not refocus on Tully. The dealer had never asked to break bread with him before. Tully's words caused the dealer to suddenly notice him as if startled. "Only credits."

"Yes, credits, and you shall have them." Jak paused. He seemed confused, as if he had just awoken, and was still trying to remember in what room he had fallen asleep. "Only there are sometimes more important things than credits."

"Yes, I suppose there always are," said Tully.

The two men stared at each other in silence, their roles changed, and Tully not quite sure what was expected of him. Jak was normally the one hurrying the process along. They'd done this many times before with little variance, and Jak's jittery attitude left him unsettled. Tully did not like that feeling, not after having just discovered himself again after so long a time adrift. If Xi had not been there, perhaps the silence would never have been broken.

"We might as well eat here," she said. "I have a feeling that I will not see an inhabited planet or even an inhabited station like this again for a long while. I'd best learn what I can."

"If that's really what you wish," said Tully. He turned to Jak, whose hand still absentmindedly stroked the urn. "We'll leave you alone to examine the piece further, and then be back when you're ready to close up."

Tully turned, but before they could leave, Jak was suddenly beside him, having sprung across the room to place one hand on his sleeve.

"Wait!" Jak muttered, almost to himself. Tully had to strain to hear the man. The words were almost beneath a whisper. "Before you go, may I speak to your friend alone? Please."

"I don't know," Tully whispered, positioning himself more solidly between the merchant and Xi. He reached out and took one of her hands, fighting the urge to back quickly out of the room. He would not have been able to explain his discomfort to Xi if he'd tried.

"What could be wrong with that?" said Xi, her fingers wriggling to loosen his grip. And then she said softly, close to Tully's ear so that only he could hear it, "He seems harmless enough."

"They all seem harmless enough."

"They?" she asked.

Tully shrugged. He didn't know what else to say to make her understand, since he didn't fully understand his feelings either.

"Go on," he said, speaking slowly. "I'll wait right over here."

Tully stood in the doorway, anxious to go, and watched uncomfortably as the two spoke. Xi seemed huge beside him, looking as if she could have crushed him if not careful. Tully was not a man given to hunches or intuitions, and so he suppressed the ones he was feeling. He wondered if he was being silly. He studied Jak as the man whispered to Xi, and he tried to tell himself that all was well, all continued as it had before. Jak suddenly noticed Tully's gaze, and the man tried to spin Xi around so that their positions were reversed, but when he could not move her, instead he moved between her and Tully and quickly turned his back. Jak's voice grew louder, and when Xi began to back away, Tully had to admit that what his gut had told him has been correct—Xi had been made upset. Jak lunged for Xi, and Tully rushed across the room to grab Jak's wrist. Jak held on tightly, the man's fingers deep into Xi's forearms, as Xi attempted to pull away.

"You mustn't leave me," Jak shouted. "You've got to stay here. You must! Can't you see how I feel?"

So strong were the trader's fingers that Tully had to pull them away one by one. As Tully bent back Jak's hand, Xi stood there, silent, more a witness to the tableaux than a participant.

"I love you," the man said. Jak's words stung at Tully, but for all Xi reacted, it was as if she had not even heard them. "Stay here with me. Don't go off with Tully. What do you need him for? I'll give you all I have! That's how much I love you."

"Jak," said Tully, his voice near a growl. "What's with you? Calm down!"

Jak made a clumsy move to push past Tully, but the spacer held him tight. He would keep Xi safe at his shoulder; he would do that forever. The more agitated Jak grew, the tighter Tully held the man's arms pinned to his side.

"I don't know what's come over him," said Tully, as Jak began to cry in his arms. "You'd better wait outside, Xi."

Xi retreated out the front door of the shop, and Jak's wriggling lessened. The trader crumpled to the floor and began weeping, his hands ripping at his hair. Tully did not know where he found the reserve to kneel beside him and place a hand gently on the man's back.

"Jak," he said softly. "Why?"

Jak made no answer, not with any conscious words. He just continued to emit the sound of agonizing weeping. Tully tried to make contact with what was in anguish within Jak, but whenever he looked into the man's eyes, he could tell that Jak did not see him. He stood and backed away, hoping that this fit would not cause Jak to hurt himself after he left. Tully picked up their artifact and left the shop to join Xi out in front.

But when he got to the outer corridor, their past and future tucked under one arm, she was nowhere to be seen.

Without her, the ship was too much for Tully to endure. As soon as he discovered that she had not returned to the *Future*, he searched for her in every inch of The Wheel that he knew, and a few places he was surprised to discover he hadn't even known existed.

He made a tour of every dive he had visited in the years before he had met Sal, and the aeons afterwards, finding people who had seemingly never moved in all that time from their private corners of Hell. He described Xi's manner to a number of old friends, the way she moved and sounded and smelled, and even felt moved to speak of her to a few of his old enemies. He called in every favor he had outstanding, and indebted himself by asking for new ones, but the favors yielded nothing. He hacked onto the security link, the defenses of which were as usual more amusing than frustrating, but found nothing there that could lead him to Xi. He visited the places where the dead men lived, and discovered nothing but that a little piece of him was dead as well. He told himself that the reason he did all this was in hopes of successfully finding her, but at the same time he knew in his heart that if she did not want herself found that he would never see her again. The truth of the matter was that he searched mainly because the only other option—sitting back in the ship and staring at the places she had been, the corners she had made hers—was too much for him. When he was too exhausted to continue looking any further, and only then, Tully returned to the *Fortune*, because his only alternative would have been to drop where he was, and that would have meant abandoning what last shred of hope he had.

Tully found Jak waiting there beneath his boarding ladder, his shoulders sunken, seeming as if exhaustion had defeated him as well.

"Did you find her?" Jak asked, but there was nothing in the man's eyes that allowed of that possibility.

Tully could not bear to look at him. There was a black hole within the skin of the man he once thought his friend.

"If she doesn't come back," said Tully, with a calm certainty the source of which surprised him, "I think I'll kill you."

The trader started to speak, but instead sputtered into tears before the words could get out.

"It wasn't my fault," he finally said. "Believe me, Tully, I couldn't help it. I would have if I could. What I felt was so powerful I had no control over it. It was an urge I could not shut off. The feeling just came over me." Jak paused, and looked down at his hands. His shame was palpable, but quickly turned to pride. "But that doesn't make it any less real. So don't say that it does!"

"Right," said Tully, with a dead voice. Jak's manner, one moment funereal, the next moment giddy, was too ludicrous to endure. "Now let me pass. I've had a big night. And as much as I liked you once, I have to say that there's no more time in it for you."

"We've been friends, Tully," said Jak, standing, placing one hand on Tully's arm. "Yes, I insist, friends. Not just businessmen together. Always more than that. You've got to know I'd never intentionally interfere in your private life. I never went after Sal. Never."

Tully shrugged off Jak's hand and moved one foot to the ladder's lowest rung.

"Don't talk about Sal," he said. "Or I won't wait to kill you. I don't want to ever see you again, Jak. I don't care whether the way you acted was deliberate or not. The outcome is the same. You've put at risk the only thing that still matters to me."

"I can make it up to you," Jak called out as Tully brushed by. "Let me do that for you. After I calmed down, I did the further research I said I would on that artifact you've found. It's priceless, do you know that? Normally I wouldn't just come right out and say that, but now, I figure I owe it to you. I've never seen one of its kind before. And neither has anyone else. Do you realize what it is? It's more than just a funereal urn. Inside are the remains of two aliens, a couple, blended together forever. Mixed there is an entire species, one that could live again. People will pay for this artifact. Politicians, scientists ... artists. I can help set you up good. You'll be able to get a better ship. You'll be able to bend yourself to bring Xi back. And even if she won't return to you, well then, you'll be able to buy everything else you could possibly need to forget her."

"The only thing it will ever make me happy to forget is you," muttered Tully from the top of the ladder. "Goodbye, Jak."

Tully foolishly hoped that when the lock opened that Xi would be there, but of course, she was not. He found the artifact and set it beside his bed. With one hand on its smooth finish, he fell asleep. He did not dream of Xi, or of anything or anyone else.

"Your people are crazy," Tully suddenly heard Xi say, her voice and her translator merging into poetry. His eyes snapped open. He could smell her before he could see her. The light that streamed over Xi from the busy port outside as she stood in the open doorway cast a shadow across his face. He did not dare to turn, so he kept his head still and just let his eyes trail towards her. He was afraid to move, almost as if she were a small animal he thought might startle. "Your people cannot be trusted."

"Don't make this about your people and my people," he said. "This is about you and me." He had no idea how long he had slept. He noticed that the fingers of his right hand were numb where they still rested on the artifact. He did not dare to move them. "Where have you been?"

"Then it is *you* who cannot be trusted," she said, ignoring his question.

"Please, Xi. Where have you been?"

She took a further step into the room and the door slid shut behind her, sending them into darkness once more. All there was was the smell of her, and when she spoke, the perfect sound of her voice. Hidden, he placed his hand across his chest and felt the life come back to his fingers.

"Do you realize how difficult it was for me to get back here unseen? There are humans all over The Wheel. Crazy humans."

"But I don't get it," he said, letting himself sit up in the darkness. "Why did you go? Why didn't you wait for me outside of Jak's in the first place? I would have gotten you safely back here."

"Did you look into your friend's eyes?"

"I was too busy paying attention to what he was trying to do with his hands."

"You should have looked there, Tully. That would have explained it all. Because what I saw there in his eyes was the same look I see in yours. You two might as well have been twins back there."

"I don't know what you mean, Xi. Jak was trying to hold onto you against your will. I was trying to free you. We're as different as could be, not just today, but in everything—he's trapped down here, I'm wandering out there where you want to be. The way he acted before, that was an aberration. Even Jak realized that. He came by earlier to apologize for having lost control."

"Tully, don't you realize by now what's going on? If he'd found me here, there wouldn't have been an apology. No. It was more than one human losing control. All of you are mad."

"That can't be," he said, slapping a light alive. He was no longer able to abide by the darkness, not when she was there. "Here. Let me look at you."

"You'd better not," she said, bringing the darkness back with a wave. "Maybe looking at me is what sends you astray."

"Xi—"

"Just try to listen, and try, try hard, to forget that it's me talking. I learned something valuable today, Tully, something that changes everything. You humans. Do you think I *wanted* to stay away from you this long? I admit I was upset this morning when Jak went wild, but once I left that man's place I intended to head right back here. And I started to, I did, I truly did, Tully. But I could not make it here. Your species was determined to be an obstacle course. Every human whose path I crossed for even a fleeting instant professed undying love for me. Just like you. Every one of them wanted to live by my side forever. Just like you. And not one of them, man or woman, would take no for an answer. Just like you."

She fell silent, waiting for a response he did not know if he had the words to give.

"This has to be some kind of mistake, Xi. Haven't I proven my love for you during our long trip back here? I'm not like all the others. There is no one like me. This has to be some sort of sick coincidence. What I feel for you is real. It's real, Xi."

"Is it? Then why did I have to move through this place like a hunted animal, racing as fast as I could away from humans, hiding until there were none nearby, sneaking around as if the smell of my skin was a perfume that induced insanity. Who knows what it was—my smell, my fur, the color of my skin, some secret signal I sent out by the way I walked? The specific reason doesn't matter. Its existence is enough. But this must be why my people have made it a taboo to travel off our planet. This has to be why they've hidden themselves away. They had to make sure that none of us would never run into Earthlings. Don't you see? That's got to be why you feel the way you do, Tully. Locked in together as we were for so long during our trip back here, I've become imprinted on you. What you feel for me isn't you—it's like a disease. You're *sick* of me. Literally sick of me."

"I don't care. I'm not looking for a cure. I'm not looking for anything. How can I make you understand? There's nothing more to look for."

He heard her sigh in the darkness. The closeness of the sound told him that she had moved deeper into the room even as the import of her words seemed to move her further away. When she spoke next, he could feel her breath on the side of his neck.

"And that, Tully," she said, "is exactly why there is a problem."

He could not stand the darkness a moment longer, and he hoped that she would forgive him. He brought back the light, and luckily, this time she did nothing to stop him. Tully turned and reached out a hand to Xi. She made no move to take it, so he scuttled closer and slipped his fingers into hers.

"This thing we have cannot end so quickly," he said softly. "That is what would be the madness, not this. Not love. We've barely found each other. What can I do to make you believe in me? There must be something that will erase all that. Something that will turn you back to me."

His fingers tingled in hers, and as he looked down at the picture they made, blue flesh and pink flesh, as close as flesh could be, that made him think once more of the urn they had brought so far. He could not bear to turn away to acknowledge it, to lose Xi even for a moment, but he was suddenly overwhelmingly aware that it was there, challenging them both.

"We must be like *them*," he whispered. "Lost forever in forever."

She put a stubby finger on his chin and tilted his head back so they could look into each other's eyes.

"Them? I don't know what you mean, Tully."

He looked at the muscles twitching in her face and saw her confusion there, saw her desire to understand, and seeing that, able to interpret her alien flesh into earthy emotions, told himself that this must mean he was meant to gaze on those indigo planes forever. Her confusion had to fade. He told her what Jak had told him earlier, of the one final secret of the world of the dead and the love that transcended it. Of how much Jak had offered for the artifact that was evidence of an eternal love, not that Jak had seen it that way, of how easy their lives could be afterward if only they would sell it to him and move on. They would not know need. He offered to take care of her forever and show her the universe, use that dead love to justify their own living love. He spoke these things as if they were the last words that he would ever utter, as a sort of final confession that if spoken with enough truth and intensity would let him know peace.

Looking at her, though, exhausted by the effort, he could see that words were not enough.

"There's nothing wrong with knowing need," said Xi, slipping her fingers from his. "I have never asked or expected that life would lift it away from me, and you, Tully, as for you, I fear that you will grow to know it very well. But looking at you now, knowing what I know, I do not think that I will be the cause of it. Maybe, if you are lucky, you will forget me. I think you will. I hope you will. I will move on, and you will move on, each to our own separate place in the universe, and after a while I will dim in your mind. Whatever part of me that has over this recent time lodged itself in you will wither and fade. And it will all be for the best."

She paused, though he knew that she had not said all she needed to say. He looked up at her standing there and watched a drop bead by one eye until it splashed upon his cheek. He welcomed it as it fell.

"Xi, you are crying."

"I am crying, yes, but I have cried before. I wonder how hard the one cried who was the first to know why my people and yours should stay far apart. It must have been a terrible thing to have to learn. I guess … I guess I should go back. The elders, though they would not tell us why, though they may not even have known the reality behind the customs themselves, were right. But I can see why they did not tell us. We would never have believed them. We would not have wanted to believe them. Who could live in a world where love and trust and desire are only a virus?"

"But that's what it's always been," he said, reaching up to trace the damp lines upon her face. "And none of that matters."

Tully dropped to his knees. He wrapped his arms tightly about her broad waist, fingers straining to graze fingers. If he could encompass her with his arms, with his soul, perhaps she would stay.

"Come," he murmured into her belly. He listened to the sound echo there. "Let me prove to you that before I would forget you, I would forget myself."

He waited. He was willing to wait as long as it took until she realized the truth. Eventually, he could feel her fingers run through his hair. They moved slowly there, feeling his skull beneath the skin, and he could sense her holding back, could almost taste her bewilderment at having come so far to stand together in this way with a creature whose head was so oddly shaped. Her hands dropped away to his shoulders.

"Tully," she said. "Tully, Tully, Tully."

The slow whisper with which she spoke his name carried a sadness so sharp he thought he might begin to bleed from their cuts, yet her syllables also bore a touch so soft he did not know whether he could bear their absence if she were to stop.

As they landed once again on the planetoid where they had discovered each other, the rutted surface beneath seemed to Tully to welcome him like an old lover. Though his trip back had not been as comfortable as he had at first hoped—Xi fought a war with herself, struggling to remain distant, often failing or forgetting, but always allowing those cold emotions to reassert themselves—Tully knew in his gut that now that they had arrived back where they'd begun, things could be made right here. Things *would* be made right here. He was so sure of how this day would end that he could almost feel Sal waiting silently on the surface, happy, content, and preparing to say goodbye.

Tully came up beside Xi as she looked out onto the crisp landscape through the ship's transparent walls. He looked out with her, saying nothing, strong feelings of awe and gratitude welling up within him. When he veered from studying the path they would take back to their discovery, he noted that Xi's gaze had turned elsewhere: she was instead looking off to where her ship had once been, a ship that had by now long returned to her sequestered home.

"Don't worry," he said, trembling as he placed a hand on her shoulder. "If you want me to take you back to your home, I will. You can trust me on that. If I must, I will take you there. Though it would kill me, I would do that for you. Do not be afraid. You are not trapped, neither here, nor with me. That is how much I love you."

"Love," she said in a strained whisper, as if that single syllable was so painful in her throat that she had to force the word out or die. "Why is it that I always worry when I hear you say that word so easily?"

"Let's get into our suits," he said. He had no other answer for her than to simply take her by the hand.

They were silent as they donned their suits. Though there was an endless world of words he wanted Xi to inhabit, a lifetime of telling that would bind her to him, he knew she was not yet ready. There was still something he had to do, a proof that had to be handed over to the universe, after which his words, and hers, would flow. As he listened to the thrum of the airlock engines, he stared not at Xi, because he knew it would have been painful to see her deliberately not staring back, but instead at Sal's empty suit hanging there on the rack. For the longest time, seeing it there, pretending in some shameful part of himself that Sal might one day rise up to inhabit it again, was the only comfort he had. And now, at last, there could be more moments of hope than that. A future finally waited.

Stepping out of the ship, he clumsily hugged the urn as they moved down the ladder. Xi offered a hand as he struggled, but Tully would not let her help him. Not yet. If he could not do this one thing for her, what sort of message would that be sending her? They shuffled quietly along, making their way to where the wall of the dead began, and followed the sculpted path until it led them back to the planetoid's lone empty alcove. Tully returned the urn to the niche where it had rested undisturbed for centuries, and where, if all went as he hoped, none would rediscover it for many centuries more. Words were necessary here, but he found his heart thumping so wildly that he could hardly speak.

"This is where they chose to be," he said, taking comfort in the steady sound that the radio gave him of Xi breathing. It was a gift without which he would not have been able to continue. "Together forever. We have no right to move them, no matter what difference it would make to our lives. No matter what burden it would lift off our backs. This is where they should remain forever."

He turned to her and paused, expecting, no, *hoping* that she would speak, hoping that his decision to have done this would mean something to her. Xi did not look back towards him. She stayed motionless and kept her silence.

"Don't you see? No one ever asked why they were together like that. Jak acknowledged it, but didn't care. At first, I didn't care. But I do now. We do not know who they were, but we know this. These two were so in love that they chose to remain entwined this way until the end of time. Shouldn't we do the same?"

He reached out to take her hand, but still she did not move. He decided that he would hold that hand out before him as long as it took. He would wait. She remained motionless as his arm began to ache, motionless and silent for so long that Xi might as well have been one of the ancient wall carvings that loomed above them.

When his muscles eventually failed and his hand fell limply to his side, finally, she spoke:

"And now what?" she said. Her words were brittle. He wished he could hear her real voice layered beneath the translation, as he could back in the open air of the ship, but he knew even as he made that wish that he'd find no comfort there.

"And now what," Tully repeated leadenly. It had not been enough. His gesture had not been enough. "And now what?"

"Yes."

"And now ... wait here. Yes. There's one final thing I must do before we leave this place and never return. Will you wait? Will you give me that much?"

As Xi stood dwarfed and alone in the bleak mausoleum, staring at the artifact the return of which Tully had obviously thought would mean so much to her, she marveled at her absence of fear. She supposed that she should be afraid that Tully would never return, leaving her to die on a world she had fled her own world to find. She felt foolish that she could not find that emotion in her, because there was that possibility. That might be Tully's easiest way to deal with the news she had given him, to treat her like a literal plague, and leave her behind, cutting her out of his life. Her people, if the news of her abandonment and death ever made it off this airless surface, would say that hers was an end to be expected for one who could not obey their society's rules. She did not mind. Let them think that. Xi might not have found exactly what she'd left her world to seek, but what she had found had been enough. It was enough. The stars were bright above, even if her future was not.

As she waited to see whether she was right to feel no fear, her eyes only occasionally flickered to her oxygen reserve gauge. It was falling, though not yet disastrously so. That would come eventually, if she let it, she knew. He loved her, he said, endlessly and with seeming sincerity, but what good would that love do if she could not breath?

She could go home, she knew. Her people would welcome her, if not with fully open arms—as no one living would have a memory of one who had left and then returned, or, in fact, one who had ever left at all—but they would welcome her as best as they were able. They had to. Maybe she could return there and tell herself that she had seen enough of the universe. Maybe she could make herself believe that. She could try. But she knew her people, the way they would look at her, the fact that they would remove any chance possibility of her ever straying again. And she knew that she could not be happy there. She'd even settle for less than happiness. Happiness was not a promise life made. She'd settle merely to be … content. But at home, the home she remembered, she did not think that she could have that either.

Her muddled confusion worried her. She was not someone who usually found herself lost in internal debates this way. If she were, she'd never have left in the first place. She checked her oxygen once more, hoping to blame her racing thoughts on something other than herself, something other than what Tully had done to her, but no, whatever muddle she found herself in was hers alone.

Did Tully love her, in truth? It had seemed so real to her, and until she discovered the underlying truth of it all back on The Wheel, she'd felt her heart starting to answer him back, but she'd learned enough of life to understand that whatever the situation seemed to be was not necessarily what it was. He loved, she could believe that. But did he love *her*? Or would he fall helplessly and equally in love with the next of her species they encountered? For truth was all that mattered. She lived her life for that. That's how she ended up at this place at this time.

She placed a palm on the urn they'd taken and brought back and tried to imagine the lives of those within. The creatures lived hundreds of years before and she could not possibly know them, but still. Had those inside really loved each other? Had they known for sure that they did? Or was it all a lie that those who placed them together here afterwards wanted to believe? There were so many questions, and there seemed to be no answers.

So intent was Xi on tracing a finger around the urn's sealed mouth that it was not until she heard Tully speak that she knew he was beside her again.

"I'm back," he said. She turned, and he was so close that his faceplate filled her entire horizon. "You knew I'd come back, didn't you?"

"I never doubted it for an instant," she said, at first not knowing as she said it whether her own words were true, until she realized that they had been. That that was why she'd known no fear out there alone beneath the stars. And then she noted what he'd brought with him, what now lay in the dust between her feet.

"That's Sal's spacesuit, isn't it?"

"Yes. It doesn't belong to me any longer. It belongs here, in this place. It belongs with the dead."

"You've held on to that for a long time, Tully. Are you sure this is what you want to do? Are you sure?"

He did not give her words, but only nodded. He began to arrange the suit so that it leaned against the urn, so that it seemed as if it was being embraced by a living being. She could hear him breathing heavily from the effort.

"I've been holding on to her for too long," he said slowly, as he stepped back and studied what he had done. "There's something else I need to hold on to now."

"You can't be sure of that, Tully. Maybe you could with someone else, with a human lover, or with someone from another alien race. But not with you and me. Not with what you've learned about us."

"I'm as sure as I ever was before. I've only been in love, real love, twice in my life now, and I know what it feels like. I know what love is."

He opened a hip pouch and removed a folded sheet of paper. He knelt for a moment and placed the sheet in the empty fingers of the suit's right hand. Xi remained silent until he was done, and did not speak until he had gotten to his feet again and backed away.

"What does that note say?" she asked, when he was beside her once more.

"It says goodbye," he said, his thin fingers taking her own. "Come. It's time to go back to the ship. We have things to do there. I have to keep telling you how much I love you."

"But what about the truth?" she asked. "What if this is as I told you? What if it is all just a lie? What if our biochemistry has you brainwashed?"

He looked at her with shining eyes that showed her a million stars.

"Does it really matter?" he said.

And for them, at that time, in that place, it didn't. At least that's what they spent the rest of their lives telling each other.

Choosing Time

Back in the summer of 1988, I published a strange little short story titled "Buffalo" in Ice River magazine, a journal of slipstream fiction published by David Memmott. Who knew then that this would, a decade and a half later, make me eligible to appear in a commemorative trade paperback published in celebration of Memmott's press, Wordcraft of Oregon?

Chris Reed, publisher of Back Brain Recluse, worked with Memmott to assemble the anthology Angel Body. My piece in the volume was a time-travel story with an odd twist, one in which the reader has as almost many choices as the lead character. But as for what those choices might be, I'll let readers discover them in the story itself.

One

"Free food tastes best," Arthur had told Helga that morning, needling her with one of his favorite lines. She had been standing in the doorway to their apartment, carrying two grocery bags full of meat and vegetables with which to prepare a stew for lunch at the shelter, and was both much too shocked and too desirous of harmony to argue. Though what she told herself at the time was that she didn't have the time to spare.

Hours later, as she stirred the pot of stew in the Avenue A Shelter, her husband's words bubbled to the surface of her mind, and she felt the anger that she should have allowed herself to instead feel that morning. Those damned smug words of his! They formed the same mocking sentence Arthur used when supposedly showing off his skills as a provider by taking her out to a fancy dinner and sticking it to AcuMarkeTech, Inc. on his corporate American Express card.

It was only later, as it always was, that she thought of all the things she could have said in return to his belittling what she was doing. But then again, also as always, when she got home, by the time he arrived home from the job and tucked in beside her and they watched the late news, side by side but far apart ... she'd forget them again.

What was it that she should have said?

a) "Arthur, Arthur, Arthur ... all these poor shelter people know is that the free food as you call it that we're donating is better than no food at all. Not that that's something you've ever had to worry about, dear."

b) "Maybe, just once, if you came down with me to the shelter, really, just once, and saw the way things are down there, you'd stop making fun of this. Life is not a television movie. Besides, getting involved in something like this was your idea."

c) "Damn it, Arthur, don't talk to me like I'm a child or an idiot. I've told you before. I won't put up with it much longer. I mean it. Really."

Two

"**E**arth to Helga, Earth to Helga!"

Helga jerked up her head and saw that Yvonne had come up beside her while she had been staring into the swirls made by her stirring. She'd been gripping the wooden spoon too tightly, and some of the stew's tomato base had sloshed over onto the flames from the gas burner.

"Where were you?" says Yvonne, as the spillover crackled. "You certainly weren't with us. You were beating that stew like you were trying to put out a fire."

Helga wasn't quite sure herself where she had gone. She only knew that it was to a place in her mind where things seemed clearer than they were most of the time, where life did not appear as lock-stepped into routine as it was most days.

Where she actually seemed to have choices. Choices were intimidating to her, for she saw them so rarely, but though they were frightening, they were better than no choices at all.

"I guess I was thinking," she said.

"This place can do that to you," said Yvonne. "Especially when you're new. You start thinking, 'There but for the grace of God,' and all that ..."

"I know what you mean."

And though Helga did understand Yvonne's point, she didn't completely agree. To Helga, the concepts of God and grace implied a person had no control, and she knew that at one time, though no longer, she had that measure of control. The life she was in, she knew, was one she had chosen, even though she did not feel it was a thing that she could any longer un-choose. The very spot of flooring on which she stood was one toward which she had unwittingly steered.

The two women loaded the food onto a cart and wheeled it out into the larger meeting room, where the hungry waited. There were two dozen of them for lunch today, and to Helga, they still seemed like a shapeless mass. She'd only been doing volunteer work there for two weeks, and she hadn't yet figured out how to differentiate them all. Their overwhelming feature seemed to be that they were so miserable, and that paint of despair subdued everything else. She didn't think about them as separate others yet; for now, they only made her think about herself. She did not spare time to wonder about these men and women, and who they might have been if they had not made their own wrong choices long ago. She only had a time to wonder about her own.

What other would she have become had she not followed the turns in her path that led her to this destination? What if, when Arthur had proposed, she would have instead handed back the ring?

a) She'd still be living at home with her widowed mother, and never-married aunt, a household of three crazy women, like the witches out of *Macbeth*. And when she got to her mid-forties, like now, she'd be forced to work to support them and not dither around on volunteer work while a workaholic husband supported her. She'd have still been a receptionist, answering phones for the ones doing the important work, never questioning why she was never given a chance to do the important work herself.

b) If not Arthur, she'd have found someone else to marry. Or rather, someone else would have found her, because she'd have long since given up, and stopped looking. And it would have been, she was sure, to yet another with more talent for money than love, and in small ways it would have been completely different, and yet where it counted all so the same.

c) She'd have married for love. Yes, she could have. Someone would have come along. Someone would have had to, if she'd only have waited long enough, if she hadn't been so impatient, and jumped at Arthur the way those in the shelter jumped at the smell of food. Far less foolish things than such a possibility had provided moments of hope and happiness.

Three

She should, really, get to know them, shouldn't she? After all, that was what she was there for, wasn't it? So as she watched the poor and homeless eat, and wandered through their midst serving some of them seconds, she studied the room for someone who appeared as unthreatening as she thought she was herself.

At a distant table, a woman sat alone, ignoring her surroundings, focused only on the food. To Helga, this one more than any of the others seemed squashed into her current state, and to have given up fighting against the precocity of her life prison. Helga could understand a person like that. She sat beside the woman, who did not pause in the eating of her stew to look up.

"How are you making out?" asked Helga, and then cursed herself for so foolish a question, especially delivered in so chipper a voice. She couldn't help it; Arthur insisted on chipper. But anyone wanting to know how this sad woman was making out only had to look. "Do you like the stew?"

Spoon paused in midair, the woman turned to her. A carrot floated in the broth, a carrot Helga was pleased to think that she herself had chopped.

"I was in Philadelphia once," the woman finally said.

"Really. That's nice."

"I shouldn't have pushed the button, you know. It's all my fault. You know what I mean."

Helga didn't know how to respond to a statement like that. The woman stuck the spoon in her mouth. It looked to Helga as if she was going to chew off the bowl. The woman was obviously mad. Life had made her that way. But still, Helga thought, patronizingly, she did deserve food and a warm place to stay. The woman began racing, lifting the spoon again and again so quickly she was almost tossing it against herself. Helga was repulsed by the broth dribbling down her chin, but she managed to find the strength to pat her hand.

"Don't worry, dear," said Helga. "There's plenty of time."

"Time," whispered the woman. "Time," she repeated, and then her eyes went wide. "Time!"

Shouting, she slammed her fist against the table, catching the side of her bowl, which flipped over and dumped its contents half on the long wooden table and half on the woman's own lap. Helga jumped to escape the red tendrils. The woman leapt up and turned to her, eyes wide.

"I'm running out of time!" she shouted. "You're running out of time. We're all running out of time!"

Helga didn't know what to do. She hadn't received any training, other than to be told by Yvonne to treat them like the people they were. Helga backed away, her hands held out, pleading for peace in a gesture of supplication Arthur would have recognized. But there was no Arthur here to tell her that everything was okay, that he would protect her. Helga looked around the room for Yvonne—she'd been here forever, Helga knew, so she would know what to do—but Yvonne was nowhere to be seen.

"I know you," the woman said.

"No," said Helga. "You couldn't possibly know me."

"Leave Art. You must. Before there's no more time. Before ..."

The woman paused. The emotions faded from her face, and she sat before her overturned bowl.

"What happened?" asked Yvonne, suddenly beside her. Helga found she couldn't answer. Neither her brain nor her mouth could function. "Did Jane have another one of her fits?"

Helga backed away, ignoring Yvonne's insistent questions. She ran through the kitchen, out a side door and into the street, not looking back. She kept asking herself, in near hysteria, what had happened?

a) The bag lady, no, homeless person, no, apartmentally challenged, no, *Jane*, Yvonne had called her—had read Helga's mind. Jane had known what she'd been thinking about her superficial life with Arthur but which she had been trying to ignore.

b) Jane must have overheard Helga talking about her life to Yvonne, and though nothing outrageous had been said (Helga would never badmouth Arthur the way she had heard other women talk about their husbands), put two and two together, just from the way Helga talked, from her intonations as she said her husband's name. Yes, Jane was poor, and had no home, and apparently her brains had been rattled around by a teasing world, but that didn't mean the woman did not know of life. What Helga always feared had finally been confirmed—that every other woman who saw her saw into her, and knew that she was living a lie.

c) Helga has been hearing things, hallucinating. She'd been so flustered about trying to interact with a person like that, someone not of her own world, that she'd just imagined it all. Made sense of nonsense, read into untranslatable growls her own guilt. Jane could never really have said what Helga had thought she said. But what had really happened no longer mattered for, after the way Helga had reacted, how could she ever go back there again?

Four

She didn't think she ever would. When she first got home, in fact, she didn't think she would ever calm down enough to do anything. She wandered the apartment aimlessly, trying to remember what it had been like to live in such a protected place, with security guaranteed. She couldn't seem to wind down. She wanted to talk with Arthur about what had happened, and shift her burden. She wanted to call him, but didn't allow herself to give in to the urge. He never liked it when she called him at the office, and the few times she did she had to pay for it later with sullen expressions and strained conversations.

By the time Arthur finally got home, Helga was riled up and nervous from her endless pacing and thinking. He appeared to never notice. She thought he would have had to, her distress written all over her as it was, but she chose to say nothing.

She welcomed the next morning, for it rescued her from a night of strange dreams of being chased through dark streets by Jane, who was wielding a large wooden spoon. She took a hot bath to wash off the invisible film that had descended on her, soaking long past the time when her fingers were puckered. She tried reading a book to relax, but all she was able to find were some of Arthur's military fiction novels, and their escapades seemed so ridiculous, now that the world appeared headed for peace. (But why wasn't she being carried along?) She even tried watching TV; but the quiet of the apartment seemed too fragile, so that no matter how low she turned the set, it seemed too loud.

She knew she couldn't take being alone in the apartment like that any longer, but what else could she do?

a) She could try to reach some of her friends. Well ... not her friends, really. Wives of her husband's business acquaintances, rather. Helga wasn't quite sure that she had friends anymore. Not like those she knows she must have had when she was younger. Yvonne, maybe, Yvonne might be a friend. But if she reached these supposed friends she now had, she would get together with these women, and then they would want to know all about this new little hobby of hers, and what the homeless were like, talking about them as if they weren't even people, and then she would want to tell them about Jane, because finally her need to try to explain it to someone would become too powerful, but she still wouldn't be able to find the words. And even if she could find the words to describe her unsettling feelings, she was sure they wouldn't be able to understand.

b) She could go for a walk. Break the routine. See new sights in an attempt to overwrite the memories of the day before. But walking, she would surely see some of the homeless. They were all over the city these days, and seeing them would force her to remember just how she had at the shelter made herself a fool. In a city like this, there could be no escape.

c) She could go back to the shelter. She would have to. In the end, there was no other way. That was where she'd be able to find the only person she could talk to who might really understand.

Five

"I can understand that you'd be a little angry with me."

"A little angry. More than that, Helga. I'm disappointed in you. Can you understand that? I expected more. So I guess I'm really angry at myself. I thought this was something more to you, that you weren't like the others."

"I don't know what you mean."

Helga felt cowed by Yvonne's harsh words, especially since Helga had seen how kindly she acted towards the homeless. She'd never expected Yvonne to talk to her just the way that her husband did.

"I thought you could be one of the ones who truly cared. Maybe it's my fault for expecting too much. But, Helga, I see you women all the time. Rich wives who get bored and think that helping the homeless will take your minds off that. Sort of like needlepoint. They flit in, raise hopes, and vanish back to their uptown apartments. With you I had hopes."

"You saw that in me?" Helga felt strangely pleased to have this woman mad at her like this. "Well, you see, I actually did come back."

"Yes ... you did. But what happened? Was it something Jane did? I know she isn't always connected with reality. She didn't try to hit you, did she?"

"No, it's not that. It's just ... all that shouting. And then she ..." Say it, Helga. It doesn't matter how ridiculous it sounds to say it, Yvonne will understand. "She starting saying ... things about me. Things about Arthur."

"When did she say these things?"

"Right after she leapt up and overturned her bowl."

"Helga, I was right in the room when that happened. I heard what Jane was shouting. I couldn't help it, she was so loud. But Jane is harmless. She was just spouting a bunch of nonsense. I didn't hear her say anything about you or your husband."

"But ..."

"Are you sure you weren't just overexcited by all the noise? By the whole situation?"

"Maybe you're right, Yvonne." Yvonne was right. As Helga had learned, the others always were. "It's just that I've never seen a woman go wild like that before. I mean, except on television or in a movie. It must have unnerved me. Oh, Yvonne, I feel so silly. Will you let me have a second chance?"

"Applicants aren't exactly kicking down my doors ..."

"Thank you! You'll see I'm able to stick with things, I really am."

She found herself thinking of Arthur.

"It's almost lunchtime," said Yvonne. "I had to do all the cooking, so why don't you help me serve."

Helga followed Yvonne out of the kitchen, and noticed Jane in the meeting room immediately. Yvonne kept her distance, forcing Helga to be the one to put the plate in front of Jane. Helga tried to place it there silently, but it didn't seem as if her care mattered, for Jane kept staring off into an unfocused distance beyond the walls.

"What's wrong with her?" Helga asked Yvonne once the serving was done.

"We don't really know, other than that there's nothing physically wrong with her. She just showed up one day like they all do. And like a lot of them, we don't quite know where she came from. And if she doesn't want to, or can't, tell us, I guess it's not really any of our business."

"There's something wrong that's more than lack of money, isn't there? Have you ever had a doctor look at her? Shouldn't she be safe in a hospital?"

"We do have a doctor come in once a month to make sure our clients are as healthy as possible under the circumstances. But medicine can't do it all. And hospitals ... I don't know. When you've been doing this as long as I have, you won't think of them as the easy answer. You haven't seen what hospitals can do to them. They're here because they can't live by society's rules, and hospital rules can be even harsher. Sometimes they go in ... but they don't always get back out. By this time, I've figured it's sometimes better to let them just be themselves."

Helga looked at the self which Jane had over the years allowed herself to become, and knew that she had been foolish to let such a pathetic person frighten her so. Helga would have to speak to her, to completely end the fear. She sat down next to Jane, who was staring into her soup, looking for something that wasn't there.

"You can eat now, Jane."

Jane looked at Helga then. Perhaps because it was the first time she'd said her name. Jane nodded slowly, and then began to eat. Helga leaned forward and whispered while Jane slurped, not really caring whether the woman heard or understood.

"You didn't really say anything to me about Arthur yesterday, did you? If you did, do it again now, when I'm ready for it. I just imagined it all, didn't I?"

Jane turned away from her soup and looked at Helga for a moment. Jane moved her face close to Helga, and squinted. Helga squirmed beneath that gaze, as if she were a butterfly in its final attempt to avoid a collector's pin. Jane finally nodded, and returned to her soup.

"I thought so. I guess I've been thinking about Arthur too much. A wife's prerogative, right? Inescapable. He's always on my mind, so it isn't a surprise, I guess, that I should think that everyone is talking about him. Shouldn't they be? After all, he's the most important person in my life."

Helga sighed.

"Most of the time I fear that if you asked Arthur, he would tell you that he was the most important person in his own life, too. I sometimes hope for more than that. But I never tell him. You've known people like that before this, I'm sure, people who have no time for anything but themselves. I think that's why when I decided I needed something to keep myself busy during the long days when Arthur was at work, and he thought it would be better if I found a hobby instead of a job, that I came to work here. I hoped that if Arthur could see me able to care for someone other than myself, that perhaps he would ..."

Helga touched her cheek and was surprised to find it wet. It had been a long time since she'd cried in front of anyone.

"Look at me. Going on like that. Why am I doing this now, with you of all people?"

a) "I need someone to feel better than today. Anyone will do, even you. It would be nice if I could be able to feel superior to someone with a normal life, but for now, I'll take whatever I can get."

b) "Somewhere I read, maybe in a tabloid while standing in line at a supermarket checkout, of people who have gone into deep, seemingly irreversible comas. And their families have gathered around them, talking, reading, touching, singing, sure that somewhere inside the dull shell remained a human being. And then eventually, because of their hard work, their faith was rewarded. The person came out of the corpse. I hope if I keep talking to you, that the same will happen here. Only I'm not too sure which of us it is I'm trying to revive."

c) "I know that however much I speak to you, whatever guilty secrets I reveal, you're not going to answer back. You can be for me the non-judgmental listener I don't seem to be able to find anywhere else."

Six

Helga folded her hands in her lap, her fingers twined tightly as if she was hanging on for dear life to another.

"I guess we've had quite enough of *that*. I feel so silly rambling on like that."

Helga pushed away from the table, but Jane did not seem to care whether she was there beside her or not. Helga spoke to Yvonne, and together they planned what supplies Helga would buy the next day; Arthur wasn't going to care about the money going into this, not when his friends' wives were busy collecting the contents of the city's better shops.

Life seemed clearer when Helga left that afternoon. As she walked uptown back to the apartment, she was pleased that she had repaired the rift with Yvonne. She felt so much calmer than she had been the day before, and was able to laugh at herself for having been caught in that transient delusion.

Waiting at a corner for a light to change green, Helga heard her name. She turned, and there was Jane, pushing a battered shopping cart. The left front wheel kept shimmying, threatening to pull Jane into the gutter. The cart was full of junk, but Helga was sure that Jane's eyes did not see it so.

"What is it, Jane? What do you want?"

Jane wiggled her fingers in Helga's general direction, and then turned, moving back the way she and Helga had just come. Helga wasn't quite sure what the woman wanted until Jane turned and tilted her head.

Helga followed as Jane led her down several side streets Helga had never seen before. Helga had stayed mainly to the wide avenues in her life, so that the abandoned building Jane finally brought her to was unfamiliar to her. Jane pulled aside a board that looked to Helga securely in place, and then clumsily wheeled in her cart over a pile of fallen bricks. Helga followed, and found herself inside a small alcove, barely the size of one of her closets at home.

"This is where you live?"

Jane didn't answer, but instead simply moved aside another piece of board that led to another slightly larger room. Inside was a pile of even more junk, similar to what Jane had been dragging about. No. Not just a pile. The assemblage of junk was twisted together in what could almost be called a sort of sculpture. Fan belts danced with twisted wire coat hangers. Broken clocks of all kinds bounced from the ceiling on springs. Jane started unloading the newer junk, equally as worthless from Helga's point of view, from the cart, and piling it at the base of the sculpture like an offering. She gestured that Helga should help. After a few moments, Helga sighed, and she did.

"What is this?" asked Helga, gesturing at the odd creation.

"This is for you," said Jane.

Helga found herself whispering in the small room, and she wasn't sure why, but for some reason it felt right.

"Did you used to be an artist?" asked Helga. "I'm sorry. I didn't mean it that way. *Are* you an artist?"

Jane shook her head, and began attaching junk to the main sculpture, choosing pieces slowly, frowning, deciding. Helga found herself handing pieces to Jane one at a time. An egg beater. A pair of eyeglasses. A car battery. Another clock. Jane found a place for each.

"What is all this for? I still don't get it. Is it supposed to be art? It doesn't look like anything I've ever seen in a museum, but then, I wouldn't really know. I like things to look like what they are."

Jane did not answer. She stood silently, a car muffler cradled in her hands, frustration in her face. She moved to the sculpture, holding the muffler up at an angle, and then went round the other wide, and tried to hook it up. It would not fit, and Jane shook her head furiously. She tried to push the muffler into place, and grunted when a nearby wire snapped. She threw the muffler to the floor and beat her fists against the unwieldy sculpture.

"No, no, no!" she shouted. "It's not working."

Jane collapsed, sobbing, her head wedged between her thin knees, herself society's junk surrounded by her own. Helga stayed as far away as she could, her back pressed against the cool brick.

"Calm down," said Helga. "Everything's all right. This isn't so important. No need to get so worked up. You'll work it out, whatever it is."

"No, you're wrong. It is important. It's the most important thing there is. You just don't know it yet." Jane banged her fists against her temples. "But neither do I."

"But what is it?" said Helga, her voice trembling. "What is it supposed to do? What is it supposed to be?"

"I don't know," said Jane, her voice dull. She grimaced as she stared at the fragments of her creation that she had scattered around the small room. "There something in all of this ... something to do with Arthur."

Helga's voice was suddenly dry. She had to clear her throat before she could speak.

"Then you *did* say something about Arthur."

"He's going to hit you, Helga," said Jane, without considering Helga, without turning her eyes from the debris. "It's going to stop him from ever hitting you again."

"But Arthur doesn't hit me. He would never do anything like that. Maybe he's a little cold sometimes, but he's definitely not a hitter."

"Not now, perhaps. But soon, he will be."

"You're crazy, you know that," said Helga, edging towards the hole in the brick that led to the streets, and her old normal world. "You're making this all up. I thought I could do something, thought I could help, but it's all so foolish. So pointless."

"I thought I could help, too. But I should never have pressed the button. That's where it all went wrong."

"What are you talking about? What do you know? You're just a lying crazy lady who's let life get to her. Well, I'm not like you. I'm never going to be like you. I'm going to fight back. Now get out of my life."

Helga stormed out to the street, while Jane wailed behind her. Walking angrily home, this seemed to Helga to be some kind of turning point. What, she wondered, should she make now of her life?

a) She was never going back to any place like this place again. No shelters or side streets for her. This time she swore it. She had snagged Arthur and arranged her life in such a way as to lift herself above ever having to concern herself with the threatening masses. How could she have been so stupid as to voluntarily dive back into the midst of them again? She would return to an ivory tower life, without sparing a thought for Jane or those like her.

b) She would try to forget about Jane, but fail. Once a year, usually near the Christmas season, she would respond to an urge to mail a check to charity. She would tell herself that she was doing the best she possibly could, and would manage to believe that.

c) She would try to do nothing. Try for no visits, no checks, and no thoughts for Jane or her life. But one day, however, while driving in a cab to the then hottest Broadway show, as they are forced to stop for a light, an old woman with a rag will slowly wipe their windshield, and Helga will think for a moment of Jane. She will want to share with Arthur her dim memories of Jane and the silly things that the poor woman had to say, but no matter how much Helga will want to broach the subject, she will be unable to bring herself to do so.

Seven

The apartment seemed particularly empty that night, even more so than the night before. Helga thinks that perhaps she should get a pet. Nothing she'd have to walk, though. Maybe a parakeet or a gerbil. Something that would make noises other than herself, that would keep her from thinking that even though she was married, she somehow lived alone.

Arthur had called to say that he would be working late yet again. It happened so often that she wondered why he called. Arriving on time would have been the anomaly. Though she wouldn't have been able to tell him what had occurred, still, it would have been nice to have him by her side so that she could at least have pretended that she might have.

She wished that night that she had a hobby, but she had never had any special interests. That was what working in the shelter was supposed to have been about. A hobby to make her forget the emptiness of the life she had forged. The life she had chosen. Once, Arthur had been her hobby, but that was before he got so busy. No, none of those substitutes would work. No small animal could take the place of Arthur. What she needed to do was to make him her hobby again.

She would approach him that night, she had decided, before she had time to vacillate as she did on so many things. She will ask him to make an effort to come home earlier. Ask him for more time. After all, what's the worst he could do?

a) He could laugh. She'd heard him do it a thousand times before, molding her, training her. Heard him laugh with that belittling snort of his that let you know that whatever it was, you had to be insane to ask.

b) He could ignore her. She thought that would be worse. He could keep looking at the large color screen, keep breathing heavily, and eventually say, "Did you ask me something?" He'd then pretend to have fallen asleep. Or really fall asleep, not even having to pretend. That, too, would be worse.

c) He could hit her. She could push him too hard with her words and he could grow so rattled that he'd reach out and hit her. She would hold her cheek and wonder at what her words had wrought, and even as her husband's face blazed before her, think of nothing but Jane. Jane, Jane, Jane, and her ridiculous accusation.

Eight

Jane had been right after all. Helga, locked in the bathroom, sat with one hand placed against her face. Occasionally she would stand and look in the mirror, in an attempt to see there the imprint of Arthur's fingers. Outside, she could hear the TV's low voices in the bedroom, still playing as background to the marital scenario, even though both the participants had left the stage.

Jane did, somehow, impossibly, know her. And not just her. She knew what was going to happen. Being able to predict that her husband would do such a thing told her that there was something stranger than a street-dazed woman involved here.

She unlocked the bathroom door and returned to the bedroom. Only the flickering orange light from the TV that splashed on the rumpled sheets was there, but nothing else. Her husband was no longer in the room. She got dressed once more in the clothing that she had worn that day and then slipped out into the hallway. She found Arthur in the kitchen, wearing his robe, sipping with a sour face a cup of tea. Another cup of tea had been placed at Helga's place.

"Where are you going?" Arthur seemed startled to see her out of her nightgown again. "I thought we could sit and talk awhile."

"Maybe later, Arthur. I'm going for a walk."

"Look, it was an accident, Helga. A slip. I didn't mean to hit you. You just don't understand the stress I'm going through. Making plans to start out on my own. Keeping this family going."

"Family. What family, Arthur, there's just you and me. You said we didn't have time for a family."

"Helga, I swear I won't ever hit you again."

Helga shook her head sadly, knowing he was telling his truth. But that truth was no longer enough.

"You're wrong. You *will* hit me again."

"How can you know that? One mistake doesn't make me a beast. How can you be sure?"

"I know."

She went out into the night, back to the secret place that Jane had shown her, needing to talk, needing help to sort things out. But Jane was not there. Nor was her shopping cart. Helga knelt and burrowed through the morning's rubble. Such strange odds and ends. She wondered how Jane could find them valuable. Bits of electronic machinery from what gadgets Helga could not tell. Pieces of a stretchy metallic fabric wrapped around ball-bearing joints. A few large coins, dollar and half-dollar pieces, fused to the endless clocks, none of which still kept accurate time, or any time at all. What could Jane think it was all for? Helga picked up one of the coins and tossed it high in the air. She'd have to wait for Jane to come back. Because Helga had been right that first day.

Jane knew.

Helga dozed off in one corner of the inner alcove, and woke to the sound of metal scraping against concrete. Jane was dragging the remains of a bicycle to the center of the room. Helga sat quietly and watched as Jane rebuilt her creation, this time with the skeleton of the bicycle as its heart. As Jane attached tin foil to the bent spokes, Helga realized she still had one of Jane's coins in her hand. She wondered where Jane had gotten a silver dollar, and studied the coin in the dim light. Staring to the left was a bald-headed president she did not recognize. A president who had never been.

"Where did you get this?"

Jane jumped when Helga shouted from her corner.

"What is it?" said Jane.

"This, this!"

Helga stumbled forward, her hand out far before her as if she was carrying something dangerous. Jane wrapped a hand around Helga's wrist, and pulled her closer. Jane's fingers felt warm feverish.

"It's just money," said Jane. "Just money. Look at you. Look at the clothes you're wearing. Haven't you ever seen money before?"

Jane touched her temples, almost as if she was trying to smooth away a pain.

"There is something wrong," said Helga. "Something you're not telling me. Or could it be that for some reason ... you can't tell me?"

Helga looked at the coin, and then once more at Jane's strained face.

"I think I know what's happening here, but ... can it be possible?"

"I don't know what you mean," said Jane, softly, painfully. "What are you talking about?"

a) "I'm going crazy I really think I am, joining you in your delirium. It's finally happened. Life with Arthur had pushed me to the edge, and I was ready to tip into the abyss. Meeting you was all it took. Holding on was so hard, and I was ready to let go."

b) "All of this is a hoax. Just another way Arthur figured to show me up. Don't you see? He's got enough money, he can do anything as long as he can muster the imagination. He encouraged my hobby. He hired an actress, a forger. He wants me to swallow all these 'facts' and make my delusional accusation, and then he will leap from the shadows to show me up, to brand me a fool. Is he back there somewhere, in yet another hidden room? I don't think that Arthur has the creativity for something like this in him, but still, as a way of putting me in my place, it would be in line with all of our lives that have gone before."

c) "You're from the future, aren't you? From another time. Come back for some reason to do with me. How else would you know about Arthur? Where else would you have gotten this coin? You had a message for me. Something you needed to tell me to fix my life. Only some terrible thing happened, and you can't remember what. And what you're trying to build here, with all these wires, all these clocks— it's a time machine, isn't it? You're trying to get back to the future, aren't you?"

Nine

"If you say so," said Jane.

"No, no, no. Not if I say so. Don't say it just to please me. Only if it's true."

Jane looked down again to Helga's cupped palm, and the coin within. She touched it gently with one trembling finger, as if afraid a spark would fly.

"I'm from the future," she whispered.

"Are you?" asked Helga.

a) "You must be out of your mind. How could a person be from the future? And I'm supposed to be the crazy one!"

b) "Future? I … I don't know. I don't remember anything. No future. But no past either. But just keep feeding me lunch, and I'll be whatever you want me to be."

c) "The future! Yes, of course. It's obvious! That's what I must be. That's got to be what this is all about. And I came back in time to save your life. Isn't that the way life always is?"

Ten

Helga fell asleep while sitting on her bed trying to choose, unable to decide what to do, unable to figure out what this all meant, whether a virtual bag lady could somehow rescue her from an uncertain future, bringing a message that could change the past, her present. Helga felt drunk with the thought that the future could be different.

She dozed off that way, concentrating more intensely than she'd ever had to before in her life. She slipped into a dream that contained Jane as she might have been, before her mind had disintegrated and her body followed along. Helga saw her neat and clean, arriving fresh from the future into today, her face gleaming with a mission. And then what had happened? Helga was just about to see it, when she woke to Arthur's hands on her, shaking her shoulders.

"Where did you get this?" he shouted. "Are you trying to pull some kind of joke on me?"

He let go of her to show her the coin in his hand, the coin that she had left on the kitchen table after reheating the cold cup of tea that had been his peace offering. Seeing the coin where she had not intended it, she guessed that she had wanted him to find it. So she told him everything.

He believed her, and the things she told him, though in his own way. So after having calmed down and listening to her very intently, he said:

a) "I can see it now. That woman has come as a lesson to us both, to help us remember that we have to work if we want to save our marriage. Thank God she showed up before we were too far gone."

b) "Let me put this as delicately as possible! Seeking psychiatric help is no longer the stigma that it once was. I hope I'm not being too blunt, but it has to be said."

c) "It sounds fantastic, but if only it were true! I need that woman, Helga. If she's really from the future, think how much she could help me. Help us. She'll know things, Helga. She'll have the tools I need to help me strike out on my own. This woman could be our salvation! If I knew what the day after tomorrow was going to be like, I could say goodbye to AcuMarkeTech. Just think of what a company I could build. All of our problems would be over."

Eleven

Arthur insisted on seeing Jane immediately, but Helga was able to convince him that at this hour of the night, Jane would be off wandering the streets in search of more refuse, and thus unfindable. Helga promised that she would make sure that the three of them would get together early the next morning, but that first they each needed sleep.

Helga lay there, pretending to be asleep, amazed at the skills her marriage had taught her. Eyes closed, breathing slow, she listened as Arthur fell asleep, and realized with a trace of fear that perhaps he was only pretending as well. But she had to take the chance; what she had to do was too important. She stole from her bed and out into the night.

When Helga arrived at the alcove, Jane was there racing about, her eyes bright and clear. When the woman spoke, her voice seemed crisp and sure, as if a new intelligence had cracked from a dull chrysalis.

"You were right," said Jane, when she saw that Helga was there. Just like that, no need for introduction, no shock at her presence, no surprise. "I *am* from the future. And I *did* come back to see you. Both of us, me and my partner. Only she couldn't take the way life was in these days, the difficulties, the differences, the sadness. Living unstuck in time was too much for her, and she ... she killed herself. Deep inside, I blamed myself for being unable to stop her, to help her, and so I lost all caring, and became as you saw me. But seeing you the way I was supposed to, and talking to you yesterday, things coalesced, and I became myself. I remembered why I'd come here. I remembered that there was someone else I could help. You."

"But why? What am I to you?"

"Allison—my partner—was your daughter. She had spent a lifetime working on the device. She wanted to save you from this time, from what your life was going to become with Arthur."

"I never had a daughter."

"Not yet."

"I'm almost too old to have children. But you really mean it. Arthur and I get to have ..."

Jane briefly paused in her running to nod.

"I came along because Allison needed me to help. But I suppressed all of it. And now thanks to you I remember. But we don't have much more time to talk now. It's almost time to go."

"Go where?"

a) "Away from Arthur, away from everything you know, to end up like me, yet another crazy woman on the streets in a world where going crazy is the only sane thing left to do. For you're imagining all of this, you realize, of course. It won't be long before you'll be living in a refrigerator box. You'll spend the day mumbling to yourself about visitors from the future, and sometimes when people pass you they will nod their heads and drop change in your cup."

b) "Where? You will go back with Arthur, because having third best is better than having nothing at all. Each day that passes you will wonder what is wrong, and some days you might even come close to putting a name to it, but you will do nothing to change your life. Eventually, this little episode will vanish from your mind completely."

c) "To the future, of course."

Twelve

"I don't know if I'm ready for that yet. I never thought I'd have to make my mind up this soon."

Jane smiled as she answered, almost a smirk.

"Well, you'd better get ready, because I'm almost done."

As Jane went back about her work, Helga puzzled at the strange contraption that had been built. In the center of the room, the bicycle was supported by two wooden crates. Cast-off costume jewelry and crumpled tin foil that had been painstakingly smoothed out decorated the spokes of each wheel. An antique pump was mounted to the rear wheel. A hundred clocks hung in a halo above the construction. A huge pyramid of car batteries filled one corner of the room. Wires wove throughout it all and then out the door.

"That's supposed to be a time machine?"

"It's not important that you understand it, Helga. You just have to be willing to use it. Because it will take both of us to make it work."

"You're not going anywhere."

Helga spun at the sound of her husband's voice.

"You're not the only one who can pretend to be asleep," said Arthur. "I followed you all the way here. So is this the one? Is she the one telling lies about me? Is she the one from our future?"

"She's either telling the truth about neither or both," said Helga.

"You can't pick and choose."

Arthur held the coin out towards Jane.

"This is no toy, this is real, isn't it? I can tell. My father used to collect coins. Nothing short of the U.S. Mint could have done this."

"It's real," said Jane, not pausing in her final modifications. "I used to see them every day. I'll soon see them every day again."

"You can't go anywhere. There's so much I have to know. Tell me. What's going to happen to the economy? Will I get my own company off the ground, the way I always wanted to? Will I be successful? If you've come back to see Helga, you must know."

"All I know is that my visit is over." She hopped up on the bike. "And that it's time to go."

She slowly began to pedal, and sparks and flashes flew.

"I need you now, Helga." Jane pointed at the bellows in the back. "You have to pump while I steer."

Helga stood framed between Jane and Arthur. She felt dizzy, on the lip of some great crevasse that she had long avoided nearing. Jane pedaled furiously, and the air became alive with a shower of light. Arthur's hands were at his side, the coin held loosely, about to drop from his fingers. And they were both calling for her, eyes wide, voices loud. Telling her what to do. What course she was supposed to choose. The pull each exerted on her was equally strong. The only problem was, what was she going to choose? Not what Jane or Arthur would pick for her if she allowed them the power, but what did she, Helga, want?

    a) She would take her husband's hand, and turn her back on Jane. Together, she and Arthur would have a child and would struggle to make their marriage work. There would be no more hitting, and few harsh words. Helga would try to forget about cosmic warnings or messengers from the future. If she thought at all of Jane, as her own future moment by moment became her present, it would be as a wild street person who shouted at her and threw her food. Helga had trusted, and then had chosen time, and had made it work wisely.

b) She would take her husband's hand, but before returning to their apartment, she would pause to apologize to Jane for stranding her in their time. She would say, "No matter what, I've got to see my daughter," with a fervor that surprised both Arthur and Jane. She would try to forget that the fates had promised not just a baby, but beatings as well, and when the former came without the latter she hoped that she had changed a future, and escaped a heavy fist. But as the years passed she learned that she'd have to live through both, and that just because she chose the time to change, it did not mean that she could.

c) She would leap behind Jane on the bicycle, and pump the bellows hopefully and uncomprehendingly until her husband's form and all else around her began to fade. She abandoned Arthur, her past, and the daughter she had not yet had. But she did not care, for she had at last seen her choice, and had chosen time, pure time, fresh time, where she would at last have the freedom to start making other choices as well.

Eros and Agape Among the Asteroids

Is the science-fiction field incestuous? Yes. Is that a bad thing? I'm not entirely sure. If editors are buying substandard stories from writers merely because those writers are their friends, I believe that to be wrong. But if what is happening instead is that writers and editors who like each others' stories develop a friendship as an outgrowth of that, then that seems more like serendipity to me. Which is the cause and which the effect? We can never be sure.

The anthology Once Upon A Galaxy *seems to be a prime example of this. Back when I was editing* Science Fiction Age *magazine, I published a number of stories by Wil Mc-Carthy, including a novella titled "The Collapsium." That story, a hard-SF tale told in a fairy-tale tone, was nominated for a Nebula and later expanded into the novel* Collapsium.

Time went by.

When I heard that Wil was editing an anthology of hard-SF stories with a fairy-tale voice, a la the story I'd bought from him years before, I completed the circuit by selling him a story, our roles suddenly reversed.

If that's logrolling, I guess I'm a lumberjack and that's OK.

Late one night, Expeditor First Class Meryl, who could dance across the asteroids as effortlessly as dirt-bound men skipped from one paving stone to the next, paid what he feared could very well be one final visit to the Belt Boss. All was silent on the asteroid of governance, a place that out of hope and memory they had learned to call Earth. All seemed to be asleep save the dying bureaucrat—none could divine the cause of this sudden onset of illness, and none could contemplate a cure—and the messenger who came to comfort her.

The Belt Boss lifted her white eyebrows when Expeditor First Class Meryl entered her chambers. A smile, quivering and slow, crept across her features, but then, all of the Belt Boss' movements were now quivering and slow. Thousands of colored lights on the walls, blinking like stars seen through an atmosphere, told them that all went well around the Belt this night. And all was going well, except for the fact that Expeditor First Class Meryl had to visit the Belt Boss in such a state, with death fast approaching.

Meryl had noticed that with each passing week, the Belt Boss needed less sleep, as if she was shrugging off one death-like state for another, and he felt that he should help fill those haunted hours. She had lost the power to find rest in dreams. Others knew that, Meryl would swear it, and yet only he came to her side to fill her nights with something other than loneliness and regret. Though Meryl knew that loneliness could not be numbered, its agonies immune to measure-ment, these sad, final hours had taught him one thing: There was no one more alone than a dying Belt Boss.

"So you come to me still," she said. Beneath the annoyed tone there was both pride and pleasure. "Why do you bother? The others probably think you more of a fool than they think me."

"You know why I come. I come because I cannot find it in myself not to come."

"That is your nature. And that is good. Would that the others felt so. Exeter weaves a dance of death about me, and instead of coming to pay his final respects to a dead woman, he plants spies, taps the comm links, and spends his days and nights testing the weather of politics. Are you sure you do not feel yourself to be wasting your time here, Meryl?"

"I do not."

And so they talked, as they'd done each night for weeks, of the things which concerned them. They talked of the balance of a life lived on such a tiny ecosystem, and how wearying it could become, but also how beautiful. They talked of Earth, not this one that had been carved from airless stone, but the one neither would likely see again. They talked—yet again—of the miracle that allowed him to be the first to stumble on the ancient alien artifact that bound itself to him with its technology that made him capable of doing what he did, with the Belt Boss insisting that his find was destiny, and Meryl equally as insistent that it was only luck, and pure, dumb luck at that. They talked of how they missed true days and nights, rather than those that space had forced them to invent, and how glad they were that they at least existed somewhere, and how lifetimes had their days and nights as well—a topic that seemed to give the Belt Boss no trouble, but which Meryl felt most uncomfortable discussing.

And as all conversations tend, when the participants are giddy with talk and lack of sleep and waking dreams, they talked of love.

The Belt Boss sighed. Her lips moved as if she was chewing something bitter, and trying to decide whether she would swallow it to save face or spit it out as she really wished. She looked away from the Expeditor First Class, and cocked her head, and when she spoke it was with an unapologetic suddenness.

"I have told this to none save my own soul, Meryl," said the Belt Boss. "And even there I have had trouble speaking the truth. At four-score years and two, with most of those days spent in the confines of this room, I still do not know the meaning of love. No, no—do not be embarrassed by this revelation, Meryl. I have done nothing, or rather, been guilty by inaction of anything of which to be ashamed. A Belt Boss must think more of ruling than of love. The years pass by, years of the Belt always coming before herself, and though she allows herself to know something of men, she allows herself to know naught of love."

Meryl cleared his throat, suddenly finding it difficult to speak. He knew her far too well. Managing the tens of thousands who lived and died on these hurtling rocks, ruling a country that consisted not of land mass but of a ragged necklace of beads hung about the neck of an uninhabitable world below, these things left little time for friendship. Keeping the oxygen farms pollinating, the space grooves unimpeded, the nuclear chords vibrating, took a level of dedication that left time for little else. And that required level of obsession with the job ill-served her as the end neared. People who looked at the Belt Boss never saw the person behind the authority, but only the power of the position, and when the promise of future favors faded, supplicants stopped visiting, and the comm stopped chirping. But she was not alone in her loneliness.

"Belt Bosses are not the only ones afflicted so," he finally said.

"As I thought."

The room fell silent once more as the two eyed each other, and Meryl grew anxious in that silence. He nodded and requested permission to leave.

"Not yet," said the Belt Boss. "Stay with me but a little while longer."

The Belt Boss had always needed him. Hers was the brain that kept civilized the community that had over the centuries sprung up circling the unforgiving planet below; his were the eyes and ears that helped her do so. But this need seemed different.

Expeditor First Class Meryl tried to banish the choking quiet with more conversation, but to each subject he introduced, the Belt Boss would give no response, and would simply lay back, propped up by pillows watching Meryl squirm in his seat. Meryl finally abandoned his attempts, as the Belt Boss evidently wanted to have no more discourse on the algae fields, or the plasma conduits, or the difficulty of carving out new asteroid caverns at a rate to keep pace with their growing population, and the chambers were silent once more.

"I would like to send you on a quest," the Belt Boss said abruptly, ending the silence with a thought Meryl recognized as having been beneath the surface during all their verbal parrying. "You know that the Physician Master Class has told me that I have but a short time to live, and what my senses tell me of myself agree with what I have been told. I am soon to exit this world, but before I go, I must unravel one last puzzle. I must know what love is like. I have experienced all but this. Meryl, I can travel no longer, and I want you to be my eyes and ears on this, as you have been my eyes and ears on so much else. I need you to journey to each Master around the Belt and ask all of these wise men and women what they know of love, and then come back and share with me your findings before I die. Will you do this for me, Meryl?"

"You know I will," said Expeditor First Class Meryl, stunned. This talk of love! Death was hard enough to stomach, but the delusion that *this* topic could know boundaries was even more difficult to bear. Still, Expeditor First Class Meryl knew without a doubt what his actions would be in response to what the Belt Boss bade him do, and so his promise sprang to his lips. "Whatever you ask."

"Go now," said the Belt Boss, suddenly tired. "I will program the navigation codes so none will be able to see your travels or map your progress. Until you return, you will be invisible. And when you have discovered love, come back to me and show me where it lies."

Meryl could think of nothing more to say, and backed away from the Belt Boss, who was deep asleep before he had even left the room. When the iris was fully closed behind him, Exeter, who coveted the title of Belt Boss in a more unseemly manner than most, appeared at his side.

"The Belt Boss, she is, ah, doing well, eh?" said Exeter. Meryl did not like the thought of him lingering so close to her cavern.

"Not as well as she once was," said Meryl. "But then—who is? It is so good of you to ask after her health."

"You have been visiting her a great deal these days," said Exeter. "Far more often than the parameters of your job would require."

"She seeks my counsel during this trying time. I had not realized anyone would consider that anything worth taking note of."

"You'd be surprised at what people take notice, Expeditor First Class," said Exeter, reaching out to touch the medallion that hung about Meryl's neck. "Be careful how you plan your days. Be careful of your loyalties. Remember—the Belt orbits about the planet below, and not around any one of us."

"I am always careful," Meryl said, and to show Exeter that he did not feel he had to be so with him, he turned, and moved away to the iris of the outer lock. Exeter would not dare follow him there, knowing what Meryl was about to do. There was only so much envy that some people could stand.

Meryl smiled to see the clumsy pods arrayed within. The bulbous drones were the method of transport that everyone else on the Belt but he was forced to use. He was, yes, no matter how the Belt Boss wished to perceive it, lucky.

What if he had not been the one wrestling ore planetside when the alien device was blasted free during their mining? What if it had therefore adapted to someone else instead of him? Then Meryl would have remained a Miner all his life and never been an Expeditor, let alone an Expeditor First Class, and certainly never have met the Belt Boss. He felt overwhelmed with gratitude, as he always was the moment before activation.

He thumbed the medallion that hung at his neck, and the air shimmered about him. A field, microns thick, suddenly separated him from the stagnant, metallic air of the lock. He signaled the puter to open the lock door.

Nothing ahead of him but free space, he ran past the docking bay. Protected by a subatomic film he did not understand, he leapt towards the frigid wasteland of sky. Sometimes, as he built momentum, it was as if the stars wanted him, and he often found it difficult to hold back from launching himself out of the well of gravity coursing from the planet below. But he never made that greatest leap of all, never did more than merely think of it, because doing this one thing exceedingly well had made him invaluable to the Belt Boss, and that made him happy. His bound took him the several thousand kilometers to the next asteroid in an instant, as if he had folded time and space. He did not know how he did it, only that he could. The alien technologies had only been able to give him so much.

This first rock up from Earth was barren—none was allowed to live so close to the center of it all—and so he skipped further up the line. The Belt Boss wanted answers from the Masters, and so Meryl hopped from rock to rock until he approached the asteroid of the Astronomer Master Class.

He came to rest lightly near an igloo of rough stone. He was tempted to rap his knuckles against the wall, but with one such as the Astronomer Master Class, Meryl knew that was not necessary. The vibrations of Meryl's approach alone was enough to upset the man's instruments and send him scurrying to investigate.

After a moment, Meryl sensed through the soles of his boots a vibration not of his own making. The entire dome lifted slowly open as if attached to the ground by a hinge. A small, circular window, flush with the asteroid surface, was revealed underneath. Meryl could see the Astronomer distorted through the glass, a wizened old man with skin like that of an asteroid's surface.

"Who is that who's come so far to bother me?" he transmitted, blinking in the starlight. "It's almost time for me to begin my watch. I've no time for visitors, not now, not when there's so much to be done. Who's that out there?"

Meryl took a step nearer the window, and the Astronomer squinted as if just beginning to see him.

"It's Expeditor First Class Meryl, on a mission for the Belt Boss. Don't you recognize me? Who else do you know who can pay a visit to you on foot?"

"On foot or in a pod, an interruption is still an interruption. Not even the Belt Boss can stop the motion of the stars. If we must talk now, come in quickly. We'll have but a short time for conversation before the Belt brings us to the proper slice of sky for the stars. We'll converse as I prepare. But afterwards, only silence, for watching the stars is a holy act."

The dome slammed down around Meryl, and he could hear the rhythmic cycling of the air pumps. In another moment, the window at his feet slid back. He climbed down a ladder into the darkness, and when his feet touched a rough floor, he staggered for a moment, bumping against something hard and cool.

"Do not move!" shouted the Astronomer Master Class from somewhere in the darkness, now a warm voice rather than just a digitized transmission. "Let your eyes adjust before you take a step. The instruments of man are not the only tools which must be prepared for the watching of the stars. There are also the instruments of God. Let your eyes be welcomed by the dark."

Soon Meryl could see, though not as well as he had seen outside. Though he imagined that perhaps the Astronomer Master Class suffered no distress, from years of living here. Meryl watched as the man scurried quickly about the huge circular room, checking mathematical calculations that floated before him as on invisible sheets, and fiddling with dials which adjusted minutely the direction in which the huge telescopic instruments which filled the room pointed. Then it was back to the calculations again, on and on, back and forth, without stop. The Astronomer Master Class noted Meryl's gaze following him about the room.

"So you can see already. You have better eyes than most. So tell me what the Belt Boss desires." The Astronomer Master Class did not cease in his actions as he talked, nor as he waited for Meryl's reply, continuing his preparations.

"The Belt Boss desires to know of love," said Meryl, feeling foolish even as he broached the subject. "She wants your opinion on the matter. She has sent me out to speak with all of the Masters. You are the first."

The expression of the Astronomer Master Class was unreadable in the dim light.

"Love? Ask an astronomer of love? Might as well ask a soldier of peace. I can tell you nothing about love. I have lived here most of my life, alone, watching the skies ever since I apprenticed to the last Astronomer Master Class. I can't see that I would know anything unknown by the Belt Boss."

"Let the Belt Boss decide."

The old man paused in thought, and sat.

"If you wish. Though I truly can give you no advice. Nothing I know of love is witty enough to be made into an epigram, nor wise enough for another to emblazon over his mantle to live by. So let me instead just tell you a story, and may the Belt Boss get from it what she will.

"Once there was a boy in love with a star."

Meryl nodded, hoping that this would yield the Belt Boss what she thought she needed.

"It was his star, he thought, and no one else's," continued the Astronomer. "He first saw it high above on the very first night he was allowed to step out onto an asteroid's surface alone. That it was out of reach he did not learn until he tried to caress it, jumping as high as he could, and it was not until his legs were aching from the strain and could leap no more and his skin was raw from scratching against the inside of his suit when falling and could bleed no more that he was content to sit quietly and look at it. By the time he was ready to quit attempting to embrace his star and content himself with merely gazing at it, his oxygen was running low and he had to bid farewell to his beloved star.

"In his memory it was perfect, a thing above and beyond anything he had ever known. That following day was filled with disdain, for as he compared all about him with what he had seen during the previous day's excursion, he found himself unable to contend with their inanities. His parents thought him feverish, and so called a doctor, who put him to bed. He did not mind. The world inside his asteroid held nothing for him anymore. When his parents finally fell asleep, he sneaked from his bedroom to the monitor and winked at his beloved star, and then he slipped into his suit and ran to a place where he could commune with his star without the intruding presence of humanity.

"The heavens seemed the right place for it, he thought, as perfection had no place in a flawed world. He would go to it, he decided that night, and not make it come to him. His dreams that next day, as he slept in the bed where his parents once more placed him thinking him sick, were concerned with uniting himself with his star. He dreamed of sprouting wings and flying there. He dreamt of taking one of the pods he had seen the grownups use to move from asteroid to asteroid and blasting himself to the roof of the universe. He had dozens of fitful dreams that day, all of them on the topic of uniting himself with his love.

"That night, as his parents retired to dreams of their own, primarily ones of fear for their son's health, their son woke and once more escaped from his room to keep his vigil. If anything, as he gazed at his star, his love was stronger. Peacefully contented, he fell asleep on his back, the beauty of his star stealing any discomfort. His father found him that way the next morning. When awakened and questioned by his father, he did not want to tell him what he had been doing, until he realized that if he did not tell his father the truth his suit would be locked away and he would never see his star again. His father nodded and grunted as the boy told him how he had found a star he loved, a star that none had seen before, a star that none but him would ever know. His father listened and then led him home, where a wave of his hand brought a map alive to float before them. A map of the stars. The boy froze as his father made it spin, and then pointed at a pinprick which represented a star.

"His star.

"The boy shouted and screamed and ran from the room, and collapsed fatigued as far from his cavern as he could run.

"And when he next opened his eyes, he saw his star, only it was not his star anymore. It belonged to the world. Others now knew it. It did not seem quite so perfect anymore. He looked at it for hours, trying to find in himself the love he'd had for it before, but he could not. He rose and went home, leaving the star still high in the darkness behind him.

"His parents smiled at him, knowing how boys will be, and he smiled back at them, a smile of hate. At that instant in his life, he decided that he would find himself another star to love.

"Only this time, he would tell no one."

The Astronomer Master Class paused. Meryl waited, dizzy. When next the Astronomer spoke, his voice was thick.

"Enough of this. Come. Let's look at the stars."

The Astronomer Master Class leapt to his instruments again, leaving Meryl to ponder about what he had heard. Had he heard truth and fact? Or was he listening to allegory? Had there been such a boy? Was that boy the Astronomer Master Class himself? Or was it all just a lie to fulfill the Belt Boss' request? Meryl could not sort this out, but hoped that the Belt Boss would be able.

"I'm afraid that I have no time to look at the stars," said Meryl. "The Belt Boss, she is ..."

"I know," said the Astronomer Master Class, who let him climb to the surface once more, where he turned his back to the planet below, and contrary to what he had just told the Master, did pause to look at the stars. He could reach them, he knew it, all he had to do was point the way and he would be taken there by an invention of aliens long dead. He wanted desperately to make that great voyage, but not when there was one who still needed him, not when there was one who...

Meryl pushed it out of his head and then thrust himself off from the asteroid face and leapt across three barren rocks until he came to the next Master.

Inside his scooped-out cavern, the Teacher Master Class addressed an invisible audience that watched his hologram across the Belt. Meryl interrupted the man and explained the nature of his quest.

The Teacher Master Class snapped his fingers, dismissing his class, and the mathematical equations which glowed in the air around them vanished. With a sweep of his hand, he drew a large circle, three meters tall, the full height of the room. Then he delicately drew another circle beside it, so small that it was almost not a circle, but a dot.

"This," he said, pointing at the smaller circle, "is what we can know."

Then he passed his hands through the air in a great arc describing the great circle within which he stood.

"And this is what is knowable."

He put his hands behind him, and bowed his head.

"I want to tell you about one of my students," he said, lifting his head. Meryl could see that the man's eyes were moist. "I want to tell you about my *best* student. Or who I supposed at the time was my best student."

Meryl sensed from the tone of his tale that this was not the first time he'd shared it. This was a ritual that the Teacher Master Class had gone through many, many times before.

"My student was in love with learning. I mean this not in the way a scholar is in love with learning for the love of manipulating facts in search of the truth. Nor the way a student will revel in learning in search of high grades. No, the boy loved learning for itself, loved the very process of learning. A literal thrill would course through his body each time he soaked up something new. He loved to learn and could not live without it.

"His parents were poor, unable to afford schooling in those days before the holosystem finally made it inexpensive for all. They begged me to accept him. I asked to see him alone before I made my decision. His parents waited outside this very room while I spoke to the boy in here.

"The lad told me that he was thirteen years old, but he certainly did not look it. He was thin, with long, scraggly hair over a prominent forehead, and if I'd had to guess his age I would have thought him a tall eleven. I asked him a few questions about the basics of mathematics, but he knew nothing. He could not read. I asked him what he thought made him suitable to join my class. He blushed and turned away when I asked him this question.

"'Come, you must tell me,' I said.

"He looked back at me, smiling.

"'I just enjoy to learn,' he said. 'That's all. Ask my parents.'"

"'You just enjoy *learning*,' I'd said, correcting him, and when I told him so, a slight shiver passed through his body, and he thanked me.

"I spoke to his parents. It turned out that he was quite a helpful lad in their Belt-scavenging business. They only had to show him something once for him to know it forever. I was surprised that they would part with such a valuable helper, if indeed he could do all they said he could, but they both wanted what was best for their son. He was their hope. Pity.

"I agreed to take him. I was dubious at first because of what little he knew in the academic way before coming to me. But he picked up the basics quickly and I could see that he was an incredibly fast learner.

"After his first month in my class, I began to notice a strange change coming over him. It appeared to me as if his forehead had grown. I did not know to what to ascribe it, and so I ascribed it to an illusion. I thought perhaps it was the result of cutting his hair short in the style of the rest of the boys that had made his head seem so much larger. But I was wrong. It was, impossibly, the knowledge up there that had made his head so big. Whereas with the other boys the nanobots merely aided in their retention of knowledge, with this one, something quite different had happened. With this one, the nanobots were responding to build him a better brain commensurate with all he had learned.

"By the middle of his first term, I noticed that his head had grown to the size of a watermelon, and he had to carry it about in his hands, as his neck could not support it all alone. He had to duck to fit inside his transport pod. His parents never complained, for they believed it was best for him. They believed that he would have what they had not; he might even become Belt Boss someday. He stayed after school to get extra assignments from me, he hungered for knowledge so, but still I did not see where it would lead. I was a blind scholar. I appreciated his enthusiasm, and aided in every way I could his thirst for knowledge.

"As we studied the maps and he ingested the new worlds the explorers of the Belt had discovered, his head grew to larger proportions. As I got deeper into the mysteries of the Earth we have all agreed to leave behind, his head became like a perfect sphere that threatened to rival the moons. And when we discussed the history of our new kingdom, it was as if within the brain he had hidden history entire.

"The nanobots continued to replicate, continued to build him greater storage capacity until he could no longer fit his head through my door. He would sit outside during class, watching me through the viewports. And the more he learned from me, the larger still his head grew.

"Eventually, he came to me with complaints. His ached all the time. I advised him to take his studies more slowly, that he had forever in which to learn.

"'Forever is not long enough to learn it all,' he said to me, sighing.

"His headaches grew worse, and I fear that I was not wise enough to do what I had to do. I could not bear to bar him from my class, for he was the best of my many students. His presence there came to be the only thing that made teaching worthwhile.

"One day, class began without him, and I was in the middle of lecturing on the War of the Inner Belt when the boy's father landed outside the classroom.

"'Teacher, you must come quickly,' he demanded. 'My son is dying.'

"I dismissed the class, and rushed to the scavenger's asteroid. He warned me to be in control of my emotions, and then led me to his cavern. I was shocked by what I saw there. The boy's head had grown to fill almost the entire room, from wall to wall, from floor to ceiling. Sticking out from under his gigantic head were spindly pairs of arms and legs, as if in his growth his head had swallowed all the rest of his body. He opened the tent-sail lids of his eyes and I could hear the whirring of the nanos as he peered at us. He greeted me, and I begged to know what had happened. He gestured then with one of his withered hands at a stack of disks close by the entrance.

"I recognized the disks at once. They were school's master encyclopedia containing all recorded wisdom. The lad confessed that, growing impatient with the rate at which he was acquiring knowledge, he had borrowed the set and hidden it in his pod (having first talked one of the other boys into doing the actual physical work of pilfering it from my library, since he himself could no longer enter it). Arriving home from school the previous day, he proceeded to spend the entire evening reading it as it flickered by on his puter, until he swooned from the pain. He did not wake until I found him there.

"He had lost consciousness, he told me, halfway through the final disk, and because his own head now blocked the screen from him, he wanted me to read it to him. I refused. Any more knowledge and the boy would surely die. I realized that then.

"'What will we do with you, what will we do?' I said, shaking my head and leaving for the docking bay. I tried to think of a way to save my student. While my mind roamed, looking for a solution to his problem, I felt a tremendous explosion, and rushed back to the family living area.

"It was as I feared. Inside the cavern, there was only blood and splintered circuits. The mother, who had been coming after me at the time of the explosion, told me what had happened. When I had left, refusing the boy's request to aid him in what I knew would be his death, the boy pleaded with his father, and his father gave in. Even though he knew the boy would die, he wanted him to die happily.

"I sometimes picture that man, squeezed in beside his son, slowly picking out the words from the screen as best as he could, not getting any sense out of the syllables himself as he tried to pleasure his son. He knew his son was dying, but did he know that he would go in quite that way? I must admit that I had no such clue. Did the father know that he would be taken with his son? Sometimes I wonder. Sacrificing that way, there was real love."

The Teacher Master Class composed himself. Meryl slipped away and left the Teacher Master Class to resume his holoclass. Meryl should have been teary-eyed from the Teacher's story, but he felt strangely distant. Would all the Masters speak to him in veiled riddles, offering him metaphors as their messages? He'd expected to hear of more personal matters, rather than fables about others.

But that's the way it proved to be for most of his journey skipping from asteroid to asteroid, talking with the other Masters of the Belt. The Mathematician Master Class had no private passions to share, but instead told a tale of how numbers could not help but breed, which is what led to them stretching towards infinity. The Explorer Master Class gave no hint of unrequited love, but talked only of his own love for the unknown. The Writer Master Class explained how the letter u so loved the letter q that it tried to follow it everywhere. It wasn't until he reached the habitat of the Xenobiologist Master Class, a most unlikely Master from which to learn of humanity, that Meryl first heard what he considered to be matters of consequence.

The asteroid of the Xenobiologist Master Class was on the far side of the planet from Earth. Meryl was astonished to realize that he had already danced halfway around a world, and he wondered what it would be like to keep on going further and further away from the center of his universe, but he could not bear to leave the Belt Boss behind with her quest unfulfilled. A cylindrical room rode them through the asteroid like an elevator, until they were at its heart.

"I'm sorry that my wife won't be able to join us," said the Xenobiologist Master Class, once they were alone together, and Meryl had explained his mission.

"Love," said the Xenobiologist Master Class softly. "I'm still trying to figure that one out for myself, you know. In my numberless years out among the stars, I have met thirty-one different sorts of aliens. There have been sixteen humanoids, ten animal-like creatures who exhibit human intelligence, three machine races who were programmed for intelligence eons past and who have since achieved full sentience, and two races who have no forms at all, but are alive in free-floating intelligences. And all of them—*all* of them—are as confused by the concept of love as we are."

"I don't think that's the sort of answer I should bring back to the Belt Boss."

"No, I suppose not. Then let me tell you, as truthfully as I am able, about one man, and one, well, one woman."

At last, thought Meryl. At last we come to reality.

"He was a trader in artifacts, exploring out among the distant stars. As a result, he had cause to travel the galaxy far beyond the limits accepted by the rest of our race. So he was able to see the effects of love in others than just those like ourselves. He confronted species with customs far different than our own. Why, in one, the aggressor actually served up a part of his own body to the pursued for sustenance, in order to prove the seriousness of his intent. In another, two actually meld their intelligences into one.

"The methods differed, but the madness always remained the same.

"Our trader was a single man, and the stars did not give him many opportunities to change this station. He rarely saw another of his own race. And then, on a distant planetoid not one of his species had ever visited, he unexpectedly met an alien who was also far from her own home planet. She was also about as far from his idealized dream lover, the one perfect thing he had sought in an imperfect world, as was possible. Her form was inhuman, with eight snaking protuberances that acted as the arms and legs of her short, squat body; her skin, rough like rock, with growths that blossomed and then fell off at a touch. But her soul, ah, her soul was all too human.

"And though he never thought the act would occur to him, he fell in love. He was as overwhelmed by his emotions as a schoolboy. The strength of that ardor was amazing to him, and with that strength he won her over. She told him, or rather, signed to him, because what they had existed beyond translation, that she had never known such love, never been the target of such a passion.

"Bound by love, they traveled the galaxy together and alone, far from civilization, and there was no impediment to this affliction of the heart until on their travels they needed to return to the Centrum to restock supplies and sell their wares. And there, at last in contact with others, all whom they met flung themselves at the feet of the trader's beloved—not that they could really be called feet—declaring an undying love, just as the trader himself had done. The species of the enthralled did not matter. Neither did the gender. At first our lovers tried to deny it, but as the numbers of the afflicted grew, they had to admit to themselves one horrible fact.

"They realized that these men, these women, these other aliens, could not help it. Because his beloved—or what he thought of as his beloved—released alien pheromones that were irresistible to any but her own species. It was only the fact that her race rarely traveled off their homeworld that prevented this from being known. He could not help but be smitten, nor could they. That was the effect she had. And he began to worry—what did that mean for his own love? Was it real? Or was it brought about solely by alien body chemistry?

"For a great while he tortured himself with this.

"It could very well be that he was a hostage to love, having no choice whatsoever in the matter. But what if he would have fallen in love with her anyway, and this scientific curiosity was a great coincidence?

"As for the female, think how she must have felt as the chosen recipient of such love. To discover that when they were together, that when she with any other races had intermingled, love was not an emotion, but rather an allergic reaction! What comfort could ever be found in such a love?"

The Xenobiologist Master Class fell silent then.

"What did they decide?" prompted Meryl. "Are they together still?"

"They were greatly disturbed by this confluence at first, and thought of ways to test their love. At first, he donned a spacesuit all times he was with her, to see whether he would still feel that love if he did not have the sense of her self in his nose. That indeed gave them troubled times, but they could not perceive whether this was due to the falloff in pheromones, or simply the stress such a barrier would cause to any couple. Then, for awhile, he made her wear overpowering perfumes, to see if he could still love her in spite of such noxious odors, and when this, too, caused problems, they could not for sure say why. Could you love with someone so adorned? There is more than enough stress in any relationship without deliberately introducing more.

"And so, they finally decided—"

"Yes?" asked Meryl.

"They finally decided that it did not matter. Their love was irrational, brought on by random causes, not subject even to their own whims. But isn't that what all love is? How is that different from what the rest of the sentient beings in the universe feel? And so to protect their love they decided to live in such a way that she would see no more of others, so that her alien scent could embolden none but him, but also, that he would seek a new profession, and travel no more, so that he would see no more other of her race, so that his love would not be torn in two by desire. And, I must say, they lived happily ever after."

"Never knowing if their love was real?" said Meryl.

"If their love was not real," said the Xenobiologist Master Class, "then no love ever was."

Meryl nodded. This at last gave Meryl much to ponder, and would surely do the same for the Belt Boss.

"I am sorry that I could not have met your wife," he said.

"So am I," said the Xenobiologist Master Class. "So am I. Believe me—you would have loved her."

As Meryl continued on his journey, he was glad to have finally heard something of worth, for the Engineer Master Class, the Geologist Master Class, and even the Psychologist Master Class were useless, spinning metaphors akin to those to which he gave ear during his first stops. The Physician Master Class told him of the way germs used love to spread throughout the universe, but that was of no help to a human, trying to figure it all out. The Historian Master Class (who was the least help of all) offered no wisdom of his own, but wasted Meryl's time by demanding that he repeat all the stories he had heard for his own files.

Totally confused, having in weeks circled a Belt that would have taken months in a pod, Expeditor First Class Meryl approached the asteroid of Earth from the opposite direction from which he had left. Meryl thought of all that he had heard as he bounded toward his home. He weighed the evidence as he skipped back, trying to make unified sense out of the contradictions, but he was unsuccessful. He had no idea what to tell the Belt Boss, other than that on this one subject, even the Masters fell silent.

Exhausted, Meryl went to his chambers to freshen up before he visited the Belt Boss. He asked the puter to recap all that had occurred since his futile quest began. To his horror, he discovered that the Belt Boss had died in his absence, finally succumbing to her mysterious weakness. He fell upon his cot in shock and sorrow, and after an untimed slumber felt hands upon himself. He was being summoned for an audience with the Belt Boss.

Meryl was confused for a moment, for he knew the Belt Boss was dead, but as he awakened he remembered that though he had known but one, the Belt was never without a Belt Boss for long; there were limitless volunteers for the job. It was the new Belt Boss who wanted to see him. As he made his way along a familiar path through the corridors, two guards walked before him, and two behind, and he saw fear in their eyes, an emotion Meryl had not often seen in others when his Belt Boss had been alive. He could not imagine why this would be so, but he did not have to imagine long.

As he passed the irises that led to the caverns of other Expeditors, he saw there occasional circles of blinking black lights there, apparently placed at random. But soon he recognized a pattern, for the doorways so decorated marked those who had been loyal to the previous Belt Boss. He was stunned, for the ceremonial patterns meant that they were no longer among the living. Could it be that it was only his absence during the tumultuous transfer of power that had kept him alive?

As Meryl was ushered in before the new Belt Boss, he was not surprised to see the grim features of Exeter in the familiar chair, surrounded by the blinking lights that had once framed another. No matter that they told him all was well along the Belt, Meryl knew that things could never be well again, for in the man's eyes Meryl saw that his suspicions were true—Exeter was indeed brutal enough to dispatch any who might be perceived as a threat to him.

"You have been gone from Earth a long time, Expeditor. Too long, and at a strange and difficult time. It seems odd to us that you would leave the side of the Belt Boss in her dying moments. Odd, and some might think, almost a treasonous thing."

Meryl's face flamed as he explained the mission on which the Belt Boss had sent him. As he began to speak of his journey and the many stories he had been told, a smile broke out on the Belt Boss' lips.

"Stop, Expeditor, tell us no more." The Belt Boss just barely suppressed his laughter. "It was obviously just a senile wish on the part of the former Belt Boss that sent you away. I do not think you yet understand how lucky you were that she did this. Let us speak of it no more, and let no mention of it be made to anyone else. I will allow you to continue to use that gift of yours. I, too, will be needing eyes and ears of my own."

The Belt Boss waved impatiently, excusing Meryl, and in the man's eyes he saw, and in the seeing, knew—Exeter had been more than just a witness to the weakening of the former Belt Boss. He had been a catalyst. Dazed, the Expeditor First Class backed out of the cavern which he had last seen inhabited by another Belt Boss.

Overcome by the weight of his luck, he wandered through the corridors to his chambers, where he repacked what he had just hours before returned to his shelves. He had the computer show him an image of the Belt Boss he had known for so long, the Belt Boss who had with her quest given him a gift greater than any love, and afterwards, gazed for one last time at his room. Then, shaking with tears of joy and tears of sadness, he made his way once more to the outer lock which would lead him from Earth.

This time, thanks to a love he'd dared not admit until now, it would be forever.

My Life is Good

When F. Brett Cox and Andy Duncan asked me to contribute to their anthology Crossroads: Tales of the Southern Literary Fantastic, *Randy Newman was the first thing that came to mind.*

Actually, the first thing that came to mind was, "Are you sure?" Since I'd spent my first thirty years in Brooklyn, I didn't feel myself to be an obvious contributor to such a project. But they assured me that since I lived in Maryland, and had been on the southern side of the Mason-Dixon Line for more than a decade, I was an honorary Southerner. And who am I to argue with not one, but two editors?

The opening line of my story will be familiar to anyone who's ever heard the song "Rednecks," which appears on the Randy Newman album, Good Old Boys, *and proceeds to reference Huey Long, Kurt Vonnegut, and of course, the life and songs of Randy Newman. But don't worry—you won't have to be familiar with the entire Newman oeuvre to appreciate the story ... though certainly, the more you know, the richer the experience.*

1. Political Science

Last night I saw Randy Newman on the time machine, with some smart, rich New York Jews. I still had hours to go in my shift, and was already at that familiar point in my day where I was so sick of his smug face as to worry that I wouldn't be able to find the stomach to see it through.

Since The Visitors had come, this mind-numbing study of each vapid moment of Newman's life was a daily irritant for me, and up until then it had been another typically boring evening. The time machine had been bringing me only scenes that I had already witnessed before, recapping a life dedicated to mocking the privilege that had molded it, but the tableaux that this time confronted me on the screen was new to me.

I waved a hand to dim the subbasement lights so I could make out his features more clearly on the tiny window to the past. Newman was smiling, but dressed as he was, I don't see how it was possible for him to maintain that grin. He wore a plaid suit that could only have been bought at a store that catered to unsuccessful used car salesmen and the most insecure of television evangelists. The tie that strangled his fleshy jowls was a chaotic patchwork quilt of overlapping confederate flags. This garish ensemble was out of character for the man I'd unfortunately come to know, and on top of that seemed completely wrong for its intended audience.

Perhaps he thought he was being funny. I'd learned right at the beginning of this that being funny had always been one of Newman's greatest problems. Or rather, *thinking* himself funny had been, when in fact he'd been far from it. The man on whom The Visitors had me waste so much of my time spying was literally addicted to satire, a flavor I despised, and I had no further patience for his uncontrollable habit.

But this outfit, this setting, seemed more than the usual idiocy; things were too off-kilter, even for him. For one thing, during all the hours I'd put in studying the man, I'd never before caught him willingly in a suit and tie, garish or otherwise. One of the other things I'd learned quickly was that when he'd lived, Newman had not been a formal sort of man, and was unlikely to have kept that unflickering smile when trapped in such a getup.

The picture made little sense to me. At first I thought that the time machine had captured Newman at a costume party of some sort, but since the rest of the crowd that milled about him in the oak-paneled ballroom had forgotten their costumes, I cast that theory aside.

The women dressed as rich women did in that not-so-long-ago time by the calendar but which the arrival of The Visitors had now made inconceivably distant. They were statuesque in their jewels and furs, and the plastic surgery which gave them the appearance of youth and firmness had obviously been obtained from the best, for their scars were barely visible. The men did not bother to trouble themselves over their physical appearance. Their doughy forms were stuffed into dark wool suits, and they'd already had too many drinks. They laughed too loud. A few of them had checkbooks in their hands, and one was already pressing a folded donation into Newman's breast pocket with fat knuckles.

I'd long been looking back to keep my eye on Newman, but I'd never before seen anything like this. It worried me, but not so much that I was yet willing to alert The Visitors upstairs and have to look into those saucer eyes again. My worries were still more about the future than the past. My hopes were that it was the machinery, rather than the timestream, that was askew. I called Pall, the technician, and had him examine the equipment. He was happy for the chance to be in the room while the time machine was operating, because The Visitors did not give him much opportunity to do so. They trusted me, and me alone, to be a witness to Randy Newman's life.

Unfortunately, Pall found no hardware problems. The troubling picture was real. Something had happened that had never happened before. I let Pall continue to huddle with me before the small screen, Visitors be damned.

"What do you make of it?" I said. "I've never seen anything like this before. Look at his face. Look at those eyes. It's as if those aren't the same eyes. He's changed somehow."

We watched the normally-awkward Newman move through the crowd as if he had been born to it, shaking hands, clapping the men on their backs like brothers, kissing the women on their cheeks until they flushed, and collecting more checks in the process.

"Is there any way we can hear what they're saying?" I asked. "As soon as this scene started, the sound crashed."

"There's too much static," said Pall. "I don't know why. But why don't we try this? Let's detach the focus from Newman himself. Unlock the gaze and let the machine's point of view wander. Maybe that will show us something."

I manipulated the controls to stop targeting Newman, the maker of my weary days. The image slid from him sluggishly, and shifted to let us see glimpses of the rest of the room. At first there seemed no answer to the mystery there. A bustling wet bar. A coat rack. A buffet table overflowing with bowls of jumbo shrimp, decorated with an ice sculpture of Huey Long, a man whose profile I would not have recognized without having been forced to study him thanks to Newman.

But then we both saw a tall poster, ten feet high, filled by Newman's face. Pall didn't know enough of my mission to react, but the sight made me dizzy. I was stunned to see that above the smiling photo were the words:

Every Man a King

Below the photo, in large red, white and blue type, was written:

A Newman For a New Day
Randy Newman for President

"Something has gone terribly, terribly wrong," I said. My gut inflamed at what this meant my next step would have to be. Those eyes. I would have to suffer them again. "I'm going to have to tell them."

"You lucky bastard," Pall whispered.

His words pushed me back from the screen. I'd had enough of Newman for this day or any other day.

"You can have my luck," I said coldly, immediately regretting the tone I took with Pall. It wasn't his fault. The blame rested entirely with The Visitors. "You can't possibly know how sick and insignificant I feel when I have to face them."

"But you realize what this means, don't you? This must be what they were waiting for all along. This must be what this project is all about. You *are* a lucky bastard."

And then Pall, in a voice washed with awe, uttered the words I never thought I'd live to hear.

"They're going to have to send you back."

2. The World Isn't Fair

I once thought I had a life of my own, but now I only have his. Randy Newman's. A minor American singer-songwriter with a voice like a tortured cat and a heart like a pumice stone whose tunes were more smirk than sincerity.

Maybe I was only fooling myself about that life business, though. Before it all changed, I'd been lost in the world of theoretical physics, stepping beyond that arena only to do what I had to do to stay there, and as little as possible beyond that. So perhaps maybe I never really had any life at all. Maybe living Newman's life vicariously for twelve hours a day is better than having none at all.

But upon reflection, I don't really think so.

Until The Visitors came in their shower of blood and thunder and set me to the task, I'd spared no time for popular music. Other people may have needed it to give their lives meaning, but I had the more basic poetry of the quark. I was deaf to song, and not entirely by choice, either, but rather by constitution. As I studied particles dancing just beyond the edge of perception, the songs the singers sang were unintelligible to me.

Randy Newman, with whom I've been ordered to spend my days, created the most unintelligible of them all. With his uncle Alfred scoring Hollywood movies and winning Oscars in the process, Randy Newman was born to make music. Instead, he only made noise.

The fact that he'd been able to garner any fame at all is as senseless as the songs themselves. He had the superior attitude of the frat boy, without the substance to back it up. He sang that "Short People" had no reason to live, but he meant us to understand that he really didn't mean it. "I Love L.A.," he wrote, but from the words, who could really tell? He called southerners "Rednecks," but didn't seem to mean it in a pejorative way, and wanted license to call African-

Americans "niggers" in the name of his supposed art. Why did he think people would want to struggle to unravel meaning and intent from a song, when all they were seeking was a distraction? Give me a song that is what it presents itself to be, with no ambiguity. There is enough mystery in the world without adding more.

No wonder that when The Visitors summoned me to set me to my task, the difficulty of my research was almost overwhelming, because in this century, Newman's musical corpus seemed as dead as his physical one.

Regardless of my difficulties or distaste, I could not protest, only submit. After the day that they announced themselves and gave that first terrifying proof of their power, no one dared question The Visitors. Whatever they wanted, they got. With their inarguable supremacy, they could have plucked the treasures of Earth.

Luckily for the world, they didn't want much.

Unfortunately for me, one of the few things they did want ... was me.

I didn't know why. I still don't. I was as far from suitable for the assignment as it is possible for one human to get. When I was taken from the university and told by my government that henceforth I would be using a time machine given us by their alien technology to peer into the past, I was ecstatic. I thought that everything my life had been headed towards was about to be fulfilled. I'd finally arrived at the fruition of my impossible dreams. But it turned out that none of my physics training was to mean anything. They could have grabbed any semi-comatose couch potato, thumbs thickened from wrestling with the remote control, for all the manipulation I ever had to do of the device they gave us. I was to watch the pictures of Randy Newman as they paraded by, and report on any anomalies.

The promise I'd thought the universe had kept had instead been broken. I lived my days in pain, as if in the grip of a disease.

I could never tell them that. I'd decided I'd rather live. They wanted me, and so they had to have me. But though I'd suffered in silence, that suffering still raced through my mind as I waited to tell them the news of the aberration. I tried to avoid meeting with them, did my best to share the information with them over a holo, but they forced me to stop before I could tell them what I had found.

They wanted to see me in person.

I did not like the way I could look into those large, liquid eyes and see myself looking back. Their gaze made me feel as if they were able to read my mind. I am not a paranoid man, and yet, they were able to make me feel like one, and I did not want to have to stand there and let them see again how stupid I felt wasting my life this way for them. I could barely hide my discomfort from Pall and the others I was assigned to work with, so how could I hope to hide it from them?

But I had no other choice.

As I sped inside the high-speed elevator from the subbasement that housed the project to where The Visitors dwelled on the skyscraper's top floor, I wondered if Pall could possibly have been right. Was this what we all had been waiting for? Would it really cause me to be sent back in time?

As the doors began to open and reveal a place I dreaded, all these thoughts emptied from my mind. What was left was fear. That fear grew when I saw their tall, attenuated forms and realized that though I'd never before seen more than one of them at a time in person, there stood two. So something out of the ordinary had indeed occurred, and they already knew it. They stood at opposite ends of the large, windowless room. The elevator that left me dead center of the room recessed into the floor, placing me pinned between them in the dimness.

I could not tell the two Visitors apart. They had no distinguishing features to individualize them. No difference in eye color, nor scars, nor variation in tone of voice. Seeing them this way made me wonder about my past visits to the top floor, whether either of these had been the one I had seen my few luckless times before, and in fact, whether their sameness now meant I had never seen any Visitor more than once, but had only thought so.

I stayed silent until they spoke, not due to any conscious decision to show respect, but rather because, this time as always, their presence left me speechless.

"You have news to report," said one, sliding closer.

"I do not understand why, but the subject is not who he once was." So great was my anger at Randy Newman for wasting my life this way that I did not like to say his name aloud, particularly in front of The Visitors, who would surely hear my contempt. I spoke to them formally because that was the only way I was able to bring myself to speak at all. "Something has changed about the past. I have looked at this moment before, and each time all was always as it always was, but now he is no longer a man who writes music. The timestream has altered. He appears to have entered politics."

"That is ... not good," said the other, taking its own fluid steps closer to me.

"He must be ... protected," said the first.

"But he's in the past," I said. "How could he be in need of protection? What's happened has happened."

Said one, its voice becoming louder as it approached, "What's happened has not happened yet."

Said the other, "What's happened never really happened."

"You're speaking in riddles. What does that mean? Is the past truly fluid? Has the past put the present in danger? Will this alteration catch up with us here? Tell me, please. Is something terrible going to happen to our timeline if he is allowed to become president? Am I going to the past to protect our future?"

I was rambling on, verging on hysteria as the distance between us shrank. I was going to say more, but then they were suddenly upon me, and words were no longer a part of my palette.

"You must fix this," said one.

"Go now," said the other. "Put it back as it was."

One of The Visitors reached out a hand towards me. I shrieked as the elongated fingers grew near. I started babbling, speaking as I'd never dared to speak before, questioning them out of a greater terror than I'd ever known.

"Why?" I shouted. "Why do you care? Why have I been doing this? Why does it matter to you?"

My questions would have horrified Pall. In challenging The Visitors, I was risking everything, including my own life. But with a Visitor about to lay hands upon me, all propriety had fled.

"Just go," said the other, answering my frustrated questions by beginning to reach for me as well.

When their flesh touched mine, an explosive energy coursed through me, blinding me, and they, the skyscraper, and all of the world I knew, were gone. For I had come unstuck in time.

3. Mama Told Me Not to Come

I popped back into existence on the 27th floor observation deck of the Louisiana State Capitol, a setting which on its own merits told me that this was an earlier century than my own. I felt a sense of freedom to be back in a time before The Visitors had razed such buildings to the ground to get our attention, but it was only a momentary emotion. I knew I was not truly out of their reach, and could not pause to enjoy this place. I had to get on with it.

I blinked into the morning sun and admired the Mississippi as it rolled towards the Gulf of Mexico. Louisiana's state capitol building, when it still stood, had been the tallest of such buildings, which was a good thing, for it meant that the structure contained enough square footage for The Visitors to have found a spot in which to have me appear that would not attract attention.

I'd had no time to prepare for this trip. Luckily, The Visitors had prepared for me. My tunic was gone, replaced by a finely woven suit that could easily allow me to pass as a member of this century's elite. As I stood there, the wind had a different feel to it that morning, and when I touched a hand to my head to figure out why, I discovered that my shaggy hair had also been altered. It was now closely cropped in a style I loathed. I could only hope that when at the end of all this nonsense I was allowed to return to my own time, my hair would return as well.

My physical shell wasn't the only thing that had been made right for this time. How else would I know without a doubt the spot on which I stood? How else would I know instinctively that I was hundreds of feet above Baton Rouge, and that if I walked mere yards to the south, I could look down on the grave of Huey P. Long, the former governor of Louisiana, felled by an assassin's bullet to then be musically commemorated by Randy Newman? As I walked along the deck so I could study where the martyr was buried, I felt as if I belonged here, and I realized that The Visitors had filled me with enough of the essence of the time and place to pass as one of them.

And then I realized something else. I was not alone.

I did not at first recognize the man who was leaning against the rails. My approach took me up to him as he stood with his back turned, and that was a side of him that the time machine, focused on telling me his story as it was, had never let me witness. As I drew to the right side of him, could see him there with his eyes closed, I was momentarily stunned. Randy Newman, whom I had known up until then only as an historical figure on the flat screen of a time machine, was before me as a living, breathing man. And I once more cursed The Visitors and mourned the loss of those I would have chosen to see on my first excursion back in time—Galileo, swearing that the Earth still moved; a young Einstein, still working at the Swiss patent office; my parents, before they'd met, before the thought of me had even entered their lives; my own self, paradoxes be damned.

Newman's head was bowed, and beneath the halo of his graying curls, he seemed lost in prayer. His forehead rested against the fleshy fingertips of his clasped hands. What was he praying for? To be the next president?

Even though almost everything I had seen of him during my long hours with the timescreen had offended me, this offended me more. And not just because I was the first human to travel through time, and I was trapped having to pay attention to this. But because I knew who he was supposed to be, and this was not it. I preferred to think of who we are as immutable. He was supposed to be mocking governors, not being one, and certainly not one on the road to the White House. From all I'd learned of him, from the clowning deviousness of his songs, I knew he was a buffoon, not a statesman. Maybe that would be good enough for Louisiana, but not for the rest of the country. That must be why the Visitors wanted him stopped, why this fracture in the timeline had to be extinguished. If Newman could not be turned from this path, something bad would come of this, or why else would The Visitors have expended so much effort? Maybe, if allowed to proceed unchanged, this timeline could ripple forward to catch up with our own, and end the present as we know it.

Randy Newman had to be stopped.

The Visitors had given me information, but not a plan on how to use it. Standing there, staring at him, I was frozen. How do I begin to change the universe? Better that they'd sent someone else. Someone who was a strategist, or a private detective. Someone who did not hate Randy Newman so much. Someone who could see what had to be done.

Yet I had to get through this somehow. Without that, I knew that there was no getting back to my own time.

Newman opened his eyes, but kept his head bowed against the early morning sun, and took a moment to survey his city. He lived. He breathed. I was still startled to behold him. I could not take my gaze off of him until he started to turn his head in my direction, and I lowered my own before he spotted my hungry attention. I shifted my look to Huey Long's grave, and quietly said a little prayer, but it was not the one Newman thought.

"I'm usually the only one who feels a need to take in the view this early in the morning," he said. His voice seemed friendly, in tones that were now familiar echoes to me, but there was a wariness to it as well.

"You're not the only one who feels the need to commune with the governor, Governor," I said.

I was startled to discover that The Visitors had not only altered my brain and my body, but also my voice. When I spoke, it was with a lazy Southern drawl. I bid him a good morning, just to hear myself speak, and then laughed softly at the sound of it. He didn't seem to take it amiss.

He nodded towards the sacred spot hundreds of feet below.

"They would like to laugh at him, you know," he said. "Laugh at us. Let them, I say. So he was a cracker. Well, I'm a cracker, too. From the sounds of it, so are you. But he bound the people together like no one else before or since."

He laughed.

"Look at me. I'm getting goddamned maudlin on you. But that isn't just a metaphor. Why, do you know that you can't get from one end of the state to the other without passing over at least a half a dozen of the 111 bridges he built us. And the roads! The son-of-a-bitch added over 2,300 miles of them. In 1931 alone, the state of Louisiana employed 10% of the workers involved in building roads nationwide. Man, what I would give for the power to do that. He was a unifier, in more ways than one."

"You'll get no argument here, governor."

"I like the man. Without him, Louisiana wouldn't be what it is today."

"With your love of Louisiana, I don't see why you'd want to leave it. I don't see how a man of your temperament could stand the air of Washington."

"I couldn't leave Louisiana behind, no matter where I end up. It's in me. But, you see, there's so much more that I can do, not just for the people of my state, but for my country as a whole. The world isn't fair. I'm just doing my best to make it so. And that's a job I just I can't do from Louisiana."

I was suddenly startled to realize that I liked him better this way. It's as if that part of him that was inside-out had been burned away, leaving what was pure and true and honest. And at least this way he wasn't singing and writing any more of those sarcastic songs.

I was tempted to leave him this way. He could surely do no more harm to the world than his other self had with his endless cynicism. But I knew that the aliens wouldn't see it my way.

"But why? Why do it? Why care enough to make that sacrifice?"

He leaned in close to me, and whispered.

"Now, you wouldn't happen to be a reporter, would you?"

"I'm just a fellow southerner, like yourself."

"Then come with me."

I followed him inside, where two bodyguards were surprised to see me with the governor. The four of us took the elevator down to the first floor executive corridor between the House and Senate chambers.

"This is where they got him," he said. His voice quivered as he pointed at the spot. "If they hadn't gunned him down, he'd have been president for sure. So since he can't make it, I will have to be president in his place."

Newman was silent for a moment as he stared at the site of Huey Long's assassination, and then his face hardened.

"When I was a small boy, my mother often took me to get ice cream. Ice cream can be a very powerful motivator for a small boy. If only it wasn't."

He scratched his full stomach and laughed ruefully.

"One day, we went to one of those one-man ice cream wagons," he said. He spoke as if he was not there, as if he was not chatting up a potential contributor. He was far away, traveling in the only time machine most of us ever know. "There were signs on the side. One side of the cart was meant for Whites, and the other side was for Colored. You don't look quite old enough to have ever seen such signs yourself. Two black children were already being helped there when I arrived. The man turned from them the instant I appeared, and ignored them both. I didn't think it fair, but I did let it happen. Because I wanted the ice cream, you see. We all want the ice cream. Only—we can't always be allowed to have it. Or else, life isn't fair."

"But why did it have to be politics? Why not choose music? After all, both of your uncles ..."

"When has a song ever changed the world?" He hesitated then, and looked at me oddly. He took a step back, and glanced at his beefy guards. "You seem to know an awful lot about me and my family."

"No, I assure you, I don't." I'd sent the wrong message, but I had no idea how or why. "No more than any other proud Louisianan, governor."

Newman stared down with wide eyes at the spot on which he stood, where an earlier governor had fallen, and blanched.

"Oh, no," I said, realizing where his thoughts were heading. "I would never do such a thing. Please don't think that."

But he did. And as he started to shout for help, I turned and ran.

I heard shouts, followed by a gunshot. Then another. I have no idea whether it was the bodyguards who fired, or some other good Samaritan. This was Louisiana; undoubtedly half of the building was armed.

I felt no pain, but I must have been hit, for the world faded away and I thought, *how meaningless, to die, here, for this.*

4. Good Old Boys

I returned to myself not yet dead on a blazing summer day, the only relief from the heat being the cool ice cream melting down a stick onto my fingers. I winced under the assault of the sun directly overhead, my eyes and mind still back in the damp cavern of the Louisiana State Capitol. I had no memory of purchasing an ice cream bar, and no hunger that would have caused me to do so. I had only an anxiety that caused my temples to pulse with the tension of it. I tilted my hand so the drips would hit the dusty pavement instead of running down my shirt cuff.

I was in yet another past, one even more distant from my own time.

Randy Newman's past.

I looked around for the ice cream cart that I knew had to still be near. That's why The Visitors had not yet brought me back. My first excursion had been for information only. There was still work to be done. The wagon was half a block away, surrounded by children. From this distance, I could pretend that it did not bear the signs marked White and Colored. Not only had he told me about it in his time, mere minutes ago that were impossibly still decades in the future, but I had been forced to listen to him sing about it in my time. Over many months, The Visitors had insisted that I listen to that part of his oeuvre and all else. I moved closer to see what was to come.

An elderly woman walked by, dragging behind her a small cross-eyed boy. She sneered in disdain at my sticky hand. The boy looked at me with one eye and away with the other, and from his split stare I realized it was Newman. The painful operations to fix those eyes would not come until later.

As the woman tugged him along, it became clear to me that he hadn't been looking at me at all, but rather at the melting confection in my hand. He wanted it very badly. A chill went through me at that desire, for I knew then with a certainty that not only was this boy a young Randy Newman, but that this was the pivotal day as well.

Still holding her hand, he skipped slightly ahead of the woman so that he was pulling her along instead of the reverse. He pointed at the ice cream wagon, and the pleading began. Even with the weight of this event heavy on my heart, I could not help but smile. The young were always able, whatever their time. It didn't take too much pouting to get her to acquiesce, and she reached into her purse to find a coin. She planted herself where she stood and watched as he skipped down the street to the cart. I dropped my ice cream bar to the pavement, and muttered to make the action seem accidental. I needed a reason to pull near, and so I grimaced and looked at the cart as if deciding whether to buy a replacement. The Visitors had made an actor out of me.

I moved closer to young Newman, his nose as yet unbroken by all the things that would come later, and watched as he stepped up behind two small black girls, only to be shooed by the jeering vendor around to the other side of the cart. I stepped up behind him and watched as one of his eyes read the sign that said Whites and the other seemed to study the two girls who had just been abandoned by the server.

"They were here first," said Newman in a high-pitched voice.

The server coughed.

"Don't tell me how to run my business, son," he said. "What'll it be?"

Newman turned and looked at me. Well, *half* looked at me. I was an adult, and he hoped that I would solve this for him. But I could do nothing. Yet.

"Mister, you saw it," he squeaked, his voice a whistle. "They were here first."

I grunted. What was I to tell him there, with others still listening? That life wasn't fair? It wasn't time for that. He would learn that soon enough himself.

"Well?" asked the ice cream man, seeming to take joy in Newman's discomfort.

The boy shifted his stance, turning his back on the girls, as if that was the only way he could find within himself the ability to place an order. He looked at the coin that had been dropped in his hand.

"Do you want an ice cream or not?" said the man.

"I do, I do, only—"

"Only what?"

Newman bit his lip and, unable to speak his order aloud, pointed to a picture printed on the side of the cart. The man thrust it in his hand through mist from the dry ice and then looked at me, the two girls still ignored. I quickly got a bar to replace the one I had dropped.

Newman had not yet gotten too far, his relative still a short distance away. I quickened my steps to catch up with him, trying at the same time to look casual about it for anyone who might be watching, as if I'd just happened to approach him on the way to somewhere else.

"E pluribus unum," I said to him.

"What was that, mister?" he said, blinking, unsure I was talking to him.

"E pluribus unum. It's a phrase the founding fathers decided to put on our money. It was stamped on the coin you just gave the man. It means, 'Out of many, one.' One people, all the same and equal. Because that's what the founders envisioned this country to be."

Newman stuck out his lower lip, his ice cream momentarily forgotten.

"Someone should make it be that way, then. Someone should change things so that they're the way they're suppose to be. If I were president—"

"Oh, no," I said. "Not president. If I were the sort of lad who wanted to make a difference in the world, a president would be the last thing I'd be. Presidents don't really change things."

"Well, who does then?"

"No, definitely not," I said. "Not politics. Politics is definitely not the way to go."

"Well, what then?" he demanded petulantly, snapping at his ice cream bar in frustration. "What am I supposed to do?"

He looked back at the wagon where the seller, without a smile, was still attending to the first of the little black girls.

"You know who really changes the world?" I said. "Writers. Particularly writers of—"

"Randy! Come over here this instant!"

A stern voice cut me off, and I looked up to see the woman striding towards me, holding her purse as if ready to use it like a weapon.

"Get away from my boy this instant! You, sir, are being far too familiar!"

I stumbled away, having run out of time.

"Remember, Randy," I cried out. "Remember what I told you. You must remember that."

I walked swiftly away, the woman continuing to stride past the boy so she could further hector me. I raced around a corner to escape her and found the hot street suddenly gone, for I discovered myself cloaked in the cool dark of a New York City hotel ballroom.

5. Maybe I'm Doing It Wrong

I realized that I was back in the same room that with its fractured glimpse of Randy Newman had begun my trip through time. And not only was it the same room—I sensed that it was also the same crystal of time that had held that catalytic fundraiser. The South was behind me now, if the South could ever truly be said to be behind me as long as I was forced to focus on Randy Newman. Perhaps Pall was up ahead in the future, watching me now, studying the moment to see how things were going as I had once watched, peering into the past to see if the timeline had changed. There was no way for me to tell; I could not return his gaze. But at the same time I felt reassured by seeing around me in person the same dark wood paneling that I had once watched—or rather, would watch in the future—on the compact screen of the time machine.

As my eyes adjusted to the dim room, I was relieved to see that the walls had no posters blaring of a presidential run. People were squeezed into ragged rows of chairs that faced an empty podium. I saw neither furs nor pinstripes around me, nothing that smacked of the elite fundraising crowd that had been there earlier. (Or was that later?) The crowd contained T-shirts and long hair, scraggly beards and a general sense of poor hygiene. The rich had been replaced, and now I was surrounded by an army of songwriters.

Newman came into the room then, and he, thank God, looked the way I remembered him. A blinding Hawaiian shirt draped his gut, and he had the sardonic twinkle in his eyes that I had come to expect. I did not realize that I'd been holding my breath until I sighed. I'd done it. This is how that earlier scene had obviously meant to be. A crowd of songwriters gathered to hear from the songwriters' songwriter. (He obviously wasn't, and never would be, a lay audience's songwriter.) My words had nudged him in the right direction. It was over.

He stepped behind the podium to applause. He smiled as a few attendees started to whistle and hoot, waved and smiled at someone he spotted in the front row, and began before the sound that had greeted him had stopped.

"I love you sons of bitches," he said, and the room filled with laughter. It felt good. Things were right again. *I sure don't love you, you son of a bitch,* I thought.

I leaned back against the wall behind me, and waited to be returned to my own time. My own life. I'd soon be back to it. It was a miserable life, but it was my own. Maybe now that the puzzle of Newman's life had been put back the way it should be, now that my mission was over and I had accomplished what The Visitors had intended, they would leave me alone now. I would be freed from the bondage of studying a man I did not like on the screen of a time machine I envied. I don't often pray, but I prayed then to be taken from this place, as I was taken from the Louisiana State Capitol, as I was plucked from the hot summer streets of an even more distant past.

Instead, when I opened my eyes I was still trapped listening to the buffoon talk. What more did The Visitors want of me? Why did they want me to undergo more of this suffering?

"You're the only ones to pay attention to what really matters in this world," continued Newman. "Others may waste their days delineating the mundane, wasted lives of college professors, but only you know that there are galaxies being born right next door, and that somewhere there are civilizations being snuffed out as galaxies die. I am home here, with the only people who understand me. The hell with the talented myopics who can only write stories of things that are thrust under their noses, when the issues that matter can best be described with metaphors that don't yet exist, that we can only imagine—aliens and planet-hopping rocket ships and time machines. You know who the real audience is for my novels? You are. I'm so proud to be one of you."

He paused, choked with emotion. It appeared that there was more he wanted to say, but could not. He returned his index cards to his pocket, and could only repeat:

"I love you sons of bitches."

I was dazed by his confusing words. What did his ramblings mean? Why was a tunesmith talking to his peers about novels and time machines? Randy Newman had never written a novel in his life. As far as I was concerned, he had barely written songs.

I was the only one who seemed bothered by any of this; the audience ate up every word. Looking at them more closely, I could see that some of their T-shirts bore pictures of scientific formulae, others had spacecraft, and the faces of aliens looked out at me with visages much like The Visitors themselves. I raced to the closest audience member and grabbed a booklet from his hand. Newman's face was on the cover of the pamphlet, but by the words that accompanied the caricature, I could tell that this wasn't the gathering of songwriters I'd originally thought it to be. Instead, this was a science fiction convention! That was the reason I was still trapped here, pinned to the past by my pain.

I'd only been half right. My message had gotten through to him as a child, but I had been interrupted before I'd been able to deliver the whole of it. I screamed my frustration to the world, but by the time the audience turned from Newman to me to see what had caused the commotion, I was no longer there to be seen.

6. *Last Night I Had a Dream*

A square of moonlight hit the boy's face as he drooled against the pillow, dreaming of ... of what? That's what this was all about, wasn't it? I sat uncomfortably on the other side of young Randy Newman's dim bedroom, contorted in a chair meant for a child. Looking at him, with his smooth face and his mussed hair, the boy did not look like someone destined to cause me pain, seemed indistinguishable from any other sleeping child, but there was potential in him I had to derail. A potential for what, I did not know. But he had become fractured from what the universe had originally planned for him, and it was up to me to set his life back within the groove before disaster struck.

Gazing at him, I could not tell, now that I was back once more in the deeper past, whether this moment was a time before or after the incident at the ice cream wagon, or even, perhaps, some other timeline entirely.

It struck me that this was one of the few times I'd ever seen him without his glasses. He appeared peaceful and serene.

I don't think I've ever felt such hate.

If he were to die right then, I thought, I would be far better off, and so would the world. He would never then grow into the man who would make music that was more curse than song, and would never attract the attention of The Visitors. I would never be sitting there where the Visitors had put me, a place where I had no right to be, hoping to be freed from this. Perhaps that was the way to solve this, by ending the matter entirely rather than trying to reinvent him. It seemed the far easier way to stop whatever disaster they meant to prevent.

Those thoughts fled when I heard the murmur of a voice, and I tensed, fearful that the approaching sound was his mother creeping up the stairs. But then I realized that what I was actually hearing was a low humming, as of someone preparing to sing. It scared me, until I realized that the vibrations were coming from my own throat. Then it no longer scared me.

It petrified me.

I have never been a person with an inclination to song, another reason why the whole assignment has been so painful for me. During my commutes, I always chose talk radio of any kind over music of any flavor. Yes, I understood music scientifically, the relationship of one note to the next, the effect they are supposed to have on the listener, how music can make emotions rise and fall, but I find no pleasure there, nor a true empathy for the pleasure it causes in others. If you were to tell me that music was a hoax, I would think, "Ah, yes, finally they tell me the truth," and believe you.

Yet here I was, readying myself in a dark room to sing a small boy some sort of reverse lullaby. Instead of putting him to sleep, I was to wake him to a new potential.

Without even knowing what was to come next, I found myself singing the opening verses of "This Land is Your Land." Surprisingly, I didn't sound half bad. In addition to everything else The Visitors had given me for this journey, a decent voice seemed to have gone with the package.

Little Randy Newman awoke halfway through, and I continued on to the final verse that is rarely sung, the one that rails against the private ownership of land. He rubbed his eyes as he looked at me, but did not say a word. So I told him about Woody Guthrie, and the various causes he championed, and how he'd had inscribed along the edges of his banjo the phrase, "This Machine Kills Fascists."

I sang songs to him from times that had come before him, but also times that had not yet occurred, though it was doubtful he'd see the difference. I sang him Joe Hill's "Casey Jones—The Union Scab," followed with "I Dreamed I Saw Joe Hill," and sketched in the effect they both had on the beginnings of the American labor movement. His eye grew wide as I told him the story of student protesters shot by the National Guard, and sang Neil Young's "Ohio." I told him of the civil rights movement and how "We Shall Overcome" helped power it. I told him about the antiwar efforts of John Lennon and sang "Give Peace a Chance." I sang "The Times They Are a-Changin'," but I don't know that he got the full effect, because the voice The Visitors had given me was better than Bob Dylan's. I did my best to let him see how people paid more attention to songwriters than they did to politicians or novelists. That much I could give him. The cynicism that would put him back the way he'd been still had to come from within.

When he finally spoke, it was to say, "I'm still asleep now, you know, mister." His voice was insistent as he pushed out his bottom lip. "I think it's time I had a different dream."

He closed his eyes. Searching for another song, I found nothing. I had run through them all. I waited there until he opened his eyes again and glared at me.

"Go away," he said.

I would have liked nothing better. But the choice was not my own. I would not know I was ready to leave until I was gone.

"Just remember what I told you tonight, Randy," I said. "Remember what the martyred Joe Hill said. He wrote that a songwriter is the only kind of writer that has meaning in this world. He wrote, 'A pamphlet, no matter how good, is never read more than once. But a song is learned by heart and repeated over and—'"

The door opened suddenly, cutting me off with a shaft of blinding light. His mother stepped into the room and moved towards her son, his arms flung over his face.

"What is it, dear?" she said. "I thought I heard you cry out."

I tried to slip out behind her into the hallway, but the floor creaked beneath my heels, and she turned to see me.

"You!" she shouted. "You're that man who was bothering us yesterday!"

It was only then that I realized I was in the same time stream I had visited earlier.

"I can explain," I said weakly as I backed away, then said nothing more. The Visitors had filled me with knowledge, but had not given me the words to deal with this.

She raced from the room, but did not look afraid.

"Now you'd really better go," said Newman. That smug look on his face reminded me once again why I hated him so.

"Just remember," I said. "Please."

There was no way to explain to him that that was the only way I'd ever get home.

I slipped out a window and dropped to the yard below. As I limped along the quiet street, a shotgun exploded behind me. After a life without violence, gunshots were chasing me for the second time that day. Between the blasts I heard a high-pitched voice shout, "Mother, no!," and then all went black.

One way or another, I prayed for it to end. I no longer cared how.

7. The World Isn't Fair

So silent was my pop back into existence in my own time beside Pall that at first he did not even realize that I had returned. I was at his elbow as he stared at the time machine, and on the screen I caught a glimpse of myself vanishing from the dark street just as bullets breezed through the spot I had just been inhabiting. The picture then vanished to be replaced by static. Pall cursed at the blizzard and backed from the screen, and only noticed I was there as he bumped into me. Turning, his cursing increased. He lifted me up in a bear hug as I complained.

"You did it!" he said. "You traveled through time."

"Yes," I said, reaching out to touch my world of now, the chairs, the walls, the blank time machine before us, almost as if I thought they would all be quickly taken away from me again. "I traveled through time."

"I witnessed it," he said quietly. "All of it. They let me see you. What was it like?"

"I don't know," I said quietly.

Pall shook his head.

"I can't accept that. You were the first human to go backwards in time. I know you. I know what that must mean to you. You must feel *something*."

I looked inside myself, and all I saw were things I needed to forget. What I felt could not be expressed in words without driving me insane. Even thinking them as abstract emotions was difficult enough, but to make them concrete ...

All my life I had wondered if such a thing as what I had just accomplished was possible. If it were possible, I would surely be the man to figure that out. There were so many things I wanted to see and do on such a voyage into history, so many precious moments I wanted to collect.

To have it handed to me in this way, like spare change tossed to a beggar, that made it worthless. And to be led around the past on a leash for as insignificant a reason as Randy Newman, that made the whole thing even more insulting still. Some pain was not meant to be endured.

So all I could say was, "I feel ... nothing."

And then hope to forget.

The interference on the screen faded, and there was Newman again, as he had been all those months before, as he had come to haunt my dreams. There he was as a young boy watching his uncle Alfred conducting an orchestra on a sound stage as snippets of film flickered above them. There he was meeting his first wife, and then later writing a song about their marriage dying, and yet later again writing another about how stupid he felt to be still loving her after all. There he was, losing an Academy Award, which pleased me. All the pieces came together into the cynical mosaic of his life as it always had.

I had succeeded. I had saved the world from whatever great unknown it was The Visitors had foreseen. Maybe they would now let it end.

"So what was that all about, anyway?" asked Pall. "Did you save the world? What was he going to do as president? Did you avert a nuclear war?"

I sat in the chair that had owned me for too long.

"I don't think they'll ever tell us."

I hoped that it was over. Now that all was well within the time stream, perhaps I would not ever have to watch Randy Newman again. I reached behind the machine, unplugged it from the wall, and sighed.

It was a good sigh.

That was when the voice in my head said, "Turn it back on."

8. *That's Why I Love Mankind*

Myy life is good.

At least I, unlike many others since The Visitors have come, have a life. I must be thankful for that.

I have grown used to spending my days as I do. The pain of it is duller than when I started my vigil. It has become bearable. I accept that though I have watched him be born, watched him live, and watched him die, I will be forever deaf to all he does. Even as I wince at it, I accept that I must be his eternal witness.

I have grown to know the rhythms of Randy Newman's life as well as I know the pulse of my own blood, the music of my own lungs. I watch constantly, and when an aspect of his life goes awry, when he jumps the track of his enforced destiny and creates something other than those infantile songs of his, I can sense the disturbance immediately. And almost before I can alert The Visitors to what needs to be done, I am gone, sent back by them again to set things right.

I have seen him become a short order cook, a comic book artist, a television weatherman, a vagrant, a school teacher, a radio deejay and more, and each time I have put him gently—and sometimes not so gently—back in his place.

I have been doing it for years now, and I still do not know why. I have asked The Visitors and have been given only silence. So I no longer ask. I try to find comfort in Pall's belief that I have saved the world many times over, but I gain no solace from that. I cannot be sure of that. I can be sure of only one thing.

I once had a dream, but now only have dreams of him.

I was going to be the one who would figure out how to unravel time, only I have instead found myself knotted in it. I was a man who liked his music straight and honest, if forced to have a choice in music at all. I was a man with little use for irony, and yet Randy Newman serves me a portion every day, mocking slavery, making fun of the homeless, and meaning neither. Or so he says.

How ironic that the last person on Earth who should be doing this job is the very one forced to do it.

How ... ironic.

As that thought began to gel, another thought intruded on my own:

"Come to us," it said.

I slumped in my soul and went to join The Visitors. It never got any easier. I was terrified to see, when the doors opened around me and the elevator slipped back into the floor, that this time there were a dozen of them. Never before had I seen more than two at a time, such as when I was launched on my first mission, and the ones that followed. As far as I knew, no human had ever seen more than two at once. I tried again, petrified, to distinguish them one from the other, looking for scratches, discolorations, differences in appearance of any body part. I hoped that their increased number could help me find distinctions. But they could have been stamped out by a machine, so identical was their flesh. It was hopeless.

"Do you know why we have called you?" one said.

I could not speak, could not even shake my head.

"We thought perhaps you already understood," said a second.

"It is time," said a third. Or maybe it was the voice of the first speaker again. I could not be sure. Their intonations were so similar that they could have been speaking with one voice.

"It is time," one of them said again.

"Time?" I asked, my voice a dull croak. But even before I finished spitting out that single short syllable, I already knew what they meant. They intended, at last, to explain it all.

"Then tell me," I whispered. "Why, then?"

After years of sparse and cryptic sentences, the words came this time in a torrent, first from one, then another. So many words after so long a time. I try to avoid attributing emotions to aliens, but now it was as if they were as excited that this time had come as I was. I looked quickly from one to the next, trying to keep track of who was speaking, but soon their voices melded together so that I did not know which of them had spoken. The unleashed sentences came barreling out of them so rapidly that what I heard carried the qualities of an uninterrupted soliloquy.

"We thought you were smarter than this, little one," they said. "Don't you perceive it? Don't you yet see the truth? You know, you were on the verge of figuring it all out when we called for you. You were so close to the answer, so close that you almost thought it yourself. You should not have to ask us why. You will undoubtedly figure it all out on your own soon."

I feared for a moment that they were dismissing me. If they had brought me this close to the brink only to leave me dangling, if they intended to send me back to the time machine with no answer, I did not think I could survive it. If this moment was just meant to be a malicious tease, I doubted that I could live much beyond the day. I needed to know.

"Do not worry. We will be the ones to tell you so that we can see your face as it happens. Think back. What was it that you were thinking when we summoned you? Do you not recall it? You were thinking that you were the last person on Earth who should be doing this job. Well, you are right. You meant it as a metaphor, but it is true ... literally."

I grew dizzy, and flung out an arm, but there was nowhere to support myself in the bare room.

"And we would know. You see, we have come to love irony. Irony, we have discovered, is the most delicious of all emotions, a thing we have learned well in our travels throughout the universe. It is our hunt for the highest degree of irony that put you in charge of this project these many years, and it is irony that has left you there."

"You're saying I am here precisely because I shouldn't be?" The anger is my voice for the first time overcame my fear. "That I am the most unfit candidate for the job, and you know it? So you're torturing me deliberately? You mean you crossed a galaxy for that? What kind of creatures are you? You came up with a stupid project designed to be the opposite of who I am just to watch me wriggle?"

"You must not call Randy Newman stupid!"

The sound in my head was deafening, and I fell to my knees. Their words continued to bombard me, each one opening a new wound.

"Do not pride yourself in thinking that it was you who came first. This wasn't designed around you, it was Newman, first, last, and always, and it is you who were chosen around him. It is this project that takes precedence. Why is it that you think we came here? Do you think that Earth's sunsets are more beautiful than the ones on other planets, or that your air smells sweeter, or that your goods are worth our export? Actually, we can see that you *do* think that. But that is not so. We come here for one reason, and that reason is Randy Newman. Without him, do you think that we would bother to keep Earth alive? No, without him, Earth would be a ball of ash. We have seen the universe entire, and we know that Earth produces the most flavorful taste of all, for he is the king of irony. You are engaged in the only thing worth doing on this planet, which is keeping his life on track, so that he can continue to produce that delicacy."

"But I thought you were trying to prevent him from going astray because of something horrible he might do, not to protect the things that he did do."

"You hoped that you were saving your planet from a nuclear holocaust? We would not care if your entire race save one went up in flames. No, we needed you to keep the shifting timeline on track, to make sure that nothing occurred that would keep Randy Newman from blossoming in all the fullness of his spirit. He sees life as it truly is. He is the only one of your entire species. As for you, there is only one reason why you and your exacerbated frustrations are involved, a reason you were close to realizing on your own. You were chosen because of your potential, because now the story of your life is as full of irony as any of Randy Newman's songs. It's all very simple, you see."

I could not speak for the horror washing over me. I covered my ears so I would not hear the judgment that they were about to deliver, so I could avoid the summation of my life, but their words seeped through my fingers anyway, and drove straight to the core of my brain.

"We want you to hurt like we do."

Scott Edelman has published more than 75 short stories in anthologies such as *The Solaris Book of New Science Fiction*, *Crossroads: Tales of the Southern Literary Fantastic*, *MetaHorror*, *Moon Shots*, *Mars Probes*, and *Forbidden Planets*, and in magazines such as *Postscripts*, *The Twilight Zone*, *Absolute Magnitude*, *Science Fiction Review*, and *Fantasy Book*. His first short story collection, *These Words Are Haunted*, appeared in 2001. *What Will Come After*, a complete collection of his zombie fiction, was released May 2010 by PS Publishing. He has been a Stoker Award finalist five times, in the categories of both Short Story and Long Fiction.

Additionally, Edelman currently works for the Syfy Channel as the Editor of *Blastr*. He was the founding editor of *Science Fiction Age*, which he edited during its entire eight-year run. He has been a four-time Hugo Award finalist for Best Editor.

CPSIA information can be obtained at www.ICGtesting.com
Printed in the USA
BVOW060040250512

291056BV00001B/55/P